D1262887

PACIFIC POISON

A YAKUZA THRILLER

DAVID LISCIO

COPYRIGHT © 2020 DAVID LISCIO
ALL RIGHTS RESERVED.

No part of this book may be used or reproduced in any manner whatsoever, including Internet usage, without written permission of the author, except in the case of brief quotations included in critical articles and reviews.

This is a work of fiction. Names, places, characters, and events are fictitious in every regard. Any similarities to actual events and persons, living or dead, are purely coincidental. Any trademarks, product names, or named features are only used for reference, and are assumed to be property of their respective owners.

This book is dedicated to the law enforcement officers, judges, government prosecutors, investigative journalists, special-ops teams and military units worldwide, who choose to make a difference by keeping evil in check.

1

A DANGEROUS SURF

SAIPAN

NORTHERN MARIANA ISLANDS

DECEMBER 1989

HOURS BEFORE DAWN on a moonless night, two compact, muscular men struggled to remove from the trunk of their dented and coral-dusted sedan the plush oriental carpet in which Mikito Asaki's naked and elaborately-tattooed body was rolled.

The surf at the bottom of Banzai Cliff pounded furiously so that little else could be heard, not the symphony of bush crickets or the cries of seabirds. The pair lifted the cumbersome carpet by its ends and began carrying it toward the edge, dragging the bundle whenever it became too heavy. Yuki, who lead the way in the dark, wore his shiny black hair in a long braid that flip-flopped against the back of his flowery, Hawaiian-print shirt as he trudged ahead. Twice he stumbled on loose rocks and finally lost his grip on the carpet, causing Kira, his shorter companion bringing up the rear, to topple onto the hard ground. The carpet unrolled and spilled the corpse like ingredients from a burrito.

Yuki cursed as he switched on a mini-flashlight and shined the beam toward Asaki's body. For a moment both he and Kira stopped to marvel at the powerful Japanese underworld boss whose eyes remained open, the lids swollen and bluish, reminding them of sea bass displayed on mounds of crushed ice at Tokyo's fish markets. The eyes were a haunting message, for both men knew the ancients believed open eyes at death indicated the deceased feared the future, presumably because of past behavior.

Asaki's mangled arms and legs lay askew on the grass, giving the impression of a marionette puppet waiting for its master to lift the strings. His hands were raw and bloody, the thumbs and two fingers missing from each. The tips of the remaining fingers were blackened, the fingernails removed. Two men's dress socks filled with a mix of beach pebbles and sand had been tucked into the carpet along with Asaki's body and now they, too, rested on the ground.

Though both Yuki and Kira had gleefully participated in the torture, they remained astonished by the massive destruction their ministrations had caused. Asaki had not gone to his death willingly. For hours he resisted their cruelty, giving up no information about the millions of dollars missing from the crime syndicate's heroin smuggling operation. He fought like a samurai until overcome by the repeated blows to his head and chest, administered mercilessly by Kira who had filled Asaki's black socks with the sand and stones, tied them together, and used them as a blunt lethal weapon.

Asaki had at one time been Kira's *oyabun* or boss in the *Ichiwa Kai*, the second-largest organized crime family in Japan's underworld. Respected by many for his ability to bring peace among the warring families, Asaki was also feared for his ruthlessness in dealing with enemies.

Yuki joked in Japanese as he nudged the weighted black socks with his foot. "Asaki-san won't need those where he's going." His lips curled into a cynical smile.

Kira absentmindedly rested the back of his hand atop his shaved head as he gazed upward at the night sky. His vulnerable expression — lips pressed together, eyes squinted as though signaling pain — was impossible to ignore, perhaps because it contrasted sharply with the fierce lightning bolt tattoo on his left cheek. Upon regaining his composure, he looked directly at Yuki. "You wouldn't say that if Asaki-san was alive. You shouldn't say it now. His spirit will hear you. Things come back around."

The knotted socks had formed a garrote used to strangle Asaki. Other forms of torture had preceded the victim's final breath, including the wiring of his genitals to a car battery.

Asaki's arms, legs, torso and chest were covered in a wild mosaic of tattoos. Despite the darkness, the flashlight made it possible to see blotchy contusions from the beating amid colorful designs of snakes, birds, koi carp and dragons.

"Be quiet, you fool. Let's go," Yuki snarled. "We've spent enough time with this piece of dung. We should have shot him and been done with it. He gave us nothing."

The two *kobun* stared down at the jagged rocks hundreds of feet below where the Pacific pummeled the limestone of Saipan Island. In the darkness, the sea was visible only as glimmers of foam that resembled crooked white lines on a black canvas. The men grabbed Asaki by the wrists and ankles, groaning as they swung him back and forth to build momentum until the pony-tailed Yuki gave the command to let the broken body fly. Neither looked down to see where Asaki landed.

Yuki brushed the coral dust from his loose-fitting white trousers that had been torn at the knees during his stumble along the rocky path. It was impossible to see if the fabric was flecked with blood but Yuki didn't want to keep the flashlight switched on because it might attract unwanted attention. Japanese families mourning their dead frequently visited Banzai Cliff to light votive candles that burned late into the night.

Yuki managed a sardonic smile. "Goodbye, Asaki-san. May you enjoy crossing the Sanzu. I think the river will be full of rage wherever you swim."

Out of habit, Kira again nervously touched the lightning bolt tattoo on his cheek with two fingers. "Leave him be. Perhaps there are things about Asaki-san we don't know, good deeds that will allow him to wade peacefully across the river in the shallows. Maybe someone will even wash and dry his clothes."

Yuki laughed heartily, exposing a smile that showed the gap where two front teeth had been knocked out in a bar fight. "And press his underwear with a hot iron," he said, recalling the seething anger Kira had once shown when Asaki ordered him to wash a pair of underpants heavily soiled during an international flight.

Hurriedly they rolled the bloodied carpet, hoisted it upon their shoulders and trotted toward the battered Toyota Corolla. They haphazardly stuffed the carpet into the car trunk, planning to set it afire before morning, then drove to the private oceanfront home leased by their boss, Orochi "Big Snake" Tanaka, a man they would not dare fail.

2

DEPARTURE PLANS

Tokyo, Japan
January 1990

After their third brief and secret meeting, Yoshi Yamamoto had begun to trust the American man and woman who offered him a way to escape from the death sentence imposed by Tanaka.

Over the course of several months, CIA officers Dan Stevens and Candace Cahill had convinced him to provide vital information about the region's heroin trafficking in exchange for safe passage and an anonymous haven in the United States, where Yoshi and his 21-year-old adoptive niece, Hiraku, could spend the rest of their lives in relative peace, free from the tentacles of the yakuza.

"Mikito Asaki was a friend," Yoshi told them during their most recent meeting, referring to the yakuza underboss found floating in the surf at Banzai Cliff. "We had similar thoughts and aspirations. He often wrote poetry. He prayed daily. He was a great artist and an honorable man."

Stevens and Cahill offered condolences as they sat with their confidential informant in a Narita International Airport parking lot about an hour's drive from downtown Tokyo and shared a box of Pocky chocolate biscuit sticks. They knew Yoshi enjoyed the snack and would appreciate the gesture. The CIA officers hoped to assuage Yoshi's fear that he and Hiraku were next on Tanaka's hit list. Yoshi repeatedly had described how his body and that of his lovely niece would be hacked to pieces and fed to the sharks off Saipan's Marpi Point if suspected of leaking information about yakuza activities.

"Once we have all the information, we'll set a time and place where you and your niece will meet our extraction team. You'll be flown out of the region, but not aboard one of our diplomatic aircraft," Cahill explained matter-of-factly, as though giving friends directions to a soccer game. "You'll travel by other means. No need for passports. You'll have a complete set of unique identification documents by the time you touch down in the United States."

Yoshi seemed relieved. "I want to trust you. There are many in our yakuza family who do not believe in profiting through the sale of drugs. We know what heartbreak it can bring."

Stevens nodded respectfully. "We're on the same team, Yoshi. Help us put an end to this madness and we'll make sure you have a good life in America."

The CIA officers were demanding yet fair. They made it clear Yoshi needed to obtain a few more bank account numbers, drug-smuggling routes from Thailand to the United States, the identity of ships or planes involved in the operation, and delivery schedules on land and at sea – then they'd be ready to go. Yoshi shared the news with Hiraku upon returning to the small Tokyo apartment they shared ever since a tragic automobile accident had claimed the girl's parents eleven years earlier.

"Do you really believe Tanaka wants you dead and not just punished? Maybe he wants only a finger. Maybe *yubitsume* is enough."

"He'll stop at nothing until I'm dead. He's a snake who wants nothing more than to sink his fangs into my flesh and devour me."

"Then we should leave soon."

"If anything happens to me, Hiraku, you must still meet with the Americans. They've promised to take you to safety and I believe them."

"Nothing will happen to you, my beloved uncle. We'll leave together while there's still time and start a new life. No more yakuza. We'll live in America – maybe in Philadelphia where I will eat delicious cheesesteak sandwiches for breakfast and Smartfood popcorn for lunch and buy beautiful new clothes at the shopping mall every day while you smoke your pipe."

Yoshi smiled Buddha-like, peacefully, as though embracing his niece's dream, but deep inside he felt a dark undercurrent and sensed fate had something completely different in store. The ancestors were reaching out, calling for him to join them.

3

DEATH ALONG THE POPPY TRAIL

CIA HEADQUARTERS
LANGLEY, VIRGINIA
MARCH 1990

STUART ASHWOOD SWUNG his legs off the antique wooden desk in his office, folded his arms and stared directly at the two CIA officers sitting before him in wheeled swivel chairs.

"Looks like you two are headed to the Pacific."

Eighteen months earlier, Ashwood had replaced Preston Barlow as the CIA's Deputy Director of Operations. Barlow had bungled a major agency operation in Cuba and the international embarrassment and political fallout it had caused was still rippling through the power corridors of DC.

Hannah Summers and Bill Carrington — the two agency operatives now hyperactively twirling their chairs — were well aware of the details, having done their utmost in Cuba to keep the situation from further unraveling.

Ashwood leaned forward, hands planted firmly on his desk.

"For the time being, let me lay this mission out in an abbreviated nutshell and then we'll get into specifics."

A picture of health in his mid-50s, with a toned physique and thick, smoky gray hair neatly parted to one side, the affable Ashwood was known behind his back as Smilin' Stu. But today he wasn't smiling. The deputy director seemed uneasy as he adjusted his regimental striped tie and tugged at the white cuffs of his powder blue oxford shirt. He brushed a fleck of lint from his tailored navy suit jacket and cleared his throat.

"What I'm about to tell you comes straight from President Bush. Last September, in his first televised national address as Chief Executive, he called drugs the greatest domestic threat facing our nation today. I'd have to agree with him. The tragedy and trauma that drug abuse causes to American families is immeasurable."

Hannah stopped fidgeting in her chair and rolled it closer to the deputy director's desk. Carrington did the same.

In Ashwood's opinion, President George H.W. Bush had sent an incomplete message when he held up a bag of seized crack cocaine during that speech and told his fellow Americans the drugs were being smuggled into the country from Central and South America. The President had pointed a finger at Colombia, where a steady stream of misery was fueled daily by greedy narcos like Pablo Escobar. The President's televised broadcast had been used to announce the authorization by Congress of funding and military equipment that would be provided to an alphabet soup of law enforcement agencies to fight corrupt and powerful drug cartels south of the U.S. border. President Bush made no mention of Japan's criminal underworld, about twenty organized crime families otherwise known collectively as the yakuza, which was responsible for smuggling heroin into the United States at an unprecedented rate.

Hannah's face paled. She gazed off into the distance, lost in thought, replaying the painful memories from thirteen years earlier that refused to die, images and words that forever captured her younger sister Rachel's near-fatal cocaine overdose.

Hannah had called 9-1-1 and requested an ambulance after the sixteen-year-old complained of chest pains, nausea and feeling overheated. When the girl began to vomit and a series of tremors and spasms overtook her body, Hannah suspected the symptoms were caused by drugs, and not by an allergic reaction to undercooked cheeseburgers from the local fast-food joint, or some errant airborne virus traveling on a stranger's sneeze.

When Hannah sniffed her sister's breath, there was no odor of alcohol. Hannah had heard stories of how her younger sister could keep up with the boys when it came to pounding down beers or drinking shots. The girl's pupils were dilated.

Hannah would never forget the sight of her angel-faced sister in the back of an ambulance, IV fluids flowing into her bloodstream, oxygen mask pushing enriched air into her lungs, ice packs strategically placed to help reduce her body temperature, the two paramedics working furiously to keep her alive, monitoring her vital signs, hoping to ward off a seizure, stroke, or heart attack. There was no magic prescription drug to counteract a cocaine overdose. It was more a matter of trying to keep the patient stable until the drug ran its course.

Hannah wondered whether her sister had snorted a full gram of cocaine, perhaps two, or had been given a speedball – a dangerous mix of cocaine and heroin made further toxic by the substances used to cut it. She'd read horror stories about dealers cutting cocaine with everything from laundry detergent, talcum powder, and laxatives, to painkillers like Lidocaine, and even Strychnine, an ingredient commonly found in rat poison.

While waiting for the ambulance to arrive, Hannah had

demanded her sister tell her the truth. The girl swore she hadn't ever used cocaine and never would. Hannah knew it was bullshit but saw no advantage in getting her sister to admit it. The blood tests at the hospital would do that. She felt grateful that her older sister, Molly, was away at college, because the woman usually became emotionally unstable in a crisis and caused more harm than good.

Hannah remembered seeing her parents standing at the curb, their faces surreally bathed in the red and blue flashing emergency lights. They looked confused and defeated. She felt sorry for them, and for herself as well. Her thoughts had been more focused on the upcoming senior prom than scoring a ball of coke from some sleazy dude in the parking lot behind the shopping mall. She detested the local drug dealers, but more so the kingpins who set the supply in motion. She also blamed herself for not noticing Rachel's frequent nosebleeds, sniffles, dilated pupils, and her increased aggression. It was a lesson on the need to think about others.

4

A HISTORY LESSON

CIA HEADQUARTERS
LANGLEY, VIRGINIA
MARCH 1990

STU ASHWOOD'S voice had returned, distant at first, but now was back to normal volume and apparently being directed at Hannah and Carrington. Hannah realized she had spaced out thinking about her sister. She felt embarrassed and hoped her momentary lapse of attention had gone unnoticed, though she doubted it. Ashwood hadn't been promoted to deputy director of operations at the CIA because he was obtuse.

Ashwood was saying, "What the President purposely didn't mention during his broadcast is the heroin smuggling that's going on in the Pacific Rim. There's a lot more to the drug epidemic here in the U.S. It's not all about cocaine. The influx of heroin is just as bad, if not worse. But the President didn't want to spread panic. Instead, he called me, and I called you."

Hannah and Carrington automatically morphed into models of concern, sitting erect on the edge of their chairs.

Ashwood unrolled a large map of the Pacific Ocean that nearly covered his desk. Saipan Island was marked with a red dot near the center. The map extended northwest to include Japan and the Philippine Sea, northeast to the Hawaiian Islands and the West Coast of the United States, and south to Papau New Guinea and Australia. He lit a cigarette, keeping his eyes on Hannah, a formidable expression on his face. Old School in his methods, he preferred paper maps to images shone on a projection screen.

"This is strictly black ops. We'll have all the funding and resources we need, some satellite coverage, and even a Navy sub at our disposal in the Western Pacific. But as always, we need boots on the ground."

Hannah felt a chill run through her — black ops, Navy subs, satellites, unlimited resources. Whatever Ashwood was about to unveil was big.

Ashwood's intense blue eyes seemed somehow too small for his face behind tortoise-framed eyeglasses but they bored into the two CIA officers seated before him. "We need to find out how tons of heroin are making their way from the Golden Triangle — namely Thailand — to secret drug labs in the Philippines for conversion to white powder, and eventually to Hawaii and the streets of San Francisco."

Carrington stood and stretched uncomfortably, as though he needed to move in order to digest what Ashwood was saying. "That's a tall order."

"So it is. But we need to destroy or at least plug the pipeline because it's flooding the United States with heroin and it's affecting our national security. Most people think the illegal drugs are coming only from Colombia. But the yakuza are doing their share."

Hannah stood and moved closer to Ashwood's desk where she could get a better look at the map.

"I'm all for cracking down on drug trafficking, whether it's in Colombia or Japan. But honestly, how do we tackle something this big? Where do we even begin?"

Ashwood leaned across the map and touched the city of Tokyo with the index finger of his right hand. "That's the power center. But if our latest intel is accurate, most likely the answers we need will be found on Saipan," he said, referring to one of the fourteen volcanic dots that comprise the Northern Mariana Islands in the middle of the Pacific Ocean and due east of the Philippines. "You'll need to tap into the pipeline and find out where it goes from there."

Ashwood was well liked at Langley and most of those working in the operation's sector were thrilled Barlow had been forced out. Ashwood was fair-minded and less motivated by politics than his predecessor. He cared foremost about the safety of the field operatives under his command.

"Japan sounds good to me. I like sushi," said Carrington, attempting to inject a bit of levity.

Known informally at Langley as Wild Bill, Carrington at forty-five was handsome, fit, and one of the CIA's top operatives. He exuded a boyish charm most people found attractive, especially women. With ash-blond hair that extended nearly to his shoulders but tamed by a short ponytail, he was dressed in tattered tan carpenter pants, a black t-shirt with paint flecks across the front, and ratty boat shoes. He might have been mistaken for a deckhand on some billionaire's yacht.

Carrington's vibrant blue eyes glanced over at Hannah who, though appearing sheik and sophisticated in her navy Ann Taylor V-neck sheath dress, was grinning inside like a schoolgirl. Hannah was thrilled by the prospect of another international assignment, especially in a region of the world she'd never visited. Chasing mobsters and mercenaries in Cuba had left her with a taste for this kind of adventure. At thirty-one, she was in excellent physical condition, her 5-foot-7 frame kept taut and trim by a daily run and visits to the gym.

Ashwood frowned. "Any more helpful comments before we continue?"

Hannah's gray-green eyes came alive with their usual playfulness. "Well, I've heard March is a spectacular time to visit Japan," she said, the tiny scar at the right corner of her mouth twitching slightly, as it did whenever she was anxious. "We can actually see the cherry blossoms blooming in their native land instead of waiting for their transplanted relatives to show off their petals in DC. Oh, and by the way, I don't own a kimono. Can I put one on my expense account?"

Ashwood took a long pull from his cigarette, sending the smoke out his nostrils in a powerful plume. He liked both operatives and was well acquainted with their spycraft abilities. Besides, he didn't trust the more obsequious CIA officers at Langley, the ass kissers who agreed with everything he suggested just to stay on his good side and help assure their ascension through the ranks.

Ashwood stared at Carrington, paused a moment, then fixed his eyes on Hannah, his lips formed into a twisted grin. "I'm glad you both find this amusing. Hannah, I'll see what I can do about the kimono. If I recall correctly from your file, your favorite color is green. But right now we've got a few more important matters to consider."

Ashwood tossed a glossy, 8-by-10, black-and-white photograph on his desk where Hannah and Carrington could see it and sat back in his chair. "For the past couple of months, a yakuza underboss named Mikito Asaki has been stiffening up in the morgue out there in Saipan, unless he has been cremated against the instructions of our Justice Department and his charred bones are already in Japan, picked from the ashes with chop sticks and spread across the family table like some spiritual board game. From what our sources tell us, his murder could be linked directly to the heroin smuggling."

Hannah picked up the photo, which showed Asaki walking along a Tokyo street in suit and sunglasses, a tan trench coat casually tossed over one arm.

"When was this taken?"

"Some time last year. I assume people in the Asian underworld are talking. Let's see if Asaki's untimely death can lead us to what happened to Dan and Candace in Tokyo. They went dark the second week of January and we have little reason to suspect they're still alive."

That was the bomb Ashwood had waited to unleash. The mood in the room shifted instantly from light-hearted and playful to dark and ominous.

Hannah and Carrington were silent, their somber faces reflecting surprise and deep concern. Until that moment, they were unaware that CIA officers Dan Stevens and Candace Cahill were unaccounted for. The pair made an enviable team in the spy world — attractive, seasoned and savvy. It would have taken professionals of the highest order to get the best of them — or a traitor.

Carrington had worked with both agents on various assignments and knew them well. He wondered where and when they'd made a fatal mistake. Stevens was always so careful. He'd made his bones at the FBI and later the CIA as an "electrician". Although his commercial work vans advertised Dan Stevens Electric — Residential and Commercial — his forte lay in installing electronic surveillance systems, particularly "bugs" hidden in offices, homes, and hotel rooms. He was a pro at eavesdropping and a savvy field agent.

Ashwood rubbed his chin thoughtfully. "We found the last vehicle they drove abandoned in the Ginza. It was wiped clean. No blood. No fingerprints. No sign of a struggle. The vehicle had been reported stolen from Narita Airport on New Year's

Eve. The steering column was pried open and the ignition hot-wired. We believe Stevens and Cahill stole the vehicle and drove it into the city. We don't know what happened after that. Obviously we'd like to find out who is responsible for their disappearance and get a little payback."

"I say let's do it," said Carrington, forcefully slapping the corner of Ashwood's desk before thrusting the fingers of both hands through his blond hair, combing it straight back from his forehead. It was more a gesture of exasperation than vanity. "I'm ready. When do we leave?"

"Later this week."

Hannah seemed puzzled, her mouth slightly open in surprise. "Why wait? Why not leave today?"

"You won't be going in on a black insert. We need you visible, on a commercial flight. Personally I'd like to send you both on your way this afternoon because we're already a month behind on this. The FBI sent two of its people to Saipan last week. Since the island is a U.S. protectorate the Feebies assume they have jurisdiction. I'm sure the local police were not pleased to see them. They don't like being told how to run their own island. You two, on the other hand, will be flying to Tokyo and taking connecting flights to Guam and Saipan where you'll be visiting as beach-loving tourists. Hannah, you'll be representing an Argentine travel company interested in setting up Saipan flight and hotel packages that focus on surfing and parasailing, scuba diving and beach volleyball. You know the drill. And Billybong, you'll be tagging along as her business associate."

Hannah's eyes swirled open, radiating disbelief and amusement. "Did you just call him Billybong?"

"I did. Forgive me. It goes back to our days in Vietnam. He often mingled with the locals to get intel on VC movements and the political climate, and in doing so was forced to partake in smoking a few bowls."

Carrington was smirking. "All in the line of duty. It was an insult if you didn't take a hit or two from the bong or hookah if it got passed your way. Same with the Thai sticks."

"I see," said Hannah, a wry smile plastered to her face. "Nothing like first-hand knowledge."

"Well, let's make sure we keep it at that level," said Ashwood, chuckling. "Heroin is a different ballgame, especially with these people. And who knows, we may learn something about how all this white powder is getting from Thailand to Saipan, and how it manages to leave the island without a trace. That's what Stevens and Cahill were trying to find out."

Hannah shifted in her seat. "Were they able to get any intel?"

"Some, but not all. Cahill spoke fluent Japanese. She lived in Tokyo for a year while in college, and she was comfortable traveling throughout Asia. Over the past four years, she's built a trusted network of sources."

"So what went wrong?"

"I wish I knew. They'd made contact with a celebrated tattoo artist in Tokyo, a businessman named Yoshi Yamamoto with ties to the yakuza and apparently some financial interest in a casino and hotel resort on Saipan. Cahill begged him to create a dragon tattoo on her wrist, which is how she eventually got him to start talking. The guy was unhappy and afraid that his life was spiraling out of control. He was willing to tell them all he knew about the drug trafficking, gunrunning, and a few other activities in return for starting life over in the U.S. under new identities for him and his niece. We had a witness-protection plan ready to go."

"What happened to him?"

"He's also gone dark."

"And the niece?"

"Her name is Hiraku and, unfortunately, she has also disappeared. From what we know, she may very well be key to bringing down their operation. Based on our last report from Cahill, a powerful yakuza boss named Orochi Tanaka had taken a liking to the girl. Her uncle feared Tanaka might kidnap her. Not so unusual when the yakuza are involved. So it looks like the girl may have gone into hiding. Stevens was scheduled to file a follow-up report with more details, but he never did."

Ashwood pulled another black-and-white photograph from his desk. "Orochi Tanaka. His nickname is Big Snake. A foul human being if ever there was one. Right now he's in position to become shogun of heroin smuggling throughout the entire Pacific Rim. If that happens, it'll be almost impossible to bring that situation under control. He'll be unstoppable. So the stakes are high."

Hannah fiddled with a few strands of her wavy blonde hair. "And the girl, the tattoo artist's niece, why is she so important?"

"Because there's a good probability that she, just like her uncle, has the information we're looking for – the names of the players, the smuggling routes, the contacts in each location, and how the money is being laundered. According to Cahill, the girl is an important key to the puzzle, but she never got to explain precisely why. It's my gut feeling that Yoshi Yamamoto is dead, but if we find Hiraku, we can still win this war. If we don't, America's streets become a heroin shooting gallery and we can watch as the fabric of our society unravels. We've got to find her and get her back here in one piece. Hopefully we're not too late."

Hannah was still struggling with the news about her two colleagues. Her throat was dry and swallowing difficult. She immediately recalled Candace Cahill's zany sense of humor that usually made her colleagues double over with laughter. Cahill was young and good looking, with four years of field experience, and now she apparently was dead.

"And you think this Asaki might have had direct involvement in the heroin trafficking? Why would..."

Ashwood palmed up his right hand to halt Hannah's next question. "I didn't say that. Right now all we know for certain is that Asaki had some sort of business interest in the same Saipan casino and hotel where Yoshi Yamamoto worked as a manager. Shortly before Christmas, a Japanese tour group spotted Asaki's body bobbing face up in the surf at the foot of Banzai Cliff. The Saipan police weren't exactly shocked. Apparently suicides are common there."

Carrington nodded, as though familiar with the location and the custom. "I recall reading about the Battle of Saipan in a course at the war college. If I remember correctly, during World War II, entire Japanese families living on the island flung themselves over the edge of the cliffs to their deaths rather than face what they imagined would be torture by the thousands of U.S. Marines storming ashore."

"You've got a good memory," said Ashwood. "Mostly it was Japanese soldiers who died at Banzai Cliff. There's also Suicide Cliff nearby, where about six hundred other Japanese jumped to their deaths – men, women, old, young, some going over the side with babies in their arms, whole families holding hands as they headed for the afterlife."

Hannah pursed her lips and glanced at Carrington, who had folded his arms on his chest while Ashwood continued the briefing.

"The landing zone at the bottom of Suicide Cliff is craggy rock, as equally unforgiving as the pounding waves at Banzai. During the Battle of Saipan, or I guess you might say in its aftermath, the Army Signal Corps recorded these suicides on film — countless horrible images. Loudspeakers were set up on land and aboard Navy ships anchored just offshore, and translators were hired to tell the people they wouldn't be harmed if they surrendered to our Marines, but it didn't do much good. They jumped anyway. Honored to commit suicide for the emperor. At least most of them did. The survivors surrendered or were found hiding in the caves. Saipan has no shortage of caves."

Hannah moved uneasily in her seat. "Jesus," she said. "I'd better catch up on my history."

"I'll be glad to fill you in," said Carrington. "We'll probably have to start with the attack on Pearl Harbor."

"I know about Pearl Harbor, you idiot," she said, playfully kicking him in the shin. "Dec. 7, 1941. The Japanese sank our fleet in Hawaii. Tora! Tora! Tora! FDR on the radio. The Day of Infamy. America declares war on Japan."

"Hannah, you obviously saw the movie and, well, not all of our fleet..."

Ashwood stopped him mid-sentence. "I'll let you two get back to your history and cinema studies later. And when you return from Saipan, if you pass the first quiz, you'll get little silver stars stuck to your foreheads, or glued into your personnel files, whichever you prefer."

"That's really sweet, Stuart, but I'd prefer a silk kimono."

Ashwood laughed aloud for the first time as he lit another cigarette. "I'll sign off on your kimono, Hannah. But let me give you both a word of caution: the Japanese, especially the yakuza, play by different rules and they typically don't pull any punches. So learn their game quickly and don't let your guard down. I don't want two more of my people missing."

5

A DRAGON'S DELIGHT

KOMODO ISLAND
REPUBLIC OF INDONESIA
MARCH 1990

OROCHI TANAKA SAT beneath a palm tree in a folding lawn chair and thoughtfully sipped a fruity rum cocktail from a fresh coconut while watching his underworld partner struggle against the ropes that lashed his hands and feet to a thick wooden pole pounded deeply into the sand.

Tanaka, whose first name translated roughly to Big Snake, was amused by the fear in the eyes of the man who, he was convinced, had betrayed him. As far as Tanaka was concerned, betrayal was the biggest of unforgivable sins and this man had committed it.

"Orochi, please. Don't do this," pleaded the man tied to the pole who wore only a white loincloth like those favored by sumo wrestlers. "I didn't betray you. I honor you. I respect you. I would never do such a thing. We have been friends for years."

The captive man was taller than the average Japanese, strongly built, with a head shaved close to the scalp and a mosaic of tattoos on his arms and legs. He tugged at his hemp-rope bonds but they were securely fastened. Rivulets of sweat spilled down his face but he was helpless to wipe them. The sand was hot but the sun was waning, the tree branches casting long shadows on the idyllic beach.

Tanaka, a barrel-chested man in his late forties, was despite the heat clad formally in a black, western-style, two-piece suit. He wore a long-sleeve, white linen dress shirt, wide purple necktie, and aviator sunglasses. If it were not for his bare feet and tiny toes methodically curling into the coarse sand, he might have been headed to a corporate board meeting.

"Yoshi, you and I were like brothers. How many years did we work side by side? Twenty? I'm saddened it has come to this," said Tanaka, loosening his silk tie and taking another sip of rum. "You knew Saipan was mine and still you tried to take it, you and Mikito. Look where it got him, and now you're no better off. When you're gone, the world will have lost a master tattoo artist, maybe the best ever. That is the biggest shame."

"I did nothing. People offered me gifts in return for information about you, but I always turned them away."

Yoshi tugged against the bonds, his body glistening with sweat. "Please believe me, Orochi. I've told you a hundred times. I didn't take your money. Someone has miscounted, or they have fixed the ledgers to make it look like I'm a thief."

"If only I could believe you. If only you and Mikito had not run off with what belongs not just to me but also to other yakuza families. How do you think that makes me look in their eyes? I'm disgraced by your actions."

Tanaka twice pounded the arm of his chair, a signal to two men dressed in baggy shorts, t-shirts and sandals, M16 automatic rifles slung over their shoulders. Normally the men worked as park rangers on Komodo Island but had agreed to turn a blind eye to Tanaka's activities in return for what amounted to a year's pay for each. The park rangers, who wore their t-shirts inside out to hide their government unit shoulder patches, casually walked in opposite directions into the underbrush. Tanaka's four armed bodyguards checked their Uzi machine pistols and nervously glanced at their surroundings, not quite knowing what to expect. Like the others, they were still jetlagged by the seven-hour flight from Saipan to Bali and then to the small fishing village of Labuan Bajo on Flores Island, all aboard Tanaka's Gulfstream III jet. A chartered helicopter had ferried the group on the final leg to Komodo Island. The pilot and co-pilot didn't ask why one of the passengers was drugged or sick and barely able to walk. They had been paid handsomely to fly and remain with the helicopter once they landed on the island.

Nobody spoke as Tanaka rested in the chair and calmly buffed his fingernails with a sandpaper file. Ten minutes passed. Then twenty. The two-way radio in the pocket of Tanaka's suit jacket beeped four times. Tanaka held it up so all could hear as the speaker crackled with an excited voice. "Ready. Coming your way."

The bodyguards drew their machine pistols and braced for the unknown. Tanaka, a handsome man who many people said resembled a Japanese version of the 1950s American movie star Clark Gable, flashed a full set of oversized white teeth. His high cheekbones were flushed pink, his eyes, with their long lashes, alive with excitement.

One of the bodyguards frantically pointed to a rustling in the underbrush less than a hundred feet from where Tanaka was seated. Tanaka raised an arm, signaling his bodyguard not to open fire. A Komodo dragon exposed its reptilian head through a break in the tall grass and repeatedly flicked its divided tongue as though sensing nearby prey, more like a snake than a lizard. Yoshi gasped in horror, which caused Tanaka to grin until his lips were stretched to the fullest.

The rustling continued as two front legs with sharp claws appeared, followed by the rear legs and long tail. The dragon, part of the family of monitor lizards, was at least eight feet long.

"No, Orochi. No!"

The dragon moved cautiously toward the sweating prey. The bodyguards, guns drawn, formed a protective flank in front of Tanaka but he ordered them to step aside.

"Please do not obstruct my view of this beautiful moment," he said, sipping from his coconut drink.

As the guards stepped aside, Tanaka leaned toward the tripod and switched on the video camera.

Yoshi began to recite Buddhist prayers aloud. The dragon moved closer, sniffed the prey with its tongue and without warning sunk its serrated, razor-sharp teeth into the man's left leg. A horrific scream sent the nearest birds flying in all directions and again Tanaka chuckled.

The dragon's jaws glistened with saliva as it ripped away a chunk of flesh and swallowed with little effort. Blood spilled into the sand. Yoshi wailed in pain, which was followed by a remorseful moan that Tanaka knew affected his bodyguards who were trying hard to show no emotion. Tanaka was convinced his men would remember this day and, at some point in the near future, tell others about it. As a result, his reputation would grow and many more would fear him.

The reptile stood on its hind legs and bit into Yoshi's right arm, again tearing away flesh. Another woeful scream burst from the throat of the dying man. Tanaka ordered one of the bodyguards to freshen his drink with a rum double. The bodyguard hustled to the Igloo cooler that rested in the shade of a palm tree where he nervously added more rum and ice to Tanaka's coconut and inserted a new plastic straw.

A second lizard, smaller than the first, skittered toward the wooden pole and attempted to join the feast. The larger animal hissed but didn't attack his competitor, content to chomp into Yoshi's stomach, spilling and devouring his intestines, the blood soaking into the white loincloth so that it turned red. Yoshi's last thoughts were of his adoptive niece Hiraku, the beautiful young woman he had nicknamed Little Peacock. The moaning soon stopped.

Tanaka switched off the camera and returned to fine-sanding his fingernails. Before boarding the helicopter he made certain the park rangers would dispose of Yoshi's body in a place where it would never be found, presuming the Komodo dragons didn't gnaw it to the bone.

6

WATCHFUL EYES

SAIPAN

NORTHERN MARIANA ISLANDS

MARCH 1990

HANNAH AND CARRINGTON casually walked from the commercial airliner parked on the tarmac to the Customs office where they joined the line of tourists, residents and other visitors headed inside the small concrete building. They appeared an unhurried couple on vacation with plans to relax. The flight from Tokyo's Narita International Airport to Guam and finally to Saipan had taken several hours during which they napped, read and chatted about matters unrelated to their profession.

Hannah was wearing a red, flower-patterned, wide-leg jumpsuit and leather sandals. Her hair was piled atop her head in a messy bun. Carrington had donned khaki surfer shorts, a Pearl Jam band t-shirt and well-worn Topsiders. His Wayfarer sunglasses rested atop his head, nestled into his ash-blond hair. Both he and Hannah had checked suitcases in addition to their carry-on bags. They'd done this purposefully, filling the suit-cases with bathing suits, paperback books and tubes of sunscreen. If Customs agents sifted through the contents, they'd most likely surmise these two were tourists headed for the resort town of Garapan and popular Micro Beach.

Hideyo Mashima, a detective with the Commonwealth of the Northern Mariana Islands (CNMI) police, leaned his lanky frame against an exterior wall of the Customs building and studied each arriving passenger. He was primarily looking for yakuza. If a male passenger was missing a pinky finger, or a portion of it, very likely this was the result of *yubitsume*, the practice of severing one's own smallest digit as a way of self-inflicting punishment for having made a poor decision or having engaged in behavior unacceptable to his underworld boss. The amputated finger was usually wrapped in clean white cloth or preserved in a small glass vial until it could be person-ally delivered to the offended person.

Although *yubitsume* was a solid clue to yakuza membership, Mashima found the severed pinky fingers difficult to spot from a distance. He knew the yakuza were a wily bunch, and wasn't surprised when a cottage industry sprang up to provide fake pinky-finger extensions for those attempting to evade detection by police or customs officers.

Tattoos were far easier to spot, especially since many yakuza were proud of them and so left the artwork exposed when at the beach. The tattoos often depicted snakes, dragons, carp, or peacocks. Traditionally, most yakuza left a bare strip in the center of their chest, running from neck to stomach and void of tattoos. This allowed them to wear shirts or sport jackets unbuttoned without revealing their ink.

Mashima moved closer to the counter as a Customs officer began questioning two yakuza who had strutted toward the arrival building as though they did not intend to stop at the gate. The men spoke abruptly and disrespectfully to the

Customs officer who had asked them to open their suitcases. Mashima could tell they were yakuza by their stride, so unlike the average Japanese tourist whose gait was more humble. Voices were getting louder and it seemed a confrontation would erupt as Mashima approached.

With a slight bow, he greeted the two visitors. "Good afternoon, gentlemen. Although this may seem an inconvenience, this officer is merely doing as he has been instructed. I'm sure you would do the same if your superior had spoken."

In a show of great annoyance, the men unzipped their suitcases and flung the lids open. Folded clothing shared space with cartons of cigarettes and bottles of scotch, far exceeding the import tax limit. Mashima pretended not to notice. He was more interested in the possibility of finding weapons and drugs.

"Are you here to spend days lounging at our beautiful beaches, or is this a business trip?"

Both yakuza ignored his question. Mashima didn't anticipate an answer. He knew the yakuza had a penchant for rudeness and disdain for authority.

The Customs officer held up a box containing dozens of condoms and inspected it with a wry grin. He opened one flap and peered inside as though the box might contain a surprise. The two yakuza shared a personal joke that apparently referred to the need for so many prophylactics. The Customs officer tossed the box atop the other items in the suitcase, closed the lid and nodded for the next passenger in line to come forward. Both yakuza grunted and headed for the counter where their passports were stamped. Mashima wondered if they were the first wave of a rumored large-scale yakuza meeting among the various families. He was well aware the yakuza bragged a membership of nearly 80,000 spread over about twenty organized families or clans. If so, other representatives would likely arrive within the next day or two, perhaps one or two per family. That's how it typically worked.

The detective prepared to brace himself for the brash gaggle of younger yakuza or sons – known as *kobun*. These were often the troublesome tourists whose primary responsibility was to cater to their *oyabun*, or father, ensuring his every whim was satisfied — carrying his bags, lighting his cigarette, or answering questions with exaggerated politeness.

It was well known among the international law enforcement community that the yakuza – with the exception of the Yamaguchi-gumi, Japan's largest organized crime family – were involved in drug trafficking. Many yakuza clans dealt primarily in amphetamines and heroin. And each treated the details of their smuggling operations and delivery routes as highly-guarded trade secrets. Giving away such information was punishable by death.

Some days, the only clues Mashima gleaned were from passport stamps indicating the person had traveled extensively between Bangkok and Manila, or Saipan and Honolulu. If those travelers were serving as mules by smuggling heroin, Mashima hoped to catch them red-handed. But given the massive quantities of white powder reaching the streets of America, he knew the transportation methods involved something much larger – tankers, freighters, private aircraft capable of flying over oceans.

Mashima also prided himself on his ability to pick out undercover American agents arriving on his island. Though these visitors attempted to blend in with the tourists, to Mashima they stood out like sharks amid a school of parrot fish. Despite their flip flops and flowered shirts, their hyper-alert eyes always gave them away.

The brief altercation between the Customs officer and the two yakuza had not escaped Hannah's attention. She quickly determined the local cop with Japanese facial features, who had interceded during the heated moment, was not a yakuza fan, unless he was putting on a show for someone else's benefit. He had shown no fear. The extensive burn scars covering the left side of his face gave him a menacing look, but the undamaged side was pleasant and kind, handsome even.

Hannah sensed the police officer had immediately pegged her and Carrington as something other than tourists. By the time they reached the Customs officer, Mashima had returned to his observation post, which left him in the shade of the building canopy with his back pressed against the wall of cool cement. The detective lit a Dunhill cigarette and watched as Hannah and Carrington allowed the Customs officer to inspect their suitcases and carry-on bags. Moments later, another Customs official stamped the passport of Argentine citizen Mariel Becker and recorded the arrival of U.S. resident Jake Marson. Welcome to Saipan.

Mashima followed them at a distance as they stepped into the sun-bleached street, the harsh light reflecting off the white coral pavement. Just outside the airport's main building, three taxi drivers rested against the front fenders of their battered American sedans and awaited passengers. Mashima already knew from their entry cards that Becker and Marson – names he suspected were false — were staying at the Chalan Kanoa Beach Hotel. The place was not among the island's luxury resorts. It was nearly ten miles from the commercial stretch in Garapan near Micro Beach where most of the hotels, casinos and other tourist attractions were located. Garapan was where the tourists flocked to gamble and perhaps indulge in Saipan's prospering sex trade. Mashima assumed the two visitors had chosen Chalan Kanoa because the hamlet would allow more privacy. He made a note to speak with the hotel owner.

PEACOCK IN A CAGE

SAIPAN
NORTHERN MARIANA ISLANDS
MARCH 1990

WHEN TANAKA RETURNED to his Saipan home perched on a bluff overlooking the sea, he found Hiraku seated on the couch. As soon as she saw him, the young woman folded her arms across her small breasts and pouted.

"Where is my Uncle Yoshi? I want to talk to him."

Tanaka shrugged. "Nobody has seen him. Perhaps he has run off with a *saseko*, or maybe a case of sake."

"He wouldn't leave without telling me. Something has happened to him. He has been gone almost two weeks."

The young woman wore bright pink shorts and a florescent green sleeveless top, which provided a glimpse of the intricate tattoos that flowed like sleeves from her shoulders to her wrists. Her glossy black hair was punk styled, spiked in a few places with streaks of orange and blue. She was barefoot, which caused Tanaka to stop, as he always did, to admire the peacock feather tattoo that adorned her left foot.

Hiraku stood but kept her arms defiantly crossed, a scowl on her face. "I want to return to Tokyo. You can't just keep me here."

Tanaka offered an amused grin. "Sit down," he said, though atypically it was more a request than a command. "Until we find Yoshi, it's best that you remain here."

"So I'm a prisoner."

"You are my guest."

"If I'm your guest, then I want to leave. Now. If you don't let me go, I'm going to call the police."

Tanaka smiled, exposing his large and perfectly straight white teeth. Slowly he approached Hiraku, reached around and roughly grasped her buttocks with both hands, lifting her so that she was pressed against him.

"Get your hands off me," she said, beating her fists into his shoulders. "They call you a snake, but you're really a pig."

Tanaka laughed gregariously as he set her down. He could still feel the warmth of her bottom on his fingertips where he'd massaged the soft skin. It made him recall the first time he'd ever seen her six years previous. She was barely fifteen and appeared at his Tokyo apartment door early one morning, carrying what she described as a very important package from her so-called Uncle Yoshi. Tanaka had been expecting the delivery but not the girl. He invited her inside but she declined, saying she was already late for school. He remembered how sexy she looked in her navy blue blazer, white blouse, short plaid skirt and buckle shoes, the uniform of her private girls' school.

Although he'd occasionally seen her with Yoshi after that, it wasn't until her eighteenth birthday party at a Tokyo restaurant that he first noticed the peacock feather tattoo on her foot. The tattoo details were exquisite. Perfect artistry.

Tanaka knew by the design quality that Yoshi had created it. He had been so taken by the tattoo that he'd asked Hiraku to remove her sandal so that he might fully admire it. Hiraku had blushed. The moment was awkward, but Tanaka was a powerful yakuza boss. His requests were really orders in disguise. So Hiraku slipped her foot from the sandal and gently twirled her ankle. Tanaka had to stop himself from reaching out and kissing it.

Yoshi had invited five of Hiraku's girlfriends to celebrate her birthday in the Ginza. The mood at the table was festive, all of them drinking plum wine, sake and beer, and nibbling on trays laden with sashimi, yakitori, tempura, sukiyaki, and even a stack of cheeseburgers with French fries – the latter a special request from Hiraku.

Tanaka had brought along two younger yakuza — handsome fun seekers, unlike other *kobun* in his crime family who practiced looking stern and fierce but offered little joy. He was infatuated with Hiraku and hoped to share some moments with her alone. As such, he had pre-arranged to receive a phone call during the birthday celebration regarding an emergency at The Lucky Carp casino and hotel on Saipan. The caller was instructed to say it was a delicate matter involving a prostitute seriously injured by a customer and a situation that only Yoshi, as the most-recognized co-owner of the establishment, could handle. According to Tanaka, the Saipan police were already threatening to shut down The Lucky Carp. Hundreds of thousands of dollars potentially would be lost from nightly gambling proceeds, prostitution, and routine money laundering until the problem was resolved.

Tanaka assured Yoshi he would transport Hiraku and her companions to their respective homes when the party was over. Yoshi was grateful his boss and business partner was also a trusted friend. He bowed respectfully and departed for the airport.

Bellies filled with food and drink, Hiraku insisted they all go dancing at an American-style discotheque. She wanted to dance and sing the latest from Madonna, Janet Jackson, and the Pet Shop Boys. It was well past three in the morning when the nightclub closed its doors. Tanaka suggested they continue the party at his penthouse apartment and everyone thought it was a great idea since it was only a 15-minute limo drive from the nightclub. Once at the penthouse, the girls chatted, sipped more plum wine and danced with the two *kobun*. They soon fell asleep on the couches in the spacious living room with its panoramic view of the glittering city.

At mid-morning, the *kobun* drove Hiraku's friends to their homes. Tanaka convinced Hiraku to stay and wait for Yoshi rather than return immediately to the tiny apartment she shared with her uncle in a far less opulent quarter of the sprawling city. The yakuza boss knew the phony business to which Yoshi had been dispatched would keep him occupied for at least two days. The flights each way between Tokyo and Saipan would consume many hours. More time would be spent discussing the incident with the casino night manager and the police, who would be confused by Yoshi's concerns since no such assault had occurred. When it came time to report his findings to Tanaka, Yoshi would be told a rumor apparently had gotten out of control and led them all astray at The Lucky Carp.

Hiraku agreed to remain until nightfall, when she would take a cab back to her apartment. She was not afraid to stay there alone. She'd done so many times when Yoshi was in Saipan. Besides, she was enjoying the luxurious surroundings, the fashionable furniture and artwork, a kitchen made for a gourmet chef, and a master bathroom with sauna, steam room, and a glass-enclosed shower where faucets sprayed water from six nozzles.

She read magazines, watched TV and tried to relax, but the

sound of Tanaka's agitated voice as he paced the room while conducting business on the phone disturbed her mood. She decided to take a shower, helping herself to two of the white, fluffy, oversized towels that were among dozens neatly stacked on a teak shelf. She was shocked when Tanaka entered the shower where the gush of warm water was working wonders to wash away the previous night of partying. She screamed. She knew she had locked the door. "What are you doing in here? Get out!"

Tanaka was naked and erect. "Hiraku is a beautiful name. It means radiance, and you are truly radiant," he said, stepping into the shower and wrapping his strong arms around her.

"Please let me go." She tried to wriggle from his embrace but he held her tightly, pushing himself between her legs.

"No. Stop!"

Tanaka persisted. He had imagined this moment many times – although in his mind it occurred on a bed of rose petals, not in the shower. And in his vision, Hiraku was willing – perhaps the initiator, possessing innate charms he did not have the words to describe.

Hiraku felt an excruciating pain that pulsed across her abdomen as Tanaka pushed inside her. She screamed loudly, scratching Tanaka's face and shoulders, causing him to momentarily thrust deeper before he released his grip and withdrew.

Thin streaks of blood were swirling toward the floor drain. Hiraku began to cry.

Tanaka stepped out of the shower and turned to face Hiraku. "Get dressed," he said. "I'll have someone take you home."

Hiraku couldn't stop crying. She was in disbelief. She wrapped herself in a towel and ran to the bedroom where she and two of her friends had slept the previous night. She closed and locked the door and sank to the floor. "My uncle will kill you," she shouted. "Do you hear me? He'll find a way to kill you."

Tanaka put his lips close to the door. "Listen to me carefully, Hiraku. If you mention any of this to Yoshi, he may try to do something foolish and you will never see him again. That I can assure you."

Three years had passed since then, though to Tanaka it seemed only yesterday. But he felt no remorse for having raped the young woman.

Tanaka's reverie was abruptly shaken when Hiraku slapped him hard in the face, leaving the imprint of her delicate fingers and claw marks from her long fingernails.

"Didn't you hear me? I said you're a pig, a fat disgusting pig. And a rapist," she shouted. "I want to talk to my Uncle Yoshi, now. And I want to leave here of my own free will." She poked a threatening finger into his barrel chest and again her shrill voice filled the room. "I'm going to call the police."

When Hiraku attempted to slap him a second time, he grabbed her wrist, twisted it as though breaking a tree branch and pushed her down on the floor. Staring at her with his chilling snake eyes, he said, "Enough games, Hiraku. I want to know what you told the CIA."

8

THE RISE OF HIDEYO MASHIMA

SAIPAN
NORTHERN MARIANA ISLANDS
MARCH 1990

HANNAH CONTACTED the local tourism office to introduce herself as an Argentine travel company representative. She was prepared to set up discount packages for hotel and beach vacations with water sports and resort-based gourmet dining. She even suggested a Sunday cock-fighting event in the remote village of San Antonio that might appeal to adventurous tourists with cultural interests, looking for more than paddling a kayak over the reefs of the atoll or taking a nature walk along a trail clogged with a plethora of large lizards.

The woman who answered the phone at the tourism office didn't seem interested in what Hannah had to say, but promised she'd leave a message for her supervisor. Hannah paid no mind to the lax response. She was more concerned should anyone later follow up, they'd confirm Mariel Becker made a phone call that supported her travel company cover. It was part of her establishing a paper trail. It was also the way things worked on Saipan.

In an effort to remain low profile, Carrington rented a dun-colored, sub-compact Nissan that they drove to Micro Beach in Garapan, posing as tourists while doing a recon of the village layout and its main attractions. Once on the white sand beach they spread two beach towels beneath a palm-thatched umbrella. They tossed their books and water bottles atop the towels and jogged into the warm surf.

Hannah wore a two-piece polka-dot bikini that Carrington found so distracting he forced himself to take a solo walk to the far end of the beach. He knew his married days were numbered, but until a judge signed the still-to-be-drafted divorce papers, the wet blanket of guilt hung heavy on his shoulders.

Hannah's feelings for Carrington were a jumble. She loved his boyishness. And then there were the little things that made her smile, like his enthusiasm for high-quality knives, flash-lights, backpacks, climbing rope, antique spyglasses, state-of-the-art binoculars, night-vision scopes, portable radiation detectors, top-notch hiking boots and polarized sunglasses. All these items she referred to collectively as his Boy Scout arsenal. She often razzed him about the number of backpacks he owned, and each time he'd assured her the packs were quite different from one another and designed with special purposes in mind.

While some people might have accused Carrington of being an equipment junkie, Hannah appreciated the fact that he actually used these possessions as a CIA officer. Those at Langley who had worked with Carrington trusted him implic-itly because in the world of dark ops, he ranked among the best. It was well known he spent more hours in the agency's innovation lab than most other officers, discussing field scenarios and possibilities with the agency's top craftsmen, scientists and engineers.

Looking out at Carrington jumping and splashing in the waves, Hannah couldn't stop smiling. Carrington looked like a joyous ten-year-old, immersed in a magical world as he dove into the crests. Her heart swelled, which made her wonder if what she was feeling was mere amusement and attraction, or some form of love, something deeper and scarier. She was filled with a sense, and more than a little afraid, that it might be the latter.

Carrington certainly came with baggage – namely a wife and two children — but he was cool, intelligent, and would do everything possible to protect her when the bullets started flying.

And then there was Decker, who also claimed a piece of her heart. Hannah knew he was off on another mission to some unfriendly land and probably taking far too many risks. She feared one of these days he'd come home in a body bag. And since he was CIA, it would all be hush-hush, no shiny coffin draped with an American flag and the major television networks with cameras rolling to record a hero's return.

It was during moments like these that she second-guessed her decision to join the CIA. The organization didn't leave much room for a normal life, yet there were times she wanted nothing more than a husband, a house, and a baby. But how, after becoming romantically involved with anyone in the spy business, could she possibly bring him home to the folks in Kansas City, Missouri?

Hi Mom and Dad, this is Decker. He's a spy and so am I. We go on missions together and sometimes we have to kill people. He's not a vegetarian, so Dad can grill up the biggest steaks!

Or Carrington. *Yes, he's married. Yes, he has two kids. No, he barely sees them or his wife. They're estranged. He's a spy, too, like Decker. But nobody calls us spies. We're agency operatives. CIA offi-*

cers. *And if the people in charge at Langley want to push the distance between them and us even farther, then we're simply known as contractors, like plumbers or electricians.*

The same dilemma played out when at twenty-five she met and began dating the renowned Boston surgeon Chandler Hughes – two decades older, highly intelligent, often obnoxious and belittling. No way would she ever introduce him to her parents. They certainly wouldn't deserve it and her father would bristle at the doctor's age and arrogance. Looking back, she seriously questioned her judgment and prided herself on never introducing him to her family or friends.

Hannah knew if she told her girlfriends from high school or college what she was doing they'd be in awe, envisioning a high-stakes life of glamour, adventure, intrigue, and international travel, never giving a second thought to how it might prevent her from finding Mr. Right, settling down, and maybe having a baby! A BABY! And why not? At thirty-one the chimes of her biological clock were clanging deep down. *Reproduce! Go forth and procreate! Become a mom!* Imagine, a mom!

When she last saw those friends over the Christmas holiday nearly two years ago, the youngest was pregnant and bursting with anticipation, while two others were gushing about their lives as new moms. This was life among the Missouri middle-class. The young women talked non-stop about diapers, strollers, and visits to the babyGap store *"because they have these really cute outfits, like little farmer jeans and crewneck sweaters and even babyGap workboots."*

Hannah had sat and listened, conscious of her tendency to roll her eyes at vacuous statements, and tried to be excited for them without showing any trace of envy.

Though the friends still treated her like the prom queen she'd been back in 1977, she couldn't help feeling a sea change had occurred and now they were the lucky ones, even if their daily challenges didn't measure up to what was heaped on her plate at Langley.

Later that day, the women's words still fresh in her mind, Hannah envisioned submitting a letter of resignation to the CIA, not knowing whether such a thing was allowed. The possibility made her smile, but the joy ended when she received a priority beeper message hours later from Preston Barlow, then deputy director of operations at Langley.

Hannah telephoned the encrypted number. Barlow was terse. Another unforeseen mission was about to get under way. She was needed back at the operations center – ASAP – in other words, immediately. No apology from Barlow was included. A private jet would be standing by at Kansas City International.

Hannah knew the danger of allowing her mind to roam. She had been graced with steely logic and it played against any whim upon which she might act. She adjusted her sunglasses and stared out at the turquoise sea. Carrington was paddling a surfboard.

A question recycled through Hannah's head: *How did things get so complicated? It wasn't supposed to be this way.*

Mashima saw his opportunity to approach the blonde woman while she was alone. He felt awkward traipsing through the soft sand in his brown, leather wingtip shoes, but going barefoot seemed too unofficial.

"I hope you are enjoying your stay on Saipan," he said, standing off to Hannah's right, hands clasped in front of him.

Hannah flinched. Over the sounds of the surf she hadn't heard him approach. "Do you always sneak up on people?"

"Forgive me. I thought it more impolite to shout."

"You're forgiven. We saw you at the airport. Customs?"

"No. CNMI police. I'm Detective Mashima."

"Well, hello detective. What can I do for you?"

Feeling self-conscious and bashful, Mashima turned his

head so that Hannah wouldn't see the raised scars on the left side of his face. "Please don't take offense, but I have the feeling you are not truly the representatives of an adventure travel company."

"What are you saying?"

"If you have come to learn more about certain activities on my island, perhaps I can be of assistance. Your accent sounds American, as does your companion's. I know it well from my college days. I was educated in the States."

"And what sort of activities are you referring to?"

"Two representatives from your FBI are already here on Saipan, looking into an unfortunate murder which occurred in late December."

Hannah pulled a gauzy cover-up over her bathing suit that seemingly had made the detective uncomfortable. "I wouldn't know anything about that. I sell travel packages."

"If that's so, I wish you supreme success in your business. If not, then my offer of assistance still stands."

"Have you helped the FBI agents who are here?"

"The two special agents made it clear they did not want my assistance, even though I speak Japanese and am an island native. My father is Japanese, but my mother is Chamorro. She was born and raised here on Saipan. I, too, was born here. I understand the people and the culture, which at times can seem confusing to outsiders."

"And why is that?"

"Because everyone here on the island is related, in one way or another. And that can make learning truthful information very difficult."

Carrington picked up his pace when he spotted the stranger talking to Hannah. As he neared the blanket, he affected the tone of a stoned-out surfer dude.

"Jake," he said, thrusting a hand toward Mashima who reluctantly shook it in bro fashion. "Is everything cool?"

"Why would everything not be cool?"

"Well, we're new here. We don't know anybody, so I figured you might be a cop. And then I thought, well, if that's the case, we might have broken a local law without knowing it. I'm pretty sure our rental car is properly registered."

"You're correct in one way. I am a police officer, a detective. But I'm not here to interrogate you, nor do I suspect you of engaging in any illegal activities. I was merely offering my services to Miss Becker."

"Services?"

"He thinks we're American spies."

Carrington burst out laughing. "That's me, all right. 007." He swirled into a crouching position and feigned holding a handgun, his arm outstretched and pointing toward the water's edge. "Bam bam! Take that you evil doers."

Mashima's calm facial expression revealed nothing. He remained convinced these were no regular tourists. The man's surfer-dude act didn't ring true, nor did the woman's faintly Spanish accent, which he presumed was faked.

"Let me leave it this way. I shall tell you something and if you find it both truthful and useful, then perhaps we shall talk again."

Hannah smiled. "Please do."

"I believe you are attempting to learn what has happened to two of your colleagues, and also to a man named Yoshi Yamamoto who evidently was their ally, or at least someone with whom they were conspiring."

Mashima paused, as though awaiting a reaction. When none came, he continued. "I believe you are also interested in a young woman named Hiraku, the niece of Yoshi Yamamoto. Unfortunately she has not been seen for the past twelve days at The Lucky Carp, the casino and hotel in Garapan where Mr. Yamamoto is among the owners. Nor has she boarded a flight to

Tokyo where she shares an apartment with her uncle when they are not on Saipan. We would know if she had."

"This is a fascinating story," said Hannah. "Sounds like this Hiraku has gone into hiding or else she has been abducted."

"That is my presumption, although her fate by now could be far worse."

Carrington affected a look of bemusement. "Why are you telling us all this?"

"Please, let's not play games, Mr. Marson, if that is actually your name. Time may be of the essence."

Hannah chimed in. "Have you tried to find her?"

"Of course, but Saipan is an island with many secrets. If certain people with power want her to remain hidden, it's unlikely anyone searching for her will have success. The yakuza are feared because they live by a code of violence and do not hesitate to eliminate those they believe are their enemy."

"Did you tell this story to the FBI?"

"I did. They were not interested. They only want to know who murdered Mikito Asaki, the yakuza boss whose body was thrown off Banzai Cliff. For them, it's a homicide case and because Saipan is a U.S. protectorate, they're here to solve it and make an arrest. Nothing more."

"And you think we're here for a different reason?"

"As you Americans say, I feel a vibe."

"I'm Argentine," Hannah said coyly. "Jake is American. Maybe it's coming from him."

Jake feigned offense. "You say that with such distain, Mariel."

"Not at all, Jake. But apparently you do have that special vibe only Americans possess," she said, kicking some sand at him with her bare foot.

Mashima blushed, realizing they were flirting with each other. He made a mental note and handed them his business card. "I'll leave you in peace to enjoy such magnificent surroundings. Contact me anytime, night or day, if you wish."

"Thanks for stopping by," said Hannah. "If you're interested in a hotel and beach vacation package in Buenos Aires, I'm your best source."

Mashima smiled knowingly, again showing the handsome side of his face as he envisioned what sort of action he'd have to take if the pair caused trouble.

9
_____

A BOX OF ROCKS

SAIPAN

NORTHERN MARIANA ISLANDS

MARCH 1990

DETECTIVE MASHIMA and two CNMI officers stood facing the relentless wind at the top of Banzai Cliff. The spot was precisely where blood had been found that the local police and the FBI were convinced belonged to murder victim Mikito Asaki.

Mashima pointed at four cardboard boxes stacked near their police vehicle. "Put six heavy stones in each container," he said with authority. "We want to make our packages heavy enough so that they drop straight down, like a body."

The two uniformed police officers loaded the boxes with the largest stones they could carry and secured the lids with duct tape. Over the course of six hours they collected additional stones and dropped the boxes over the edge on Mashima's command at 90-minute intervals.

The tide flowed slowly and persistently inward, until it

nearly touched the third box where it had landed on the rocks.
The box rested just above the wrack line, the natural mound of
seaweed and flotsam deposited by the previous high tide. The
forth and final box landed only inches from the water's edge,
though it was not yet high tide.

Mashima was pleased with the results of their field test.
"This confirms Asaki's body landed on the rocks and remained
there until the tide rose," the detective said. "On the morning of
the murder, there was a high tide with a plus of two-and-a-half
feet. That is when his body was washed out to sea, at approximately 10:55 a.m., when the tide was highest."

Mashima needed the tidal information to establish a time-
frame for the crime that would eliminate alibis when suspects
were questioned. He was delighted that his forensic team had
found blood atop the cliff along with tire tread tracks, but the
crime lab was having difficulty saying for sure whether the
blood was from a human, a dog, or a fish. Mashima knew any
defense attorney would use that evidentiary weakness to great
advantage.

10

A NIGHT OUT IN GARAPAN

SAIPAN

NORTHERN MARIANA ISLANDS

MARCH 1990

HANNAH AND CARRINGTON parked their rental car on the village outskirts and walked toward Garapan's commercial strip — a few hotels, small casinos and tiki bars catering to tourists. They passed several local watering holes that were little more than half sheets of plywood laid across a pair of rusted 55-gallon steel drums, a rickety plastic shelf for the liquor bottles as a backdrop, and a galvanized tub filled with ice shaded by a tarp for the beer. A handful of restaurants, dive shops, beachfront surfboard rentals, and mom-and-pop grocery stores were spread out along the white coral street. The only visible marked police vehicle was parked in front of the JoeTen food market but no officers were inside it.

Hannah smiled at Carrington. "Sort of like Rodeo Drive, only different."

"I think Tiffany is right around the corner. Or is it Van Cleef and Arpels?"

Hannah flashed a dazzling smile. "More likely Coconuts Are Us."

The street was crowded with shoppers on foot and drivers on motorized scooters, forcing Hannah and Carrington to weave through the persistent prostitutes gathered in doorways. Several of the women reached for Carrington's arm as they passed but he politely shrugged them off.

Hannah rolled her eyes. "Must be your cologne."

"Oh, Ms. Becker. How can you so easily discount my animal magnetism?"

"Keep it in your pants, buster."

"Yes, ma'am."

It didn't take long to find The Lucky Carp, with its orange and blue neon sign and flashing marquis that appeared to have been liberated from a theater in New York City's Times Square in the 1960s. Live Nude Girls. Sex Show Tonight. Tourists Welcome. Win Cash.

Hannah shook her head in disgust. "I thought this shit was illegal unless you're in Vegas or Amsterdam."

Carrington shrugged. "Garapan may be the G-string capital of the Pacific. The police overlook it for whatever reason. Undoubtedly there are perks involved. How do you say kick-back in Chamorro?"

Seconds before they entered the casino, Hannah spotted a four-door sedan parked along the road shoulder where the streetlamp was dark. Two men in navy polo shirts slouched in the front seats, baseball caps partially covering their faces.

"Feebies," she said, cocking her head toward the car. "So much for blending in."

"Saw them. Maybe they're waiting for a later show when the admission price goes down."

"Let's go inside and see if we can find somebody who will talk about Yoshi Yamamoto and his niece."

Carrington held open the grimy door with a flourish. "After you, my island princess." he said. "By the way, are we on a date?"

"Only a guy nicknamed Billybong would ask that."

"I take it that's a yes."

Hannah glanced at the girls dancing topless in cages set high on pedestals along both sides of the room. She headed straight for the bar. The place shuddered with electronic dance music emanating from massive loudspeakers in every corner. Orbital's *Chime* blasted out from the walls, followed by New Order's *Blue Monday*.

The dance floor was packed. The EDM crowd was mostly young Japanese women on holiday dancing with each other and in some cases with Japanese men of varying age. At least twenty locals – Carolinians and Chamorros – leaned against the far walls and sipped beer as they observed the tourists. Carrington lightly pressed a hand against Hannah's back, which was fully exposed in her white linen dress. He ushered her to an open spot amid the dancers where they happily began moving to the beat. They danced for three songs, which consumed more than thirty minutes considering the EDM mix relied on extended tracks. Both were sweating when Hannah announced she'd had enough and needed a drink.

Tony, the beefy bartender, was an ethnic Chamorro — the indigenous people of the Marianas. He looked directly at Hannah and Carrington but didn't ask what they'd like to drink.

Hannah flashed an engaging smile. "Two cold beers would be just fine. Something local."

Without a word, Tony plunked two beaded bottles of Pabst Blue Ribbon on the bar. Hannah slid a twenty from her purse, presuming correctly she would receive no change unless she made a point of it.

Carrington shamelessly studied her dress and the long, shapely legs that extended from beneath the hem. "You look spectacular. The last time I saw you in that dress, we were in Havana. And if I recall correctly, you didn't keep it on for long."

"You're such a bad boy."

"Maybe so. But I love you."

When *Clear* by Cybotron began playing, Hannah grabbed Carrington's hand and led him back to the dance floor. She loved to dance and was having fun. She draped her arms around his neck and kissed him seductively as her hips writhed to the music.

After a few more songs, Hannah retreated to the restroom where two young Japanese women were holding up the head of a third who was vomiting into a toilet. Another woman with reddish hair, pink highlights and a freckled complexion ignored the goings on as she applied a fresh coat of lipstick while seated with her legs crossed on the edge of a sink. A skimpy halter and ruffled miniskirt that could have adorned the stage at a Cyndi Lauper concert left most of the redhead's body uncovered. Hannah sensed the woman might be an ex-pat living on the island. She definitely wasn't native. Her skin was milk white.

Hannah attempted to strike up a conversation. "Love the color. I usually go for bright red but I think the dark red works for you."

The woman slid off the sink, batted down her fluffed mini skirt that quickly returned to its ruffled flare, and indulged in a protracted glance in the mirror. "Thanks. In case you hadn't noticed, black or dark blue are big lipstick hits with the Japanese. But I think us Haole girls should stick to tradition."

"Haole?"

"White girls."

"Speaking of white girls, do you happen to know where I might find a Japanese-American girl named Hiraku?"

"Why do you want to know?"

"Actually I was looking for her uncle Yoshi Yamamoto, who is a friend of a friend. I thought she might be able to tell me how to contact him."

The punked-out woman pulled a slim paper packet from the waistband of her nylon pantyhose and laid out two lines of white power on the sink countertop. She rolled a twenty-dollar bill and snorted a line. "Second one is all yours. Best cocaine in the Pacific." She handed the rolled bill to Hannah.

Without hesitating, Hannah snorted the line, feeling its impact as a rush between her eyes and a sudden sense of hyperawareness and energy.

"That's very generous of you."

Hannah was suddenly overcome by a pang of guilt after years of denouncing illegal drug use. Her mind flashed back to the sight of her teenage sister Rachel in the back of an ambulance.

The freckled woman tucked the slim packet back into its hiding place and thrust out a hand. "Krill. And yes, I know, it's definitely a weird name. It was my father's idea. He was a marine biologist fascinated by whales."

Hannah responded with a contained smile and extended her hand. "Mariel. My mother's idea. I have no idea why she chose it. Some days I like it, but other times it seems too French. I was told it means bitter, but I prefer not to think about it because I don't feel that way."

Both women laughed as they shook hands. Krill made direct eye contact with Hannah before she spoke. "Nobody has seen Yoshi for weeks. Sometimes he goes to Tokyo on business, but most days he's here. Not sure what's up."

"What about his niece?"

"You must mean Hiraku. Beautiful girl, smart, and very kind. She often seems sad, but aren't we all? Haven't seen her either. Maybe they're both in Tokyo. Yoshi always calls her his Little Peacock."

"Why is that?"

"Because she has a beautiful tattoo of a peacock with lots of feathers. It's one of Yoshi's masterpieces. It covers her entire back and wraps around her shoulders and waist. I've never actually seen the whole design, though I'd love to, but I guess she'd have to be naked for that."

Krill's tone suggested she would be equally comfortable with a male or female sex partner. "People say Yoshi is the best tattoo artist in all of Japan, maybe in the whole world. His wealthy clients fly him thousands of miles just to touch up their designs or add new ones. They're happy to pay whatever he asks."

Hannah rubbed her nose as she listened with interest to Krill, hoping the woman would not begin asking questions about how the two knew each other.

"I'd heard he had become a true master. Do you have any tattoos?"

"Just one, and it wasn't done by Yoshi," said Krill, brashly lifting her skirt to reveal a delicately-inked pufferfish and next to it a red-and-blue feathered arrow. The arrow was aimed at the apex of her thighs. Beneath the shaft was the word Heaven in script.

Hannah wasn't sure what to say so she simply nodded, as though a tattoo pointing the way to your vagina was in no way unusual.

"In my wilder days," said Krill, by way of explanation, shaking her head slowly as though still stunned by that impulsive decision. "I thought Heaven was more tasteful than Meat Garage. What about you?"

Hannah burst out laughing. She appreciated Krill's sense of humor. "None for me. Not yet, at least. But I have thought about it. Maybe a simple yin and yang, but I don't know where I'd put it."

"No special guy's names?"

"Special guys, but no tattoos. Maybe it's because I want to forget them. Tattoos would only lengthen the memories."

"Well, if you decide to get one, wait until Yoshi comes back from wherever he has gone. You won't regret it."

Hannah sniffed repeatedly as the cocaine enlivened her nostrils, then glanced at her wristwatch, the Cartier she'd been given by an extraordinary man in her life, ex-Special Forces soldier, lover, and accomplished sniper Emmett Decker who as far as she knew was currently on a CIA mission in Iraq, Kuwait or Afghanistan. It seemed Decker was always in one of the world's shit holes.

"I'd better be going. My friend will wonder what happened to me. You've been very helpful. I'll stop by the casino again later in the week. Maybe Yoshi will be back by then."

Hannah knew her chances of that happening were unlikely as she recalled Mashima's words. Back in the bar, she ordered two more bottles of Pabst Blue Ribbon, which she and Carrington carried out of the building and into the humid night. It was nearly eighty degrees despite the midnight hour. They strolled casually hand-in-hand for about twenty minutes until they reached Micro Beach where the surf splashed playfully against the soft sand. Carrington kicked off his Topsiders and tossed his shirt, trousers and underwear atop them. Hannah followed, leaving her clothing behind as they frolicked in the gentle waves. Feeling buzzed by the cocaine and beer, she wound her arms around his neck and her legs around his waist, sighing as he entered her. She tried not to think about sharks.

Through his night-vision binoculars, Mashima watched

them from behind a sand dune, feeling a pang of envy and a hint of anger. He needed to be sure they were CIA and not just tourists on holiday. He concluded they, in some ways, were both. If they proved disruptive, Mashima thought he might be forced to kill them and bury their bodies in the sand where the crabs roamed in uncountable numbers.

11

SEARCHING FOR LITTLE PEACOCK

SAIPAN

NORTHERN MARIANA ISLANDS

MARCH 1990

DETECTIVE MASHIMA relentlessly pursued his underworld contacts in an attempt to find out where Hiraku was being held captive or perhaps buried. He was reluctant to entertain the latter possibility. Although he never had been introduced to the young woman, he recalled seeing her on many occasions accompanied by her uncle and thinking she was remarkably beautiful.

Homicide detectives in Tokyo confirmed to Mashima they were looking into rumors that two CIA officers were slain by Tanaka's men, their bodies taken to shark-infested waters, chopped to pieces, and tossed overboard.

As a professional courtesy, the detectives told Mashima the vehicle in which the CIA officers were last seen was a Chevrolet Blazer, reported stolen from Narita Airport. A paid informant had told them he saw what looked like a man and woman hot-wiring the ignition and speeding away from an airport parking garage. The detectives assumed the informant's observation was about fifty percent accurate, maybe less.

Learning that two agents had disappeared was a new and painful experience for Stuart Ashwood, the CIA's deputy director of operations. Tip-toeing his way through State Department protocols in an effort not to ruffle political feathers, Ashwood sent a forensic team to closely examine the SUV where it was abandoned in the Ginza. The vehicle had been hot-wired, but no useful evidence was recovered.

Mashima suspected there was more to the story but he didn't pressure the Tokyo detectives. The yakuza had many connections within Tokyo's prefectural police force as well as the Criminal Affairs Bureau.

Mashima assumed a tipster had spotted Stevens and Cahill talking to Yoshi Yamamoto, recognized the master tattoo artist, and passed along the information to police in return for money or favors. The CIA officers were always so careful, which meant whoever gave them up was an insider, someone they trusted.

Mashima asked the Tokyo police if any criminal activity had been reported at or near the address where Yoshi lived when in the city. The detective who returned his phone call acknowledged that a break-in had occurred at Mr. Yamamoto's apartment. It was unclear whether anything of value had been taken, although the place was torn apart during what apparently had been an intensive search. Light fixtures and electrical outlets had been removed and inspected as possible hiding places. Gaping holes had been made in some of the walls, the toilet tank dismantled, the stove and refrigerator moved, and every piece of upholstered furniture slashed open.

The interior of the modest wood-frame home Yamamoto owned on Saipan was also ransacked. When Mashima arrived, it looked as if a grenade had exploded. The detective donned a pair of latex gloves before touching anything, but he knew the odds of learning what the intruders had been seeking were slim.

Later that day he visited The Lucky Carp where Tony, the bulging Chamorro bartender and bouncer, unlocked Yoshi Yamamoto's cramped office where he handled casino business. Desk drawers were open, papers strewn across the desk and floor, photographs and calendars removed from the walls. The safe door was hanging by twisted hinges.

Tony swore nobody but the managers had been in the office for the past two weeks. At least not while he was working.

"I can't say what happens overnight."

"Where do you put the money at the end of the last shift before closing?"

"In the safe."

"So you have a key to the office and a combination to the safe?"

"Not me. I have a key to the office. I can't open the safe. But there are others who can."

"I'm listening. Who are they?"

"Asaki had the combo, but of course he's dead."

"Who else?"

"The night manager, Krill."

"Any others?"

"Maybe. I can't be sure. I'm just the bartender. Yoshi had several business partners. Yakuza guys. But I'm sure you know that."

"Whoever broke into the office was looking for something specific. Any idea what that might be?"

"Cash. Drugs. Lots of desperate, strung-out people around here these days."

"So who's running the casino now that Yoshi isn't around?"

"Krill. She likes her blow but she doesn't steal. She never seems interested in money. She's cool."

Mashima knew he wasn't getting anywhere with the bartender, whose teeth were stained red from chewing betel nut. "Thanks, Tony. If you hear anything, I'd appreciate your letting me know."

Tony nodded his head, unconvincingly, and spat his reddish saliva through the open window. *"Hafa Adai."*

12

DAWN RAID IN TANAPAG

S AIPAN
N ORTHERN M ARIANA I SLANDS
M ARCH 1990

D ETECTIVE M ASHIMA quietly made his way in the dark from
one police officer to the next as they crouched amid the
mosquito-infested underbrush composed mostly of tangan-
tangan trees and tall grasses. More than two hours had elapsed
since they'd gotten into position within view of the tiny
cinderblock house with its corrugated tin roof.

The rural village of Tanapag was asleep, the sky above
sparkling with stars that would be invisible to the human eye in
places with more light pollution.

The ragtag tactical team included five CNMI police officers
armed with .38-cal. revolvers, 12-guage pump shotguns and AR-
15 rifles, and a rugged American police lieutenant named Louis
Brick on special assignment as an anti-drug consultant. The
men were eager for the operation to get underway.

FBI Special Agents Brent Palmer and Sean O'Reilly hunkered at a distance, making it unclear to everyone present whether they planned to take part in the raid or merely intended to observe. Both were wearing body armor and packing 9mm SIG-Sauer P226 handguns.

Detective Mashima chuckled to himself when roosters began crowing to announce the sun's anticipated arrival. Boonie dogs barked in reply, setting the police officers on edge for fear the suspects would be awakened and incite a gun battle. It was what commandos call first light, when the sun is about twelve degrees below the horizon and rising.

Mashima flashed the OK hand signal to Lt. Brick and whispered into his handheld, two-way radio. "Team members one and two, flank to your right. Team members three, four, and five fan out to your left. Everyone stand by."

The radio crackled with static and what sounded like an acknowledgement of the detective's orders. Mashima had instructed his men to double-click the transmit button on their radios as a signal that his message was received and understood. But the men continued to push the talk button and respond with words.

As the police officers shifted their positions, the boonie dogs followed suit, skulking warily between the scramble of rusted cars and trucks in the yard, some with foliage bursting through their shattered windshields and open hoods.

Moments later, the sun crept over the island, illuminating the small house guarded by strutting roosters and clucking chickens. Mashima pushed the transmit button on his radio. "One minute to green."

"Team one, received. One minute to green."

More radio static. Mashima's face showed concern. "Second team, acknowledge."

Static again. Garbled words.

"Good here. Team three and four. One minute and we go."

"Team five, report."

"I'm here. Team five ready for action."

Mashima drew his 9mm Glock and glanced back at Palmer and O'Reilly, the two federal agents, but they remained poker-faced. He held the radio to his lips. "Thirty seconds and we go." Mashima carefully followed the second hand on his wrist-watch. "All teams go. Green. Green."

Mashima was first through the rickety wood door, which splintered and easily gave way after a single boot kick. Lt. Brick and the CNMI police officers were right behind him, weapons set to blast away at the slightest sign of resistance.

Two men asleep on rack beds in the first room were stunned by the sound of the cracking door and the sight of guns pointed in their faces.

Mashima's voice left no doubt he was in command. "Hands where we can see them."

The men looked fearful, eyes wide, hands above their heads.

"Don't move."

Rustling sounds in the back room let the adrenaline-pumped police officers know there were other suspects in the house. Shotguns aimed, three CNMI officers burst into the back room followed by plenty of shouting.

Minutes later, two additional suspects were brought out into the dawn light, their wrists secured with plastic handcuffs. They were roughly shoved into the open bed of a Datsun pickup truck and ordered to sit quietly. Although none asked questions, Mashima informed them they were being arrested on unspecified charges connected to the murder of Mikito Asaki.

The CNMI officer standing in the doorway to the house clutched a rusty machete and gave a thumbs-up. He waved the menacing blade to direct everyone's attention toward the rear of the property.

Inside a small goat shed, wooden floorboards were scattered about, revealing a shallow underground chamber. Mashima spread his arms in the doorway to keep others from getting near the cache.

"Don't disturb anything. We need to take these weapons back to the station for testing. They could be linked to crimes on the island that remain unsolved."

Mashima photographed the cache with a point-and-shoot 35mm camera. An olive green canvas duffel bag like those used by soldiers lay in the hole next to two hunting rifles and a sawed-off shotgun. Mashima carefully hauled it from the hole and laid it on the floor. His eyes narrowed as he peered into the duffel stuffed with U.S. currency, the top layers in small denominations of fives, tens and twenties. He ordered two officers to put the duffel into the rear cargo bed of the SUV.

One CNMI policeman was posted at the truck while the other four officers fanned out onto the property where they quickly discovered fields covered densely with marijuana plants.

The youngest officer, still in his teens and dressed in camouflage fatigues, began waving wildly as he stood amid a jungle of healthy plants. "Umbilico," he shouted proudly, announcing he had found a system of hidden irrigation hoses. "Now we know how they water the money trees."

The round-bellied sergeant, approaching with some difficulty as he navigated the uneven terrain, simply chuckled at the sight of the younger police officer holding the black rubber hose.

"Be careful it's not a snake," he said, rolling his eyes. "Or a booby trap."

The teenage officer quickly let go the hose and stepped back from it, looking at the sergeant for guidance. The sergeant chuckled again as he pinched a bud from one of the thriving female marijuana plants so that his thumb and forefinger came away coated with a sticky resin. He sniffed his fingers and smiled. "Best harvest in five seasons. We should come and cut some plants before the chief gives orders to burn the field."

The younger officer seemed uncertain whether the sergeant was being serious or just joking, so he remained silent. He kicked away the black hose with his boots and shrugged his shoulders.

13

PLUCKING LITTLE PEACOCK

SAIPAN

NORTHERN MARIANA ISLANDS

MARCH 1990

HIRAKU WAS NO LONGER ALLOWED access to the entire house. Tanaka first locked her in one of the ground-floor bedrooms. When she protested by pounding on the door and hurling an original Tiffany table lamp against a wall, Tanaka jabbed her in the stomach with iron-stiff fingers. The blow took her breath away and left a bruise.

Hiraku dragged herself to the bed and climbed atop it. She hadn't eaten a meal in the nearly two days with the exception of water and a dozen Oreo cream-filled cookies found stashed in a bedside night table, which were Tanaka's favorite. The Oreos had been made in America, at least it stated so on the package label, because Tanaka believed cookies baked under the Oreo brand name in Japan were inferior.

When the pain subsided, Hiraku again began to shout and

pound the door with her fists and feet. Tanaka barked orders and two men roughly escorted her to the windowless, typhoon-proof cellar room with its thick cement walls and steel entry door. The room was more like a cell, with a toilet, sink, and a four-poster bed against one wall. The floor surface was concrete and slightly pitched to reveal a rusty drain in the center.

The following morning, or perhaps it was the middle of the night since there were no windows or clocks, Hiraku was jerked from sleep by the sharp crack of a flat wood paddle across her buttocks.

When her eyes focused, before her stood a middle-aged woman no taller than five-feet-two, wearing a black Lycra body-suit and red Converse high-top sneakers. The woman's short-cropped hair was coal black and her face fully tattooed, as presumably were her arms, legs and torso. She wore a dark blue headband scrawled with Kanji symbols in white ink, but the cloth was folded sloppily, making it impossible for Hiraku to read the words.

The small woman in black smiled clownishly, revealing her rotted brown teeth and the red stain of betel nut. Her eyes had an intensity found typically among crazies or those high on hallucinogenic drugs.

"Good morning. I hope you were not awakened from a pleasant dream."

Hiraku sat on the edge of the four-poster bed, legs hanging off but not touching the floor, rubbing the pain in her lower back with both hands. The flesh of her buttocks was stinging. She stared defiantly at the woman who was gripping the flat wooden paddle in her left hand and a samurai sword in her right. The woman oddly bowed and quickly swirled. Her sword made a musical zinging sound as it slashed through the air in looping circles. The woman began to hum deeply as she swirled, as though engaged in some ancient tribal dance.

Hiraku flinched when the sword easily lopped off one of the four wooden bedposts that had been carved into the shape of a pineapple. Tears wetted her eyes but she did her best to retain courage.

"Who are you? What do you want from me?"

The woman again bowed, this time respectfully. "Only that you cooperate. Tanaka-san would like some information and it is my task to obtain it for him."

"I don't know anything."

"And how would you come to that conclusion when I have not yet asked you a question?"

"Because I know Tanaka. He's a snake. That's what the name Orochi means, isn't it? He thinks I have contacts at the CIA and that I've told them about the heroin shipments."

"Did you?"

"No. I said nothing to anyone. It's not my place. And drugs are not my business. I don't want to know anything about it. I just want to be left alone to live my life."

The interrogator squinted and smiled as she slapped Hiraku hard across the face with one of her bony hands. The blow sent Hiraku tumbling back onto the bed.

"Let us not waste time," she said, tossing aside the wooden paddle that clattered to the floor. "We know you and your uncle met with the CIA agents – Stevens and Cahill — and now they are no more. So you are alone."

Hiraku unstably got to her knees on the soft bed. "My uncle will kill both you and Tanaka when he returns."

The interrogator belly-laughed as she expertly swung the sword. A split-second later another wooden bedpost pineapple skittered across the floor. Hiraku recoiled and curled her body onto the bed as though attempting to make herself smaller.

"Your Uncle Yoshi has joined those two CIA agents in the after life."

"What are you saying?"

"Tanaka-san has not told you?"

"Told me what?"

"I will leave that pleasure to him," she said, suddenly pressing the tip of the sword so that it barely touched the skin between Hiraku's breasts. "My name is Akumu. It means nightmare, and I will be yours if you don't start talking. So tell me, what information did you give these agents? Did you tell them about the plane?"

When Hiraku refused to cooperate, the interrogator applied more pressure until the blade sliced through her t-shirt, leaving behind a thin line that glistened with blood. Hiraku screamed as her hands examined the flesh wound.

"You cut me!"

"Next time, the sword will go deeper. Now tell me, how much does the CIA know? What did you tell them? Do they know about the ship?"

Hiraku closed her eyes and prayed Stevens and Cahill were still alive and about to rescue her at any moment. She felt certain they would come charging through the door, tossing flash bangs and smoke grenades, shooting down whatever opposition they encountered. She merely needed to stay alive until that happened. She imagined, too, that Uncle Yoshi would rejoin her once he was no longer delayed. Whatever was causing the delay must be truly important, she told herself. Otherwise, Yoshi would be at her side. He was her protector.

"If you hurt me, my uncle will find you and kill you. Make no mistake about it."

"Perhaps you didn't hear me. Your uncle will kill no one because he's dead."

Hiraku sat up and spat into the woman's face. Just as quickly she was propelled off the bed and across the room by another bony slap. Once again she curled her body into a fetal position on the cold floor and began to weep.

"Your uncle took money that did not belong to him. I'm sure he mentioned it to you. I'll bet you know where it's hidden."

Through her tears and choked voice, she said, "My uncle is an honorable man. He doesn't steal. He runs a successful business at The Lucky Carp. He doesn't need more money."

Akumu, in her finest interrogator mode and with almost superhuman strength, lifted Hiraku by her ankles and tossed her back onto the bed. The samurai sword whirled, creating a whooshing sound before cleanly decapitating a third bedpost. Hiraku cringed as the interrogator slashed the bed, cutting deep furrows into the mattress. She tried to hold back her tears.

"You were saying?"

When Hiraku spat again, Akumu lost her temper. She tore off Hiraku's t-shirt and bra and beat her bare back with the paddle, coming down hardest on the pictorial tattoo where the peacock's wings began to spread upward amid a kaleidoscope of dragons, koi fish, plants, words and numbers, some in English, others in Kanji. Each blow left a red welt. Just before Hiraku passed out from pain, she heard Akumu say, "That is the most magnificent tattoo I have ever seen. Such a pity it was wasted on you."

14

THE LUCKY CARP CASINO

SAIPAN
NORTHERN MARIANA ISLANDS
MARCH 1990

WITH HIS PRIMARY business partners Mikito Asaki and Yoshi Yamamoto both dead, Tanaka began spending more time at The Lucky Carp, reviewing the long-term financial records while keeping close tabs on the daily casino and bar operation. He considered bringing in an accountant whose only job would be to conduct a forensic audit, but he was wary about trusting anyone outside his immediate circle. Letting a stranger know about your financial status was just as dangerous as talking about your medical or marital problems. If weakness was revealed, a competitor might use it as an opportunity.

Although Krill was supremely competent as casino night manager and Tony confidently handled the bar, Tanaka trusted neither. He was still seething over the embezzlement of two hundred million dollars by the two men he had been foolish enough to call his close friends.

Tanaka knew the money had not been siphoned from the casino, hotel, or the restaurant and bar. He had studied the two ledgers of profit and loss, each maintained for a separate audience. The ledger kept solely for the taxman showed marginal profit in some categories and a slight loss in others. The private ledger kept for the three partners and a handful of lesser investors in Tokyo, displayed the truth – massive earnings from gambling, prostitution, gun running and heroin smuggling. Since owning a handgun in Japan had been made illegal at the end of World War II, a single pistol could easily reap $7,000 on the black market. The yakuza had plenty of guns for sale.

Tanaka had equally divided the major shares of the Saipan enterprise among Yoshi, Asaki and himself, which made him wonder why they had nonetheless chosen to steal. After a close look at the books, it was evident the amount of cash missing could not have come from the roulette wheels, Black Jack tables, overpriced drinks at the casino bar, marijuana sales, or the Asian sex slave workers. It had been skimmed from one of the bigger operations — gun running or heroin smuggling.

When had it begun? Did they hide the cash as though it were some pirate treasure, maybe buried it in the sand on Managaha Island, or stashed it in one of Saipan's many remote caves next to the bones of long-dead Japanese soldiers and their rusty Arisaka rifles? Had they taken only a few thousand dollars at each grab, small amounts that likely would not be missed, no different than an unscrupulous bank siphoning nickels and dimes from its unwary depositors? Were those millions now stored safely in a private account in Tokyo, or had his associates been clever enough to send the money to an offshore bank? The Caymans came to mind. It brought his blood to a boil and he scolded himself for killing Yoshi, but his temper had gotten the better of him once the torture methods had failed.

Tanaka was at a table counting stacks of American dollars when Hannah walked in and sat at the bar. She was wearing a strapless yellow sundress that showcased her bronzed shoulders. Her yellow rubber flip-flops matched flawlessly. Designer sunglasses were nestled atop her hair, which was coiled loosely in golden strands. Three Rastafarian-style weaves hung to the left of her forehead, giving off a Bohemian accent. She was carrying two paperback guidebooks on how to travel efficiently and affordably in Micronesia.

Hannah set her leather clutch purse on the bar but before she could say a word Tony the bartender placed a napkin and prepared to take her order.

Tanaka stood and casually nudged Tony aside.

"I'll get her whatever she needs," he said with an air of authority and a flirtatious grin that Hannah found repulsive. "We're here to please."

Hannah ignored Tanaka and looked squarely at Tony, who seemed suddenly uncomfortable. "I'm in the mood for liquid lunch — a frozen margarita with Patron – if you have it. If not, Cuervo will do just fine."

Tanaka rested an elbow on the bar directly in front of Hannah. He glowed with self-importance. The Lucky Carp stocked Patron tequila, which had been introduced to the liquor market the previous year, but he wanted to show Hannah that he, too, was sophisticated when it came to drinking spirits, perhaps more so than she.

"Patron, certainly, if that's your wish. But I have something rare that you can find only in Mexico, and only if you have the right connections. I have a bottle of Fortaleza, tequila like none other you will ever taste, and made especially by my friend Guillermo who has taken over his family's distillery. This tequila will not even go into production until next year, so you'll be among a select few to savor it beforehand."

"Why the special treatment?"

"Let's just say it's a way of offering friendship to the most beautiful woman I have ever seen in Garapan, or all of Saipan, or maybe even all of Micronesia."

Hannah faked a smile. It was a lame line from a stranger and she'd heard versions of it dozens of times since she began dating in her teens. Clearly the bullshit was getting knee deep. She was amused that Tanaka had actually winked at her, something no man had ever done. It seemed preposterous, something from a past era or an old movie. But then again, she'd already heard he was extremely weird.

"Flattery will get you everywhere," she said coyly.

"That's the idea."

"And you'll be joining me in this special tequila moment?"

"Certainly. It would be an honor."

Tanaka disappeared into a back room and reemerged with his precious bottle of Fortaleza. "It seems a waste to dilute such fine spirits with ice and bar mix. I suggest we simply sip it from shot glasses, or a larger glass if you prefer."

Hannah forced a pleasant smile. "So now you want to pound down shots of tequila in the middle of the day? And here I thought you were a responsible businessman and member of the community."

"Sorry to disappoint you. Miss? I don't believe you mentioned your name."

"Mariel Becker."

"Miss Becker. Sipping tequila in the middle of the day would be more accurate than pounding down shots. But if you are game, that's exactly what we'll do."

Tanaka gave Tony some sort of signal that caused him to mumble about an errand that needed doing immediately in the back room. There were only four other customers in the place, Japanese men seated at a table near one of the dancer cages, as though hoping a nude woman might suddenly appear and begin to shake and grind. The next show wasn't scheduled to start for another two hours. Tony served them a round of drinks before he departed, leaving Hannah and Tanaka seated at the bar.

"Where is your boyfriend?"

"Boyfriend?"

"The blond-haired man who arrived in Saipan with you."

"He's a business associate. That's all. We work together."

"I saw you walking along the road with him. He had his arm around your waist. You seemed close."

"Like a brother."

"And where is your brother today?"

"Not a clue. Probably surfing. Or drinking beer on the beach. Maybe just hanging with the locals at one of the surfboard rental shacks. He loves to surf. Definitely not working, though he should be. He can't get too far because I have the keys to the car."

Hannah purposefully let slip the name of her luxury travel company and her title as a business partner and consultant, knowing if Tanaka tried to check it out his call would be instantly routed to a CIA operations desk and her story verified.

Tanaka carefully poured two shots. As he reached for one of the glasses, Hannah's hand intercepted. "I'll take that one."

Tanaka grinned, registering his companion's survival skills. Perhaps someone had once slipped a roofie into her drink.

"And your toast?"

"To enjoying the best things in life."

Tanaka clinked his shot glass to hers and took a sip. Hannah followed suit, making a purring sound as she swallowed the warm spirits.

"Tell me, Miss Becker — or may I call you Mariel?"

"Mariel is just fine."

"What are the best things in this life, Mariel? Money? Love? Power? Big houses? Fast cars? Perhaps a gleaming yacht?"

"I like to think the best things are sunny days, good friends, fun parties, and wherever those celebrations might lead me," she said, disgusted by her own answer loaded with sexual innuendo but knowing she had to dangle the bait. It took Tanaka all of two seconds to nibble at it. He was already aroused.

"If I were to meet you at a party, I would not want to leave without you. I would insist you come home with me and together we would have the time of our lives."

Hannah wondered how many times Tanaka had uttered those same words to countless women. Had any of them fallen for it? Sad if they did. And the whole 'time of our lives' line was obviously something he'd borrowed from a book or, more likely, a movie soundtrack. He didn't seem like the type with patience enough to read a book, to sit by a roaring fire and devour sentence after sentence. She wouldn't have been surprised if at that moment Tanaka flicked a switch under the bar and the ceiling speakers filled the room with his picks of romantic music – Montovani, or Percy Faith and his orchestra.

"Well, maybe we'll meet at a party. Only I don't know enough people on Saipan to get invited to one."

Tanaka blushed for the first time. Hannah had caught him off guard as he unveiled his predatory thoughts. Tanaka had been imagining taking Mariel Becker back to his home overlooking the sea and seducing her, but then he remembered Hiraku and the ruckus she might cause. Even if the girl was locked in the basement, she still might do something to arouse suspicion. The girl was a pain in the ass. He silently cursed her and her Uncle Yoshi and Mikito Asaki. Once again, the trio had managed to rob him, this time of an opportunity to engage in sex with a tall Argentine blonde, among his favorites of all the female types, better even than those he had bedded from Australia and Sweden. German women repulsed him because he had found they did not always shave their armpits and that was something he could not endure. He was a self-admitted clean freak and he preferred bodies, including his own, be shaved in the most private places, particularly if sex was in the offing.

"Are you hungry? We have fish that you won't find any fresher. In fact, we can catch whatever you like and cook it immediately."

"Actually, I'm more in the mood for gambling than eating. I noticed you have a healthy assortment of electronic poker machines in your casino."

"So you're a gambler?"

"Not really. But I'd be willing to risk losing this soggy twenty," she said, pulling a damp $20 bill from her purse. "I forgot I had tucked it into my bathing suit when I went for a dip earlier."

Tanaka raised his shot glass. "To taking risks. Sometimes they are necessary."

"To taking risks."

Krill sauntered into the bar just as Hannah and Tanaka set down their glasses. Her pinkish orange hair nicely framed her face with its delicate features, and her pouty mouth was coated with dark blue lipstick. "Well, if it isn't my friend from the ladies' room. I didn't know you two were acquainted."

Hannah smiled, trying to hide her alarm. "Please join us."

"No. The customers might get the wrong idea if they see the lowly night manager drinking with the boss."

Tanaka's facial expression showed his surprise that the two women had previously met, but he quickly recovered and once again became the suave player.

Hannah had taken notice of Tanaka's demeanor as she continued to smile coquettishly. "So you own The Lucky Carp? Silly me. Here I thought you were simply the handsome manager who'd taken a liking to these wonderful surroundings as his favorite watering hole."

"Yes, I own the casino and hotel with a group of partners,"

Tanaka said, attempting to override his pride with a matter-of-fact reply. "It seemed like a good investment opportunity."

"And has it been?"

"We make a modest profit. Only so many dollars can be made from beer, mixed drinks and cheeseburgers."

"But that isn't all you sell."

Tanaka visibly reddened, his eyes narrowed to slits as he studied Hannah. "I'm not certain what you are implying. We are not a house of prostitution."

"I guess it's legal, at least here in Garapan."

"Men come to see the dancers and in doing so spend their paychecks on overpriced drinks. I believe that is not an unusual or unorthodox business model, even in Argentina, Europe, or the continental United States."

"I was kidding," she said, playfully punching his arm near the shoulder. "Just trying to get through that reserved Japanese exterior."

"Ah, I see," said Tanaka, looking visibly relieved. "If you are aware of a more lucrative method to earn a living, please inform me and I will look into it. I hold an MBA."

Hannah reached out and clasped Tanaka's hand. It was clam cold, but she held it. "Orochi – may I call you Orochi?"

"Please do."

"Orochi, I sometimes have a sense of humor learned in my Argentine homeland. It can be blunt, but that's only a sign of affection. In Argentina, those who don't joke with you aren't your friends."

"I will take that as a compliment," he said. "We should drink another tequila."

15

AFTER THE RAID

SAIPAN

NORTHERN MARIANA ISLANDS

MARCH 1990

THE FOUR PRISONERS seated in the Datsun pickup were coated with coral dust by the time the convoy pulled up in front of the police station in Susupe. Their wrists were still bound with plastic handcuffs. None spoke or made eye contact with their captors.

Detective Mashima unlatched the truck's rear gate and cocked his head, signaling the prisoners to follow him. A dozen police officers cradled their weapons and flanked the entrance to the building, though their stance showed more exhaustion than aggression because in some cases the men being led into the police station were relatives or friends. It had been an intense morning and afternoon and the work day wasn't over. A reporter from the cable television station in Guam was doing a live stand-up in front of the police station, Sony video camera mounted on a tripod. He'd been tipped off to the raid but didn't arrive in time to actually accompany the task force to Tanapag. Donley had been counting on the publicity that would showcase his anti-drug task force in a positive light.

As police and suspects entered the jail, Mashima ordered the CNMI sergeant to remain behind to guard the SUV where the confiscated weapons were piled beside a duffel bag stuffed with cash, presumably proceeds from marijuana sales.

Once the prisoners were secured in their holding cells, Mashima and Lt. Brick began the task of counting the seized money. It took them nearly an hour to straighten and stack the crumpled bills. The haul totaled $36,015 and was mostly in well-worn tens and twenties. Mashima turned the money over to CNMI Police Sgt. Alfred Torres, supervisor of the department's evidence locker, for safekeeping and to ensure the chain-of-custody procedure was followed.

By late afternoon, the prisoners were in Garapan, standing with heads bowed before a judge and facing arraignment for their alleged crimes that still remained unspecified. The justice system on Saipan was a hybrid of its own making, a mix of U.S. law and island tradition, a situation that perplexed prosecutor Ray Donley because he was powerless to change it. During his first week on the island, an elder Chamorro had whispered some advice in his ear. *You cannot come out here and expect to change anything. You will have to learn to accept or ignore it, or certain things may drive you a little crazy.*

Tired and sweaty, Mashima and Lt. Brick stood beside Donley, who loosely described two of the men arrested as suspected yakuza associates and the other pair as pot farmers, operators of a marijuana plantation with a sophisticated irrigation system and camouflage designed to evade aerial reconnaissance.

When Mikito Asaki's criminal history was read into the record, Donley didn't defend him before the judge. "Mikito

Asaki lived a gangster's life and died a gangster's death. But nobody had the right to murder him."

Donley alleged two of the four defendants were formerly Mikito Asaki's bodyguards who had been pressured by an as-yet-unidentified but high-ranking yakuza underboss to turn against him. Donley described the two men as mob assassins but offered no further details because his argument was based on speculation and rumor.

Instead, Donley showed the judge photographs of the victim, beaten and strangled by his killers, his body bloated and battered by the sea. Donley requested the photos be marked as evidence. The judge agreed and quickly slipped the gruesome photos into a manila envelope, to which the court clerk affixed a label.

FBI Special Agents Brent Palmer and Sean O'Reilly stood at the rear of the courtroom, waiting for their turn before the judge if summoned. The agents had found tire tracks and blood traces at the edge of Banzai Cliff. The tire imprints matched the tread on a Toyota sedan found torched behind a run-down automobile repair shop near Tanapag. The blood samples were at the police lab but no results were expected for at least a week, maybe much longer.

Donley requested bail be set at $10,000 for each of the alleged pot farmers and $100,000 for the two suspects associated with the yakuza. The court-appointed defense lawyer — a gaunt, middle-aged man whose pallor suggested he'd never been outdoors when the sun was shining — objected on grounds the alleged pot farmers had only minor offenses on their criminal record while even less was known about the so-called mob assassins.

The judge set individual bail at $500 cash for the two alleged marijuana growers and $5,000 each for the other two defendants who were loosely charged with serving as accessories to a homicide.

Relatives and friends quickly raised $1,000 to free the pair charged with growing pot. The other two defendants were ordered held in lieu of bail, but within an hour a courier representing Orochi Tanaka arrived at the courthouse and posted the required $10,000 cash.

Police Chief Joe Napuna and his law enforcement superiors in the U.S. strongly emphasized the FBI would be given full credit for the arrests. Napuna conveyed as much to Mashima, adding if he didn't like it, he should prepare to spend the rest of his career at a desk in a windowless police station on one of the outer islands, deciphering illegible reports written by illiterate police officers.

Mashima turned over his fingerprint files and witness statements – the most rudimentary facts of the investigation. As a result, the FBI agents celebrated the arrests but could offer the court no motive for the slaying. None of the suspects were talking.

Hannah and Carrington monitored the situation through conversations with friendly trial court officers and whoever else would talk. In Saipan, it was more effective to learn the behind-the-scenes story than what was actually happening in the courtroom.

Hannah rubbed her chin, as though in deep thought. "Interesting that Mashima didn't tell the Feebies about Tanaka or why he might have wanted Asaki dead. Something tells me we'll be hearing from the detective very soon."

As though on cue, Mashima knocked on their hotel room door at the Chalan Kanoa Hotel. Hannah studied him through the peephole before opening the door.

"Sorry for intruding. I wanted to let you know the four men who were arrested, not all of them are guilty of crimes, and certainly not of murder. I'm not convinced any of them killed Mikito Asaki."

Hannah invited Mashima into the hotel room. "Please have

a seat on that lovely couch," she said sarcastically, calling attention to the gaudy fabric pattern and numerous cigarette burns
in the upholstery.

"I try not to notice such things, but being a detective, sometimes they're hard to overlook," he said.

Shedding his surfer-boy act, Carrington went straight to the
point. "So, detective, why are you here?"

"Because the FBI does not care about motive, only arrests."

Hannah arched her eyebrows. "What about the motive?"

"The FBI has attributed Asaki's murder to underworld rival-
ries. That's the term used in court. A generalization. No further
explanation, most likely because no more information was
available. The news media, eager for a story, is often willing to
accept such generalizations, as is the public."

It was muggy in the room despite the sea breeze coming
through the balcony's sliding door. Hannah poured a glass of
bottled water for herself and offered one to Mashima who
gladly accepted. Fresh drinking water was scarce on Saipan.

"I believe Orochi Tanaka was convinced that his business
partner, Asaki, was stealing from him, which may be true," said
Mashima, who reluctantly brushed what appeared to be bread-
crumbs and cat hair off the upholstery before sitting on the
dilapidated couch. "We know that billions of dollars in drug
sales have been laundered by Tanaka and his associates over
the past few years. We also know The Lucky Carp casino is
among the businesses used for that purpose, although we
cannot prove it."

Carrington nodded, as though accepting the possibility. "So
what you're saying is, for some petty thievery, they threw this
guy Asaki off Banzai Cliff? No option to repay the debt over
time? What about loan sharks? Certainly the yakuza have a few
of those. Wouldn't it have been wiser to let him live and eventually get the money back on the installment plan?"

"You do not understand the yakuza. Not everything is about

money. Asaki dishonored Tanaka and that cost him his life. And it was not petty thievery as you suggest. The amount was far greater — one hundred million stolen by Asaki, possibly more."

"And what about Yoshi Yamamoto? You seem to think the yakuza erased him as well?"

"Same situation — a matter of dishonor for the *Ichiwa Kai* – the crime family to which Tanaka swears allegiance. Only the *Yamaguchi-gumi* family is larger, and the news of Yamamoto's death will spread quickly among its members, so that Tanaka may hold his head high. Such action shows Tanaka will not tolerate his own soldiers stealing from him. If he did, all order would be lost. In my opinion, the large amount stolen also played a role in Tanaka's decision to eliminate Yoshi."

"So now the FBI can go home, satisfied they have done their job," Hannah hissed.

Mashima looked down at his shoes. "That's correct. Now the real work begins. We must find Yoshi and Hiraku, although we may be too late. Lt. Brick, an American police lieutenant assigned here because he has had much success in cracking down on drug dealers back in the States, may also be of assistance. I know he would be willing to help. He's not here looking for glory, so he would keep things confidential."

Carrington eyed Mashima warily. "We? Us?"

"If we work together, even if Yoshi has been eliminated, maybe we can still save Hiraku."

"I'm all right with that," said Hannah. "Where do you think she is?"

"Somewhere here on Saipan. My first guess would be Tanaka's house, but getting inside would be nearly impossible. He has dozens of guards and the place is wired with alarms. But we need to know what Tanaka is thinking. We need somebody close to him," said Mashima, staring oddly at Hannah.

"What? Why are you looking at me like that?"

"Orochi Tanaka is a womanizer. He prefers tall, young, beautiful blondes, not unlike you," he said, embarrassed by his own words and observation.

Carrington abruptly stood and held out a hand like a traffic cop. "Wait, wait, wait. Are you trying to suggest we bait Tanaka with Hannah? Dangle her in front of him like some piece of meat?"

"That is exactly what I am saying, though not in those precise words," said Mashima. "I think in your spy vernacular it is referred to as a honey trap."

16

THE EVIDENCE IS MISSING

Saipan

Northern Mariana Islands

March 1990

The sight of thousands of dollars in small denomination U.S. currency – some of the bills soiled, wrinkled or torn, but all neatly stacked and banded in a cardboard box — stirred the blood of CNMI Police Sgt. Alfred Torres. He set the box on a storage shelf in the department's evidence locker cage. Before closing the lid, he pressed both hands atop the bills and ran his fingers across them, imagining what he'd do if the money were his to spend. He envisioned a lovely fishing skiff, painted bright red, with a shiny Honda outboard engine hanging from the transom. He saw every line of the skiff. It was hauled up on the sand of Micro Beach, and next to it was a brand new pickup with crew cab, raised suspension and brush guards on the grille. As his mind wandered and his imagination soared, he saw the swimming pool behind his modest home. It was surrounded by comfortable patio furniture just like his wife was always daydreaming about, and the laughter of his children could be heard above the splashing. *Haves and have-nots,* he thought. *It just doesn't seem fair.* Everywhere he looked, the Japanese seemed to have it all, at least those who had visited his island over the past two decades with bundles of cash, ready to long-term lease the beaches and build their luxury high-rise hotels, while he worked six days a week as a low-paid cop, struggling to feed, shelter, and clothe his family.

As midnight approached and the sergeant's work shift neared completion, he took the box from the shelf and opened it. His first instinct was to grab a thick wad of bills, whatever he could clamp in one hand, and return the box to the shelf. But once the stack was in hand, the temptation to take another was too great. He grabbed a second, enjoying the weight, feel, and smell of it.

For what may have been a half hour or more he sat at the steel table holding the two stacks, one in each hand, his eyes closed, his mind awhirl in a wondrous purchasing spree. New bicycles for his children. Fashionable dresses for his oldest daughter. A state-of-the-art satellite dish that would allow him to watch his favorite sports on a brand-new large-screen television set. And for his wife, a set of fine china to impress dinner guests, and new livingroom furniture upon which no sharp springs threatened to impale anyone adventurous enough to sit.

Abruptly he stood and tossed both stacks into the box, pushed them down atop the others, neatly pressed the lid closed and carried it to his truck. He imagined blindly that nobody would miss the cash, not even the judge who had announced in court that the confiscated drug money would be used to help pay for police security details at the airport. If the money were actually used for that purpose, just about every CNMI police officer on Saipan would have benefitted from the overtime.

The sergeant began whistling a favorite tune as he drove home with the box of cash on the front seat. About half way to his destination he pulled a sudden U-turn on the narrow coral road and headed for Round Two, the casino hotel in Garapan a 10-minute drive from his desk at the Susupe police station.

The electronic video poker machines and roulette tables were in full swing, the place a cacophony of light and sound, brimming with tourists and locals drinking, eating and celebrating — or, more often than not, cursing their lack of good fortune.

Torres nodded to the CNMI patrolman working a security detail at the front door but didn't stop to make small talk. He was determined to double the amount of money in the cardboard box before the night was through, thinking he would keep his winnings and return the borrowed amount to the police evidence locker before anyone knew it was missing.

Torres was $7,000 down at Round Two when he decided to try his luck elsewhere. With three beers and a shot of tequila in his belly and $29,000 in cash in his pockets, he steered the short distance along the beach road to The Lucky Carp. The voice in his head wouldn't be silenced. *It's a setback, but I can still make this happen. I'm feeling lucky. And when my wife sees all the money I've won, she's going to be happier than she has ever been in her whole life.*

Tony was stacking cases of Budweiser beer behind the bar. The massive Chamorro crossed his arms over his chest and locked his eyes on the police sergeant. "You still on the clock?"

"Why do you say that?"

"Because you're in uniform."

At that moment, Torres realized he had been so preoccupied with getting to the casinos he'd overlooked his appearance. "Thought I had a change of clothes at the station, but I guess I left them at home."

Tony was about the same size as the police officer, maybe a tad larger but far more muscular. "You want a t-shirt? XXL from the Surf Shack?"

"That'll work fine. Don't want your customers to get nervous having some local cop around when they're trying to score some blow."

"And I don't want you to lose your stripes because somebody reports that you were gambling in uniform."

Tony tossed the florescent green t-shirt across the bar and Torres caught it. Walking toward the men's bathroom he turned around briefly. "I owe you."

Although he still wore his striped uniform trousers and duty boots, the t-shirt made him less conspicuous as he sat amid the video poker machines and roulette tables.

Krill was seated at the bar, her skirt carelessly hiked and exposing most of her thighs when the sergeant entered the room wearing the shirt.

"Woo-hoo. Look at that t-top. Hey, surf's up, Alfred."

"Don't be a wiseass, Krill."

"I like the style. Really I do."

"Oh yeah, that's because I look just like one of your blond surfer boys."

"You should lighten up, Alfred. Besides, I don't fuck surfer dudes."

"What you see before you is Alfred lightened up. You going to get me a cold beer or are you going to leave it up to Tony now that you're night manager?"

"It's just a job title."

"Well, I hope Tanaka pays you something for it."

Krill set a beaded bottle of Budweiser on the bar. "It's on me."

"Thanks, Krill. I'm going to hit the machines for a while."

"Good luck, Alfred."

17

TANAKA'S RAGE

TANAKA FUMED when he heard through his informants that $36,000 was seized during the police raid in Tanapag. It was his money earned from the sale of pot grown in his fields, using his water on an island where fresh water was a precious commodity. The cash should have been in his casino safe by the end of the week, not buried in the ground under some farmer's goat shed. But the men hired to oversee the harvest were simple farmers and had been in no hurry to deliver the cash to Tanaka. Now it was in police custody. The yakuza boss cursed aloud. "Idiots. This is an island of idiots!"

Tanaka's mood worsened upon learning that the cash, which had been stored in an evidence locker at the police station, was already missing. Every last dollar had disappeared, or was misplaced.

As soon as Mashima picked up the receiver on his desk phone and identified himself, Tanaka launched into a tirade in Japanese.

"Detective, my name is Orochi Tanaka."

"I know who you are."

"Is it true that the money seized during your drug raid in Tanapag has been stolen from the police evidence room?"

Mashima had already monitored the police station gossip. The officer in charge of the evidence locker was an inveterate gambler.

"I know nothing about any missing evidence, Mr. Tanaka. And if I did, I would not be at liberty to share that information with you."

"But surely you can tell me if such a theft has occurred."

"What makes you so interested?"

"I run a casino where lots of cash changes hands. I want to make sure it's safe to do so. Or should I be concerned that someone might attempt to steal it, maybe even a police officer."

"We do everything in our power to provide a safe environment for the residents of Saipan and those who conduct business here," said Mashima, knowing his reply sounded like something being read from a training brochure on community policing.

"So you'll tell me nothing?"

"If a theft has occurred, it's a police matter. If you'd like to report a crime, I'd be glad to take down the information."

Tanaka resumed his cursing as he slammed the phone into its cradle. He vowed to find out who stole the cash from police headquarters. "I swear on my mother's soul the cops will pay for this."

Sgt. Torres considered calling in sick the following morning, but he sensed that would only make matters worse. As things stood, he would act surprised when informed of the theft. He would swear the money was secured in the evidence locker when he left the building for the night and must have been stolen sometime before dawn, by someone familiar with the building and police procedures.

Detective Mashima was already waiting for Torres when the sergeant walked into the police station ready to start his shift.

"You're up early."

"We need to talk, Alfred."

"What can I do for you?"

"Where's the money?"

"Sorry, I don't know what you're talking about."

"The money that's missing from the evidence locker."

"Money? Missing?"

"Don't play games with me, Alfred. The $36,000 seized during the Tanapag raid is gone, and you were the officer in charge of the evidence. So where is it?"

The sergeant acted offended, as though he had been deeply insulted. "If there's anything missing from the evidence room, I'll look into it and find out who took it."

Mashima stared at the sergeant. "I think you took it, Alfred."

"Fuck you, Mashima."

"You should probably get yourself a lawyer."

"What are you saying? Are you accusing me? You want to arrest me?"

"I want you to tell me the truth."

Torres moved past the detective, knocking him with his shoulder. "Excuse me. I have to get to work."

"Alfred."

The sergeant stopped but didn't turn around. "Unless you have some kind of proof that it was me who took the money, I suggest we end this conversation."

"We're going to do a lot more talking – today, Alfred. The chief has already authorized a lie-detector test and he wants you to take it."

"Never going to happen. The chief is my cousin."

Shortly before noon, Detective Mashima informed Torres he was being placed on administrative leave pending the outcome of the theft investigation.

"You can't do this, Mashima."

"I just did."

"I'm not leaving the building."

"Then you'll be arrested for trespassing."

"Is that the Japanese half of you talking? You've never been one of us."

Mashima remained expressionless. "Alfred, you refused to take a lie detector test. That alone could be grounds for termination, but for now, as a courtesy to you, we're letting it slide. Now please gather your belongings and go home."

Torres lunged at the detective who agilely stepped out of harm's way before delivering a precise open-hand chop to the back of the sergeant's neck. The blow sent the sergeant crashing to the floor but he quickly rose to his knees and attempted to stand. Two uniformed police officers grabbed his arms. Torres fought back, struggling to break their grip. Mashima joined the fray and soon the massive sergeant was face down on the floor. Although it was unnecessary, Mashima handcuffed the agitated sergeant to make a point that he meant business.

"Alfred Torres, you're under arrest for assault and battery on a police officer, for resisting arrest, and for the alleged theft of police property."

The big man looked strong enough to break the handcuffs as he rose to his feet, his arms still restrained by the uniformed officers.

"I'll get you for this, Mashima, you Jap bastard."

Mashima showed no outward sign of emotion, but deep inside he was filled with rage aimed at the irresponsible sergeant who had tainted the police department.

During the night, a cup of urine was poured on the prisoner as he slept. A tray of food lay untouched on the floor of his cell out of fear it might contain poison or been otherwise tampered with.

Less than twenty-four hours later Torres was in front of a judge in Garapan, where the defendant was released on his own recognizance.

The judge was not pleased with the prosecutor. As he put it, "There's not enough evidence to support the allegation of theft, and if this man had not been accused, there would have been no scuffle at the police station, and therefore no assault and battery."

A pre-trial conference was scheduled for mid-April, until which time Torres would remain on paid administrative leave unless the case was resolved sooner.

18

AKUMU'S PREY

AFTER RETRIEVING his battered pickup from the police station parking lot, Sgt. Torres drove slowly, not wanting to give his law enforcement colleagues any reason to conduct a traffic stop and lure him into an altercation. Akumu tailed the sergeant's truck along Beach Road and into the Joeten Supermarket parking lot. She waited in her small Datsun station wagon until he emerged carrying a twelve-pack of Budweiser bottles, a handle of tequila and a bag filled with snacks. He hadn't eaten in over twenty-four hours and his stomach was rumbling loudly.

Instead of heading home, Torres drove sluggishly north along Marpi Road, passing through Tanapag where the fateful drug raid had occurred. Occasionally he flung an empty bottle from the truck. Akumu counted five bottles along the roadside by the time they crept through the village of San Roque. She tailed at a discreet distance, trying to keep at least one vehicle between them and hoping to stay out of his rearview mirrors.

The sergeant finally parked the truck near Suicide Cliff where he stuffed his face with popcorn, Doritos, Fritos, and two chocolate candy bars. He removed his duty boots and walked barefoot toward the cliff, holding a beer in one hand and the tequila jug in the other. Once the beer was gone he tossed the bottle over the edge. The sun beat down as he took three long pulls of tequila, closing his eyes each time he swallowed. He needed to numb the pain of failure. Akumu watched him through her compact birding binoculars as he stood staring out at the sea without moving. It was as though the man was in a trance or made of stone.

Twenty minutes elapsed before he began stumbling along a trail that led into the dense, green jungle growth. He stopped abruptly, leaned unsteadily against a thick tangan-tangan plant and urinated. The trail soon opened onto a small clearing with a panoramic ocean view. Torres sat with his back resting against a banyan tree and sipped from the jug. Moments before falling asleep, his mind filled with dark thoughts and he reached for his handgun, only to realize it was in the top drawer of Chief Napuna's desk along with his badge.

Akumu stealthily moved through the high grass until she was behind the tree. She could hear the sergeant snoring loudly. The handle of tequila lay on its side, the contents slowly dripping into the thirsty soil.

Akumu unrolled a five-foot strand of climber's webbing she carried in her pocket and deftly wrapped it around the sergeant's neck. She pulled it tight, bracing her feet against the back of the tree as he awakened, realized what was happening, and started to struggle. She held the pressure until the man was unconscious.

Torres felt the water droplets on his face. His wrists were tied behind his back with webbing, his ankles bound with duct tape. A petite Asian woman with short black hair and facial tattoos was standing over him.

"Welcome back."

"Who are you? And why did you try to kill me?"

"Never mind that. I need some information."

The sergeant began to wriggle and tug at the restraints. Akumu kicked him low on the spinal cord. When he cried out in pain she kicked him again.

"What do you want?"

"I want to know what you did with the money. Is there any left over or did you spend it all at the casinos?"

"You must have mistaken me for somebody else. I don't know what you're talking about."

Akumu kicked him a third time. "Did you steal the money from the police station?"

The sergeant shook his head.

"You're lying."

Another slow head shake.

"Did you spend it all?"

"Let me go. Take these damn cuffs off of me or you'll be under arrest."

"You're not going anywhere until you tell me where you hid the money." She swung her lead-filled leather slapjack so that it struck between his legs. The sergeant's eyes bulged. "Maybe that will help you remember."

"You're crazy."

"No. I'm Akumu. Now tell me about the money you stole because it belonged to someone I know and he'd like it back."

Tears welled in the sergeant's eyes. "You're making a huge mistake. I'm a police officer, not a thief."

Akumu began to softly sing a Cole Porter tune in her Japanese accent. *"In olden days a glimpse of stocking was looked on as something shocking, but now heaven knows, anything goes."* She did a little dance step and curtsy, then struck the sergeant's nose with the leather-covered slapjack, causing rivulets of blood to spill over his lips and chin. *"Good authors too who once knew better words now only use four-letter words, writing prose, anything goes."*

"I didn't take any money."

"Don't you like Cole Porter? He wrote the most wonderful songs."

The sergeant tried to roll so that he would be in a kneeling position. Akumu let him do it.

"I get a kick out of you. That's also a Cole Porter song."

"Untie me now."

"I'm afraid not. You've been very bad. People who are bad need to be punished," she said, plunging the ice pick into his lower back.

Torres screamed.

"Were you trying to tell me something?"

"You stabbed me."

"Oh, it was only a little pick that made a teeny-tiny hole. Stop being such a baby. Now tell me, did you take the money?"

The sergeant nodded.

"Is that a yes?"

"Yes."

"And did you spend it at the casinos?"

Another nod.

"Shall I presume that's a yes?"

"Yes."

"All $36,000?"

"I've told you everything."

"No. You didn't say which casinos and you didn't tell me if all the money is gone." She stuck him in the back again with the ice pick.

The sergeant looked up at Akumu with eyes seeking mercy. "Round Two."

"That's the only one?"

"The Lucky Carp."

"How much money is left?"

"None."

"I don't believe you."

"I blew it."

"Yes, you did," she said, pushing the ice pick into his chest until it pierced his heart.

Torres's expression suggested he was having difficulty believing this was really happening to him. Akumu dragged his body into the underbrush, untied the webbing and cut away the duct tape. She knew Tanaka would be unhappy with the results of her mission. That made her sad because she was hoping to show her loyalty and deliver better news about the whereabouts of the $36,000. Now she'd have some serious explaining to do. Tanaka had warned her about keeping her temper under control. She vowed to become more patient when such situations arose, though she doubted her need to kill could be kept in check. Tanaka would just have to understand that whenever she killed, she did it for him.

19

YAKUZA JUSTICE

Saipan

Northern Mariana Islands

March 1990

News that a local police officer was found stabbed to death near Marpi Point in the northernmost region of Saipan traveled at lightning speed despite the island's limited telecommunications network.

A fisherman's wife collecting driftwood had literally stumbled upon the body amid the rugged terrain near Suicide Cliff, where Tanaka's parents had flung themselves to death during World War II. The victim, though barefoot, was otherwise clad in his police sergeant's uniform. Flies were buzzing about the body, which in the heat of the day already had begun to swell, making it appear as though the victim had donned clothing two sizes too small.

FBI Special Agents Palmer and O'Reilly cancelled their

return flights to San Francisco and joined the investigation. The directive from FBI headquarters was awaiting them at the Saipan airport terminal, along with another rental car. Minutes later, they were studying the roadmap that would lead them to Marpi Point and the dead police officer.

Detective Mashima was already at the crime scene with Lt. Brick when the FBI special agents arrived. He greeted them with a slight bow and a hidden expression of frustration. The agents barked questions at him, stomping through the tall grass to where other police officers were gathered around the body.

Mashima shooed the haze of flies away from the dead man's face as he leaned over the body. He had already smeared Vaseline up his nostrils to ward off the smell of death and decay. The detective was glad Torres's eyes were closed because he felt a pang of guilt, as though his actions had somehow brought the sergeant to this unfortunate end.

The victim had been stabbed three times with an ice pick, one of the wounds puncturing his heart. Although his name was being temporarily withheld from the local newspaper and cable television station reporters from Guam, the island drums had already identified him as CNMI Police Sgt. Alfred Torres. At least two police officers at the scene were distant cousins of the deceased and visibly upset.

The victim had less than twenty dollars cash in his pockets and a jumble of coins. Had it not been stolen, the $36,000 was to have been turned over to authorities at the Saipan airport and used to pay for police security details at the terminal, but it was gone, every last dollar. And yet there was no absolute proof that Torres had taken it.

Mashima suspected the police sergeant had blown the entire amount in two of Garapan's most popular casinos – Round Two and The Lucky Carp. Oddly, it was not considered unusual for an islander to lose thousands to the electronic poker machines.

Such unbridled gambling had begun in the 1970s, ever since Japanese developers had followed their country's "Look South" policy by investing heavily in Saipan. Although only native Chamorro and Carolinians could own land, they were not prevented from long-term leasing to the Japanese for fifty to one hundred years. With plenty of lease money in hand and few options available for spending it, the newly-rich locals headed for the casinos.

Mashima soon tracked down where the dead police officer had gambled away thousands of dollars and, not surprisingly, it was primarily at The Lucky Carp.

During his investigation, he asked Krill, the night manager, and Tony, the bartender, if they had seen Torres at the poker machines. Both acknowledged they had.

Mashima shook his head in disappointment. Eyes narrowed and focused studiously on Krill, he said, "Did it ever occur to you he might be spending money that wasn't his to spend?"

"Why would I think that?"

"Please. This is a small island. The Torres family has not leased their land. It's too far from the beaches to have any value to those in the business of developing resorts."

"You obviously know more about him than I do," she said.

Mashima turned to the bar where Tony was nervously drying a wine glass. "You knew Alfred. Didn't you ask him how he suddenly had so much money to put into the machines?"

Tony stopped drying the glass and set it down on the bar. "I'm just the bartender. I don't tell people how much they should spend here."

"But both of you agree he was at the machines for three, maybe four hours?"

Krill and Tony nodded like two bobble heads.

"And neither one of you spoke to him during that time?"

Tony spoke first. "Whenever he wanted a mixed drink, I brought it to him. Vodka and soda. Alfred was always saying how doctors and lawyers drink vodka because it's hard to smell, which helps in case they get pulled over by the cops for drunk driving. He also had several beers. Budweiser. His usual. And a couple shots of Cuervo. Nothing fancy."

"Sounds like Alfred was on a mission of self-destruction. And what about you, Krill? Did you speak to him?"

"I waved when he first came in. I give a little wave to all our customers. Just being friendly. But no, I didn't speak to him. The place was hoppin'. I had a lot more things on my mind than whether some dumb cop wants to gamble away his paycheck."

Mashima bluntly asked them what they had heard about the stolen money being Tanaka's illegal earnings from the sale of marijuana and seized during the Tanapag drug raid. As expected, Tony remained stone-faced while Krill acted as though she was offended by the suggestion she might be privy to yakuza goings on.

"Detective, I have a child to feed at home — a daughter who needs me. And I need this job. I don't want to lose it. I work hard every fucking night and when I'm done I leave. I go home. Nothing more. I don't ask questions because I don't want to know the answers. I don't get involved in people's business, especially the yakuza."

"I wasn't suggesting you had any knowledge of criminal activity. But I am investigating the homicide of a police officer and was hoping you might offer any bit of information that might help."

Krill turned to the cash register and opened the drawer, pretending to count the cash. "Sorry. Now I have to get back to work."

Mashima planned to interview the deceased police officer's wife, Amista, on the slim chance the squandered money repre-sented their life savings, but instinct told him it was unlikely.

The case was already shaping up as a cop with his hands in the cookie jar, only in this instance, he ended up being ice-picked to death for his greed. Mashima mused. *It might have been safer had the sergeant robbed a bank. At least, once apprehended, he would have gone to jail instead of his grave.*

20

WHITE POWDER ON SUGAR DOCK

SAIPAN

NORTHERN MARIANA ISLANDS

APRIL 1990

TANAKA HAD a premonition his shipment of processed heroin, being transported by plane from a jungle hideout in the Philippines to the airstrip on Tinian Island — was in jeopardy. The premonition had come in the form of a bad dream and it had left him feeling unsettled. Millions of dollars were at risk and he wasn't about to lose a single ounce of the precious white powder.

The battered C-47 cargo plane, built to carry twenty-eight heavily-armed troops during World War II, was flying on fumes when it landed on Tinian during the night without any difficulty despite the absence of runway lights. Capable of hauling up to six thousand pounds, the plane's factory range was 2,600 kilometers. A few engine modifications since the 1940s helped put the distance from Manila to Tinian at slightly over the maximum range. The skilled pilot, assisted by fair winds and a bit of luck, had brought the C-47 safely to its destination. Tanaka was eager to unload the cargo and prepare it for the next leg of the journey.

Yuki and Kira — Tanaka's most-trusted men — were ferried to Tinian by two Saipanese fishermen in their twenties who chewed betel nut throughout the day. One was missing some of his front teeth and the betel nut dyed his exposed gums a bright red. His brother was taller but his back was permanently hunched from hard labor and bar fights. His knuckles were covered in blurry jailhouse tattoos. Both men had gladly accepted a generous wad of cash with the understanding they and their families would be executed if ever a word were spoken about the round trip.

The two *kobun* inspected and found intact the shipment of 1,200 tightly-packed bricks of white powder wrapped in clear plastic. Yuki punctured one of the bricks with his knife and licked the gleaming blade. He was obviously delighted with the quality of the product, trusting out his lower lip and nodding enthusiastically. "*Totemo yoi.* Tanaka will be pleased."

Kira poked a finger into the slit made by Yuki's switchblade and tasted it. "*Totemo yoi.* Let's hope all of these bricks are the same quality."

Since heroin has a long shelf life, transferring it to a cargo ship for the long passage to Hawaii was a matter of manpower and shuttles rather than a time crunch. Over the next week, the same rickety fishing boat that ferried the two *kobun* became a shuttle between the make-shift loading platform on the Tinian shoreline and the rusting vessel tied to the crumbling industrial Sugar Dock pier on Saipan.

Tanaka insisted the approximately twelve hundred pounds of white powder be transferred to the freighter in three equal shipments. He was concerned an inadequate bribe to the local police might cause some disgruntled officers to defect and release information about the smuggling operation to the newly-formed anti-drug task force, or potentially worse, to the U.S. Drug Enforcement Administration. It was no secret on Saipan that DEA agents had visited the island in the early 1980s under a directive from then President Ronald Reagan and his "Just Say No" to drugs policy. More recently, island wags had turned to discussing Lt. Louis Brick, the aggressive American police investigator who was already carrying out anti-drug raids in the small villages. In Tanaka's thinking, if the drug task force boarded the local fishing boat while it was laden with heroin, only that portion of the entire shipment potentially would be lost.

Six *kobun* were stationed aboard the freighter and along the Sugar Dock in Chalan Kanoa to keep unwelcome police and curious sightseers away.

Mashima closely watched the activity from the bell tower of the Roman Catholic Church. Father Martin Garcia, the priest assigned to the parish, was a friend who disliked the yakuza as much as Mashima did.

Mashima first met Father Garcia at the U.S. Naval Hospital on Guam Island where the newly-ordained priest counseled patients recovering from a wide array of ailments. Then a fledgling police officer, Mashima had entered a suspected illegal drug lab on Saipan where crystal methamphetamine, known among the locals as Shabu, was being produced in large quantities. He had been horribly burned when a booby trap exploded, showering him with sulfuric acid. The left side of his face was damaged beyond recognition but doctors had hopes plastic surgery might result in an acceptable reconstruction. Mashima's spirit had fallen to an all-time low, and he had actually begun wearing a partial mask when in public, but Father Garcia helped him see the bright side. As the priest put it, though disfigured, Mashima was nonetheless young, intelligent, honorable, and perhaps would one day rejoin the active ranks of the CNMI police force. The priest's words had become reality the day Mashima was reissued his badge and gun.

As Mashima peered through the binoculars from a windowsill in the church tower, the priest emerged from the stone stairwell carrying a plate of food.

"They've been busy. Two of the fishermen are bringing cargo to the ship."

"Do you know them?"

"Only by sight. Many of the fishermen attend Mass on Sunday, but they aren't among them."

"Has the number of men guarding the ship increased over the past week?"

"Most definitely. They're posted on the dock and aboard the ship at all hours. When I walked near the dock last week, one of the guards leveled his gun at me and shouted in Japanese. It didn't take a translator to know what he was saying. *Get away or I'll shoot.*"

"Have you seen any of the local police officers go aboard?"

"I'm glad to report that I haven't. I'm sure the temptation to collect bribe money is strong."

The priest handed Mashima the plate laden with motsiyas, a mixture of ground chicken, hot pepper leaves, mint and lemon juice.

"Ah, you are so kind to remember my favorite food from Rota. I'm afraid I have no culinary skills and must depend on the generosity of others like you."

"Enjoy," said the priest, backing toward the stairwell. "Stay here as long as you like and come any time. You don't need to ask. The yakuza pay little attention to what goes on at the church."

"Thank you, Father Garcia. It seems you're always there when I need you."

"My pleasure. You are an angel dressed as a police detective."

Mashima suspected the rusting freighter was loaded with processed heroin and perhaps a shipment of stolen, military-grade weapons. But CNMI Police Chief Joe Napuna had ordered Mashima to use his time investigating the murder of popular Caucasian schoolteacher Mark Jensen and his Saipanese lover, the pretty social worker Maria Flores, instead of wasting time on the yakuza.

In the bars and restaurants, locals were outwardly accusing the island police of ineptitude and demanding the double homicide be solved. It was well publicized that the two had been shot to death while parked in Jensen's truck after dark in a remote area. Flores had been beaten and raped before she was executed. The schoolteacher had been killed with a single bullet to the head. It didn't look like a robbery. Jensen's wallet remained in his back pocket and Flores' straw purse was tucked beneath the truck's bench seat.

Mashima had listened patiently to the many public complaints. Personally he had found the burly and bearded Jensen pompous, obnoxious and self-absorbed, a man whose voice was a continual stream of tales focused on his own great-ness. It made him wonder what attracted the serene and generous Flores to such a man, but she had been reluctant to answer when he once asked and her reticence pained him.

The day Jensen arrived on Saipan to begin teaching would always be ingrained in Mashima's memory. Jensen was tall, clean-shaven, and walked with the authority of Gen. Douglas MacArthur coming ashore on Leyte Island. This was months before the teacher grew what became his trademark gray beard and long, untamed hair.

Earlier that week, Mashima and Flores had enjoyed another picnic lunch on the beach, something they frequently did as friends. Mashima looked forward to those picnics, each one bringing him closer to the woman of his dreams. But that last picnic had been different. With a never-before-seen sparkle in her eyes, Flores had excitedly described Jensen as a typical American, friendly and smiling, very outgoing and entertaining. The schoolchildren loved him, she said, and two of the other women teachers commented on his tall frame, white teeth, and commanding presence. Mashima felt sick the first time he spotted them kissing in the school parking lot.

Mashima stopped at a market where the television was blaring near the checkout. A news reporter from the regional cable television station was broadcasting a story about the murder of CNMI Police Sgt. Alfred Torres whose body was discovered less than a week previous. A photograph to Torres in uniform flashed on the screen. As an addendum to her story the reporter emphasized that no arrests had been made in the Lover's Lane case, insinuating corruption within the police force might be playing a role.

Mashima brushed aside the unflattering news stories that criticized the CNMI police and inferred that law enforcement authorities were generally untrustworthy. He had no intention of ignoring the investigation into the sergeant's death, but the opportunity to disrupt the yakuza's drug-smuggling operation had arisen and he felt compelled to take advantage of it.

Mashima knew the sergeant had a gambling addiction, but he wasn't a drug trafficker. The detective was clutching a bottle of sake when early in the evening he gently knocked on the hotel room door where Hannah and Carrington were staying. When Hannah opened the door, the detective presented the bottle with both hands stretched outward as might a sommelier at an upscale restaurant table.

"What's this for?"

"I thought the three of us could share a drink and talk about things we have in common."

Carrington's voice reached across the room, though Mashima could not see him because the door was only partially open. "And what might that be?"

"I don't want to shout."

Hannah fully opened the door. "Please come inside." She closed the door and accepted the bottle, holding it up like a trophy. "Look here Jake, Detective Mashima has brought us a gift."

Carrington had spent years in Southeast Asia and was well acquainted with the importance of ritual. He fingered three small glasses off the nightstand, quickly rinsed them in the bathroom sink, and poured a few ounces of sake into each.

Mashima nodded a mix of approval and appreciation. "I believe a large shipment of heroin has arrived by plane on Tinian. At least two local fishermen, maybe more, have been hired to bring the cargo to Saipan in their boat."

"Is this fact, or speculation?"

"I know the fishermen on this island and most of them trust me. When they tell me things, they have no reason to lie, only to help."

"So why would one fisherman tell you that another fishermen is helping the yakuza?"

"Because they are unhappy with that decision. They don't like the yakuza, especially the aggressive *kobun* who try to order them around like servants. And they don't like what's happening here because of the drugs. They see what it's doing to the young ones."

Hannah held up her glass. "Enough talk. Let's toast to things in common. An alliance."

Mashima smiled for the first time, consciously exposing the right side of his face without the scars. "To an alliance."

Carrington tapped his glass twice on the nightstand and raised it to meet the others. "An alliance."

After two more sake drinks, Mashima unveiled the details of his surveillance, along with the names and descriptions of key yakuza players in Tanaka's immediate crime family. Hannah and Carrington were surprised to learn that the freighter under surveillance at Sugar Dock was tied up just north of their hotel and within walking distance.

"I believe the cargo on board is processed heroin destined for the United States. Hundreds of pounds."

Carrington raised his eyebrows. "You're talking hundreds of millions of dollars in a single shipment."

"That's correct. From what I have been able to learn, Tanaka's connections oversee the raw poppies as they are harvested in Thailand. Once liquid from the flowers is allowed to spill onto wooden boards, it dries into a paste. Then it's collected for shipment to the Philippines by plane. I have calculated that flight at approximately 2,200 miles. The final processing takes place somewhere in the Philippines."

Hannah rubbed her chin. "Do you know where the lab is located?"

"No. Presumably well hidden in the jungle. I was hoping one of your satellites might be able to provide some itel."

Hannah glanced at Carrington. "We'll see what we can do. If we knew what island the lab was on, it would make things easier."

"I'm afraid I don't have that detail."

Carrington seemed perplexed. "There are over 7,000 islands in the Philippines. My guess would be somewhere on Luzon. Ever since Francis Ford Coppola filmed *Apocalypse Now* in the area the place has been fucked."

Hannah shook her head. "I disagree. Luzon has too many prying eyes and it's too close to Manila. I'd look south toward Davao, probably Mindanao. Lots of anti-government activity where an organized crime operation can flourish."

Mashima stood and slightly bowed his head. "I shall leave those decisions in your hands. Thank you for listening."

21

A SNAKE IN THE GRASS

SAIPAN

NORTHERN MARIANA ISLANDS

APRIL 1990

A WEEK after the murder of Sgt. Torres, Tanaka intensified his presence at The Lucky Carp where he could closely watch over the operation. He became, in Krill's words, a fixture.

Mashima conveyed this information to Hannah and Carrington in order that they might ramp up the honey trap.

Carrington was sprawled across the hotel room bed, disassembling and cleaning the two Glock 9mm handguns Mashima had provided without request. The serial numbers on both weapons were obliterated. The gift was a gesture of professional respect because tourists were not allowed to bring firearms onto the island, which meant Hannah and Carrington had come through Customs unarmed.

Carrington studied Hannah as she moved about the room. "Are you sure you're up for this?"

Hannah gazed at herself in the full-length wall mirror. She recognized her own beauty, though she seldom played that card. She preferred men who appreciated her intelligence, wit, and her occasionally dark sense of humor.

"What about this one?"

Carrington whistled when Hannah held up a spaghetti-strapped, gold-sequin mini dress. "I think that'll get his attention."

"Tanaka left a message at the hotel desk. He'd like to go sightseeing, show me around the island."

"And?"

"Well. Why not?"

"It puts you out of range. How am I supposed to stay in contact?"

"You worry too much."

"The guy's a killer. I don't want you to end up like Stevens and Cahill. You should take along one of the Glocks."

"Nowhere to hide it, especially in this dress," she said, doing a full twirl in front the mirror that left Carrington speechless.

Hannah tossed the sequin dress across the back of a chair. Carrington didn't hesitate. In seconds he was kissing her ravenously and pulling her toward the bed where the guns were disassembled. He yanked back the covers, not caring that the metal parts were jumbled in the process, and gently eased Hannah onto the clean sheets.

"Would it bother you if I told you I loved you?" Carrington asked.

Hannah pressed a finger against his lips and waited until his eyes met hers. She kissed him deeply, tongues swirling, bodies writhing. And when they'd finished an hour later, glowing with sweat and short of breath, they lay back atop the pillows.

"Does that answer your question?"

Carrington smiled as though he owned the world. "I think it does," he said, pulling her close.

Hannah enjoyed the warmth, the connection, and the back-to-back orgasms, but something about the relationship felt wrong. Sure, she cared about Carrington, but he wasn't going to be her future, and that thought alone was enough to form a constant barrier. She didn't want to be the one who broke up his marriage and left his kids to grow up without their father. When the time came, she'd muster the strength to keep him at arm's length and eventually pull away.

Hannah deftly swirled out of bed. "I'm going to shower. Tanaka wants to take me on a picnic. Sushi and champagne. Fun, fun, fun."

Carrington's expression changed from relaxation to serious concern. "And when is this picnic date supposed to take place?"

"Later today. He's sending a car."

"Today? Didn't you think to mention it until now?"

"I knew you'd pull a nutty. But we have to find a way to get to this guy. Remember what Stu said at Langley, if we don't take him down, he becomes the shogun of heroin in the entire region. Besides, I won't be alone with him. From what I've seen and heard, he always has two or three bodyguards."

"Those guys are there to protect him, not you."

"I know that. But having other people around reduces the likelihood that Tanaka will act inappropriately. He wouldn't risk having witnesses in the case that his advances are rejected. With the Japanese, it's all about face."

"And now you're an expert on Japanese culture?"

"Nope. Read it in our briefing file. I guess you skipped over that part."

Carrington quickly reassembled one of the Glocks, slammed a full magazine into the handle and pulled back on the slide to load a round into the chamber. "I hate this fucking place. Even more than I hated Saigon."

Hannah shot him a quick look of disapproval. "As you frequently remind me, William, we have to keep our heads."

Carrington loaded an additional magazine and stuffed it into the front pocket of his shorts. "When Tanaka's vehicle pulls up outside the hotel, I need you to distract him and the guards long enough for me to attach this," he said, holding a military-grade GPS tracker. "It'll only take a few seconds. Just get them to look at you. Trip, fall, pretend you're about to faint from the heat. Whatever it takes."

22

RETURN FROM SAND LAND

AFGHAN-PAKISTAN BORDER
APRIL 1990

DECKER HAD BARELY MOVED his body in more than twenty-four hours. He lay beneath a dun-colored tarp further camouflaged with scoops of sand. Navy sniper Riley "Reb" Turner – a member of SEAL Team Six until the unit was disbanded in 1987 and reorganized under the name DEVGRU (Navy Special Warfare Development Group) — lay equally still beneath the tarp.

The target had not appeared as expected, but nothing was for certain in this waiting game. Snipers were trained in patience and endurance.

Both their hydration backpacks were nearly empty and the temperature beneath the tarp was pushing 100 degrees Fahrenheit. Decker had waited far longer on other missions, some of which disappointingly did not end in a kill. But he wanted this one. He was determined to snuff out what he saw as the hypocrisy of radical religion in the Middle East. The mullah on his hit list had radicalized dozens of young Afghani boys, shown them how to build roadside bombs and booby traps that would maim the Americans and their allies and slow their anticipated counter-invasion forces. Some of the booby traps exploded when touched, often hidden in the stomachs of sick children or dead dogs.

The mullah was an expert in destruction — truck bombs piloted by suicidal drivers, poison gasses, biological agents, nail bombs designed to explode inside restaurants or other gathering places of his enemies. The latter, called flechettes, were particularly effective at inciting terror because the shrapnel left behind such devastating wounds.

A religious zealot with a penchant for military tactics, he had studied the effectiveness of the flechettes that were frequently employed by the Irish Republican Army during The Troubles in Ireland in the 1970s. The war in Vietnam had added a new bag of tricks, like the so-called rubber band grenade. A rubber band was wrapped around a grenade with its pin already pulled. The band kept the grenade's safety lever in place until the rubber melted. As American soldiers burned village huts to locate hidden tunnels or weapons, the grenades exploded.

The grenade-in-a-tin-can method was equally nasty and another of the mullah's favorites. With the pin removed, the grenade was tucked into a tin can to keep the safety lever from opening. The can was attached to a trip string, so that when a door was opened or the string pulled by an unsuspecting soldier's boot, the grenade detonated.

Decker had read the mullah's extensive file at Langley. The man had many devout followers willing to lay down their lives for Allah in a war against the infidels.

Decker cursed the sand fleas beneath his uniform, which he had already treated with Permethrin. Two years prior, when he was still a sergeant in the U.S. Army Rangers, he'd heard plenty of jokes about how Permethrin was used to treat scabies and other sexually-transmitted diseases. But he wasn't laughing now.

It seemed a lifetime ago that he was a grunt eager to strut his stuff and get selected for sniper school. That special education translated to two months spent at Fort Benning, Georgia — a time he'd never forget. Bees, fire ants, insects of all sorts ready to bite, burrow, tickle or do any number of things that might cause a sniper to move and give away his position.

The instructors watched every recruit through powerful optics. If they couldn't see the sniper, it was a job well done. But if they spotted movement and focused in on the recruit in the ghillie suit, it meant bye-bye, you just flunked out.

Decker could still hear his instructor shouting, "Snipers are force multipliers. A few good snipers can sometimes swing the momentum on the battlefield. That's your job. Shoot straight and swing the momentum."

Decker knew he could hit a target squarely from a half-mile away, and often at much longer distances with a .50-caliber round fired from his trusty Barrett M107 rifle. He'd done it dozens of times in Lebanon while listening to music through his headphones.

"Move like a sloth," his instructor had said, over and over again. "Any faster, you'll be seen."

So Decker and Reb had moved like sloths to the crest of a sand dune that gave them an acceptable field of fire. It had taken hours of crawling to get into that position, but they'd done it, undetected. Reb – at thirty-five and about the same age as Decker — was right by his side, unmoving, unspeaking, but ready to lock in on the coordinates and tell the sniper where to adjust his aim.

Just as Decker was feeling as though luck had left them behind, the whine of a small truck engine caught his attention.

Reb instinctively brushed his sweat-glistened black hair and beard with his fingers before nestling into his spotting scope.

In the crosshairs, two bearded men came into focus – the younger, lanky one in the driver's seat looked about mid-twenties, the older man in the passenger seat, thickly bearded, and wearing the headdress of a mullah. Reb quickly computed the distance to the target and what effect gravity would have on the projectile once it left the barrel. He was thankful for the absence of wind, which would have added yet another factor.

The pickup stopped in the open and the younger man got out. He sparked an M18 smoke grenade and stepped back to avoid the purple plume. Satisfied with the signal, he leaned against the truck and lit a cigarette. The mullah stayed in his seat.

Several minutes passed before a battered Mercedes Benz sedan came to a sand-tossing halt beside the truck. Both Decker and Reb watched as the mullah left the truck and approached the car's open trunk where a scraggly man cradling an AK-47 rifle was gesticulating wildly at the contents. The mullah held up and inspected what looked to them like several pair of blue jeans. Next he picked through a plastic crate containing porn films on VHS tapes. Decker seethed when the mullah smiled at the provocative cardboard covers. Negotiations were happening, presumably about the quality of the merchandise and ultimately the price. More hand gestures followed, as did another exploration of the car trunk, where cardboard boxes of Scotch whisky and American bourbon were stacked.

The younger man accompanying the mullah handed over what apparently was payment and began loading the purchases into the pickup bed, which he quickly covered with a tarp. Some odd hugging and back patting went on among the four men. The Mercedes roared away into the desert, leaving behind a whirl of sand.

Reb relayed additional shooting instructions to Decker who pressed the trigger just as the smiling mullah lifted the tarp for one last glance at his latest illicit treasure. The bullet tore the mullah's head from his body. The young driver stood motionless, as though frozen by a wave of fear. Decker watched closely through his riflescope as the shaken man finally regained his composure and scrambled toward the driver's door. Decker could have shot him as he grabbed the door handle, but it seemed too easy. Instead, he waited until the man started the engine and began turning the steering wheel. The bullet took out the windshield before exploding into the man's body.

Decker closed his eyes as a flash memory played out. Beirut, Lebanon. Early 1980s. Sniper City. Madness. Never knowing for sure if the target was truly the enemy. Listening to music on his headphones as he pressed the trigger gently, always gently. Following through when the pressure registered on his index finger. The sick thrill of sensing the heavy bullet leave the barrel. Witnessing the destruction it caused.

The shrinks at the VA hospitals in Pittsburgh and Boston had tried to make him talk about the experience, but he basically told them to go fuck themselves — partly because they often talked psycho-babble-gibberish and hadn't ever experienced combat. But mostly he didn't cooperate because he still didn't know how he felt about shooting people for political purposes. It was simply a job he had been trained to do for his country and he did it better than most.

Decker usually tried to ignore politics, but it was difficult. The mullah that he and Reb eliminated was the enemy. The religious leader had become a central player along the Afghan-Pakistan border where he regularly visited a network of madrasses. The small schools, originally established to teach religion, had been transformed into training camps where boys from poor families were indoctrinated to fight against the infidels — namely, the United States.

Decker assumed the Islamic mujahideen guerrillas in Afghanistan apparently had short memories, choosing to forget the military assistance they'd received from the United States to oust the Soviets from their country, a ten-year struggle that ended less than a year before. Ungrateful bastards is how he thought of them.

With the latest target eliminated, Decker was free to return to Langley or wherever else he was ordered. Same went for Reb – known at the Joint Special Forces Operations Command (JSOC) as Riley Turner, a Navy SEAL with an excellent sniper rating and high-security clearance, the same man Decker referred to in moments of endearment as a mullet-tossing Florabama hick who should have joined the Navy's Blue Angels in Pensacola and flown air shows for a titillated public instead of the goddamn SEALs.

Decker radioed the reconnaissance plane to request extraction by helicopter. Within a matter of hours they were en route to the forward operations base. It was there Decker found a coded message from Stuart Ashwood, the CIA's deputy director of operations, instructing him and Turner to await priority agency transport to Saipan where Hannah and Carrington apparently needed a sniper team. The message offered no explanation. It was simply an order they were expected to follow.

23

PICNIC WITH THE OYABUN

Saipan

Northern Mariana Islands

April 1990

THE PAVED ROAD to Marpi Point was narrow and badly rutted. Highway maintenance wasn't exactly a priority on Saipan. Tanaka and Hannah sat in the back of the black SUV. Each time the customized Nissan Pathfinder dipped into a furrow, the passengers were tossed, causing them to bump shoulders. Tanaka attempted to put an arm around Hannah as though to protect her but when she didn't respond he withdrew it.

Yuki, the bodyguard in the front passenger seat, grimaced when Tanaka shouted the ride was uncomfortable and they should drive more carefully. He nervously twirled his long braided hair that hung across his right shoulder and onto his chest. When the SUV struck another rut in the road, Kira's grip on the steering wheel was so fierce it turned his knuckles white.

Yuki slapped the man's shaved head. "Pay attention. You drive like a teenager."

Traveling the roads was made more difficult by the locals — many first-generation drivers who seldom exceeded 10 miles per hour. And since the chewing of betel nut was widespread on the island, it was not unusual for a pickup or car to come to an abrupt halt. Seconds later, the driver's door would open as gobs of reddened saliva were spat onto the white coral road.

After climbing a steep switchback, the SUV stopped where the land ended at the rim of Suicide Cliff. It was here that Tanaka's parents in June 1944 had thrown themselves to their deaths onto the rocks below.

Hannah leaned out the window. "Is this our picnic spot?"

"No," Tanaka said solemnly. "We are only stopping long enough for me to light the candles to honor my mother and father."

All along the cliff edge, wooden markers were scrawled with names or special messages in black ink. Some of the markers were three feet tall and a foot wide, others far smaller. Most of the words were written in Kanji.

"What is this place?"

Tanaka pointed to a flock of white birds swooping just beyond the edge of the cliff. "Do you see those birds? They contain the souls of all those who took their lives here," he said. "Before that day when the Marines landed, Saipan had no white birds."

Hannah kept silent as Tanaka approached one of the larger wooden markers, bowed deeply and struck a match to a candle protected from the wind by a glass cylinder. Tanaka's bodyguards stood at a respectful distance while he prayed.

Tanaka turned to Hannah and with a head nod invited her to step forward. "Few people come here at night. The locals stay far away from it. They say it's haunted because of the war, that it's a place of darkness. Perhaps they are correct," he said.

"When I listen closely, mixed in with the wind I can hear the cries of my ancestors, feel their pain and suffering."

"Did your parents die here?"

"Yes. Of their own will. They took my two sisters with them. I don't remember it, though I was here. I was only two or three years old. For some reason I had wandered off into the high grass. Perhaps I was guided by a survival instinct that told me to flee."

"I'm so sorry," said Hannah. "That's such a tragic story."

"Others who had decided to survive – in my case an entire Japanese family – ran from Marpi Point and hid in the caves. The father of that family carried me and his youngest daughter in his arms for many hours, or so I have been told."

"How did they find you?"

"At first they thought I was a snake slithering through the grass, which is why I was later named Orochi. That is what you might call a silly observation since Saipan has few if any snakes. But as you may imagine, my rescuers had more to think about at that time than whether the island is home to snakes. More importantly, according to Japanese legend, Orochi is an eight-headed snake, but as you can see, I have only one."

Tanaka laughed quietly. Hannah wasn't sure whether Tanaka was attempting to make a joke, so she didn't reply.

"When my saviors realized my mother, father, and sisters were gone, they made me a part of their family. They did not hesitate and I have always been grateful. Though I've never been able to forgive the Americans for what they did. When I was a young man, I engaged in a bar fight with a U.S. Marine in Okinawa and was about to push a knife into his throat when my companions pulled me off. It would have been a big mistake, but at the time, I only wanted to kill a Marine. I wanted vengeance."

Tanaka's eyes were glassy as they returned to the SUV.

"Enough ghosts for one day," he said. "Let's find a place to watch the sunset and enjoy some sake and sushi."

Hannah had no idea how much Tanaka knew about her or just how reliable his intelligence sources might be. Criminals like Tanaka typically possessed a poker face, making it difficult to determine what they were thinking. She hoped he saw her only as a vulnerable, young Argentine travel agent eager to make business connections on Saipan and explore the culture, just another pretty blonde he might add to his list of sexual conquests.

"Thank you for bringing me here," she said as they sat at a folding table with two chairs that Tanaka's men had set up. "It's such a beautiful island. I'm hoping to learn more about it, enough so that I can guide my clients in Buenos Aires to the best hotels and beaches."

Hannah listened closely to whatever information Tanaka shared and he seemed pleased by her undivided attention. They sipped sake and watched the sun begin its descent into the Pacific.

"I will be honored to assist you with your business venture. I have a deep connection to this place. In many ways, this is my island," he said.

"If I may ask, did you remain on Saipan after the war ended?"

"No. I was only a baby and the family that saved me returned to their home in Osaka. While in Saipan, the father had worked at the hospital as a general laborer, not even a salaryman. As you might imagine, the hospital became over-whelmed with casualties as the fighting worsened. Near the end, the laborers were given weapons and ordered to join our soldiers in defense of the island, but they were not able to hold back the Americans. Over the years I listened to many horrible stories but they are not worth repeating because they only prolong the suffering. Our life in Osaka was without privilege because the man who raised me could find little work. I remained with them until I was able to finish my schooling."

"Are they still in Osaka?"

"Yes. But now they are becoming old and frail. I pay for their housing and medical expenses. I have not stayed in contact with their sons and daughters. I have never considered them as true brothers and sisters. They are not my blood."

"That's very kind of you to help the family."

"It's the least I can do. I owe them my life."

Hannah wanted to ask a lot more questions but sensed it might make her suspect. Tanaka reached out and touched her thigh as she sipped the sake, causing her to reflexively pull it away. He quickly kissed her on the cheek but she dipped her head when he aimed for her lips.

"Orochi, I hope I didn't give you the wrong impression when I agreed to have a picnic with you," she said. "It was such a generous offer, I could hardly refuse."

Tanaka forced a smile. "And yet you reject me."

"Not reject. Just going slowly. We're strangers. Although I'm hoping we'll become friends one day."

"And then?"

"Who knows? You're a handsome, powerful man, educated and well traveled. I think most women would find you quite attractive."

"Do you?"

"Of course, I do. Do you really think I'd be here if I didn't? But I'm in no hurry. I plan to learn all about Saipan, so I'll be here for as long as it takes and that could be quite a while."

Tanaka tapped his sake glass to hers, breaking into a full-tooth smile in an attempt to hide his frustration and disappointment. "To island friends," he said. "I will make it my mission to show you everything wonderful that Saipan has to offer."

Hannah feigned pure delight. "I'm looking forward to it. I'd also like to hear the story of how you lost part of your finger."

Tanaka stretched his arm onto the table and stared at the partially-amputated pinkie finger. He smiled demurely, as though both embarrassed and proud. "I didn't know if you had noticed. I will tell you all about it when we meet again."

Back at the hotel, Carrington was relieved when the tracker showed Tanaka's vehicle returning. Next time, he'd shadow them personally.

24

WANTED: ONE SNIPER TEAM

TINIAN

NORTHERN MARIANA ISLANDS

APRIL 1990

CARRINGTON'S FACE was a mask of deep concern as he entered the hotel room. He had telephoned Ashwood using an encrypted line designed to run through a series of switches before actually connecting to the deputy director of operations. "I called Ashwood for instructions. He reminded me that I don't have advanced sniper training, so he's sending a Navy SEAL with a long gun in case we get into a jam and need somebody who can shoot with precision."

"Do we really need a sniper?"

"Apparently Ashwood thinks so. He doesn't want to take any more chances than necessary. The stakes are too high. He also wants some payback for Stevens and Cahill. If there's no other way to eliminate Tanaka, he wants the sniper to do it."

Hannah glanced up from the romantic comedy she was

reading on the bed. She was wearing the over-sized Nirvana band t-shirt Carrington had given her not long after they first crossed paths in Ireland while hunting down a serial killer, back in the days when she was a Massachusetts State Police homicide detective. "When is he arriving?"

"This afternoon. His name is Turner. A Navy chopper will be setting him down on Tinian. I'll be there when he lands. And by the way, it sounds like Decker may be with him, though I don't know why."

Hannah's face went pale. "Decker?"

"According to Ashwood, Decker will act as a spotter."

Hannah was suddenly uneasy. "Is it going to be weird for all of us?"

"That depends on what you want everyone to know."

"So it's on me?"

"How did you leave it with Decker? I only heard his side of the story."

"What did he tell you?"

"I'd like to hear your version first," said Carrington. "Then I'll share what he told me."

"Fair enough. Things are strained. I knew he was leaving for Iraq before he broke the news to me. He's mixed up and hurting inside. He's been like that since he returned from his last Middle East deployment."

"And then there was Cuba."

"And then there was Cuba," she echoed. "You know how that turned out. I'm not exactly sure what went on between him and Selena Delgado, but whatever it was seemed to touch him deeply."

"Are you jealous of Selena Delgado?"

"How could I be, after what you and I shared in Havana? I have no right to be jealous. Besides, Selena Delgado is dead."

Carrington glanced at Hannah with a look of pure adoration. "Do you regret them?"

"You mean our moments in Havana?"

"That's what I mean."

"I treasure them."

"But you still haven't come clean what's going on between you and Decker, or what's going on inside your head. Are you two still together? Last I heard, you were sharing an apartment in Boston. For the longest time I thought you two were inseparable. Now I don't know what to think."

"It's complicated. He saved my life. After that, we became very close."

"I read that field report at least ten times. Serial killer Luddy Pugano was about to set you on fire as his latest victim when Decker showed up to save the day, along with one of his ex-military buddies who was accompanied by a combat K-9. I wish you'd gotten the chance to personally get even with Pugano."

"We all know what happened in Ireland. Water over the dam."

"But you're still angry about it, deep inside."

"You're probably right. Back then, I would have arrested Pugano and handed him over to the authorities so that he could face trial."

"And now?"

Hannah sat on the edge of the bed, nervously rubbing her bare feet on the tattered carpet. "I'm not so sure any more. The courts, the judges, the whole American justice system — sometimes it all seems like a big joke on people who respect the law. It's as if justice were a commodity like potatoes and you only get as much as you can afford."

Carrington sat beside her on the bed, took the book from her hands and placed it on the nightstand. Gently he leaned his shoulder into hers and she rested her head upon it.

"I don't want to lose you, Hannah."

Hannah reached for Carrington's hands and squeezed them

affectionately. "You know I care about you, William. But I can't be responsible for everybody's happiness. I never wanted things to be this messy."

"Well, they are. I know you might not want to hear it, but I'm in love with you. I think about you twenty-four hours a day. Every time you walk out that door I worry you won't come back."

Hannah withdrew her hands and stood. "We have to remember our problems are always secondary to why we were sent here. We have to stay focused. You taught me that."

Carrington wrapped his arms around her but she didn't respond. Her arms remained limp, her eyes closed.

Carrington took a step back. He looked defeated. "I've got to get moving if I'm going to meet them on time."

"How are you getting to Tinian?"

"Local helicopter service. Blue Pacific Aviation. The company has a bird parked at the airport."

"Do you want me to come along?"

"Not enough room, especially if Decker and the sniper are lugging gear. Besides, I need you to meet them with the rental car at a landing zone about four miles from here."

"Right. They can't land at the airport. No passports, not to mention the rifles and whatever else they're packing."

"Don't worry, when I get to Tinian, I'm not going to say, 'Hey, Decker, good to see you, and by the way, Hannah and I are sleeping together.' I get the feeling that news wouldn't go over very well."

Hannah flopped back onto the bed, rolled over on her stomach and covered her head with a pillow. She growled, but it was muffled. A moment later she turned and gazed at Carrington with a look of disappointment on her face. "Let's keep what you and I have just between us. At least for now."

"Fine by me. I'll go sleep on the beach when Decker gets

here and expects to crawl into bed with you. I don't think I could listen to that."

"Oh, fuck off, William. You're not exactly in the position to make any demands."

"Understood. We keep to the mission."

"By the way, you never told me Decker's side of the story, at least whatever it was he confided in you."

"He told me you were too good for him, that he could never live up to your expectations."

"He actually said that?"

"He did. Whatever happened to him in Lebanon did some real damage, but he'll never admit it. And as for Selena Delgado, well, I think they were two lost souls who came together for comfort, nothing more. I don't think he was in love with her, in case that's what you're wondering."

25

THREE'S A CROWD

SAIPAN
NORTHERN MARIANA ISLANDS
APRIL 1990

THE NAVY MH-60 Seahawk assault helicopter landed on one of the two-mile-long runways built on Tinian Island during World War II to accommodate B-29 Super Fortress bombers like the *Enola Gay*, which on August 6, 1945 dropped its atomic payload on the Japanese city of Hiroshima.

The Navy crew chief opened the side door to the powerful, 65-foot, twin-engine aircraft that was built to carry up to four passengers in addition to its three-man crew. The rotor blades were still churning but no longer at full thrust. The crew chief tossed a green duffel bag to the sun-bleached runway and signaled Reb to exit.

Reb leaped the three foot distance, not losing his balance despite the padded rifle case slung over his right shoulder and a pump shotgun over his left. He did a double take at the cattle and goats placidly grazing along the sides of the runway. The animals didn't seem fazed by the helicopter. Reb's commanding officer had given him the option of returning to a SEAL team or embarking on a top-secret CIA mission somewhere in the western Pacific, never thinking the battle-weary soldier would choose the latter.

Decker instinctively scanned the terrain from the helicopter's side door before flinging his gear toward where the other duffel had landed. He handed his sniper rifle to Reb before jumping out.

Within seconds the Seahawk was airborne, returning to its berth aboard an aircraft carrier from the U.S. Seventh Fleet, one of many warships deployed to protect Taiwan from China and thwart regional aggression by North Korea.

Carrington casually strolled toward the two men who were hunkered as they moved out from beneath the rotor wash. He extended a bro handshake. "Welcome to Micronesia, the asshole of the Pacific. Glad you could make it," he said, falsely smiling at Decker as though he was a long lost brother. "Let me take your duffel."

"Why'd we land here?"

"Didn't want to attract a lot of attention on Saipan, especially at the airport. The locals don't exactly appreciate law-enforcement intervention, particularly by the Feebies and the government prosecutors. Frankly they don't seem to like any Statesiders, which is one of the nicer names they have for us."

Reb put out a hand and Carrington grasped it bro-style, locking eyes with the stranger. "Any friend of Decker's is a friend of ours. Let's get the fuck out of here."

Carrington cocked his head toward a beer-bellied man wearing tattered jeans, a soiled Ozzy Osbourne t-shirt, Nike sneakers and a Boston Red Sox ballcap. He guessed they were about the same age, but the pilot leaning against an aging, blue-and-white, five-passenger, Bell 206 JetRanger helicopter obviously was going to seed at a far faster rate.

The pilot had adopted Whirly Man as his aviation call sign and personal nickname. He was puffing nervously on a cigarette. The light-utility helicopter, with its wraparound glass windshield and generous side windows, was a fragile baby bird compared to the Seahawk. Its fuselage paint was chipped and scratched, the body dented in several places, the windshield glass showed hairline cracks and the spindly landing skids were out of alignment. The aircraft did not inspire trust and confidence. It was emblazoned with the name Blue Pacific Aviation.

Carrington shot a wry look at Decker and Reb, knowing they must be wondering why he'd arranged transport in a deathtrap. "We'll be flying with him. Only ride in town. He'll let both of you off at an LZ before he and I continue on to the airport. Hannah will meet you with a car when you touch down."

As Decker and Carrington approached, the pilot snuffed out his cigarette on the white coral. "If you guys don't mind, we'll skip the formalities. I'd like to get this bird off the ground and back home as quickly as possible."

Carrington handed the pilot Decker's duffel bag and the padded rifle case so that he could properly distribute the weight in the small helicopter.

Decker held onto his rifle as he squeezed through the rear door to the cramped passenger compartment. Reb folded himself beside Decker and gave him a hip check as he plunked down on the three-man bench seat. "This is cozy."

Carrington thrust the second duffel and a long, dun-colored Pelican case onto Reb's lap. "Plenty of room," he said, chuckling.

The rear passenger compartment was separated from the pilot and co-pilot seats by a steel mesh screen, installed because Whirly Man occasionally transported prisoners for the CNMI police.

Carrington climbed in next to the pilot who pretended to be fiddling with the controls. Whirly Man shook his head at the sight of the weapons as though they were bound for trouble. Without any pre-check, he fired up the engine and the helicopter jerkily lifted off.

Peering out the window, Reb marveled at the sight of the coral-dot islands, the low-slung atolls surrounded by reef-toothed lagoons amid an endless turquoise sea. Even while wearing headphones, it was difficult to talk inside the small chopper, so he simply tried to relax after the long hours of travel from Kuwait. He'd just about nodded off when he heard the pilot's panicked voice.

"We're taking ground fire!"

Whirly Man pushed the cyclic control, keyed his radio to signal the radar station at the airport, and shouted into his microphone. "I think some of the rounds have hit near the tail."

Decker chuckled to himself, wondering if he would ever see Hannah again or simply die in a helicopter crash. If this were the end, his death shockingly would not occur on some Taliban-infested jagged mountain peak in Afghanistan but on a magazine-cover tropical island. People who didn't know him would undoubtedly assume he died while having a whole lot of fun in a beautiful place, like a tourist in a helicopter that crashes while viewing the fiery innards of some Hawaiian volcano.

The voice from the radar station, which was a wooden shack near the airport terminal building, urged the pilot to veer off and change course.

"Already bearing east. The ground fire is coming from the fields near Tanapag. Small arms at this point, but I don't want to hang around to see if whoever is doing the shooting has something bigger in their arsenal."

"Copy that, Whirly Man. We have Blue Pacific Aviation changing course and heading east to avoid suspected weapons ground fire near Tanapag."

"Not suspected, you asshole. I've got bullet holes in my helicopter."

"Message received, Whirly Man. Please maintain radio protocol. Saipan flight radio office standing by for any further change in your status. We will notify law enforcement."

The pilot barked into his helmet-mounted microphone. "Fucking assholes!"

Carrington adjusted the microphone on his headset. In a calm voice, he asked the pilot, "Who's shooting at us?"

"Pot growers. They think I'm flying the police to get a look at their fields. I get threats all the time. I've had voodoo dolls with pins stuck in their eyes left in the cab of my pickup."

"Do you take on gigs flying the police?"

"At one time I did. It seemed like easy money. But I don't want to get shot down. It's not worth it. Happened twice in Nam and I'd prefer no repeat performances. Apparently whoever was shooting at me today didn't get the message. You guys aren't police, are you?"

Carrington grinned. "Far from it. Our concerns are business-related. And my friends here, well, they just like to go hunting."

The pilot rolled his eyes as he set the bird down in a fallow field where Hannah was waiting in the rented Nissan sedan. The possibility that the helicopter had been hit by ground fire gave him the perfect excuse for an emergency landing at a site not listed in his flight plan, a document he filled out by habit but was not obligated to since Saipan Airport had no air traffic control tower. Whirly Man needed to lose the tired-looking mercenaries and their weapons before returning to the airport with Carrington.

Decker and Carrington lugged the duffel bags to the car.

Reb slung the shotgun strap over his shoulder and grabbed the soft rifle case by its handle. Decker went back for the Pelican case and another unmarked equipment box.

Hannah had changed into a white summer dress and sandals, her hair tamed by a single French braid. She wanted to look good for Decker, still uncertain about where their relationship was headed. She waved to Decker while shielding her eyes from the brilliant sun.

Decker's bearded and sun-darkened face was the color of molasses but his teeth were still gleamingly white as he smiled.

Hannah hugged him, feeling the estrangement. "Good to see you, Decker. And you're all in one piece," she said, jerkily releasing her embrace. "We had no idea you were coming this way. It's a surprise."

"You mean Ashwood didn't mention it?"

"Not until this morning."

"Well, I didn't get much advance notice either. But damn, you look fantastic. Total island girl. You even have a tan all over, or at least the parts of you I can see. Where I just came from the women were wearing burqas."

Hannah blushed. "Thanks, Decker. You know I'm usually the pale office flower. It's nice to have a bit of color in my face."

Carrington cleared his throat as a way of breaking into the conversation and giving Decker an opportunity to introduce Reb.

"You three should roll. Lots of eyes everywhere. Hannah, this is Reb and he has no idea who you are or why you're here, but this is the ninety seconds when you get to say hello to each other and we'll go from there. Start now."

Reb thrust out a hand – warm and friendly. "Riley Turner. People just call me Reb. Glad to meet you, ma'am."

Hannah's eyebrows lifted. "Did you just call me ma'am, Mr. Reb?"

Reb blushed. "Sorry ma'am, or miss, or whatever. No

offense. Where I come from, that's what we call women we don't know."

"And where might that be?"

"Florida for the past twenty years, but by way of Alabama."

"How charming," she said, but immediately regretted her words because they sounded snarky when in fact she felt an instant spark of connection with the handsome, sweat-glossed soldier. For some reason, he reminded her of home.

Decker glared at them disapprovingly. "You two can talk southern culture later — pecan pie, NASCAR races, *Gone With the Wind*. Right now we've got to get moving. Let's toss our gear in the trunk."

"Yes sir," said Hannah, giving Decker a mock salute.

Decker turned to Carrington. "Where are we headed?"

An awkward moment of silence followed. Carrington seemed uneasy. "We only have a single room at a hotel a few clicks from the town where most of the drug trafficking seems to be taking place, but now that there are four of us, we can make other arrangements."

"Sounds fine," said Decker. "I can crash just about anywhere. I haven't slept in days."

"I'm sure you were busy."

"You could say that."

"We know Iraq is massing its military forces near the Kuwait border. Looks like they're preparing for an invasion."

"At this point, you probably know more than I do. All I know for sure is that special-ops teams are inside Afghanistan taking out high-value targets, mostly rabble-rousers preaching revolution against the west. The whole country is a shit show since the Russians pulled out with their tails between their legs."

"Well, we can talk more back at the hotel and I'll fill you in on what's going on here."

The helicopter pilot was inspecting the aircraft for bullet

damage. At least one round had pierced the tail but fortunately not struck anything mechanical.

Carrington signaled the pilot that he was ready for takeoff. He turned to the others with a forced smile. "I'll see you all later. I've got to go with our man here to the airport so that it fits with our story. He was supposedly flying me to and from Tinian so that I could get a look at the island as a possible resort location for Hannah's travel company in Argentina. I don't know how much Ashworth told you, but that's our cover and once again she's Mariel Becker. I'm Jake Marson. I hope our pilot can keep his mouth shut. We told him your passports had expired but that we had an emergency and needed to get you both into Saipan. Believe me, we paid him well, but he's a nervous fellow."

"I can see why," Reb said sympathetically.

Carrington knew he was prattling on, something he seldom did. If anything, he was a man of action and few words. But he knew once he stopped talking, Decker and Hannah would be off alone together and the thought of it was making him a little crazy.

"I suppose Ashwood could have arranged our transport by submarine and let the SEALs give us a ride to the beach in a RIB," said Decker. "We figured they'd do as much since Reb here is a SEAL."

Carrington grinned. "I guess the Navy chopper was cheaper on fuel than the nuke sub. Ashwood has to watch his budget at Langley."

Decker chuckled. "You're probably right. And speaking of Ashwood, he owes me some serious back pay."

Hannah nestled herself into the sedan's driver seat and watched the helicopter disappear in the distance. Reb twisted himself into the back and sprawled out, his legs stiffened by hours aboard planes and helicopters. Decker sat erect in the passenger seat and rolled down the window despite the fact that the air conditioner was struggling to cool the car's sunbaked interior. He lit a cigarette and blew the smoke out the window.

Hannah coughed as she glanced over at Decker and rolled her eyes. "Well, what now? We can fight about whether to leave the air conditioner running or shut it off. Or we can discuss the dangers of second-hand smoke inhalation."

Decker smirked. "What's the temp here, about 80 degrees?"

"Every day, sometimes all day."

"Well, my body is used to the Afghan desert where it was well over 100, every day, sometimes all day. I'll have to get accustomed to this chilly island weather."

Hannah switched off the AC and opened her window to the warm sea breeze. "Sorry. Sometimes I get tired of the same weather every day. Makes me miss Boston with its whacky swings of hot and cold. If we were back in Boston, there'd be snow on the ground."

Reb sensed the tension. "I'd love to see some snow. Never get any of that in Pensacola."

Decker frowned. "Snow is one thing I don't miss, especially in April."

Hannah affectionately swatted his shoulder. "You don't miss making snowmen? Skiing? You were always throwing snow-balls at me."

"That seems like a long time ago. Another lifetime."

"So what life are we in now, Decker?"

"I guess we'll have to see. Are we still friends?"

Hannah thrust her right hand toward Decker, keeping her left on the steering wheel to avoid the potholes. "Good friends."

Decker, albeit sleepy-eyed, gallantly kissed the back of her hand. "Good friends."

Reb wished he were invisible or could somehow vanish into the back seat. He had no desire to witness what seemed like a lover's quarrel. Decker had mentioned Hannah on their flight to Saipan, describing her as special ops and a close friend from Boston, nothing more. Obviously there was more, maybe much more.

Reb closed his eyes and tried to erase the scent of possibility he'd detected the moment his eyes had met Hannah's. For a nanosecond he had felt a connection, a spark, a tingle, but now, after overhearing their conversation, he was convinced his imagination had gotten the best of him. He was about to doze off when he heard Hannah's perturbed voice.

"When did you start smoking again?"

Decker exhaled loudly, the plume whooshing out the car window. "A few months ago. Just needed something to take the edge off."

"Was it bad in the desert?"

"Not every day."

"That's bad. I'm sorry Decker."

"Don't be sorry, Hannah. I chose the playlist so I'll dance to the music."

26

A NIGHTMARE IN BLACK

AFTER THE FIRST day of torture, Hiraku was allowed to sleep for what she estimated was at least twenty-four hours, although with no windows or clocks she couldn't be certain.

The next meeting with Akumu was equally unpleasant. The feisty woman burst into the room without formalities, still clad in a black Lycra bodysuit, strutted toward Hiraku who was about to stand and struck her on the side of the head with a leather-covered truncheon.

When Hiraku awoke her head throbbed and her vision was hazy. She was strapped with nylon webbing to what remained of the four bedposts. Akumu was sitting beside the bed in a folding chair reading People magazine.

"Did you know that 87 people were killed in a fire in the Bronx last month? The place was called the Happy Land Social

Club. Lots of young people were dancing to the music but somebody set it on fire with gasoline."

"No. I hadn't heard," said Hiraku, confused by Akumu's sudden change of mood. "That's very sad."

"We all have to die, sooner or later. Might as well be while we're having a good time."

Akumu tossed the magazine aside and plugged in the electric circular saw that was suspended on a rope from a ceiling pulley, its safety guard removed, the trigger taped to the on position to keep it running.

Hiraku watched in horror as Akumu slowly let the rope slide through her fingers to lower the saw, its blade screeching and whirring lethally. When the blade was almost touching Hiraku's chest, which was rising and falling in panic and fear, Akumu tied off the rope. It was a matter of millimeters. Akumu smiled devilishly and returned to reading her magazine.

"I don't like Marla Maples and I don't like Donald Trump," she said loudly over the whine of the saw, turning the pages to read more about the unfolding celebrity sex scandal.

"You're sick," Hiraku shouted over the din. "I don't know what you want from me. Please let me go."

"You know exactly what I want. If you tell me truthfully about your conversation with the two CIA agents, I'll ask my boss if you should be spared."

Hiraku twisted her arms and legs against the straps, but the exertion caused her hips to rise and allowed the blade to nick her stomach. Blood spurted from the saw and spattered the bed sheet. She thought she was about to die but Akumu hauled on the rope and the screaming saw moved upward, twirling in a small circular pattern as it dangled from the rope. Akumu unplugged the electrical cord and after a few moments the room was quiet except for Hiraku's panicked breathing.

Akumu grabbed Hiraku by the hair so that her head was lifted from the bed. She poured water from a glass directly into

Hiraku's mouth, forcing the young woman to swallow as she coughed.

"Don't you like my water?"

Hiraku shook her head back and forth. "Please stop."

"You still haven't told me what I need to know," said Akumu, who placed a wet washcloth over Hiraku's nose and mouth and began saturating it with more water.

Hiraku squirmed, trying to turn her head away from the falling water, but Akumu had done this many times and easily kept the woman's head positioned.

"Are you ready to talk?"

"Uuughhh!"

"Yes?"

More guttural sounds followed.

"I hear yes," said Akumu, removing the washcloth. Hiraku's face was a profile of sheer terror.

"Names. I want the names of the two CIA operatives."

"I thought you already knew who they were and that they were dead?"

Akumu pushed Hiraku's head down forcefully and again covered her nose and mouth with the washcloth. She poured bottled water until Hiraku's haunted and muffled screams suggested the torture was successful. Hiraku truly believed she was drowning.

"Names."

Hiraku coughed up water. "The man is Stevens. The woman is Cahill."

"Now tell me what you told them about yakuza activities on Saipan – the heroin smuggling, the marijuana fields, the weapon sales."

Hiraku felt defeated as she glanced around the damp cellar. On one table was an array of ice picks and pliers, on another two car batteries attached to wires that ended in alligator clips. She didn't want to drown or be bled to death. She described to

Akumu the places where she had met the CIA officers and gave her the specifics of their agreement – namely that she and her uncle Yoshi would gather bank account numbers, delivery routes, and the names of key contacts along the heroin trail from Thailand to the Philippines to Saipan, and then on to Hawaii and California.

Although she had cooperated under duress, Hiraku had not delivered the most important piece of information sought by Tanaka – the location approximately $80 million siphoned primarily from the heroin trafficking operation. Even when Akumu administered powerful electrical charges from a 12-volt battery attached by wires to Hiraku's genitals, no information about the missing funds was unveiled.

The outcome left Akumu frustrated and alone with her thoughts. *The girl holds the power of her ancestors. She will not break in the way others do. But I will find her weakness and then she will tell all about where the millions are hidden.*

27

HERE COME THE TATTOOED MEN

SAIPAN

NORTHERN MARIANA ISLANDS

APRIL 1990

HIDEYO MASHIMA COUNTED forty-two yakuza arriving on the island over three consecutive days. The Customs officers at the airport had also taken notice and word among the local law enforcement community was that something big was brewing.

For some Customs and CNMI police officers, the intel simply meant more private detail pay should the yakuza schedule any events or gatherings that might require a police cordon. For other police officers and Customs agents, it was an opportunity to interact with members of Japan's organized crime syndicates, if not to arrest them then to at least gain some experience in dealing with their ways.

It wasn't unusual for a dozen yakuza to meet on Saipan for a mix of partying and business, but the week's headcount was far above average. Mashima's suspicions were further confirmed by the arrival of at least twenty tall, young, blonde women, mostly from Australia but as far away as the United States, Iceland and Sweden, who arrived independently and in small groups. Nearly all the women were in their twenties or early thirties and staying at the new 14-story Kensington Hotel built on a private beach in San Roque. The luxury hotel was a 10-minute drive north from Garapan along Marpi Road.

Although most firearms were prohibited on Saipan, locals were allowed to possess .410 shotguns and .22-caliber rifles, some of which for the right amount of currency would fall temporarily into the hands of yakuza bodyguards during their stay.

Mashima suspected more powerful weapons would also become available through local gun smugglers but his department did not have the resources to investigate such matters. He knew Tanaka's bodyguards routinely carried Uzi machine pistols.

The detective decided to share his information with Palmer and O'Reilly, the FBI special agents working on the two murder cases – that of yakuza underboss Mikito Asaki tossed off Banzai Cliff, and the slaying of local police Sgt. Alfred Torres, found stabbed to death on Marpi Point. Mashima caught up with Palmer and O'Reilly as they exited the courthouse.

The detective approached with his head lowered and offered a slight bow. "Good day, gentlemen. There is some activity on the island this week that could be important to your work."

Palmer furrowed his brows as though he disapproved of Mashima's approaching them. He doubted anything the detective had to say was relevant to their mission. He had no desire to partner with local law enforcement. As far as he was concerned, they were amateurs.

O'Reilly slowed his pace. "Make it quick. We're busy taking care of homicides on your home turf."

It was a professional jab, but Mashima chose to ignore it. He showed no emotion as he explained that a meeting of many high-ranking yakuza was about to occur. Such an event might signal a change in drug-trafficking or gun-smuggling operations on Saipan, he said, or perhaps lead to an increase in the abduction and sexual exploitation of girls and young women. It was, as he put it, a significant opportunity to learn more about yakuza plans, information that if handled properly could result in a crackdown on regional crime.

O'Reilly laughed out loud. "And what do you suggest? We get ourselves invited to this big shindig?"

"That would not be possible. But if we pool our intelligence sources, we might end up with a clear picture of what's going on."

"I'll tell you what's going on," said Palmer, stopping long enough to dab the sweat from his forehead with a soiled white handkerchief. "A large group of Japanese businessmen are planning a party on your miserably-hot island. You counted some heads at the airport. That's great. If you were paying close attention, you probably saw a parade of good-looking blondes arrive since they seem to be the party girls of choice among these Japanese mobsters."

Mashima fixed his stare on the backs of the dismissive FBI agents as they resumed walking to their car. Palmer stopped again momentarily and looked back over his shoulder. "If you do get an invitation to the party, let us know. We'd love to tag along."

Palmer backslapped O'Reilly as they opened the car doors and waited for the trapped heat to escape. "What's with that guy? I think he's been watching too much *Miami Vice*."

28

WHO KILLED MIKITO ASAKI?

SAIPAN

NORTHERN MARIANA ISLANDS

APRIL 1990

JURY SELECTION in the murder case of Mikito Asaki was an exercise in frustration for Ray Donley, the American assistant attorney general assigned to prosecute the case.

"There's no fucking way we're going to impanel a fair and impartial jury on this island. Literally everybody is related or connected by some kind of friendship or business," he complained to his legal team, which consisted of Ned Hayward who, like Donley, was an assistant attorney general from Boston, Massachusetts, and a local woman named Nona who needed a secretarial job. "Nobody is going to come forward even if they know what happened."

Donley tossed a sheaf of court documents on his desk in a manner that unveiled his disgust with the case and the island's judicial system.

"We've got two defendants charged as accessories to commit murder and none willing to cooperate. Frankly, that sucks. Mashima has his nose to the ground but so far there's nothing to link these guys directly to the murder."

Hayward nodded sympathetically. "This place is fucked up, Ray. The surface has nothing to do with what's going on right below it."

Donley gulped a pint of water from the plastic bottle on his desk. "It gets weirder by the minute," he said. "Mashima is convinced Asaki may have been killed by a former bodyguard who hated him because of some shit-filled underwear. Unfortunately for us, that bodyguard isn't one of the people we arrested."

Hayward's face showed marked confusion as Donley continued. "Apparently Asaki had an unexpected bowel movement during a recent plane ride and when they touched down he ordered the bodyguard to immediately wash the stinky grunts. The guy never forgot it and considered it a personal insult. Admittedly, it's a sketchy motive for murder, but I've tried people who committed murder over possession of a TV remote control."

Donley sighed as he set his heavy leather briefcase on the desk in the small courthouse office reserved for attorneys. He was startled by a knock on the door. "Come in."

Detective Mashima bowed his head slightly. "I have some news. But it may be best if it is shared only in private."

Donley glanced at his two colleagues who were already moving toward the door. Mashima rested a hand on the wooden chair next to the prosecutor's desk. "May I sit?"

"Of course. What's up, detective?"

"I have spoken again to the family of the deceased policeman, Alfred Torres. His widow, Amista, indicates two men were seated in a car along the road to her home the same day her husband failed to return from the courthouse."

"Locals? FBI?"

"No. She believes they were yakuza."

"Did she recognize any of them?"

"No. But she described the make and model of the vehicle and was able to recall part of the license plate number."

"And?"

"The black Nissan Pathfinder is registered to a company owned by Orochi Tanaka."

"That doesn't prove anything."

"No. It does not. But it gives reason to bring in Mr. Tanaka for questioning. If we put pressure on him, he may make a mistake that will tell us more about who killed Sgt. Torres."

"Do you think Tanaka killed him?"

"It's very possible that Tanaka caused it to happen. When money is lost, anger usually leads to violence. We've seen a lot of that on Saipan these days."

29

A MEETING OF THE MOB

SAIPAN

NORTHERN MARIANA ISLANDS

APRIL 1990

WHEN TANAKA CLOSED The Lucky Carp restaurant and casino for two days so that it could host a private yakuza business convention, it angered the Chamorro and Carolingian natives and the tight-knit group of American and British ex-pats who frequented the establishment three or four times a week to drink, play electronic betting games and ogle the dancers.

On the first day of the convention, yakuza guards were stationed at all entrances and exits during the event. CNMI police officers, paid privately by Tanaka, maintained a loose buffer zone along the perimeter of the property. Some of the yakuza guards wore black tuxedos but were shirtless to show off elaborate chest tattoos. Others were dressed in American-style two-piece suits, the back of their jackets distorted by weapons tucked into their belts.

The festivities were well under way by noon. Exotic dancers gyrated on stage or from within their hanging cages. A punk rock band filled the room with hard-edged music while a second band clad in black leather despite the heat was tuning up behind a wall curtain.

The blonde women who had arrived on the island in droves were drinking, laughing and flirting with the yakuza. Some were engaged in lap dances with the men, or performing other sexual favors in the booths along the open-air wall facing Micro Beach. Several yakuza were passed out on the floor or staggering and rudely pushing their way through the crowd. In one corner, three men had stripped off their clothes and were comparing full-body tattoos. Two yakuza were fist-fighting martial-arts style in a far corner and bleeding from wounds to the face, but both seemed to be enjoying it.

In the center of the room, two heavily-tattooed men, wearing only loincloths and white socks, balanced atop separate wood logs from which the bark had been removed. The logs were held aloft on the shoulders of each opponent's supporters. Amid the shouting and cheering, the challengers feigned ferocious kicks and attempted to knock the other off his log. Tanaka gleamed with pride. This was his kind of party.

When one of the tattooed fighters was finally dethroned from his perch, the logs were set aside and the winner crowned with a rubber shark mask that covered his entire head. The shark received dozens of exuberant cheers from his yakuza brothers and countless backslaps of congratulations. One of the taller blondes was summoned to stand before the winner and expose her ample breasts. She backed away gingerly when the shark tried to bite.

As the afternoon waned into evening, more bottles of sake, bourbon and single-malt scotch were opened. The back-up band began to play, the musicians cranking out whatever was requested, mostly covers of 1980s songs: *Thriller* by Michael

Jackson; *True Blue* and *Like a Virgin*, both by Madonna; *Make it Big* by Wham!; several numbers by a Japanese pop icon band, The Checkers; an out-of-tune rendition of Julio Inglesias' *Momentos*; and the entire soundtrack to the movie *Footloose*.

As the music blared, Detective Mashima walked the perimeter of the property, keeping watch on the CNMI officers hired as a private security detail. Had it been his decision, he would have denied the request for security assistance from Orochi Tanaka, mostly because he detested the man, but Joe Napuna, the local police chief, obviously saw no harm in it. The offer of a private security detail seemed an easy way for his men to pick up some extra pay at no cost to the police department.

Mashima was aware some of the local police officers didn't appreciate his attitude toward private-detail pay. Those who understood his dislike for the yakuza, and knew the story behind his facial scars, harbored no grudge. They allowed him through the perimeter cordon so that he could better witness the festivities.

Tanaka worked the crowd, individually approaching the six most powerful yakuza in the room and whispering a confidential invitation to a special ceremony in the back room.

A simple plank table draped with fine white linen was set for seven places in a small storeroom that had palm thatch walls, wooden window shutters and carved teak door. Six cream-colored paper lanterns hung from the ceiling and several tall candles perched on wrought-iron stands illuminated the room. Tanaka made certain each man had a fresh drink before he announced the menu – *fugu*.

Mere mention of the delicacy caused a stir at the table. One man's complexion turned ashen. Another laughed uneasily, while still others cheered Tanaka in a show of bravado.

"Krill learned how to prepare it in Japan," Tanaka reassured his guests. "She is a top *fugu* chef."

Krill modestly waved at the men and bowed deeply, which

caused her mini-skirt to rise up and expose her cheeks. Some of the men were transfixed by the sight and the nearest tried to put a hand up her skirt but Krill quickly swirled out of range. Krill shook a finger at the man. "Naughty boy," she said, flashing a dazzling smile. Laughter broke out at the table. Tanaka was pleased. It was all in good fun.

When the most visibly nervous guest asked to see Krill's *fugu* competency license, Tanaka intervened with a toothy smile and the voice of assurance. "One-hundred percent certified. She was taught by the best in Tokyo."

The guest was obviously dissatisfied with the answer but didn't want to challenge Tanaka. That would be perceived as a public insult. It was important to save face.

With assistance from Tony the bartender, Krill went about displaying the puffer fish, named so because as a defense mechanism it can expand to appear much larger, which helps ward off natural predators in the sea.

As though preparing sashimi, Krill cut the raw fish into thin slices that were artistically arranged on seven small china plates. She avoided serving the liver because that organ contains the largest concentration of Tetrodotoxin, the poison found in the pufferfish's skin, skeleton, ovaries and intestines.

As the guests took their seats, in a show of fearlessness Tanaka remained standing and deftly plucked a slice of *fugu* with his chopsticks, dropping it into his mouth. He stuck out his tongue to show his guests the fish.

As Tanaka savored the taste and sensation, Krill explained that her boss was among the more adventurous pufferfish aficionados who preferred to eat it with a residual amount of toxin left inside the meat. She also noted that doing so might leave a tingling in the lips, which is the sought-after effect. She assured them there was nothing to worry about.

Tanaka clutched his neck and made a gurgling sound as though in the throes of death. When his guests realized it was a joke, Tanaka settled into his chair and smiled, lips and eyes closed, as if in a state of unbridled gastronomic pleasure. Two guests followed suit, quickly tonging and engulfing a slice of blowfish. Just as Tanaka had anticipated, the men were getting off on the thrill, the potential danger, which to some pufferfish fans was truly addictive.

Krill explained that while the toxin was key to the ultimate pufferfish dining, ingesting too much could lead to a lamentable experience. She would have explained further that Tetrodotoxin does not cross the blood-brain barrier, so the victims remain fully conscious while their central nervous system gradually shuts down, first producing dizziness and incoherent speech, followed by paralyzing of the muscles. But she knew better. Most would simply not understand. It was obvious some of the guests had almost no attention span for such a detailed explanation.

"Is anyone feeling dizzy?" she asked coyly.

At that, Tanaka burst out laughing.

"Please continue, Krill. Explain to them. Tell them what to expect."

"As I was saying, too much toxin isn't good. This can lead to asphyxia, which means you are unable to get oxygen and you start to suffocate, or possibly die."

After a theatrical pause, she added, "There is no antidote for *fugu* poisoning."

Tanaka laughed louder than Krill had ever heard him, his entire body shaking as though in a fit. He raised his glass of sake. "To those of us who live life to the fullest."

The others lifted their glasses, some with obvious reluctance.

Tanaka clenched a fist as a gesture of strength and defiance. "Now let's finish our fish. If you don't feel your lips tingle, you haven't eaten enough."

Tony poured more sake and freshened the beers and mixed

drinks while Krill set up a TV monitor on a wheeled cart.

When dinner was finished and the plates collected, Tanaka stood and spoke proudly, saying another surprise was in store. Krill blew out the candles as previously instructed and switched off four of the six lanterns. Tanaka pushed the button on the remote control. The room suddenly filled with bright light and a blank image appeared on the screen. Seconds later, palm trees swayed on an idyllic sand beach. The camera zoomed to the surf, capturing its gentle rhythm. It was a scene that could have been captured on most any tropical beach around the world. Nothing special. The men in the room seemed puzzled. They had expected some high-grade pornography, or perhaps a snuff film. It was rumored Tanaka had one of the largest collections of porn in all of Japan. But there was only the beauty of nature before them – white sand, turquoise water, swaying palms.

Tanaka raised his hands and with open palms urged his guests to be silent. The yakuza boss sipped deeply from a rum drink laden with fresh fruit. "Please be patient. I assure you it will be worth the wait."

On the TV monitor, it was obvious the camera was being carried along a trail that led through thick underbrush. Images bounced around. The labored breaths of the cameraman were recorded on the audio track along with the cries of seabirds. Moments later, a man's distinctive voice could be heard over the seabirds and the cameraman's huffing and puffing. The voice was pleading. The camera pointed at the sand beach, swirled toward the trees and then at the sky as it was secured to a tripod. The bouncy images were disconcerting and two of the men at the table complained of feeling queasy, a moment Tanaka used to jokingly suggest they had eaten too much pufferfish.

A third man politely insinuated that Tanaka was wasting their time — they hadn't traveled to Saipan to watch amateur nature films, they'd come for the party, the women, the endless drink and camaraderie, all of which was barely ten feet away on the other side of the thatch wall.

Seconds later, the image of Yoshi Yamamoto flared into view, his body tied to a thick wooden post that had been driven into the sand. The men recognized the fear in his eyes and gasped at the sight of giant lizards biting and tearing apart the tattoo master's body.

When the six yakuza looked toward Tanaka for comment, he merely smiled and sipped his rum drink. Tanaka knew the video would strike fear into their hearts and make them understand he was capable of great cruelty to those not loyal. It was a warning shot.

Only Hageshii, the oldest yakuza in the room, an octogenarian and accomplished international drug smuggler, was bold enough to speak. "I enjoyed your movie, Orochi. Yes, you got revenge for Yoshi's betrayal. But where is our money? We are missing almost two hundred million between Yoshi and Asaki. Two dead men."

Tanaka's face suddenly paled. He solemnly faced the older man and bowed his head slightly. "I am trying to find out. We believe Yoshi's niece knows where the money is hidden. It's only a matter of time before she tells us."

"And what of the local policeman who stole $36,000 of our money? Not much money, for sure. But just like Yoshi, the policeman, too, is dead, and therefore cannot repay his debt."

"I did not end his life."

"Perhaps not. But I assume you gave the order and that is the same thing. You let your temper get the best of you, Orochi. You must learn to control it."

Once more Tanaka bowed his head in respect and did not look up for several long moments, during which he envisioned slowly dipping the old man into a pool of sulfuric acid. "My

DAVID LISCIO

deepest regrets, Hageshii. I have offended you. I beg forgiveness and offer yubitsume."

Hageshii sipped his tea. "That will not be necessary. Just remember, the dead do not speak. After those living have given you what you desire, you can do with them as you please — but not before. Orochi, you must learn to be patient."

Tanaka neglected to tell Hageshii that Akumu had killed the police sergeant in an overzealous moment and had not been acting on her master's orders. Such information might lead Hageshii to conclude Tanaka lacked control over his underlings.

On the other side of the thatch wall, Detective Mashima rubbed his eyes, feeling overwhelmed and astonished by the savagery he'd just witnessed. He sometimes grappled with the fact that certain people in the world were truly evil.

30

HOME MOVIE NIGHT

Saipan

Northern Mariana Islands

April 1990

Akumu became convinced Hiraku had told everything she knew about the conversations with the CIA and what had become of the stolen funds. She wasn't looking forward to sharing that news with Tanaka. She was well aware his anger might burst into rage and turn violent.

Tanaka had been in a jolly mood since the business meeting had ended. The event had resulted in fresh partnerships and new goals, including an agreement to increase human trafficking and weapons sales.

Tanaka had taken great interest in the international clothing brand manufacturers who sourced their goods from garment factories tucked deep into the jungles of Saipan. The factories were more like prisons, surrounded by chain link fencing topped by razor wire. Security lighting on tall poles burned throughout the night. Inside, predominately young South Korean and Filipino girls worked eighty hours a week for low pay and were allowed to visit the resort town of Garapan on special occasion, but only when chaperoned by company managers. Tanaka imagined these girls would be eager to accept new opportunities as hostesses for the many yakuza-controlled bathhouses throughout Japan, unaware of their intended fate.

Trying out a new interrogation strategy, Akumu stayed away from the cellar for what Hiraku estimated was three or four days, maybe longer. Each day, a tray of food was pushed into the room by what appeared to be a barefoot young boy wearing a devil's mask and a white martial arts *karategi*. Hiraku pleaded with him each time, but the boy never spoke or made eye contact. The meal consisted of Soba noodles in a steaming broth, several spoonsful of boiled rice, a small plate of sliced cucumbers and carrots, and a glass of water. Hiraku dreamed of cheeseburgers and French fries and a cold Dr. Pepper soft drink. That was the meal she should have been eating with her Uncle Yoshi at a McDonald's in California. She knew Yoshi did not approve of fast food, but would nonetheless eat it to please her — maybe even dip his French fries in a puddle of ketchup. She hoped that day would arrive soon.

When Akumu finally returned after her unexpected absence, she entered the room cheerfully humming a song from the hit Broadway show *Cats*. Hiraku was curled into an embryonic ball on the cold floor. Her body still ached from the beatings but all her senses were alert, tuned as always during these dark days to the possible approach of her torturer.

Akumu continued to hum the bittersweet ballad called *Memory*. Perhaps she didn't know all the words, but Hiraku did.

"*Daylight*
I must wait for the sunrise
I must think of a new life

And I mustn't give in
When the dawn comes
Tonight will be a memory too
And a new day will begin."

HIRAKU WONDERED IF AKUMU WAS ATTEMPTING TO SEND HER A message, to communicate without directly speaking. She didn't have to wait long to find out.

Akumu shouted. "Stand up and remove your clothes. You stink. You need a shower. Let's go."

Hiraku felt every ache in her body as she clumsily removed her clothes. She felt dizzy as she walked out of the room and entered the bathroom at the end of the hall. The devil boy was there at the door, holding a clean towel and bar of soap. He handed it to Hiraku as she moved toward the shower in a dream state.

Hiraku let the hot water stream over her body. It felt wonderful, and though she expected the flow would be shut off momentarily, that didn't happen. Instead, she stayed under the shower for what she estimated was a half hour.

Just outside the shower stall, the devil boy was seated on a three-leg teak stool with a folded terrycloth bathrobe in his lap. From what Hiraku could tell, the boy was staring at her naked body through his mask. The boy finally stood and handed her the bathrobe. No words were exchanged.

Akumu was waiting in the hallway. "Did you enjoy your shower?"

"Very much. Thank you."

"Life here can be much easier when you cooperate."

Back in the locked room, Hiraku, still in the terry bathrobe, was ordered to sit on the edge of the bed. She felt light-headed and questioned whether she was actually seeing the piece of chocolate being offered by Akumu.

"For you."

Akumu popped a Sainsbury chocolate morsel into her own mouth while waiting for Hiraku to take the piece in her outstretched palm. Hiraku bit into the chocolate, savoring the rich flavor. Akumu offered a second piece, which Hiraku also devoured. The interrogator sat on the concrete floor with legs curled beneath her and gazed up at Hiraku. It was as though they were close friends about to engage in some confidential girl talk.

Akumu tugged down her black elastic body suit to expose her shoulders. "As you can see, I have many tattoos, but none are as magnificent as yours. You must tell me the history."

Hiraku wondered why her torturer was so interested, or was it merely the woman's attempt at gaining her friendship despite the odd captive/torturer relationship. She'd heard of Stockholm syndrome and assumed it was a condition to which Akumu aspired in an effort to build a mutual trust. But she felt no bond with this crazed woman, only hatred for her and her master, Tanaka.

Hiraku was willing to tell the story of her tattoo, if only because it would delay the next beating or means of brutality. So she began with the days prior to her eighteenth birthday when she had only one tattoo, an elegant peacock feather on her left foot, a work of art that had caught the eye of Orochi Tanaka.

At seventeen, she had wanted a tattoo, as did many of her schoolmates. But unlike the others, she was the adopted niece of Yoshi Yamamoto – recognized among the premiere tattoo artists in all the Pacific Rim. Yamamoto's steady hand and artful eye for ink design had brought him into the social circles of royalty and those with unlimited wealth. A tattoo created by Yoshi Yamamoto was prestigious. And while Hiraku did not think of it in those terms, she recognized her uncle's skill and was proud to serve as a canvas for his work.

But the peacock — with wings that elegantly spread across her back and wrapped around her sides — was quite another matter. It was he, Yoshi, who had first proposed such a tattoo to his niece. He had told her it was important that she agree because the design might otherwise be lost on a lesser subject.

Although still in her teens, Hiraku sat patiently for endless hours while Yoshi pricked and prodded, injecting colorful ink at precise times and places, until the peacock emerged. The process took months and finally lapsed into years. At first, Hiraku was uneasy, concerned she would be forever burdened by a body tattoo she neither admired nor understood. Yoshi had shown her dozens of examples from a book of ink drawings but none had connected with her heart, at least not until she saw the peacock.

When it was finally completed, Hiraku spent hours staring at it in a full-length mirror, attempting to decipher each character, symbol and number. She was thrilled that Yoshi had included the names of her parents, the date of her birth, and the image of her cat Neko. The tattoo was magnificent, just as Akumu had described it, the best her uncle had ever created. And though she often asked her uncle to explain the details, he evaded certain questions or replied in vague terms, saying only that within the beauty of the raucous bird lay numbers that would one day lead to her salvation. Such answers only made her more curious.

"My Uncle Yoshi is a great artist. But he did not explain the meaning of this tattoo. He did not tell me its story."

"I don't believe you. Lay down on the bed."

Hiraku seemed puzzled by the abrupt change in Akumu's mood.

"Move. Now. Quickly."

Akumu pressed a *Kubotan* keychain against Hiraku's wrist, inflicting immediate pain. Hiraku didn't resist. She lay on her back as Akumu again tied her wrists and ankles to the bed with webbing.

"Did you hear me? I don't believe you."

Akumu dragged a straight-back chair to the edge of the bed so that she was face to face with Hiraku. "It's time we talk about your Uncle Yoshi. I know you think he's coming back to rescue you, but I'm afraid that's not possible."

Hiraku stared back defiantly into her interrogator's eyes. "My uncle will kill you when he returns and finds out what you've done."

Akumu abruptly stood and hurled the chair into a wall, breaking one of its legs. She was manic. Hiraku held up her arms defensively to ward off the anticipate blow. But it never came. Akumu strutted to the door, yanked it open and left the room.

Hiraku wished she could wipe the tears that flowed from the corners of her eyes. She hoped somehow she would wake up from a deep sleep and find this was all a vaporous nightmare. But a look at the wounds covering her body told a different story. So here she was, three years after the first ink had been injected into the peacock, flat on her back on an unyielding bed in the cellar of a Japanese mobster who wasn't about to let her go free until she unveiled where her uncle's stolen millions were stored. She was glad she didn't have the answer.

Akumu returned moments later cradling a camcorder with a thick battery attached and a coil of connection wires. The devil boy was right behind her, struggling to carry a small, portable TV monitor.

Akumu tucked a pillow beneath Hiraku's head, shooed the boy from the room and frantically began connecting the camera to the TV monitor. She cursed the camera, the wires, and most of all Hiraku.

After more than ten minutes of fiddling with the equipment, Akumu was ready to show her videotape.

"Watch closely," she said. "You don't want to miss the most exciting part."

Akumu started the video at the beginning, where the cameraman is pushing his way through the underbrush but not having an easy time of it. Impatient, and eager for Hiraku to see the most dramatic parts, she fast-forwarded the video until Tanaka was on the screen seated in a folding chair, sipping some sort of cold drink and talking to one of his bodyguards.

Akumu stood next to the bed and slapped Hiraku across the face. "Pay attention."

The video played on, unveiling Yoshi lashed to the wood post in the sand. Hiraku gasped. She wanted to look away but forced herself to watch her beloved uncle being devoured by prehistoric Komodo dragons. When the film ended, Hiraku vomited on the bed.

Akumu was smiling. "I should have made popcorn. I just love watching movies with popcorn." She was relishing the discomfort she'd caused her captive. "I hope you understand now why I say your uncle will not be coming to your rescue. He was unable to rescue himself. So are you now ready to talk?"

31

JUSTICE IN GARAPAN

SAIPAN

NORTHERN MARIANA ISLANDS

APRIL 1990

INSIDE THE SMALL courthouse in Garapan, Assistant Attorney General Ray Donley handed a sheaf of legal documents to the informally dressed and disinterested judge seated at a large wooden desk on a dais.

Donley wiped his sweaty brow with a blue bandana and stuffed it into his back pocket. The building's air-conditioning system had quit more than a week ago. The ceiling fans were turning, but their blades hadn't cooled the courtroom.

The prosecutor stood before the bench and waited while the judge sifted through the documents. The judge didn't look up after examining the last page. Donley plowed ahead. "A lot has happened in the past few days since we were here before you, Your Honor. So thank you for agreeing to hear what the government has to say today."

Donley glanced at the judge, convinced the man wasn't listening to a word. "I've spoken to the attorney for two of the four defendants. As you know, it's the government's contention that two of the men charged in the case are marijuana growers and nothing more. Although their crime of harvesting an illegal substance is serious, we believe it should be handled separately from the homicide case. That is the intent of our motion here today."

The judge leisurely munched from a plate of local fried banana donuts on his desk. He eventually looked up. "I agree, Mr. Donley. Let's dispense with the marijuana-growing issue this morning and get on with the murder case."

Six armed trial officers brought the pair of handcuffed pot farmers before the judge.

"How do you plead?"

The court-appointed defense attorney, a waifish man who introduced himself only as Charlie B, objected to the suggestion his clients render a plea without further judicial review, but the judge motioned to remain silent.

"I'm talking to these two men, not to you, Charlie B." The judge narrowed his eyes as he focused on the two defendants. "Do you two understand what is being discussed here in this courtroom?"

Both men nodded unconvincingly.

"If you plead guilty here and now, your marijuana crop will be destroyed by the police and you will be sentenced to two years imprisonment, suspended, pending your completion of a drug-education course and dependent upon your following the strict rules of probation for two years."

The defendants looked relieved, especially the taller, wiry one, who was related by blood to the judge's wife.

"Do you agree?"

More vigorous nodding followed the question, the brothers conversing in Chamorro.

The defense lawyer again raised a hand but the judge ignored him and rapped his gavel. "Plea accepted. Probation. Two years. Don't plant any more pot on your land. And while you're at it, try to find yourselves some honest work. Let's move on. Next case."

Donley stood before the bench with the distinct feeling the judge wasn't sympathetic to his situation. "The government is having some difficulty in impaneling a jury for the other two defendants, those we assert were Asaki's bodyguards and also his alleged killers."

The judge quickly replied. "That's not my problem. Get some people in here who want to listen to the case and decide whether these two men should go to jail for the murder of Mikito Asaki. You've got a budget, Mr. Donley. Offer the jurors some money for showing up. That usually helps get their attention."

"Yes, Your Honor," said Donley, requesting a one-week postponement in order to call more prospective jurors.

"Motion granted. See you next week."

Donley appreciated the homicide case was simplified by the elimination of the two pot-growing brothers. It would make it easier for the jury to concentrate on only one issue – who killed Mikito Asaki and whether the two men accused were guilty or innocent of participating in that crime. Donley heard Mashima's words as they played repeatedly in the back of his mind and left him with a pounding headache. *These poor farmers did not kill Mikito Asaki.*

Donley still faced another legal hurdle, the ongoing investigation into the murder of Sgt. Torres. Somebody had killed a cop on U.S. soil, albeit thousands of miles from the shores of California, and the FBI wasn't happy about it. Pressure was being ramped up back in Washington to send in a special team of federal investigators and maybe even a replacement prosecutor. Donley didn't want any of that to happen because it would likely undermine his authority and derail his career.

To complicate matters, when Donley arrived in Saipan to assume the role of assistant attorney general months earlier, he inherited the double Lover's Lane homicide that was as yet unsolved. So far, there were no suspects, a situation Donley might have found hard to believe back in the States, but in Saipan anything was possible.

To further add to what had become an ongoing crime wave, a Japanese fashion model was raped at the island's newly-opened Hotel Nikko, but security cameras didn't provide any clues and, except for the black-masked rapist described by the victim, there were no witnesses. The beautiful young woman had spent the day doing a magazine photo shoot with an established photographer and his two assistants at a picturesque beach, then returned to the hotel feeling exhausted, ordered dinner from room service and gone to sleep. She was assaulted in her bed sometime after midnight.

"Your Honor, if you please, one last matter."

The judge puffed his cheeks and let out a burst of air, exasperated by the prosecutor's persistence.

"I'd like to submit a government statement contending that Mikito Asaki was a yakuza underboss and that his rank in that criminal organization may have caused him to be murdered by one or more of his own men."

The judge squinted at Donley. "Motive?"

"Revenge, sir. We believe that approximately one year ago, Mr. Asaki had an unanticipated bowel movement upon landing in a plane here on Saipan and after being driven to his hotel ordered one of his bodyguards to launder his underwear. This directive angered and dishonored the bodyguard, and when the opportunity arose in December, he used it to extract revenge by torturing and murdering Mr. Asaki. The government also contends that the opportunity to murder Mr. Asaki was sanctioned by the yakuza chain of command as a result of a disagreement Mr. Asaki had with his yakuza associates over gambling and drug-smuggling profits."

"That's a lot of contends, Mr. Donley."

"It is, Your Honor. But we believe they are accurate and provable. I'm unable at this time to name the person in the yakuza organization who gave the authorization to murder Mr. Asaki, but we hope to do so shortly."

The judge seemed half-convinced. "No evidence, no case. If you attended law school, you know that."

"The prosecutor is in full agreement with the court."

"I'm glad to hear that, Mr. Donley Though you are a busy man, there's still a dead police officer in our morgue and nobody in custody for his murder. Oh, and let's not forget about the two innocent lovers slain by God only knows while in their truck. Perhaps when you stop chasing the yakuza and all the press coverage that goes with it, you can focus your resources on who murdered that lovely couple. In case you haven't looked into the case, the woman murdered was a native of Saipan and beloved throughout the island. The people here want justice. They also want to feel safe. I'll see you at the next hearing."

The judge stood and reached for the knob on the private door behind the bench.

Donley simply nodded and swallowed the reprimand. "Yes, Your Honor."

32

WHERE IS HIRAKU?

SAIPAN

NORTHERN MARIANA ISLANDS

APRIL 1990

WITHIN HOURS of Decker and Reb's arrival, Hannah had arranged with the hotel management to rent a second room, the smallest in the building, but it would be all hers. She was not going to put herself in an uncomfortable position with two rivals, at least no more than had already become apparent. She also arranged for the three men to share an adjacent room, which had two double beds. Two of them would have to share a rack, but it was the best she could do.

When Decker learned Hannah was involved in a honey-trap operation with a violent yakuza boss named Tanaka, he lashed out at Carrington for allowing it to happen.

"Why the fuck would you let her go off alone with that animal? From what I've heard, he's as crazy as the yakuza get and more powerful than most."

"She set it up herself."

"And you did nothing to stop it? Aren't you her field supervisor? Aren't you supposed to be looking out for her? You've been doing this most of your adult life. She's brand fucking new at this game."

Carrington didn't appreciate the interrogation or the insubordination, particularly since he outranked Decker. But he let the man spew, figuring of all people Decker probably knew better than most how stubborn Hannah could be.

"I put a tracker on Tanaka's vehicle, courtesy of Detective Mashima."

"A tracker isn't good enough. They're new technology and not always reliable. You should have had eyes on her the whole time."

Hannah had given Decker and Reb a rundown on what was happening on the island and how they were attempting to obtain as much information as possible about the yakuza's heroin smuggling operation. She told them about the diligent Detective Hideyo Mashima, Krill the funky casino night manager, Donley the newly-appointed government prosecutor, and Alfred Torres, the local police sergeant allegedly murdered because he stole thousands of dollars from the police department's evidence locker and blew it on electronic poker machines.

Hannah also filled them in on the four men arrested during the Tanapag drug raid where the cash was seized, noting two of the four suspects were charged with murdering a yakuza underboss on Saipan in December, though evidence linking them to the crime was scant. But she had purposefully neglected to mention her outings with Orochi Tanaka, sensing Decker wouldn't approve. Besides, she'd made it clear to both Carrington and Decker that she didn't expect or want special treatment simply because she was a woman. She was a CIA officer, just like them, and equally capable of defending herself.

The day after his arrival in Saipan, Decker found a written note from Hannah slid under the door to the room he was sharing with Reb and Carrington, saying she was meeting with Tanaka who promised to show her the best panoramic views and beaches on the island, locations Argentine travelers were sure to enjoy.

Decker felt his anger rise up. He was fuming. If he had been awake when the note arrived, he would have stopped Hannah from going. He cursed himself for requiring sleep, but the mission in Afghanistan had taken its toll on his endurance. Reb had already exhibited his resilience by rising early and renting a surfboard. The Navy SEAL was comfortable in just about any body of water and had done plenty of surfing in California.

Decker kicked the plastic wastebasket near the room desk, sending it flying into a framed photo of a Saipan sunset. Glass exploded into shards that glittered on the carpet, adding to his sense of frustration.

Carrington was whistling as he jiggled the key into the doorknob. The first punch hit him in the stomach and he doubled over. The second was an open-hand chop to the back of the neck that knocked him to the floor.

Stunned but tuned for survival, Carrington blocked the kick that was aimed at his head. He locked onto Decker's bare foot and twisted it until both men were wrestling wildly and rolling in shards of glass.

Within seconds they were on their feet, poised in martial arts stances. "Did you just drive her to meet Tanaka?"

"Yes."

Decker bared his teeth and lunged at his opponent but Carrington quickly sidestepped the attack and picked up the wooden desk chair. "That's enough, Decker," he shouted. "You're out of your fuckin' mind."

Decker let out a war cry and charged. Carrington swung the chair, which struck Decker's left arm and shoulder. One of the wooden legs broke off and bounced across the rug. Carrington quickly grabbed it and brought it down on Decker's head, putting an end to the fight.

Carrington was sitting in an upholstered side chair, sipping a low-ball glass of bourbon when Decker regained consciousness.

Decker pawed the lump on his skull. "Did you really need to do that?"

"Have you come back to your senses?"

"Sorry. Too long in the desert, I guess."

"You've got to get yourself under control. And beyond that, you've got to flow with the plan if you're to accomplish anything here. We work as a team."

"I just don't like Hannah being alone with that asshole. Aren't you worried about her?"

Carrington bristled. "Of course I am."

"Of course you are. If anything happens to her, it's your ass in a sling back at Langley. But I want her safe for a different reason."

"That can make a mission a lot more complicated."

"Maybe so. But I need to protect her."

Carrington sipped his bourbon, swirling the glass though it contained no ice. "You've made that very clear. So far, Tanaka has taken her sightseeing and on a picnic, always accompanied by his bodyguards. From what we can tell, he's dazzled by her looks and charm and starting to open up with personal information. We just need him to lead us to Hiraku. She could be the key to the puzzle."

As it turned out, Hannah and Tanaka decided to forgo the vacation paradise tour and instead went to the movies in Chalan Kanoa, within walking distance of her hotel. The featured films were several months behind what was playing in the continental United States, but the selections included the Italian drama *Cinema Paradiso*, Stephen King's spooky *Pet*

Sematary, and the domestic comedy *Honey, I Shrunk the Kids*. Hannah picked *Pet Sematary* because she didn't want to foster any post-film conversation about love or family — better a story about bringing a road-killed tomcat back to life.

Although Tanaka spoke English, he wasn't fluent, yet he seemed to grasp the concept of using an ancient rite to bring back the dead – even if in this case it was a cat. When the movie ended, Tanaka walked Hannah back to her hotel, flanked by two bodyguards who followed behind at a discrete distance.

Decker was waiting in the hotel lobby when Hannah returned. Tanaka had bowed and bid her goodnight at the front entrance where he repeated his promise to give her a private tour that would benefit her travel company and clients.

Hannah locked eyes with Decker. It was a silent battle of wills and Decker lost because he was first to speak.

"Are you doing this just to piss me off, or to prove you can take the lead on this mission?"

"You don't even know what this mission is about. You haven't been here long enough."

"I've been at this business a lot longer than you have."

"Sometimes that doesn't make any difference, and this is one of those times."

"So now you're the expert?"

"I didn't say that. I'm just pointing out that William and I have gotten to know many of the players here and we're trying to take the right steps to get the intel we came for."

"And that includes dating some pompous Japanese mobster?"

"We're not dating. It's a honey trap and you know it. You just want to start trouble where there isn't any."

"And Carrington agrees with everything you're doing?"

"I don't know if he agrees. But he knows we need to find out where the girl with the secrets is being held so that we can find a way to get her out of there and back into our hands. She's the key to the mission's success."

Decker seemed momentarily defeated. He stared down at his calloused and blistered feet encased in Teva sandals. "I still don't like it. And I don't think Carrington should have allowed it."

"Well, you'd better get used to it because Tanaka is picking me up tomorrow for an island tour of places my wealthy, fictitious clients from Buenos Aires are just going to love when they vacation here. And by the way, how did you get that bruise on your head?"

Reb came through the door just as Decker was about to answer. He, too, noticed the bruise but made no comment. Sensing the tension, he and kept on moving toward the corridor where his room was located. Hannah followed him with her eyes until he was out of sight.

"You were about to tell me about the bruise."

"Some other time."

33

DONUTS AND SECRETS

SAIPAN
NORTHERN MARIANA ISLANDS
APRIL 1990

DETECTIVE MASHIMA SAT ALONE SIPPING coffee and nibbling on a honey-glazed donut in Winchell's Donuts House in Garapan when Carrington pushed open the glass front door to the air-conditioned restaurant.

Carrington ordered a coffee and noisily slumped into a chair at a table directly across the aisle from Mashima. He picked up a newspaper and scanned the headlines. There was a story about the Tanapag drug raid and a self-serving quote from FBI Special Agent Brent Palmer.

According to Palmer, the FBI was able to match car tire tracks at the scene of Mikito Asaki's apparent death at Banzai Cliff to those from the tires of a car parked at the Tanapag pot-growing farm. Nothing in the story suggested CNMI police had in any way contributed to the investigation.

Carrington nursed his coffee and pretended to read. Every few moments he stopped to habitually run his hands over his ash-blond hair to keep the strands from falling in front of his eyes as he scanned the news. The locals were concerned about the U.S. Navy bringing large ships into the region from which military operations could be staged. Two letters to the editor expressed grief about the unsolved and apparently senseless murder of a local schoolteacher and the rape and slaying of his girlfriend along a secluded lover's lane.

Carrington nodded to Mashima in the way strangers might acknowledge each other's presence on a train or bus. The three other customers in the place were going about their business and seemed uninterested in anything else, but Carrington was trained to wait and observe. After an exchange of small talk, Carrington joined Mashima for a candid conversation that mostly focused on tourism possibilities for Saipan — the best hotels, quality restaurants, casinos, sandy beaches, reliable transportation services, small grocery stores and other details that might prove useful to an Argentine tourist – just in case anyone was listening.

When the other customers were gone and the restaurant staff had retreated to the kitchen, Mashima breathed a sigh of relief that he no longer needed to play the game. He immediately relayed the information he felt Carrington should know.

"I can tell you with certainty, Mr. Marson, that Yoshi Yamamoto's life was ended with much cruelty, or what your CIA likes to call extreme prejudice."

"Are you saying the CIA killed this guy Yoshi?"

"Not at all. I'm saying the yakuza are responsible."

"And how do you know this?"

"I listened closely to what was being said when the yakuza held their party at The Lucky Carp. I was just outside the party. And what I heard was very disturbing."

"So tell me."

Mashima relayed the details of the gruesome video from Komodo Island. Carrington's jaw hung open in disbelief, showing how repulsive he found the story. "Tanaka let Komodo dragons eat his business partner alive? Is that what you're telling me?"

Mashima nodded and took a small bite of his pastry. "Tanaka also may have ordered the death of the local police sergeant for stealing the confiscated $36,000 from the police evidence locker. He did it to send a message. Unfortunately, it was not made clear to me who did the actual killing."

"And you learned this also through eavesdropping on the yakuza party?"

A wry smile creased the detective's face. "Loose lips sink ships. Isn't that what the American people were told during the Second World War? You never know who might be listening, so keep your trap shut. Well, as you can see, sake loosens the lips."

"So what about the girl?"

"Only rumors that she is being held at Tanaka's rented home here on the island."

"Fuckin' A. He's got her in a fortress?"

"That seems to be the situation."

"Any suggestions?"

"The honey-glazed."

"Fuck you, Mashima. I'm trying to be serious."

"As am I, Mr. Marson."

"What do you plan to do?"

"We need to work together on this. Perhaps your Argentine travel company can assist with some overhead surveillance."

"I'll request a bird, but not until we're sure she's being held at that location. Requesting a satellite isn't like calling a fucking cab."

"I wouldn't know."

"How sure are you that she's in Tanaka's house?"

Mashima took another small bite of his donut and delicately wiped his lips with a paper napkin. "I highly suggest you order one of these. They're Winchell's specialty."

"Why are you fucking with me?"

"Because I want you to be as honest with me as I am being with you."

Carrington let loose an exasperated groan. "You weren't fooled by Mariel and me from the moment we landed at the airport. But we had no idea who to trust. Still don't. Strange island. Different customs. Lots of dead bodies turning up. We weren't about to advertise our arrival like the FBI. As you might have noticed, we don't have any agency letters stenciled on the backs of our clothing."

Mashima chuckled. "I suppose that's wise. If you've been paying attention, then you've seen the pins the yakuza wear on their lapels that identify their membership in a specific organized crime family. Not much different than letters on a jacket."

Carrington appreciated the intel. He hadn't had much time to prepare for this mission and certainly not enough opportunity to read *The Ways of the Yakuza* or whatever primer was available at Langley. He raised an arm to signal the waitress who had returned to her post near the cash register. She promptly appeared at their table, officiously clutching a pad and pencil.

"I'll have two honey-glazed," he said, looking across the table at Mashima. "I believe this gentleman would like the second."

The waitress glanced at Mashima for confirmation.

Mashima popped the last morsel into his mouth. "I'd like that very much. Winchell's is the best."

After they'd both devoured their donuts in silence, Carrington stood and slid his chair beneath the table.

Mashima smiled. "I know you are concerned that Tanaka might attempt to take advantage of Mariel, but I'm told he no longer possesses the ability to do so."

"And why is that?"

"My colleagues in Tokyo say Tanaka is suspected of murdering a nurse who was part of the team that conducted his failed penis enhancement surgery last year."

Carrington raised his eyebrows as a smirk formed on his lips.

"Apparently the operation went badly and left Tanaka in worse shape. The nurse was stabbed in the back and her throat was slashed. Although it happened on a side street after dark, two witnesses described the suspect as a large Japanese man wearing a tan trench coat. The victim was already dead when one of the witnesses rushed to where the body collapsed on the sidewalk. She indicated a black Mercedes sedan raced along the street at high speed moments later but she was unable to read the entire license plate."

"What about the doctors?"

"They have agreed to police protection, though I'm not sure how successful it will be if Tanaka decides they, too, must pay for the error."

Carrington couldn't suppress his grin. "Thanks for being a stand-up guy, Mashima. That's the best short story I've heard in a while, no pun intended. I'm looking forward to our partnership."

Mashima slightly bowed his head, his lips glued in a close-lipped smile. "I, too, look forward to a strong alliance."

34

YOU'RE GUILTY EVEN IF YOU'RE NOT

SAIPAN
NORTHERN MARIANA ISLANDS
APRIL 1990

BOONIE DOGS WERE BARKING and roosters crowing as the black Nissan Pathfinder pulled into the hamlet of Tanapag.

Tanaka's two most trusted *kobun* – Kira with the shaved head and lightning bolt tattoo on his face, and Yuki with the long braid of black hair nearly reaching his waist – hopped out of the front seat and cradled their Uzi machine pistols. They jogged toward the small house, kicked open the wood door and shouted for anyone inside to come out with their hands up.

Moments later, two Saipanese farmers were ushered out into the scorching sun and ordered to kneel in the dirt yard, the guns aimed at their heads. Orochi Tanaka opened the rear door of the SUV and slowly approached them. He was an imposing figure in his black, American-style suit, starched white shirt and polished shoes.

The men were trembling, suspecting this moment would be their last. They were told at the courthouse that Tanaka had posted their bail.

"In case you don't know, my name is Orochi Tanaka, and Saipan is my territory. My money that was in your care is now gone. You did not protect it. You did not bring it to the casino as you were instructed. Instead, you were sloppy and lazy."

The men glanced up at Tanaka as though awaiting their fate – a bullet to the brain.

"I am not here to punish you. In fact, I am here to save your lives. We all know you did not kill Mikito Asaki. But if you wish to remain on this earth, you must confess to doing just that."

The two men spoke hurriedly in Chamorro.

Tanaka was suddenly enraged. "Stop talking. If you have something to say, talk in Japanese or English. I know both of you have Japanese blood."

The smaller man raised a bandaged hand as though answering a question posed by an elementary school teacher. "English."

Tanaka towered over them. "If you do not agree to this, we can kill you here and now, dispose of your bodies, and then do the same with your families. My men may even decide to rape your wives and daughters before slitting their throats and tossing their bodies off Banzai Cliff."

The men again broke into Chamorro.

"Stop."

The taller farmer with long gray hair and a goatee spoke first in English. "We will do what you say. Please do not harm our families."

"I don't expect you to do this simply out of fear for yourselves and your families. You each will be paid — more than you can earn here in ten years."

The men's spirits seemed to rise with the prospect of staying alive, reaping sudden riches, and the removal of threats to their families.

"Here's what I need you to do. You will surrender to the authorities at the courthouse in Garapan and tell them you mistakenly murdered Mikito Asaki during a robbery attempt in the late evening, during which time you stole the $36,000 he was carrying from the casino to an unknown destination. You will say you followed Asaki as he left The Lucky Carp and ambushed him. When you realized he was dead, you panicked and threw his body off Banzai Cliff. You then took the money and buried it in a goat shed in Tanapag. You will confirm it was this money that was later discovered by the police."

35

A BIT OF BLACK MAGIC

SAIPAN

NORTHERN MARIANA ISLANDS

APRIL 1990

RAY DONLEY, the pistol-packing government prosecutor, seemed out of sorts as he once again stood before the judge in the Commonwealth Trial Court. Mashima noticed it immediately because Donley typically was not at a loss for words. He was normally articulate, opinionated and fiery. But now he was distracted, deflated and lacking his usual firebrand.

During the recess, the prosecutor shared aloud with Mashima and Lt. Brick what he had observed. He looked down at the floor as though ashamed by what he was about to reveal.

"I know. I can't think straight today. It's my wife, Cheryl. This place has her scared out of her wits. We went out to dinner last night in Garapan and when we came home, the wedding photo of the two of us in a glass frame beside the bed was missing. Or, more accurately, the frame was still there but the photograph was gone."

Lt. Brick tried to calm the prosecutor. "From what Mashima has been telling me, housebreaks are very common on Saipan. I'm not surprised. A few hundred years ago it was known as Islas de los Ladrones — the island of thieves. Maybe not much has changed."

Mashima quickly joined Lt. Brick's effort to assuage their colleague's anxiety. "True enough. We don't have a problem with car thefts because there's nowhere to go with a stolen vehicle, just round and round the island. Unfortunately, the locals do break into homes from time to time, especially those of visitors. Usually it's cash-and-carry, as the Americans say – jewelry, wallets, money left lying about, small-sized electronics, cameras, binoculars, radios, credit cards, anything that might have quick turnover value."

"But whoever broke in didn't take anything else. Only the photo."

Mashima did his best to explain. "It could be because they are superstitious and fear the power which they can see you possess. Some of the natives believe in black magic. The native Chamorro and Carolinian populations are mostly Catholic, courtesy of the Spanish soldiers and priests who arrived on our shores in the 1600s, but they also worship the old deities."

"What does that have to do with stealing my personal photo?"

"Whoever took it is no doubt convinced the image of a person holds power and, as such, if they are in possession of the image, the power will be theirs. Perhaps they cannot control you directly, but they can keep you from doing what they perceive as harm."

"And meanwhile, what am I supposed to do? We already lock all the doors and windows, but obviously that isn't enough. When I was offered the opportunity to come here, I told my wife this was going to be like working in Paradise. Saipan was supposed to *be* Paradise – sand beaches, piña coladas, happy natives. Like the movie *South Pacific*, only we'd be the stars."

Mashima wondered about such expectations. "I'll ask around. Voodoo is still practiced in some of the smaller settlements like Tanapag and San Antonio, but the young don't seem to put much faith in it."

Donley tossed his pistol into the maw of his over-stuffed briefcase. "I'd appreciate that. Any and all advice is welcome."

"I think you'll find only the elders still talk of the Taotaomona Legends. They believe the spirit of an ancient Chamorro lurks at night among jungle burial sites, in the Banyan trees and around the latte stones. Apparently over 300 years of Catholic teaching here in Saipan hasn't wiped out those beliefs."

Donley's face turned pale. "Was there ever any truth to the legend? God, I can't believe I'm actually asking you that."

Mashima smiled knowingly. "Such truths exist only for those who feel affected by the spirit of Taotaomona or another *kami*. For them, if a relative or friend seems possessed, a witch doctor must be consulted, sometimes a female witch, who at great expense can provide secret cures made from coconut bark and various herbs."

"I take it you were never a believer."

"No, not me, but rumors about such things often circulate at the Sunday night cockfights in San Antonio. I'll plan to attend this weekend. Perhaps you'd like to come along. The fights can seem brutal to the uninitiated, but they're also enlightening."

"No thanks," said Donley, pressing down on his briefcase lid until he heard the buckles snap closed. "I need to finish here and then pick up my wife at the hospital where she's volunteering part time."

Mashima pursed his lips. "I suggest you not give the missing photograph another thought. Stealing it was most likely an act of simple-mindedness and nothing will come of it."

"Thank you for that, but I'm not certain my wife would agree. She's about ready to buy a ticket and fly home to Boston. She enjoys helping out at the hospital, but I think this place is too much for her. She doesn't like surprises."

Back in the courtroom, two police officers were wrestling a middle-aged man with long gray hair and a goatee, who attempted to slash his own throat with a razor blade. The man had been quietly observing the court proceedings from a seat at the rear of the room. The razor had been hidden inside one of his rubber boots.

Donley and Mashima heard the ruckus and rushed into the room to investigate. The prosecutor immediately recognized the man as one of the two who had pleaded not guilty to being accessories in the murder of Mikito Asaki.

Blood trickled from the man's neck as the burly guards pressed him to the floor. The wound didn't look fatal, but those in the courtroom squeamish about the sight of blood were obviously ruffled.

The judge entered the courtroom through the side door to his chambers. He frowned and banged his gavel several times, attempting to understand what was happening, but the pandemonium continued.

"What's going on? Who is that man?"

One of the court officers hurriedly approached the judge. "Your Honor, he's one of the men charged in the Asaki murder case. He was released on bail."

The judge fished for his eyeglasses in a drawer behind the bench. "Why is he here? We continued that case to provide Mr. Donley more time to impanel a jury."

"Apparently he's here to confess to the murder of Mikito Asaki."

The judge furrowed his eyebrows. "Nonsense! I don't

believe it. He's clearly not yakuza. He's a poor farmer, not an assassin."

The court officer shrugged. "Right before he slashed himself, he stood up and shouted, 'I killed him. I didn't mean to do it. But I killed Asaki.' That's when everything went kind of crazy."

More trial court officers arrived. The two policemen lifted the injured man by his arms until he was upright and gave him a gauze pad to stymie the bleeding. The wound was superficial.

The judge stood behind his bench. "If that man needs medical attention, get it for him and then bring him back in here so that we can hear what he has to say."

Donley literally jogged to the front of the room until he was before the judge. "Did I just hear the court officer say this man has confessed to the murder of Mikito Asaki?"

"That's right. But I have no idea why he would do that. And personally, I doubt if it's true."

Donley appeared bewildered. "So this man surrendered himself?"

"That appears to be the situation. He's the second man today to claim he had a role in the murder of Mikito Asaki."

Donley's mouth hung open, stunned by the news. "Who was the first one?"

"The other defendant charged in connection with the murder. He also confessed, but only to being an accomplice by driving the car used to transport Mr. Asaki's body to Banzai Cliff."

"What do you intend to do?"

"I'll schedule a hearing and listen to what these men have to say. If the man who has stated he drove the car is willing to testify against the defendant who claims he killed Asaki, we can move forward and resolve this matter. In return for his cooperation, he'll receive a reduced prison term."

The judge nodded toward the rear of the courtroom where

FBI Special Agents Brent Palmer and Sean O'Reilly were standing. "The federal agents investigating this case should be equally pleased. Now they can go home."

The judge turned to Donley, whose face was flushed red. "Do you have any objections, Mr. Donley?"

"Frankly, I do, Your Honor. You've sidestepped the judicial process and not given either man an opportunity to defend himself."

"They'll both get a turn. I'm sure the powers in Washington will be elated that this unfortunate murder has been solved by the diligent work of the FBI and those responsible put behind bars."

36

TAGGING ALONG WITH TANAKA

SAIPAN

NORTHERN MARIANA ISLANDS

APRIL 1990

DECKER'S FACE was a study in contained anger as he peered through Reb's spotting scope. He watched closely as Tanaka's bodyguards opened the door for their boss and then for his companion, Argentine travel agent Mariel Becker. He winced when Tanaka placed a hand on Hannah's bare back, exactly where her blue sundress ended at the base of her spine, and ushered her toward the front entrance of the sprawling house. At that moment, if Tanaka had been alone and in the crosshairs of Decker's sniper rifle, the man's head would have been transformed into a pink mist.

Two more bodyguards appeared from the far side of the house, both carrying what looked like Uzi machine pistols.

Decker pressed the transmit button on his radio. "Tanaka and Hannah are at the house." He adjusted the focus on the scope and recorded the range from his camouflaged perch in a grove of tangan-tangan trees. "Tanaka. Hannah. Two bodyguards from the vehicle. Two more outside with automatic weapons. It looks like everybody is headed for the front door." Carrington responded. "Roger that. Any sign of Hiraku?"

"Negative. And the blinds are pulled down on all the windows."

"Give it another hour or two and then head back to the road intersection a mile east of your position. Radio when you get there and we'll pick you up. Over."

"Wait! There's a fifth party at the front door. Female. Short. Possibly middle-aged. Black hair. Wearing some kind of dark-colored athletic workout clothes. Do you copy that?"

"Affirmative. Any bowing or hand shaking going on? Or does it look like she's more subservient, a servant perhaps?"

"No way to tell from here. But I doubt she's a cook or a housekeeper dressed like that."

"Good point. Mashima has a camera with a hefty telephoto lens that you can bring along next time. Always a chance somebody at the local PD will recognize her."

Once inside the house, Tanaka strutted straight for the stocked bar that overlooked the infinity swimming pool and the ocean. He was brimming with self-importance.

"What may I get you? Vodka? Gin? White wine? Maybe some tequila."

Hannah yawned. She was feeling weary after having spent nearly three hours on a grand tour with Tanaka as her attentive guide. At each stop, she had been forced to muster false enthusiasm and interest. She had even scribbled notes and taken photos with a point-and-shoot camera. It was obvious Saipan was blessed with beaches and coral reefs, and Hannah recorded their names along with brief descriptions. Obyan, Lau Lau, Landing, Ladder, and Pau Pau were among her favorite beaches. The cliff-edge view of Bird Island and the adjacent sunken grotto were impressive, as was Wing Beach where the wing of a U.S. Navy aircraft still rested unburied in the sand. Twelve miles long and five miles wide, it didn't take long to see the island highlights.

"Water would be just fine."

Tanaka groaned with impatience. "Mariel. Please. If you won't accept my hospitality, I will have failed as a host."

"Then a cold beer, if you have one."

Tanaka smiled. "Name your brand. I have many here."

"You pick it. Surprise me."

Tanaka returned to the living room with a cold beaded bottle of Kirin and an empty glass. "Japanese. But I also have Budweiser if this is not to your liking."

"Perfect. And right out of the bottle is fine."

Hannah clinked the bottle against Tanaka's rum drink before taking a long swig. She immediately thought about rape drugs and wished he hadn't opened the bottle out of her view. She would have to sip slowly.

Tanaka seemed amused by Hannah's decision to drink from the bottle, as though the act somehow did not fit with the image he held of her in his mind. A more cultured woman would have requested a glass, but then again, perhaps that's the way women prefer their beer in Argentina.

"Please step out onto the balcony and enjoy the view. It's among the best on the island, and very private."

Two of the bodyguards returned to their outdoor posts. The other two faded into nearby rooms, as did the woman dressed in the black Lycra bodysuit and red high-top sneakers, the one who Tanaka identified as a member of the domestic staff but did not introduce.

Hannah stood at the balcony railing, her feet instinctively set in a T-stance in the event someone tried to knock her off balance and send her toppling over the edge. Her martial arts training had been deeply ingrained.

The phone rang on an end table beside the couch and Tanaka excused himself with a light grunt in order to answer it. From the sound of his voice, whatever was being said in Japanese was important and urgent.

Hannah studied the expression on Tanaka's face as he talked. She didn't know Tanaka was then learning that one of the two pot farmers from Tanapag – the one who vowed to confess to murdering Asaki – had changed his story and now admitted only to driving the getaway car.

Hannah sensed the man's mood had changed for the worse when he again joined her on the balcony, but Tanaka continued to smile charmingly with his oversized teeth as though all was well.

"What do you think of my home? Although we Japanese are not allowed to buy such properties outright, I have leased this house for fifty years. I think that's long enough." Tanaka chuckled to himself.

"It's spectacular. And so beautifully decorated," she said, sweeping an arm upward and around like a television game show hostess. "Did you have a hand in that?"

Tanaka flushed with pride. "Yes. I designed most of it. The house was already here but I have made many changes. I added the swimming pool, the sauna, a gym, the large windows overlooking the sea, and even a special room for watching movies like the one we saw earlier this week. Perhaps you'd like to see a movie here in comfort. You could even stay the night. My private chef would prepare a fine dinner and we would transport you back to your hotel in the morning."

Hannah tried to look flattered by the offer, meanwhile thinking *I wouldn't trust this guy as far as I could throw him.* "That sounds wonderful, but not tonight. I've got to head back to my hotel and start writing up reports on all the places you have been kind enough to show me. My bosses back in Buenos Aires will be very pleased."

Tanaka was startled by the sound of pounding that seemed to come from the basement. The pounding was followed by shouting and other noises, as though furniture was being hurled about. Suddenly on high alert, his posture grew stiff. "It's the housekeeper. She has seizures and recently she was sick with a high fever. Sometimes she pounds the walls and shouts out in confusion. The doctors believe she may be afflicted with Tourette syndrome. If you'll excuse me, I'll go check on her."

More muffled screams rose from the floor below and the pounding resumed. One of the bodyguards had left his post, his heavy footsteps echoing as he descended the stairs to the basement.

Hannah stepped toward Tanaka. "I'll come along. Maybe there's some way I can help."

A look of panic filled Tanaka's face. "No. That won't be necessary. This happens all the time. My men know what to do. Please help yourself to another cold beer. They're in the refrigerator on the left as you enter the kitchen. I'll return shortly," he said, departing with a gentlemanly curt bow.

37

WHAT'S FOR DINNER?

SAIPAN

NORTHERN MARIANA ISLANDS

APRIL 1990

TANAKA WAS furious when he opened the door to Hiraku's cell. He glared at Akumu. His eyes quickly scanned the room – a broken chair, a videotape player perched on a small table and pointed at the blank white wall.

"What caused this disturbance?"

"I showed her the tape of Yoshi and the dragons. I thought she would enjoy the show."

Tanaka scrunched his face as though containing some explosive reaction. "Stop your nonsense. Why did you do such a thing?"

"She needs to see she will not be rescued, not by her great uncle Yoshi or from those two CIA agents who are now shark food."

Hiraku let out another wail but Tanaka slapped her hard

across the face and she crumbled onto the bed, curling into a fetal position.

"You see. She's defiant."

"She's only a girl, Akumu. I thought you could handle her, but apparently not."

Hannah saw Tanaka's absence as an opportunity to take a closer look at her surroundings – possible weapons, escape routes, defensive positions. She clutched the black umbrella leaning against a wall in the living room, felt its weight and examined its metal tip.

The beer bottle on the side table would also be useful as a club, or as a jagged blade if shattered. The stainless steel writing pen in her pocket was strong enough to penetrate plywood, or an assailant's skull. She glanced up at the length of chain holding a chandelier in the living room. That, too, might come in handy. A razor blade was hidden beneath the false silicone scar on her thigh — one of Carrington's many recommended spy gadgets. She presumed the kitchen would be stocked with knives and the cabinet drawers unlocked.

Hannah knew the thick glass windows overlooking the sea would be difficult to break and possibly bulletproof, so she recalled the interior doors she had passed through upon arrival. While entering the house, she had spotted a separate exterior door leading to the eastern wing. The door appeared to be made of steel and had no handle or knob on the outside.

Carrington had taught her plenty about how to cause distractions using water, fire, smoke or noise. Escape was often more preferable and productive than a fight.

Nearly a half hour elapsed before Tanaka retuned to the living room, spewing apologies for his unreliable staff, his face a moving mass of frustration.

"I hope you can forgive me for being such a poor host. It can be very difficult to find domestic help here on Saipan. I'm afraid most of the island residents would rather collect their welfare checks from the United States government and sit around chewing betel nut."

When Hannah didn't reply, he added, "I hope you don't find my comment offensive, given that you are Argentine and not American."

"Certainly not. We all know how the U.S. government works in the world's poorer countries. Is your housekeeper going to be all right?"

"Absolutely. She's fine. She just needs to rest. Akumu gave her something to help her sleep."

"Is Akumu the woman who met us at the door when we first arrived?"

"Yes. She, too, is a member of my staff, but more reliable than most of the others."

"Is she a housekeeper?"

Tanaka was evasive. "She wears many hats. Housekeeper isn't one of them."

"And she's not on welfare?"

"Only mine," said Tanaka, regaining his confidence and flashing his big-toothed Clark Gable smile. "Now that we have had this unfortunate interruption, I would be honored to make up for it by having my chef prepare a special dinner."

Hannah knew Decker, Carrington, Reb, and probably Mashima by this point would begin to worry and perhaps do something rash like formulate a rescue plan. She suspected Reb or Decker had the house under surveillance, likely through the reticle of their riflescopes. "I really should be going."

"Please. I insist. I'll have my chef begin immediately."

Hannah made it seem as though she was reluctantly agreeing to stay for dinner. "Orochi, you're going to get me into big trouble with my boss."

Tanaka smiled victoriously, his mind already envisioning a sumptuous dinner followed by wild sex with this attractive young woman. He prayed his pleasure pole would stand when the time came. The next time he visited Tokyo, he'd find the doctors responsible for his misery.

Hannah returned the smile. "Apparently I'm hungrier than I thought." She had no intention of leaving until she confirmed what had caused the shouting and pounding in the basement. She needed to be sure Hiraku was alive.

Tanaka barked extensive orders into the phone in rapid-fire Japanese and poured himself another rum drink. He smiled at Hannah, staring invasively into her eyes. "My night manager from The Lucky Carp will arrive shortly and prepare our meal."

"You mean Tony?"

"No. Tony merely tends the bar. I doubt he could prepare a decent tuna steak in Finadene sauce. A cheeseburger, perhaps, on the grill, would mark the height of his expertise in the kitchen. I'm talking about Krill."

"The woman with freckles and reddish purple hair?"

"The same one you met when we were enjoying our special tequila. She is an accomplished chef."

"That's wonderful. I've always wanted to take a cooking course."

Hannah didn't mention sharing lines of coke with Krill in the ladies' room during her visit to the casino, knowing it might lead to questions from Tanaka that she didn't want to answer. She got the feeling Krill had never mentioned it either.

Krill appeared at the front door in a fluorescent green mini skirt and skimpy, electric-blue halter. Her blonde hair with purple and red streaks was styled into four-inch spikes as though she were a blend of pop singer Cyndi Lauper and the Statue of Liberty. Judging by their eye movements, Tanaka's stern-faced bodyguards were intrigued by Krill's funky appearance. A basket laden with foodstuffs was precariously tucked beneath Krill's left arm while her right hand dragged a wheeled Igloo cooler. One of the bodyguards stepped forward and lifted the lid on the basket and the Igloo cooler to make certain they contained only food.

Reb peered through his scope. "We've got a visitor. Female. Caucasian. Young. Possibly blonde. Green skirt hiked up to her cheeks. Blue top. No bra. Rainbow hair. No fuckin' idea what she's doing there."

The radio crackled with Carrington's voice. "How did she get there?"

"Datsun pickup. She parked it in the front driveway."

Had Hannah heard the radio transmission, she would've chuckled, recalling Decker's distain for Lauper's hit song *"Girls Just Wanna Have Fun"*, when he was deployed to Lebanon. As Decker had put it, the 1983 release just didn't fit the occasion in war torn Beirut where fun was a thing of the past.

Tanaka began introductions in case either woman had forgotten the other's name or their previous brief meeting at the casino, but Krill intervened. "No need. We've met. In the girls' room."

"I see. Well, I hope it was a pleasant first meeting."

Hannah laughed mischievously. "I'll never forget it. I was feeling a bit out of my element so it was refreshing to run into – what was that word – haole? Yes, another haole girl."

Krill gave the thumbs up sign. "Haole girls rock."

Tanaka rolled his eyes and abruptly turned toward the kitchen as though to leave these two to their senseless women talk. "We can proceed directly to our dinner preparations."

Krill followed him without hesitation, as though she'd been to Tanaka's home a thousand times. "Let me set these things down and I'll get started."

Tanaka had given her specific instructions about dinner. He was feeling horny, though he didn't share that news with Krill. Believing divine luck was on his side, he simply instructed Krill to add black rhino horn, which had been ground to a fine powder, into the seasoning of the grilled grouper. He was convinced the powerful animal's horns were an aphrodisiac. Krill added the rhino horn to the mix of seasonings, though she doubted it would produce the result Tanaka expected.

Next came the shark fin soup. Krill couldn't recognize one shark fin from another, but the Japanese merchant who had delivered the two fins now in her hands assured her they had been cut off a tiger shark, which was Tanaka's preference. When she warned the merchant his life was at stake if he wasn't telling the truth, the man dropped to his knees, bowed his head and swore in his mother's honor the fins were indeed from one of the most vicious tiger sharks swimming in the Mariana Trench.

Krill eavesdropped as Tanaka popped a bottle of Louis Roederer Cristal Brut champagne, knowing he had paid hundreds of dollars for the bubbly. She wondered if Hannah had a taste for champagne and whether she would realize what she was being offered.

Krill carefully removed the pufferfish from the Igloo cooler and unwrapped it. The fish was still wriggling and gasping for air. She had prepared the delicacy for Tanaka and others on several occasions and was well aware of its toxic potential.

The words of the master chef at her class in Tokyo where she obtained licensure to cook pufferfish, known as *fugu*, still echoed in her head. *The poison of one blowfish is enough to kill thirty humans – and there is no known antidote.*

The master chef had explained the word *fugu* was derived from two Chinese characters meaning "river" and "pig". The pufferfish name stemmed from the creature's ability to swell its size and appear more formidable to its enemies. Whenever the master repeated this information, he puffed his cheeks and widened his eyes for emphasis. It always made Krill laugh.

On the last day of her *fugu* training, she was ordered to

prepare and eat a pufferfish as proof of her competence. She didn't hesitate.

Although *fugu* is typically eaten raw as sashimi in thousands of Japanese restaurants, Krill had no interest in becoming a full-time *fugu* chef. She had witnessed what could go wrong if the fish was improperly prepared. A dinner party guest had complained of a tingling in his lips upon eating blowfish, followed by temporary constriction of his breathing. It was precisely this kind of symptom that attracted adventurous people to eat *fugu*.

The master chef had emphasized ingesting the toxin *can lead to asphyxia and possibly death, and there is no antidote for fugu poisoning.*

Krill understood that despite the scary warnings, the thrill of eating something that might kill you can be addictive to some people.

While Tanaka plied Hannah with expensive champagne, Akumu stationed herself in the kitchen and focused her attention on Krill, pretending to understand the *fugu* preparation. Akumu commented on the weather, but Krill ignored her because she wanted to hear what Tanaka was saying to Hannah in the next room.

Akumu felt personally insulted by the rebuff. Inside she fumed with hatred, but her face remained placid. She began to sing as she peered out the kitchen door, her eyes on Tanaka who graciously poured more champagne for Hannah. *"I get no kick from champagne. Mere alcohol doesn't thrill me at all, so tell me why should it be true, that I get a kick out of you."*

Akumu smiled at Krill. "I just love Cole Porter, don't you?"

38

FUGU ON THE MENU

S<small>AIPAN</small>

N<small>ORTHERN</small> M<small>ARIANA</small> I<small>SLANDS</small>

A<small>PRIL</small> 1990

O<small>UT ON THE BALCONY</small>, Tanaka was convincing himself that Hannah found him attractive and would ultimately share his bed. He was feeling the effects of the champagne. Hannah was playing along, laughing at his stilted, chauvinistic humor and pretending she was interested in him not only as a business contact. She wondered whether Reb or Decker could see her out on the balcony. She removed one of her sandals, held it over the railing and pretended to shake out a small pebble that was causing discomfort, her signal to Reb and Decker that all was under control.

Reb had made his way unseen through the jumble of rocks and boulders at the rear of the house where he could see the balcony. He radioed Carrington with the status report.

Tanaka seemed puzzled by Hannah's behavior. "A problem?"

"No. Only a little stone that had found its way under my foot."

"Apparently the housekeeper needs to do a better job."

"Oh, no. It was certainly a stone from outside the house."

"Is the bubbly to your liking?"

Hannah smiled coyly. She'd already dumped one glass full into a large indoor palm tree. "Absolutely. It's a buoyant wine. I can feel the bubbles in my head."

Tanaka sat on the couch and patted the seat as a sign that Hannah should join him.

He treats women like they're dogs, Hannah thought to herself as she gracefully sat, leaving nearly a foot of space between them.

Tanaka leaned closer, to where he could talk as though they were intimate friends. He imagined they were on a date. "You have no idea the joy it gives me to hear you say that about the champagne. I picked out this bottle especially for you – for us."

Hannah smiled, feigning deep appreciation. "Orochi, I can't thank you enough for showing me all the special places on Saipan where my clients will be eager to explore."

"It is a pleasure. And I have many more to show you."

"I'll look forward to that. But I feel bad that you know so much about me and have done so much for me, yet I know so little about you."

"There's not much to tell."

"I don't believe that. Not for a second."

"As you undoubtedly have guessed, I am yakuza."

"Honestly I'm not always sure what that means."

"It means I am yakuza — among the worthless ones."

Hannah furrowed her eyebrows and acted as though she was confused. "Worthless? You're not worthless."

"That is what it means to be yakuza. Hundreds of years ago,

in feudal Japan, men played the Flower Card game called *hana-fuda*. Most of them were samurai bandits, outcasts who had no master. They were known as *kabukimono* – the crazy ones."

"But why do you say you're worthless?"

"The Flower Card game is like Blackjack, which I assume you are familiar with. In Blackjack, twenty-one is a winning hand. But in *hanafuda*, nineteen is a winning hand. If you are dealt 8-9-3, pronounced ya, ku, sa, you are a loser because it amounts to twenty. You are over the limit."

"But a simple card game can't possibly reflect a person's power, especially when it comes to a man like you."

Tanaka blushed. "Hanafuda is an old game. Today, we play a new one."

"And what might that be?"

"We don't play cards. We just take what we want."

"You mean businesses? Like corporate takeovers? Or literally anything?"

Tanaka moved uneasily in his seat. He felt powerful and wanted to show this beautiful, blonde woman just how much influence he wielded. He assumed most of the men in her social circle were effete, overly polite, intellectual but not virile.

"Yakuza do not take orders from anyone, not the Japanese government, not the United States of America. Nobody tells us what to do, or what not to do."

Hannah sipped her champagne. "I see."

"No. I'm not sure you do. In Japan, it is an honor to be yakuza. But in the United States, this social standing is considered criminal."

"So you're a criminal here? In Saipan."

"*Hai.* Yes. These islands are territories of the United States, are they not? Although we are slowly taking them back."

Tanaka didn't continue immediately. He was searching for the correct way to describe himself in a manner he felt certain Hannah would find irresistible.

"Long ago, when I had opportunity to study world history, I recall reading about the creation of laws. I believe the lesson was simple. You can make all the laws you want, but they are meaningless unless you have the ability and willingness to enforce them."

"And you're saying the United States imposes laws here but the people of Saipan do what they please regardless?"

"The United States is far away — thousands of miles, and separated by a vast ocean. Their Marines came here to fight the Japanese and then they left, leaving behind only government bureaucrats to tax the natives, or to give them welfare money. There is no pride here among the native people these days. They have lost their skills and are quickly losing their culture."

"So why do you care so much?"

"Who ever said that I care about what happens to the people of Saipan?"

"I think you are still connected to the war and to what happened to you and your family."

"I weep for my ancestors. But today Saipan is no more than a business opportunity."

Hannah remained quiet. She made it clear she was thinking about her next question. "Before I came here, I heard only that Saipan was a drug-smuggler's paradise, a place without law and order. It didn't sound like a tourist destination."

"That may be true."

"There were stories in the news about creepy underworld criminals who use Saipan as a stopover for shipping drugs. It made my boss doubt Argentine tourists will want to come here. "

Tanaka gulped his champagne, belched, and thrust out his lower lip as though deeply offended. "I wouldn't know about that. I am a business man and my business is hotels and casinos, not drugs."

"I'm so sorry. I never meant to imply you were part of any drug trafficking."

"There's certainly truth in what you've read in the news. Heroin comes from Southeast Asia and somehow ends up in the United States where the people crave it like dogs eating discarded meat in a dark alley."

"I'm curious. How does that happen? Somebody grows poppies in Thailand or somewhere in that region, somebody else converts these beautiful flowers into powder, and other people figure out how to ship it to San Francisco, Los Angeles or wherever?"

"You seem to have a keen interest in the subject."

"I'm no geography expert, but I think it's the distance from Thailand to the coast of California that caught my attention. As you just said, the United States is such a long way from here with the Pacific in between. I read somewhere – maybe it was an article in Clarin or the Buenos Aires Times – that heroin is sent from Thailand to the Philippines and then to Saipan. That must be close to 3,000 miles. And then from here to the United States, it's what, another 5,000 miles?"

"Why such interest?"

"My company has very wealthy and influential clients who frequently vacation in Thailand. They love Phuket, of course, and even Bangkok — so I try to keep up with what's happening there. They expect me to be informed."

"I seriously doubt your clients would ever encounter drug smugglers while visiting Thailand. People who deal in massive quantities of drugs don't advertise. They don't attract attention to themselves."

"I suppose that's so in Thailand. I'd just like to make sure that kind of activity doesn't mar my clients' travel experience should they visit Saipan. My bosses would be horrified. So for me, it's a legitimate concern, no different than any I'd have about putting them up at hotels in certain neighborhoods of

New York City or Los Angeles. My company no longer sends clients to Colombia because of the cartels, or to Rio, which was once a fantastic destination and is now crime-ridden and environmentally polluted."

"If you are here long enough to gain a better sense of the island, I think you'll find the smugglers keep to themselves. They're mostly professional deliverymen, making schedules for shipments by plane or boat. It's all very dull in some respects."

"Well, I'm relieved to hear that. Do you know who they are?"

Before he could answer, Krill appeared in the archway leading to the balcony. She was holding a stemmed glass of red wine. Tanaka glared disapprovingly at Krill and the wine glass. He was insulted and angry she had not only served herself but had gone on to sip before them.

Krill smiled sheepishly, shrugged her thin shoulders and bowed slightly. "Your dinner is ready and will be served in the dining room, if that is your wish."

Tanaka growled approval. He grunted at Hannah as though saying follow me and marched toward the dining room. The room was stark except for a dark wood table with four straight-backed wood chairs. The bare walls were painted light blue, a color enhanced by the turquoise sea. A 3-D bamboo sculpture that resembled a cage was the sole artwork, perched in a far corner.

Reb again radioed Carrington. "She's gone inside the house."

Hannah stopped and pretended to admire the table setting. "How lovely. And Krill was so quick. Will she be joining us?"

Tanaka furrowed his eyebrows as though he did not expect such a nonsensical question to come from the seemingly intelligent Hannah. "She is a servant."

Hannah cleared her throat. "I see."

"Perhaps you are not accustomed to having servants, but in this house, I am the master."

"My apologies. I should have known that." And then, after pausing for several long seconds, she added, "Master."

Tanaka didn't seem to know how to respond, so he simply said nothing.

Krill appeared, cradling a bottle of French red wine. "May I open and pour?"

"*Hai.*"

"I've already had two beers and a bit of bubbly."

"You must at least try this Chateau Margaux. I assure you it is very special."

Hannah glanced at Krill. "Is this what you were drinking in the kitchen?"

"I'm afraid not. Just the house red."

"Well, I'd offer you a taste, but it seems you're a servant."

Tanaka flushed, but Krill kept a straight face. Hannah knew at that moment she'd made an ally. Krill uncorked the wine, expertly poured two glasses and bowed. "Your humble servant."

Tanaka offered a toast to friendship and adventure. He grinned mischievously and launched into a short explanation of Japan's tradition of eating *fugu*.

The pufferfish that had been breathing moments earlier succumbed when Krill sliced it open on the kitchen counter with her favorite carbon-steel filet knife and delicately transformed the meat into sashimi. The paper-thin slices were arranged artistically on a plate in a circle that resembled a chrysanthemum – which Hannah found a bit eerie given that the flower symbolizes death in Japanese culture. The raw slices rested upon a bed of edible flowers and sprouts.

Tanaka snatched a slice with his chopsticks and deftly stuffed it into his mouth. "Nothing to worry about. Please eat."

Hannah hesitantly tonged a slice of the deadly delicacy and brought it to her lips. Tanaka watched her closely. Krill stood near the kitchen doorway but when Hannah looked her way she slipped out of view.

Hannah let the slice lay on her tongue and waited for the anticipated numbness. "I probably won't be able to speak after I swallow this, which means you – Orochi – will have to do all the talking."

Tanaka smiled, hoping the *fugu* would numb her just enough to accept his advances. He tried not to think about the botched surgery in Tokyo. "You've barely touched your wine, and it's such a wonderful vintage."

Hannah batted her eyelashes. "Are you trying to get me drunk?"

"I would never do such a thing. It would not be honorable."

"Now why don't I believe that?"

"You are a beautiful woman. I would be crazy not to enjoy spending the day with someone like you whose veins are coursing with fine wine."

"Well, I'm from Buenos Aires and we can hold our liquor."

Tanaka chuckled. He admired her spirit.

Hannah acted as though the wine was slightly taking effect. "So tell me, Mr. Yakuza, are you really just a simple international businessman, or are you a smuggler? It all sounds so exciting to me. It's like going to a Pacific island and meeting a pirate. Orochi, are you a pirate?"

Tanaka was flattered by the idea that this beautiful woman might imagine him as a swashbuckling pirate or modern-day samurai and decided to play along with her vision.

"If I proved to you I was truly a pirate, as you say, would you treat me differently? Would I appear differently in your eyes?"

As Tanaka voiced those words he reached under the table and caressed Hannah's knees. "I've always read that pirates were irresistible, especially to refined women."

Hannah stopped his hand from probing along her thighs.

She felt a chill when her fingers touched his shortened pinky finger.

Tanaka stared into her eyes. "It was an act of apology."

"No need to explain. Just something I hadn't run into before. In Buenos Aires, if we've offended someone, we simply say *lo siento* and let bygones be bygones."

"That's very charming, but it doesn't always work in the business world where profit or reputation is at stake. *Lo siento* would only go so far. Something more might be demanded. *Yubitsume*, for example."

Tanaka held his hand with the severed finger close to Hannah's face. "In this case, something more was demanded."

"And what did you do that caused the need for apology? Perhaps you can't say."

Tanaka sifted through his memories. "I was young and inexperienced, but eager to please. I made a mistake while trying to do what I thought was the correct move. In the process, I embarrassed the *oyabun* who had taken me under his wing when I first joined the yakuza. It was no different than a son dishonoring his father. Yakuza live by the *bushido*, the warriors' code of honor. It has always been this way. Honor and loyalty are most important."

Hannah feigned shock at such social standards. "What in the world did you do to offend him?"

"I took photographs of him at the beach, photographs of his beautiful tattoos."

"Why would that offend him?"

"The photographs fell into the hands of law enforcement officers who matched the tattoos to those described by witnesses to a robbery and fatal shooting that had occurred in Thailand many years before. The police arrested him and though he was not convicted, the trouble he experienced was caused by my camera."

"So he ordered you to cut off your pinky finger?"

"Absolutely not! It was my decision. It was my way to ask for forgiveness."

"And did he forgive you?"

Tanaka laughed, recalling how the ceremony had gone awry. "It did not go well. I laid out a clean white cloth, tied a loose tourniquet and used my sharpest blade. I cut into the finger and sliced, back and forth, until blood was spurting across the table."

Hannah pressed her hands over her lips as though queasy. "Oh, my."

"I wrapped the bloody finger in the white cloth but it continued to bleed and I began to feel weak. A friend brought me to the hospital where a doctor stitched my finger."

"Did your boss hear about your hospital visit?"

"If he had not, I would not be here talking to you today. His forgiveness gave me a start toward gaining power."

Hannah put on her most flirtatious glance. "So now you are the pirate who controls an empire of hotels and casinos."

Tanaka blushed. "Not an empire, I'm afraid. At least not yet."

39

A CHAT BEFORE DINNER

As TANAKA and Hannah chatted over dinner, Krill served the grilled grouper with its heavy sprinkling of ground black rhino horn. Tanaka smiled knowingly, assured the secret ingredient would swell his manhood. Krill topped off their wine glasses and disappeared into the kitchen. When she was certain Tanaka was enraptured by Hannah's presence, she quietly approached the two bodyguards who were sitting in hardback chairs just outside the basement room where Hiraku was captive. She held out a tray with *fugu* and small bowls of soy and wasabi sauce and a bottle of sake with two glasses. The bodyguards kept their hands on their Uzi machine pistols and traded glances as they eyed Krill suspiciously. Krill plucked a slice from the tray with her fingers and swallowed it. The men eased their stance and curtly bowed as they accepted the tray but declined the sake.

Krill returned to the kitchen to serve the next course of fish soup and rice porridge. She left the door open and listened to Tanaka enthusiastically answering questions. She wondered if the man realized he was being pumped for information or whether his ego had clouded his senses. Tanaka had poured more wine. Krill thought she heard him slurring his words.

"The United States thinks their FBI and CIA are unstoppable, that they can go wherever and whenever they want without fear. Well, the yakuza have shown them differently."

"What do you mean? Who could possibly touch the CIA? In Argentina we have secret police, but only to keep order in our country."

"There was a rumor circulating only a few months ago that two CIA agents were killed by the yakuza in Tokyo."

"Was it true?"

"Who can say? Perhaps it was just a tale that others found worth repeating, the bragging of some *kobun* who drank too much sake."

"In the tale you were told, what were those agents doing that was so offensive?"

"Again, only rumor. I heard they were meddling in affairs that should not have concerned them," said Tanaka, his thoughts wandering back to the night the CIA officers were caught off guard. He could still hear the woman's screams as they boarded the speedboat tied to the darkened dock.

"Can you give me an example?"

"You ask a lot of questions," he said with a sparkle in his eyes. "Maybe that's what they were doing. Asking too many questions."

Hannah pretended she felt threatened, slightly parting her lips and opening her eyes widely. "I guess I should stop asking you questions. I don't want to end up like those CIA agents."

Tanaka chuckled. "No harm will ever come to you as long as you are a guest in my home."

Hannah smiled. "That's reassuring. I was starting to imagine you murdering people."

Tanaka guzzled his glass of champagne. "It would require good reason, such as violating the *bushido*."

"Have people done that? I mean, dishonored you or been disloyal?"

"Unfortunately, yes, it has happened."

"What did you do?"

Tanaka momentarily became lost in thought, the champagne coursing through his bloodstream. He gazed at Hannah as though contemplating how much he should tell her. He wanted her to know he was a killer, capable of taking a life at any moment, but the warning lights were going off in his head. *Be careful what you tell her. She may be beautiful, but she's a stranger.*

"When you are betrayed by close friends, that is the worst kind of disloyalty."

"And that's what happened?"

"Yes, on two occasions. One of the men was like a brother, and the other a trusted, longtime business associate."

"Did this happen when you first became a yakuza?"

"No. Those days were simpler. There was no need for killing because little offended me and I had nothing others would want to steal."

"These two people were thieves?"

"They took what was not theirs and it dishonored me in the eyes of those who hold much higher rank among the yakuza."

"So you felt shamed?"

"I was shamed and belittled."

"I'm sorry to hear that."

"If someone chooses to steal from our family, the consequences are unbendable. It is no longer a matter of *yubitsume*."

"But these two people are dead because you gave the order. That must weigh heavily on you."

"When you are a leader, that unpleasant task is something you must do yourself. It sets an example for others so that they fear you."

"And it's important that you be feared?"

Tanaka laughed heartily. "In my world, very much so. Many people fear me. One of my business partners stole millions from our enterprises. That was a very big mistake. He would have benefitted from some fear."

"Hotels and casinos?"

"You have a good memory."

Hannah carefully sipped her wine as Tanaka downed what remained in his glass and again poured both to the brim. "Thank you. My mother taught me to listen when people are speaking because it's the polite thing to do. But how did you find out he was stealing? Millions sounds like a lot of money."

"I became suspect over time because the profit margins began to decline, though the number of customers had not."

"I see. And you confronted him, I assume?"

"I did. At first he denied it, but under pressure he confessed."

"And that's when you killed him?"

Again the warning buzzers sounded inside Tanaka's brain. He clinked his champagne glass to Hannah's. "I didn't say that."

"And the man who was like a brother? What happened to him?"

"I'll save that story for another day. It might upset your stomach and we're about to enjoy a lovely dessert."

"And what might that be?"

"*Kakigori*. It may be 80 degrees outside, but here we serve shaved ice in many flavors. I hope you like pistachio."

40

SETTING THE PEACOCK FREE

SAIPAN

NORTHERN MARIANA ISLANDS

APRIL 1990

WHEN KRILL again checked on the bodyguards, they were slumped across the floor. One was already dead, an expression of anguish on his face. The other still had a pulse and was gasping for air, his eyes wide, legs pedaling on the cool turquoise tiles.

Krill found the key in the dead guard's pocket and unlocked the door. Hiraku was naked and tied face down to the four-poster bed with nylon webbing. She looked frightened. Multiple bruises marked her body but the beauty of her peacock tattoo could not be dismissed. Krill couldn't take her eyes off it. The peacock spread its wings across the young woman's back and draped over her shoulders. The feathers, each delicately etched, reached around her rib cage and spread upward to her small breasts. The overall effect made it seem as though Hiraku was a peacock, or at least partially so.

Krill sensed her fear. "Don't be scared. I'm here to help."

Hiraku wriggled helplessly. "Go away."

"I promised your uncle Yoshi that I would look out for you."

At the mention of Yoshi's name, Hiraku burst into tears.

"No time for crying. I need to tell you some very important things, but I only have a few minutes so you must listen carefully."

Hiraku stilled and nervously waited as Krill sliced away the webbing. "I don't know how much your uncle told you about the design of your tattoo, but it holds the secret to your future."

Hiraku seemed surprised and confused.

Krill quickly explained the tattoo had hidden within its intricate design a Swiss bank account number. More importantly, a chunk of the estimated ninety million dollars siphoned from the heroin-smuggling operation by Yoshi Yamamoto was in the account.

"It's all yours. He did this for you. He wanted Tanaka to pay for what he did to you on your eighteenth birthday."

Hiraku was stunned this stranger knew about such a private matter. "I don't want money. I want my uncle alive."

Krill helped Hiraku stand, albeit shakily, next to the bed. From a heap of discarded clothing in the corner she grabbed a bright red, off-the-shoulder blouse and a pair of olive green men's cargo shorts with roomy, bellowed thigh pockets. She cut a length of hemp rope for a belt and handed Hiraku the folding knife.

"Put this in your pocket and don't hesitate to use it if you have to."

Hiraku opened the knife and ran her fingers cautiously across the blade. "Hopefully that won't be necessary."

"But it might be. If you have to use it, think of your uncle. He was a good and brave man."

Tears trickled from Hiraku's eyes. "I know how he died."

"How did you find out?"

"The videotape. It's still in the projector on the table."

Krill popped the cassette out of the machine. "I'm very sorry that you've had to suffer. Tanaka was responsible for what happened to Yoshi and for Mikito Asaki as well. I'll do my best to make sure he pays for those deeds, but right now you need to get out of here. You need to run and hide. The woman having dinner upstairs with Tanaka will help you. I'm sure of it. Her name is Mariel Becker and she's staying at the Chalan Kanoa Beach Hotel, but don't go there immediately. Hide up north in the caves. Wait a couple of days. If you can't find her at the hotel, contact a detective named Hideyo Mashima at the police station in Garapan. Maybe he can help you."

"My uncle always said we should not go to the police with our problems. He didn't trust them."

"Well, your options could be limited, so let's just hope you can contact Mariel Becker."

Krill guided Hiraku along a corridor that led to an exterior door on the east wing of the house. "I know you're tired and groggy. But run and don't stop. When you can't run any farther, rest but keep out of sight."

Suddenly noticing Hiraku was barefoot, Krill slipped off her sandals. "Quick. Take these. I'll help you put them on."

Krill stuffed the videocassette into one of the front cargo pockets on Hiraku's shorts and a floppy computer disk in the other. She secured the flap buttons and set her hands gently on Hiraku's shoulders. "Don't lose these. You can bargain with them once you're safely away."

Hiraku hugged Krill tightly, holding on until she was pushed outside and the door closed behind her.

When Akumu awakened from her short nap, she cursed herself for such personal weakness. But after spending so much time interrogating and torturing Hiraku at all hours, she felt exhausted. She didn't want Tanaka to know she had needed rest but if nothing were amiss there would be no reason to mention it.

Akumu, her eyes still bleary from sleep, was startled to find her door locked and further secured on the outside by a slim wooden wedge. She pounded furiously, smashing a wooden chair against the doorknob until it broke off, but the door remain closed. Mustering her strength, she ran and flung herself against the door. She landed flat on her back. After another try, the door budged enough for her to slip out. Within seconds she realized Krill was missing and frantically began searching the main floor hallways. As she reached the bottom of the cellar stairs, she clutched the icepick in her waistband. Both of Tanaka's bodyguards lay dead or dying. The door to the room where Hiraku had been held was open but nobody was inside. Akumu instantly noticed the nylon webbing on the floor next to the bed, short lengths that had been cut.

One of the bodyguards was slightly alive and moaning but unable to speak. Akumu crouched next to him and shouted questions inches from his face.

"Where is the girl? Did Krill do this?"

It was obvious the man could barely breathe and would soon be dead. Akumu cursed in Japanese, kicked him in the ribs and ran back up the stairs.

Krill was standing beside Tanaka and poised as though about to remove the dishes from the table.

"Why are you barefoot?"

"I thought it would be quieter and less disturbing when I walk through the house."

Hannah smiled, thinking Tanaka's question odd, something only a control freak would ask. "That's very considerate of you."

Krill moved slightly until she was standing behind Tanaka. "I'll clear the plates if you're finished."

"*Hai.*"

Akumu burst into the dining room just as Krill raised her favorite Damascus-steel chef knife and pressed it against Tanaka's throat. She did a running dive onto the table, sending the dinnerware crashing to the floor. Krill hesitated, never having killed anyone, which allowed the stunned Tanaka to quickly rebound, clutching the knife by its razor-sharp blade and spattering blood from his fingers onto his dress shirt and the tablecloth.

Akumu yanked Krill by her spiked hair and pulled her to the floor. Hannah stood and lunged at Akumu in an attempt to break up the fight but it was too late. In a flash, Akumu had disarmed Krill, sending the chef knife skittering across the tiles. She unsheathed the icepick that was tucked into her waistband and jabbed it at Krill's chest like a short sword. Krill twisted her body, managing to evade the potentially fatal strike but screaming as the icepick found her right shoulder. Blood spurted onto Tanaka's face as the icepick was withdrawn.

Tanaka bellowed. "Stop. Enough. We'll get to the bottom of this." He touched his throat where the knife blade had momentarily rested to see if any blood had been drawn. His fingers were glossy red but he assumed it was from the wounds on his fingers.

Krill was already on her feet and turning toward where the chef knife lay on the floor. Akumu's face contorted into an evil smile as she spun with the agility of a practiced martial artist and with amazing speed plunged the icepick into Krill's chest, leaving the metal point buried to the hilt, the wood handle sticking up straight. Krill gasped and collapsed against Hannah, her electric-blue halter smeared with dark blood. Her startled eyes shifted toward Tanaka. When she spoke, her voice was little more than a whisper. "You may have killed Yoshi, but you will never find your money."

Hannah kneeled beside Krill and pressed a hand over what

she knew was a fatal puncture wound. "Krill. Stay with me. I'll call for help."

Akumu laughed so hard she bent at the waist.

Hannah sprang into action and kicked Akumu in the face, breaking her nose and toppling her to the floor. She followed up with two precise kicks to the woman's kidneys. She was about to rip the electrical cord off a table lamp and use it to bind Akumu's wrists when she felt a gun barrel pressed against her head.

"Those were very skillful kicks for a travel agent, Mariel Becker, though I presume that is not your real name. I'd like to know what truly brought you to Saipan. I'm sure Akumu would very much like the opportunity to help me find out."

Tanaka waited until Akumu got to her feet, wincing in pain, her face smeared with blood that trickled from her nose to her lips. "You'll live. Now get me a radio so that I can contact the guards outside."

Squeezing her nose with two fingers to halt the bleeding, Akumu limped toward the kitchen and returned with a hand-held two-way radio. She gave it to Tanaka, who continued to press the gun barrel against Hannah's head.

Akumu smirked at the sight of Hannah being held at gunpoint. She turned to Tanaka, who had raised the radio closer to his mouth. "You won't reach the guards downstairs. They're dead and the girl is gone."

Tanaka showed no expression. He pushed the radio transmit button and called the two bodyguards outside the house. Yuki, the kobun with the braided ponytail who had tossed Mikito Asaki's body off Banzai Cliff, responded instantly.

"Do you see the girl? She has escaped."

"Nothing, Tanaka-san. Nobody out here but me and Kira."

"Look around the property. She can't be far. Find her and bring her to me."

"*Hai.* Right away."

Hannah felt the gun barrel strike her head seconds before the room went dark. Akumu dragged her down the cellar stairs.

Hiraku had fled out the east door. She had no sense of direction or where to go, but she began to run as fast as her battered body would carry her. She raced along the edge of the cliff, dodging inland to the high grass whenever the trail became impassable or simply too frightening.

Reb picked out the red blouse through his spotting scope. He also saw two men who appeared to be shouting and chasing after her.

"Looks like the man in the lead has some speed. He's holding some sort of weapon in his right hand. There's also a second man who's carrying what looks like a machine pistol and having trouble keeping up."

Reb twice clicked the transmit button on his portable radio to signal Carrington. "Female exiting the house in a hurry. Through the east door. Two males in pursuit. At least one armed. Maybe both."

Carrington replied. "More description."

"Young. Twenties. Thin. Short dark hair. Maybe Japanese. Running but losing ground."

Mashima clenched his teeth. "May I use the radio?"

Carrington handed the detective the handheld. "That must be Hiraku, the niece of Yoshi Yamamoto. Can you see any tattoos on her body?"

Decker nudged Reb aside and squinted through the tripod-stabilized spotting scope. "Shoulder tat for sure but it looks like it may wrap around her back. It's some kind of bird, colorful, a peacock maybe."

Mashima's voice was filled with excitement and hope. "Yes. It's a peacock. That would be Hiraku. We're on our way."

"Looks like her company is catching up."

"How far?"

"One hundred meters and closing."

Decker's voice suddenly took on new urgency. "Two bursts just fired at the woman. But the shooters are too far away for an accurate aim. Looks more like a spray and pray."

Carrington grabbed the radio from Mashima. "If they start to close the distance and keep shooting, take them out!"

"Are you sure about that?"

"Absolutely. We have full authorization from Langley. We need to talk to that woman and we need her alive."

Decker rolled toward his rifle and rested its bi-pod on a mound of stone. He dialed in his scope while Reb rattled off the distance and elevation.

Reb peered through the spotting scope. He described the scene to Decker. The man with the braided ponytail was scampering over the rocks and underbrush like a gazelle.

"How far now?"

"Forty meters, maybe less. It's getting interesting. The woman with the peacock tattoo just fell. She's on the ground, rubbing her left arm. No, now she's trying to get up. She's on her knees. The target in the lead is closing fast. Thirty meters."

Decker sighted in on the slower of the two men. A lightning bolt tattoo gave his face a menacing look. The man was bringing up the rear, clumsily attempting to catch up to his agile companion. Decker calculated that shooting the slower man first might afford them a few precious seconds before the bodyguard in the lead realized what was happening.

He decided to check with Carrington one last time. He pushed the radio's transmit button. "Target engaged."

"Take him out."

It was a textbook headshot. The man went down a nanosecond after Decker pressed the trigger. The powerful rifle kicked when fired, momentarily forcing Decker's eyes away from the scope.

Decker looked at Reb for confirmation. Reb grinned and relayed the news to Carrington. "One down."

The second target proved more elusive, bobbing and weaving as though he knew he might be in a sniper's crosshairs, though Decker sensed the erratic running pattern was more likely due to the jagged terrain. The bodyguard's long braided ponytail swung wildly across his back as he ran. Decker was suddenly reminded of hunting with his uncle in the Pennsylvania hills, an activity he cherished every fall and early winter since he was old enough to carry a rifle.

When the bodyguard suddenly stopped and fired his machine pistol at the fleeing woman, Decker put a .50-cal. round through his skull, taking with it every bit of bone and flesh above the neck.

Reb pressed the transmit button. "Second target down."

Carrington acknowledged. "Received."

Mashima glanced at Carrington with a look that questioned the legality of the lethal shootings.

Carrington understood. "Say it, Mashima. Say what you're thinking."

"I'm a police officer, not CIA. I have an obligation to arrest those who have broken the law and ensure they receive a trial. I'm not both judge and jury."

"Would you have rather they caught up with the girl or maybe kept shooting until they killed her?"

Mashima didn't utter a word. He knew there was no right answer.

Decker peered through his riflescope, studying the terrain. He was trying to plot where he and Reb might intercept the young woman along her escape route. From what he could see, it appeared she didn't yet realize she no longer had any pursuers.

41

EVERYONE TO THE RESCUE

DECKER WAS PUFFING hard as he ran along the cliff-edge trail, followed closely by Reb who carried both rifles but was only slightly winded. Hiraku shrieked when the pair burst from the underbrush of tangan-tangan and banyan trees, sweaty and wild-eyed.

Decker held up a hand in a way he hoped she would recognize as a friendly command to stop. "Are you Hiraku?"

The young woman backed away from the soldier, whose full-grown black beard glistened in the sunlight. She teetered on the brink of the cliff, the ocean crashing into jagged rock hundreds of feet below, glancing over her shoulder as though considering a fatal escape option. "*Hai.* Yes. I am Hiraku."

"Please. Step this way. My name's Decker. This is Reb."

Decker considered extending a hand so that she might take

it and move away from the cliff edge, but there was always the chance she'd see it as a threat and leap to her death. Instead, he casually pointed a thumb at Reb. "We're here to help you, but first we need to know what's going on inside the house. Can you tell us what happened to the tall blonde American woman?"

Hiraku seemed confused. "I didn't see any such woman, only Krill. She's the one who helped me escape, though I fear she may be in great danger now."

"So you never saw a tall blonde woman?"

"No. I would remember if I had. I was locked in the cellar with no windows."

Carrington and Mashima were hustling along the trail. Reb shouted to them. "Over here to your left."

Just as Carrington and Mashima joined them, Hiraku sank to her knees in desperation, tears flooding her eyes, shoulders shaking with grief.

Reb crouched beside her and smiled. "I presume this is the girl you were looking for."

"Mashima grinned sheepishly. "Yes. This is Hiraku. A very brave young woman."

"Great. Now I'm going to find Hannah."

Decker snarled. "Stay here, Reb. Hannah is my responsibility. I'll find her."

Carrington set a hand on Hiraku's shoulder but she flinched. "Nobody is going to hurt you. Do you remember the two Americans — Stevens and Cahill – the ones you and your uncle spoke with in Tokyo?"

"They're dead."

"We don't know that for sure, but they were part of our team."

"Their bodies were fed to the sharks. That is how the yakuza work. The yakuza kill anyone who opposes them."

"You and your uncle gave Stevens and Cahill information

about how the yakuza are smuggling heroin through Saipan. Isn't that true?"

Hiraku stared at the ground as she spoke. "The American man and woman promised to take us to the United States if we provided information. We gave them many details but they wanted more. They were supposed to give us a new start in America, a new life away from the yakuza, away from Japan."

Carrington's face showed deep concern. "We'll still do that for you."

"I don't care about America. My uncle is dead. I'm alone and now the yakuza will find me."

"Your uncle's death was a great loss. From what we've been told, he was a masterful artist and a caring person who was trying to do the right thing. I can see you're very upset and I certainly understand why, but right now you have to tell us about what you saw inside in the house."

Hiraku shakily attempted to stand, her legs barely able to support her waifish body. Mashima gently braced her arms and spoke a few soothing words in Japanese that seemed to provide comfort.

"Did you see any guards?"

"Yes."

"How many?"

"Akumu is there. She is Tanaka's private servant and body-guard. The others are *kobun* — yakuza soldiers. Six or eight. Maybe more. When Krill came for me, two of the guards were on the floor outside the room where I was being held. I think they were dead."

Decker raised a fist in approval. "That's welcome news. Two more of Tanaka's bodyguards, the ones who were chasing you, are equally dead."

Hiraku seemed confused, as though she had been unaware of the latter threat. Mashima again spoke to Hiraku in Japanese, his voice little more than a whisper. He unveiled how the two bodyguards had been eliminated.

"I heard gun shots but I didn't know they were shooting at me."

Reb smiled at Hiraku as he patted the stock of his rifle so she would understand.

"*Domo arigato.* Thank you."

Reb smiled. "Our pleasure."

Mashima put an arm around Hiraku and she nestled her face into his shoulder, her eyes welled with tears. He continued talking almost intimately in Japanese and she responded likewise. Hiraku covered her face with both hands and wept.

Mashima shared what he had learned from their conversation. "It seems Krill stayed behind, perhaps to give Hiraku a better opportunity to escape. Krill pushed Hiraku out a side door and told her to run. When she looked back, the door was closed and Krill was gone."

Hiraku muffled a sob. "When he finds out what she has done, Tanaka will kill her. Or he will order Akumu to do it. Then he will come after me."

Mashima tightened his hold around her shoulder. "Nobody is going to hurt you. I can take her in my truck to the Susupe Jail, but I think it wiser to hide out in the caves until this matter is resolved."

Carrington tossed Mashima a two-way radio. "Stay in touch. Let me know your location when you get there."

"I will do that, but once we are inside the caves, the radios will be useless."

Hiraku's face paled at the mention of the caves. She had heard plenty of stories about ghosts and haunted underground chambers filled with dangerous monsters and spirits. She sometimes believed the tales of walking dead who roamed the island, their bodies made lifeless nearly four decades ago by the ravages of war. Some of the dead were Japanese soldiers, others Chamorro or Carolingian natives. What horrors had been done to them?

Mashima sensed her fear. "I've been in the caves. Even as a boy we explored them. There were no evil spirits, only rusting guns and bayonets, and an occasional unexploded round from the American battleships."

"I'll radio you when we arrive. If I don't get a response, I'll try again at midnight."

Decker checked the slide action on his Beretta 92FS handgun and grabbed his rifle. "Good enough, Mashima. Take good care of her."

Decker avoided looking directly at Reb and Carrington. "You guys can figure out things here. I'm going to Tanaka's house."

Reb picked up his rifle. "I'm going with you."

Carrington made a show of inspecting his weapons. "We'll all go to the house."

Decker pouted. "I'm going in alone."

Carrington was incensed by the insubordination. "In case you forget, this is a classified CIA operation and I'm the senior officer here. I'm telling you we're going in together – you, me, and Reb. We all want to rescue Hannah – nobody more than you or I."

Decker sneered. "Oh, I'm sure of that. But only because you're her field supervisor, right? Nothing personal."

42

GUESS WHO'S A GUEST?

SAIPAN

NORTHERN MARIANA ISLANDS

APRIL 1990

WHEN HANNAH REGAINED CONSCIOUSNESS, she was lashed with hemp rope to a hardback chair in the center of the room where Hiraku had been held captive. Her ankles were bound with duct tape. Akumu was standing near the door, an adhesive bandage affixed to her swollen nose. She scowled at Hannah.

"I need to use the bathroom."

"You can piss all over yourself for all I care."

Tanaka was eavesdropping from the cellar hallway. "Let her use the bathroom."

"I'm doing nothing for her unless it will be very painful."

Tanaka snarled. "Do as I say. Don't make me repeat myself."

Akumu grabbed a Japanese throwing knife from the array of torture implements on a small table and begrudgingly sliced the duct tape binding Hannah's legs. She immediately stepped back to stay out of range in case Hannah decided to try another kick.

Hannah sat uncomfortably on the toilet, hands still bound behind her back, while Akumu stood in the doorway, arms crossed over her chest, and stared with hatred in her eyes.

"Can you please close the door?"

"The door stays open."

When Hannah finished, Akumu ordered her to again sit in the chair. Hannah arched her back as she sat and inhaled as much air as possible, filling her chest cavity to maximum capacity as Akumu retied the hemp rope around her torso.

From her CIA training Hannah knew doing so would provide more wiggle room when she eventually exhaled and relaxed her body while trying to escape. Akumu added an additional rope around Hannah's neck, gleefully giving it a taunting tug, and again wrapped her ankles with duct tape.

"Akumu. Do not harm our guest. She will be coming with us and she must be in good condition to travel."

When Akumu failed to respond, Tanaka returned to the basement room and knocked her to the floor with an open-handed slap. Akumu didn't move as Tanaka spun on his heels and left the room without saying a word. Hannah heard Tanaka climb the stairs to the main level and wondered whether his departure was a sign for Akumu to begin her interrogation.

While waiting for what she sensed would be inevitable torture, Hannah tried to focus on how to escape, but her head throbbed from where Tanaka had struck her with the pistol and her vision was blurred.

Tanaka telephoned The Lucky Carp. Tony the bartender was chewing betel nut and spitting the shards into a rusted coffee can behind the bar, his teeth stained by the red juice. He begrudgingly got up from his seat and shuffled to the end of the bar to answer the phone.

Tanaka's voice was all business as he instructed Tony to take a detailed message. Tony assured Tanaka the information would be delivered personally. Tanaka then telephoned Blue Pacific Aviation, the private helicopter service that had covertly ferried Decker and Reb from Tinian Island to Saipan. The pilot seemed frightened that a yakuza underboss was requesting his services and insisting it was an emergency. When the pilot hesitated, Tanaka offered $50,000 cash.

"I need only a very short flight from my home to the airport. If you leave now you'll be back in your office within the hour, and $50,000 richer."

When the pilot didn't respond, Tanaka momentarily envisioned himself as Don Vito Corleone in *The Godfather* — one of his favorites movies — as he paraphrased the gangster's most famous line. "I'm making you a deal you can't refuse."

"I don't want trouble."

"There will be no trouble, Mr. Whirly Man. I merely want to climb aboard my jet and leave Saipan. Will you do that for me?"

The pilot unconvincingly vowed to land his helicopter on the roof of Tanaka's residence and fly the yakuza boss and two women passengers to the airport.

"You must come immediately."

"OK. But I need to check the fuel level before I take off. If it's down, I'll need to hit the pump."

"Check your fuel. I'll be waiting with your money."

When Tanaka hung up the phone, the trembling pilot sank into the chair behind his desk, lit a cigarette, and tried to ignore the ominous situation. He had no intention of flying his Bell 206 JetRanger to Tanaka's rescue and risking a jail term if found out. He imagined standing before the judge in Garapan and being charged with aiding and abetting a fugitive, presuming Tanaka was officially a wanted man. Nervous and jittery, he headed for the office door, planning to drive north into the mountains and hide out with an old friend who lived alone in a two-room shack, far off the main road. It would be an ideal hideaway until the present circumstances blew over. He was about to lock the office door behind him when two Japanese men dressed in black two-piece suits clamped his arms, walked him to a Nissan Pathfinder and roughly shoved him into the back seat.

The more talkative of the two — a pencil-thin man with unbridled energy and buck teeth — introduced himself as Sadashi and sat next to him as they sped toward the blue-and-white helicopter that was parked on the airport pad. Sadashi fidgeted in his seat, sniffing and wiping his runny nose on his suit jacket sleeve, his demeanor fueled by a heavy dose of crystal meth. "Mr. Tanaka is expecting you. I hope you were not planning to disappoint him. He wouldn't like that."

The pilot's face was sheen, the armpits of his Guns N' Roses t-shirt darkened by sweat. "I was going drive my truck to the helicopter. I didn't need a ride." He adjusted his faded Boston Red Sox cap and fished for his cigarettes in the side pocket of his cargo shorts. His hands were shaking as he attempted to touch the tip with his lighter.

The Nissan Pathfinder SUV came to an abrupt halt next to the helicopter. Sadashi was out of the vehicle in a flash. He flung open the pilot door on the aircraft and gestured with his hands. "Please get in."

"I need to make sure we have enough fuel before we take off."

"Make it quick. Mr. Tanaka is waiting."

The pilot slipped into the cockpit, toggled a few switches and studied the gauges. The turbine fired up and the two blades began to turn. "The fuel is good, as long as we're only going from here to Tanaka's home and back. Any farther and we'll be flying on fumes. You understand?"

Sadashi climbed into the front bucket seat next to the pilot. He rested a vintage Japanese Nambu pistol in his lap.

"You intending to use that?"

Sadashi laughed wildly, exposing the full extent of his rotted and brown-stained teeth. "Only if needed."

The pilot rolled his eyes, feeling both exasperation and fear. "Well, if you do, we're both dead. You hit the gas tank and this bird becomes a bomb in mid-air."

43

WAITING FOR A RIDE

SAIPAN

NORTHERN MARIANA ISLANDS

APRIL 1990

TANAKA PACED THE ROOF, gazing up at the endless blue sky dotted with puffy white clouds. It was a typical day in Saipan and good flying weather for his Gulfstream III jet, which he hoped by now was being refueled and readied for takeoff. He trusted Tony the bartender had delivered that message to the airport ground crew.

Twice Tanaka glanced at his wristwatch, cursing himself for such a weak show of impatience. The helicopter would be landing momentarily, preceded by the welcome *thwap thwap thwap* of its rotor blades slicing the air.

The first incoming gunshot rang out before the chopper arrived. The bullet zinged over Tanaka's head and struck the concrete wall upon which flowering vines made their home. It left behind a fist-sized hole. Tanaka instinctively flattened himself to the roof tiles and crawled toward the door leading to the house. His bodyguards flanked him, their eyes darting in all directions, expecting an attack.

Tanaka suspected something tragic had befallen Yuki and Kira because they had not answered his radio transmissions. The three bodyguards on the main floor of the house were on full alert, their Uzi machines pistols cradled and ready.

Once inside the house, Tanaka scurried to a small room on the main level. He slid open a hidden wall panel, turned two dials and studied the needle gauges showing power output. Satisfied, he switched on a series of electrical circuits and closed the panel.

An avid gun collector, Tanaka opened the wooden chest holding his prized World War II German MG42 machine gun, capable of spitting out 1,200 rounds per minute. American soldiers had nicknamed the weapon Hitler's Buzz Saw because of the sound it made and its lethal bursts of firepower.

Beneath the machine gun were belts of ammunition. Tanaka draped three belts over his shoulders, sagging under the weight. Although his bodyguards offered to carry the ammunition, he waved them aside. He hefted the gun and trudged toward the front of the house where a protective crenel allowed the gunner a field of fire without being exposed. He was pleased the gun position commanded the main approach to the house.

Despite Carrington's orders, Decker forged ahead at a pace that left the others behind. He passed by the headless body but barely gave it a thought, having seen dozens in his work as a sniper. A bit farther along the trail he came across the other yakuza soldier who had moved at a slower pace and met his death.

In his rush to be first to rescue Hannah, he ignored much of his special-ops and ranger training. Rather than avoid the well-worn route and instead cut through the underbrush, he hustled along the path leading directly to the house and was blown off his feet by a series of small explosive charges.

The blasts left him bewildered and unable to hear. He suddenly had difficulty breathing.

Carrington called out. "Decker. Can you move?"

There was no reply.

"Can you hear me?"

Again, no reply.

Reb handed his rifle to Carrington. "I'll get him."

Tanaka opened up with the machine gun, sending clumps of dirt flying just short of where Decker lay immobile. He was inexperienced with the gnarly weapon and had difficulty adjusting the aim.

Carrington spotted the crenel and the protruding machine gun barrel resting on its bi-pod. He fired several heavy rounds from Reb's .50-cal. sniper rifle that forced Tanaka to take cover. He figured they were mostly lucky shots because he had no sniper training.

Reb luckily spotted the electrified wire that was strung across a leafy tract and snaked into the underbrush. One touch and he'd be toast. He moved more carefully after that, staying off the lesser-used path as well, but it slowed his progress. More loud bursts from the machine gun forced him to pick up speed, knowing it was only a matter of time before one of the deadly rounds found Decker. He needed to get Decker off the trail. The soldier was on his back, legs flailing as though trying to run.

Reb took a deep breath and hustled toward him. A dozen or more rounds from the machine gun tore up the soil. He knew it would be game over if one of the bullets made contact with either of them. He grabbed Decker by the legs and dragged him off the trail, crashing through the underbrush and down an embankment until they reached adequate cover, the divots of churned up grass and packed soil raining upon them.

Decker moaned, thoroughly disoriented. Reb assessed him for wounds. Despite some bruises, lacerations and the obvious loss of hearing, Decker had emerged relatively unscathed. At least that's what it seemed until Reb saw Decker's eyes were barely reactive to the bright sunlight, the pupils no longer of equal size. A lump on the right side of his head suggested he had hit the ground hard after the impact of the blast.

"You need to stay right here," he said, exaggerating the shape of his mouth as he spoke, hoping Decker could read his lips and understand. "Me and Carrington will take out that machine gun."

Decker pushed him away and tried to stand but toppled to the ground. Reb recognized the effects of concussion and suspected Decker's eardrums were ruptured, his balance completely racked. "We'll come back for you. Just stay put."

Carrington heard the Blue Pacific helicopter buzzing toward the house but the dense foliage overhead made it near impossible to shoot at it. Reb made his way back to Carrington with an update on Decker's condition and suggested they leave him until the rescue was completed.

Carrington pursed his lips in concern as he handed Reb his rifle. "Let's see if we can make our way to the east entrance of the house and get through that side door."

Two *kobun* were guarding the steel entryway. The door was held ajar by a short length of lumber. One of the bodyguards was speaking into a hand-held radio, the other panning through the sights of what looked like an AR-15 assault rifle. Reb shot the armed man squarely in the forehead. The second *kobun* tossed his radio and scampered into the house, closing the door behind him. Seconds later, remotely-detonated C-4 claymore mines rigged in the trees turned the terrain into a hailstorm of deadly ball-bearing projectiles. Reb and Carrington flattened out, trying to make themselves into part of the ground until the explosions ceased. If the claymores had been positioned closer to the surface, both men would have been ripped to shreds. Apparently Tanaka had placed them more as a potential warning than a deadly deterrent.

Reb wormed his way toward a rock outcropping that could provide cover in case there were more surprises. Carrington was right behind him, Reb's boots in his face. They heard and then saw the blue-and-white helicopter approach the house and expertly make a sharp turn before lowering toward the flat rooftop.

44

FRANTIC FLIGHT

SAIPAN

NORTHERN MARIANA ISLANDS

APRIL 1990

WHEN THE SHOOTING QUIETED, Tanaka returned to the main floor of the house and shouted to Akumu.

"Bring the intriguing but ultimately disappointing Ms. Becker to the roof."

Hannah's hands were still lashed behind her back as Akumu nudged her up the stairs. She couldn't read the expression on Tanaka's face, but she sensed he was seething inside. Three of his bodyguards stood close by, their eyes fixed on Hannah as they braced for the helicopter's landing.

Tanaka felt like a fool for thinking the beautiful Argentine travel agent Mariel Becker actually had been interested in him intellectually and, more importantly, physically. Now he wanted to exact revenge and was imagining just how he might do it. One overriding thought swished through his mind: *The deceitful bitch deserves to suffer.*

The rotor wash from the helicopter as it nimbly set its skids down on the roof forced the three yakuza bodyguards to hold onto their black trilby hats. The pilot switched off the engine and the blades slowed and wobbled but continued to whirl dangerously.

Sadashi aimed his Nambu pistol at the pilot. "Get out, Mr. Whirly Man, but don't try to run."

"Where the fuck would I run to, you idiot?"

Sadashi moved the pistol closer. The pilot did as instructed, wary a stranger was about to fatally shoot him. Sadashi hustled out the opposite door and ducked as he ran around the front of the aircraft until he was standing beside the pilot, the pistol pressed into the man's back.

Tanaka scowled at him disapprovingly. "No need for that. This pilot is helping us. Give me the gun."

Sadashi hesitated but quickly bowed deeply and handed the pistol to Tanaka. He sensed any hesitation might be construed as insubordination, which would bring an end to his aspirations of becoming one of Tanaka's trusted yakuza soldiers. It might even translate to the loss of his head, or at very least a finger. Whirly Man seemed momentarily relieved, wiping his sweaty face on the sleeve of his t-shirt.

Tanaka set down the red zippered suitcase near the helicopter and smiled toothily at the pilot. "Thank you for coming. Your payment is enclosed."

Whirly Man bent and reached for the handle of the luggage but Tanaka stepped between them. "When we are safely back at the airport and I'm getting aboard my jet, you can count your money."

The pilot didn't argue. He simply looked disappointed, sensing he might never see the cash.

Tanaka barked at Akumu. "Bring Ms. Mariel Becker forward and put her in the rear of the helicopter."

Sadashi squeezed Hannah's arms hard enough to leave bruises as she was pushed into the aircraft's separate rear compartment and onto the three-passenger bench seat, her wrists still bound behind her.

Akumu watched closely. "Make sure you tie her ankles together. She's a troublesome bitch." She tossed Sadashi a length of twine, which he clumsily used to lash Hannah's ankles, never having learned to tie proper knots.

Hannah lay across the padded bench, attempting to right herself, twisting and turning in an effort to reach a kneeling position. Sadashi made no effort to assist her. He was mesmerized by the blue sundress hiked nearly to her waist and the show of elegant underwear. He attempted to join her on the bench but Akumu yanked him backward by one of his feet.

"My seat."

Sadashi bristled, confused by Akumu's pronouncement. He had already decided this was his seat in the rear of the helicopter, where he would guard the important prisoner. It was a place of honor, proof that the powerful Orochi "Big Snake" Tanaka valued and trusted him.

Tanaka maneuvered himself into the rear compartment and settled next to Hannah, purposely resting a hand high up on her bare left thigh as he helped adjust her on the bench seat. He let the struggle between Akumu and Sadashi play out. Akumu would not budge. She blocked the rear door. When Sadashi stepped forward once again, she head-butted him, kicked one of his shins and shoved him aside.

Sadashi knew he was beaten. He cocked his head toward the pilot. "After you, sir."

Whirly Man again seated himself at the controls with Sadashi beside him in the front passenger seat.

Akumu was about to take the seat on Hannah's opposite

flank when Tanaka's voice rang out from the compartment's open door. "Akumu! Bring me the suitcase. Now!"

Akumu had momentarily forgotten about the cash needed for the emergency flight. Ready to obey, she hoisted the red suitcase and pushed it toward Tanaka through the rear door. Suddenly she gasped, wide-eyed, as Tanaka fired two rounds from the Nambu pistol point blank into her chest. It was the price of overstepping her bounds.

Tanaka wrestled the suitcase from Akumu's dying clutches as she collapsed, a startled expression frozen on her face. The bodyguards seemed mystified but didn't move or speak. Sadashi smiled as though vindicated by some invisible *kami*.

Tanaka addressed the pilot. "Start your engine, Mr. Whirly Man, and fly as fast as you can."

The pilot nervously nodded. The turbine spat repeatedly before it fired. Seconds later, the twin rotor blades began turning slowly, forcing the bodyguards to move out of range. Once airborne, the helicopter ascended to two thousand feet.

Tanaka spoke into the microphone on his headset but received no reply from the pilot. Frustrated, he leaned forward and pounded the metal screen with his hands, trying to attract Whirly Man's attention.

The pilot flipped a toggle switch to connect Tanaka's headset and gave the OK sign with his right hand.

"Keep away from the land. I want to be over the ocean."

The helicopter immediately veered away from the towering cliffs. "Over the water we go."

Hannah squiggled in her seat. She shouted at Tanaka. "Can you please untie me?"

"And why would I do that?"

"Because there's nowhere I can go when we're thousands of feet off the ground."

Tanaka narrowed his eyes at Hannah who recognized the

dangerous intent. "I presume you are with the police, maybe even a member of the American task force that has been causing so much trouble on the island. So tell me, what is your real name?"

"Let me loose and we can talk."

"I think I like you better just the way you are."

"If you're going to keep my hands bound, can I at least have them in front of me?"

Tanaka roughly pushed her down on the bench, holding the Nambu pistol to her head as he slipped a set of plastic handcuffs over her right wrist. His strong grip held her left wrist until it was around her front and lay on her lap. He looped the second handcuff and pulled it so tight, Hannah cried out.

Tanaka smiled, pleased with himself. "My apologies. So sorry."

Hannah tried to push down on the fabric of her dress so that it covered more of her upper thighs, but the hem was short and unforgiving.

Tanaka ignored the dilemma and lovingly stroked her thighs, running his fingers to the rim of her underwear. Hannah pressed her legs together.

Tanaka was emboldened by her resistance. "I was hoping we could be friends, but apparently that was not in the cards. It seems I have drawn an unlucky hand — maybe 8-9-3. I'm over the limit."

"I don't know who you think I am. I confronted your servant Akumu after she murdered Krill, who seemed like a very decent woman. I would have done the same for anyone."

Tanaka roared. "Krill was a traitor. Another thief."

"I don't know anything about that. I do know she didn't deserve to die. She had a young daughter. Now what's going to happen to her?"

Tanaka shrugged to show his indifference.

Hannah puffed out a deep breath. "What did I do to offend you?"

"You're a liar," he bellowed. "Everything you have said and done since the first time I met you was a lie."

Tanaka unbuckled his seatbelt, turned toward Hannah and crawled atop her. He was convinced the black rhino powder was making him virile.

"Get off me!"

"Not until I get what I want."

Sadashi squirmed in the front seat, cursing the steel mesh that confined him to the front compartment and obscured his view. He was eager to witness his boss rape this beautiful Haole woman.

Hannah shrieked as Tanaka groped her breasts, squeezing them painfully. He pressed himself upon her, grabbed hold of her hair and held it down against the bench. When he tried kissing her neck and ears, Hannah bit him in the face, drawing blood from just beneath the left eye.

Furious, Tanaka hung his headset on a hook behind the pilot's seat, untied the twine holding Hannah's ankles together and pushed down his trousers. But he was unable to get an erection.

Hannah gambled a laugh. "Looks like some of your parts aren't working."

Tanaka grunted and punched her in the face. When she laughed again, he struck her repeatedly. He was completely unnerved. He climbed atop her, crushing her with his weight, and reached for the headset.

"Whirly Man. Do you hear me?"

"Yes."

"I want you to slow down."

"Why?"

"Because I said so."

The helicopter's forward speed dropped off as the pilot steered back toward the island. "Reducing air speed."

"Now hover."

"That will spend a lot of fuel, which we don't have."

"Just do it."

The helicopter slowed to a crawl. Tanaka flipped the latch on the rear door and tried to push it open. When he raised his body in an effort to reach the door and apply more pressure, Hannah used all of her strength to push him off.

Tanaka groaned as his body rolled on its side. He searched blindly for the Nambu pistol, clutching the barrel as Hannah kicked him repeatedly in the stomach and chest. With the pistol gripped and his finger on the trigger, he pointed at Hannah, but the angle was off, making any round fired potentially suicidal in the helicopter. She felt for the tiny razor blade that was hidden beneath the false silicone scar on her thigh, merely inches from where Tanaka's fingers had explored. Her fingernails dug at the edge of the raised scar until the razor was in her hand.

Tanaka wrapped her in a bear hug and began pulling her toward the open door. The wind that initially rushed into the compartment had diminished once the helicopter began to hover.

"*Sayonara*, Ms. Becker," he said, flashing his toothy smile and laughing madly as he nudged her closer to the open door.

Sadashi's had turned in his seat. His face was pressed hard against the steel mesh, his buck teeth snarled.

Hannah cut the plastic handcuffs and reached for the stainless-steel ballpoint pen tucked into the fabric of her dress. It was one of the items Carrington insisted she always carry. She wildly kicked her feet as Tanaka tried to tighten the bear hug.

Tanaka's rage increased. He again pointed the gun at Hannah who grabbed his wrist. The pistol fired, sending a bullet harmlessly out the door. Hannah slammed Tanaka's wrist until the pistol broke free and skittered beneath the pilot's seat. Tanaka released his bear hug, clamped his arms around her flailing legs and began dragging them toward the open door. Hannah stabbed him in the eye with the metal pen, pushing until the steel shaft was deeply embedded. Tanaka howled in pain, releasing his hold as his right hand went to cover the damaged eye. His headset tumbled onto the seat.

Sadashi shouted and banged the steel mesh with both hands.

Whirly Man didn't appreciate the shifting weight inside the small helicopter. "What the fuck is going on back there?"

Sadashi's voice was shrill. "She is trying to kill Tanaka-san. You must land immediately so that I can stop her."

Hannah slipped out from under Tanaka, braced herself against the bench and kicked his spine with both feet. Tanaka rolled toward the open door, unable to control the forward momentum. His head and shoulders banged against the doorframe, keeping him inside the compartment, but his legs went out into the slipstream. He held onto the doorframe with both hands, his one good eye filled with terror.

Hannah inched along on her stomach until they were face to face. She pulled the stainless steel pen from his eye and jammed it into his right hand, which lost its hold on the doorframe.

Tanaka was left hanging by one hand. Twice he attempted to bring the injured hand back on board but it was slippery with blood.

Whirly Man twisted in his seat, pounded the steel mesh and tapped a finger against his headset. Hannah understood. She put on the headset, keeping a close watch on Tanaka.

"Go ahead."

"If we don't break out of this hover and start moving forward, we're going to crash. And since we're over some very steep cliffs, this isn't very promising."

"You can move forward and reduce your altitude. That should save some fuel."

"Is everything all right back there?"

"Everything's fine."

"Doesn't sound like it. And all that movement is rocking the ship. Can you close and latch the rear door?"

"We're working on it."

The helicopter picked up speed and began its descent to 1,000 feet, following the rock ledges near Suicide Cliff. Hannah looked over at Tanaka. It appeared as though his lips had formed the word *please*, but she couldn't be sure because it was noisy in the compartment. Hannah fastened her seatbelt. She estimated nearly a minute elapsed before Tanaka's grip failed him.

Sadashi let out a wail of grief, unable to digest what he'd just witnessed. His face registered a mix of anger and fear. He reached for the switchblade in his front pocket.

Whirly Man set a course straight for the airport. Despite thousands of hours of flying time, he felt jittery at the controls, the fuel gauge causing a lump in his throat.

45

LZ HOT

SAIPAN

NORTHERN MARIANA ISLANDS

APRIL 1990

HANNAH SPOKE SOFTLY into the microphone. "Tanaka is gone. We can get all of this straightened out at the airport."

"I'm all for that, but I've got a very unhappy customer here who is poking me with a knife."

"What does he want you to do?"

"I'm not exactly sure. Apparently he's upset by whatever is happening back there. Maybe you can fill me in."

"Tanaka-san had to leave."

"What do you mean?"

"Let's just say he'll be on the ground long before we land."

Sadashi bellowed and wailed in Japanese as he repeatedly jabbed the switchblade into the steel mesh until the tip broke off.

Hannah spoke matter-of-factly into her microphone, instructing the pilot to hand his headset to Sadashi.

"Mr. Sadashi, do you hear me?"

Hannah saw him nod. It sounded as though he was whimpering.

"When we land, you're probably going to be charged with kidnapping – which is a federal crime — unless the police are offered a different story. If you want to save your ass, Mr. Sadashi, and not spend the rest of your days as a sex slave to some mass-murderer in a U.S. prison, put down that stupid knife and listen to me."

Sadashi momentarily felt a gush of fury, but it was soon replaced by an understanding that he was in no position to barter. "No more knife."

"That's good. Now you need to calm down. Tanaka is dead, unless he figured out how to grow wings before hitting the ground. As for you, except for waving your gun and knife at people, you haven't broken the law in a big way. So I suggest you keep your mouth shut when we touch down. Now give the headset back to the pilot."

Whirly Man wriggled the headset back on. "Did you two have a nice chat?"

"I think he understands the situation. Now let's get ready to land this bird."

46

CAVE DWELLERS

MASHIMA EXTENDED a hand and Hiraku groggily accepted it. He led her along a trail to where he had parked the police truck.

Hiraku was understandably distraught. She snuggled against the passenger cab door as they drove toward Marpi Point and the rugged, northern reaches of the island. She didn't say a word during the drive and Mashima respected her silence.

When they arrived, Mashima ditched the truck beneath a grove of mature tangan-tangan trees and chopped some fronds to help cover it. He didn't want anyone to know his whereabouts, not the yakuza or the CNMI Police Department. He was seriously contemplating leaving police work forever.

"Are you sure there are no ghosts?"

Mashima smiled warmly with his eyes. "No ghosts, Hiraku." He felt elated uttering her name aloud and liked the way the three syllables sounded as they left his lips. In some ways, it was a new feeling. It lightened his heart. Mashima's police career had consumed much of his life, and only a few key people had interfered or distracted him from it, until now.

"Bats?" Hiraku gripped Mashima's hand tightly, which filled him with joy.

"Maybe a few. But they'll be sleeping and we won't wake them."

"Snakes?"

"No snakes."

Hiraku made a whimpering sound. Mashima put an arm around her shoulders. He assumed they had much in common but never had been given opportunity to talk. He had researched the young woman's background as part of his police work, attempting to learn more about her connection to Tanaka. In doing so, he had found both he and she were native Saipanese, born within a few miles of each other, albeit nearly twenty years apart in age. Their fathers were Japanese who had married Chamorro women.

Separate life paths had taken them to Tokyo numerous times, he on police business and she with her Uncle Yoshi whenever they stayed at their small apartment in the city.

Mashima sensed Hiraku loved her uncle, just as he revered his parents who had left Saipan two years earlier for a new life on Japan's remote Hahajima Island. Family was important. And then there was the intriguing fact that, as far as he could ascertain, neither he nor Hiraku was bound to a romantic relationship or a particular religion. The police detective felt the path of his love life open wide.

Mashima slung a military-style canvas satchel over his shoulder and switched on the battery-operated spotlight as they entered the gaping Kalabera Cave. For nearly thirty feet, the limestone walls on both sides were covered with prehistoric drawings, mostly done in white pigment, which Mashima had been told was slaked lime. He had counted them as a boy. There were more than fifty cave art images. He shined the spotlight on one depicting a gecko lizard.

"No monsters. You see. Only a happy gecko."

Hiraku giggled, feeling light-hearted for the first time in weeks. She paused to study it and asked him to illuminate other parts of the wall, pointing enthusiastically to the different designs. Above and below the gecko were human figures, many of them headless. The figures were standing or in burial positions. A few were engaged in maritime activities such as paddling small boats or fishing.

Mashima purposely didn't mention what cave explorers had discovered in the 1920s. The interiors were littered ankle-deep with ash and bone. Countless skulls suggested the caves had been used as burial or cremation sites. The skulls and bones remained undisturbed until the 1940s when Japanese soldiers stumbled upon them. Japanese army engineers soon transformed many of the caves into defensive bunkers, storage facilities and a hospital, a process that increased in speed as the Battle of Saipan drew near.

"I have heard so many stories about these caves. Even my Uncle Yoshi stayed away from them, especially at night."

"What did you hear?"

Hiraku seemed momentarily embarrassed, as though her willingness to believe in superstition made her somehow less intelligent in Mashima's eyes.

"The caves in the north part of the island are haunted. People say voices can be heard coming from the caves, crying voices. The voices are filled with suffering and pain. Some are lost and trying to find their way."

"I don't hear them."

Hiraku playfully punched Mashima in the arm. "You think I'm simple."

Mashima clamped her arms gently and gazed into her eyes. "Not at all. Anything but simple. Complicated, yes. Not simple."

Hiraku avoided his eyes. "It's just creepy. I know Japanese families who still light candles on certain nights atop the cliffs. Old women come here and bow before the wooden markers, the ones with kanji messages written in black ink. They summon the *kami* and call to their dead sons, the ones taken by the war. So many Japanese soldiers were killed by the Americans."

"War is a horrible thing for all sides involved. Many American Marines also died here. I've met some of their families and they, too, feel the suffering."

Hiraku stepped backward, causing Mashima to release his hold on her arms. "Certainly. But being half Japanese, I can't help feeling sorry for our soldiers who died defending this island for the Emperor. I once heard my uncle talking about the flamethrowers used by the Marines. Fire was blown into caves filled with our soldiers who were hiding or had refused to surrender. I can only imagine the screaming. Perhaps it's these voices that are heard. The pain of their being burned to death."

Mashima crossed his arms, not knowing what else to do with them now that Hiraku had made it evident she wanted no embrace. "Thankfully neither of us was born yet when that tragedy unfolded. I hope we never see anything like it in our lifetimes."

"My school teachers often said 1944 was a very bad year in Japanese history because of the Battle of Saipan, followed quickly by 1945, which may rank as the worst."

"That's probably true. Until Hiroshima, no one had witnessed the horror of atomic warfare."

The cave narrowed as they walked. Mashima shined the spotlight on two flat stones that appeared to have been used as seats, perhaps by prehistoric cave dwellers. The stones were smoothed on the surface and flanked a larger monolith that, positioned as it was, might have been used as a table.

"Let's sit. I'll light a candle so that we don't waste the battery."

Mashima opened the satchel and pulled out a candle and a cigarette lighter. He lit the candle and set it on the stone table.

"I'll bet you're hungry. I have all sorts of treats."

Hiraku smiled. "You think of everything."

Mashima pulled a water canteen from the satchel and set it before Hiraku, along with a package of Pocky biscuit sticks.

Hiraku's eyes welled with tears.

"What's wrong?"

"Pocky biscuit sticks were my uncle's favorite."

"I didn't know. I'm so sorry. I would have brought along something else."

Hiraku opened the package and bit into one of the sticks. "Maybe this will bring him back to me, at least in spirit."

After eating two biscuits and drinking some water, Hiraku shivered. The cave interior temperature was in the mid-50s.

"I'm sorry I don't have a blanket or jacket to drape over your shoulders. I should have been more prepared."

"You've done more than enough. I could never have found my way here by myself."

"Hopefully we won't be here long. The American in charge seems very capable."

"I hope so, too. I want this whole thing to be over with."

"I know this has been an ordeal for you, but it would help immensely if you could tell me what you know about the heroin smuggling operation."

"I honestly don't know much. Sometimes I listened when my uncle would talk on the phone to Tanaka or Asaki. I realized they were using code words, but it was obvious the conversations were about drugs."

"Did they ever discuss how the heroin was being transported?"

"No. Not specifically. They would mention planes and once they talked about landing on Tinian. I think they also hired local fishermen in different locations, including here on Saipan, but I don't know who they were."

"Can you recall any names of places or people that might have been involved?"

"I heard them talk about Thailand, the Philippines, Hawaii, and a man who owns a warehouse in San Francisco, though I never heard his name. Sometimes I tried not to listen."

"Did your uncle have any close friends who might be still involved?"

"My uncle spent most of his days and nights overseeing the Lucky Carp, both the casino and the bar. He used to refer to it as the washing machine. And when he wasn't doing that, he was off to meet one of his tattoo customers."

"So he had no close friends?"

"I heard him mention Krill many times. I got the feeling Tanaka didn't like her, but I know my Uncle Yoshi thought she was a good person."

"Did Krill help you escape?

"Yes. I believe she poisoned the guards with *fugu*."

"Ah. Curse of the blowfish."

"When she came to free me, the guards were already dead or dying."

"Do you know what happened to her?"

"No. Only that she remained in the house as I fled. I thought she was planning to escape with me, but when I turned around to face her, she had already gone back inside and locked the door."

"And what about the blonde woman? Did you talk to her?"

"I never saw a blonde woman. Who would she be?"

"An associate of the three American men you met earlier today."

"I see. Is she CIA?"

"Yes."

"Can they bring me to America?

"For your sake, I pray they can. I'd like to go there myself."

Hiraku seemed puzzled by Mashima's words. "But your job and your life are here on Saipan."

"Though I'm sure it may seem that way, I'm far more drawn to a certain person who will soon be living in America."

"Who?"

"You."

Hiraku blushed, suddenly uncomfortable. "You are a kind man, and very brave. I hope we can be friends."

"Once this mess is over, the yakuza will come looking for me. They'll be angry that I helped you hide, and that I assisted the Americans in their investigation. Both the U.S. Justice Department and the CNMI authorities will also make my life miserable if they find out I allowed the CIA to kill two yakuza on my watch."

"You mean the bodyguards who were chasing me?"

"Yes. They were given no warning or chance to surrender."

"But they were trying to kill me."

"That's true, but my boss, Chief Napuna, may not see it that way. He has friends among the yakuza."

Hiraku gazed up at Mashima. Her eyes were glued to the left side of his face. "Tell me about your scar."

"Does it bother you?"

"Oh no. But I want to understand it, to know how it became part of you."

Mashima turned his head so that Hiraku could only see the right side of his face. "An explosion. We were investigating a suspected meth lab here on Saipan. We should have been more careful."

"What happened?"

"It was our own fault. We should have anticipated a booby trap, but we were young and eager to prove ourselves as police officers."

"A bomb?"

"Not exactly. Not with explosives. It was more like a shower and it burned our skin."

"So others were hurt as well?"

"Yes. Three of us. My injuries were the most serious."

Hiraku pressed a hand against his chest. "You're one of the bravest men I've ever known. You were very courageous to enter that drug lab."

"It was all a long time ago – fifteen years, maybe more."

"And now we're here, entering a cave to escape from yakuza who would prefer us both dead."

"Unfortunately they're more interested in you than me. They think you have information about their operations and would like nothing more than to prevent you from sharing it with the police or the CIA."

Hiraku suddenly remembered how Krill had been so emphatic about giving her a 3.5-inch square computer disk moments before they were separated. She reached into the pockets of the men's cargo shorts she was wearing. Her fingers found the folding knife and then the plastic disk.

"Krill gave me this. She stuffed it into my pocket at the very last moment before I left Tanaka's house and told me to be sure not to lose it, that it was very valuable and might be my ticket to a secret life in the United States."

Mashima held the floppy disk as though it was a rare diamond. He tucked the disk into his satchel.

"For safe keeping."

Hiraku didn't object. She feared the disk might fall from her baggy pockets if they were forced to run or climb.

"We won't know what's on the disk until we get access to a

computer, but I have the feeling it contains the information our CIA acquaintances are looking for."

Hiraku nodded. "At Tanaka's house everything was happening quickly, so we only had a few moments to talk, but Krill assured me the disk contains information about the drug smuggling. She told me there are bank account numbers, names and homeports of boats being used in the operation, the names of boat captains, though she doubted they were real. She even mentioned there is an old plane that they use regularly to bring the heroin to Saipan."

47

A DIFFICULT TOUCH DOWN

SAIPAN
NORTHERN MARIANA ISLANDS
APRIL 1990

UNABLE TO PENETRATE Tanaka's defenses, Carrington and Reb had rigged a makeshift stretcher and carried Decker more than a mile over rough terrain to their compact rental car. The explosion had left Decker disoriented and unable to walk without stumbling or falling.

Once at the car, they carefully settled him in the back seat before Carrington slipped behind the wheel and raced over the bumpy highway toward the airport, thinking mostly of Hannah and hoping she was still alive.

Inside the helicopter, Hannah swept her hands beneath the pilot's seat until she felt the Nambu pistol. When the aircraft landed, she was the first one out and quickly trained the gun on Sadashi.

"Get out!"

Sadashi's eyes widened. "Please, no!"

"I'm not going to shoot you unless you don't do what I say. Remember, you were only a passenger. Except for threatening people with a gun and knife, you didn't commit any crime. Understand?"

"You say I commit no crime. I will obey."

"Good. Now just shut up and put your hands over your head. There may be a dozen rifles pointed at you right now and it won't take much for one of those folks to open fire. Let's not give them a reason."

"*Hai.* Yes, yes, I agree. No reason to shoot. No shoot Sadashi."

Hannah drew a straight hand across her throat, a signal to the pilot to shut down the engine. She grabbed Sadashi by his shirt and pulled him out of the helicopter's front seat.

"Keep your head down or it might get lopped off!"

Sadashi bent at the waist and stayed close to Hannah. Whirly Man exited the helicopter as the blades slowed and drooped. He joined Hannah and Sadashi on the landing pad. "It's your show, lady."

"As I just explained to Sadashi here, don't do anything stupid because if it's interpreted as a threat, somebody we can't even see right now might decide to eliminate it."

The pilot paled. "What should I do?"

"Move slowly. Let's see if the reception committee is friendly."

The so-called committee quickly made its presence known. Lt. Lou Brick and government prosecutor Ray Donley were at the head of a detachment of CNMI police officers armed with shotguns and AR-15 assault rifles. Mashima was conspicuously absent.

The task force members fanned out as they approached the helicopter. Lt. Brick — in baggy cargo shorts, t-shirt and flip-flops — was moving rapidly, handgun at his side, barrel pointed downward.

"Nobody move! You, pilot, face down on the ground."

Lt. Brick waved his gun toward Sadashi. "You, too. Face down on the ground, hands behind your head."

The lieutenant turned to Hannah. "Please put that gun down."

"Gladly." Rather than simply toss it, Hannah slowly crouched until her hand was able to set the Nambu pistol on the tarmac.

Donley, overheated in his standard khaki trousers and polo shirt, caught up to Lt. Brick and the CNMI officers. "Where's Tanaka? What's that travel agent doing here? Why does she have a gun?"

Standing off to the side, FBI Special Agents Palmer and O'Reilly watched the operation, not interfering, but prepared to assert their jurisdiction and make arrests if the opportunity arose. As Palmer had previously put it, the powers in Washington were demanding a head on a stick, maybe two. The agents had received an anonymous tip that it might be worthwhile for them to be at the airport when the Blue Pacific Aviation helicopter touched down. They suddenly had reason to believe Tanaka would be aboard, providing them with a prime murder suspect who could face federal racketeering charges.

The pilot shouted from where he lay prone on the landing pad. "Why the fuck am I down here on the ground like some dog turd? I was forced to fly these monkeys. I didn't have a choice in the matter."

"You'll have a chance to explain. But right now, just shut up and cooperate," said Donley, who moved closer to the helicopter, Glock 17 pistol drawn and braced with two hands as he peeked into the rear compartment.

Hannah spoke flatly. "If you're looking for Mr. Tanaka, you can start at the bottom of Suicide Cliff."

Donley's jaw dropped open. "You can't be serious?"

"Dead serious. For a while I thought it was going to be me out the door. Unfortunately for Mr. Tanaka, it didn't turn out that way."

"Would you care to elaborate?"

A small Japanese sedan hummed and sputtered loudly as it raced across the runway toward the helicopter pad. The CNMI police trained their weapons on it. Donley also aimed his pistol at the approaching vehicle.

Lt. Brick excitedly held up a hand. "Guns down, gentlemen. It's a friendly."

Most of the police officers rested their rifles but a couple seemed reluctant. The lieutenant roared. "Weapons down. Now!"

Carrington slammed the car into park and rushed toward Hannah, hugging her joyfully. "You scared the shit out of us. I didn't know what had happened to you. We couldn't even confirm whether you were on the flight because we never made it inside Tanaka's house. By the way, where is he?"

Special Agent Palmer walked rapidly toward the small car and glared at Hannah. "Everybody here has been asking the same question. Where is Mr. Tanaka? It seems he is the one person tied to every bit of this case. The bureau needs to talk to him immediately."

Hannah cleared her throat loudly to get the agent's attention. "Unless you're some sort of clairvoyant, that's going to be tough. Tanaka is already mingling with his ancestors."

"What would you know about that? I thought you were some kind of beach resort consultant from Argentina."

"Let's just say both Tanaka and I got on that helicopter and only one of us got off."

Palmer kicked a small stone across the tarmac. "Are you saying you killed him?"

"Of course not."

"Everything you say can and will be used against you in a court of law."

Carrington ignored Palmer whose face was reddened with anger. "Oh, cut the crap, Palmer. She didn't kill anybody." He tightly wrapped his arms around Hannah and whispered into her ear but she stiffened and didn't smile.

Palmer kicked another stone. "Fuck. Fuck this case and fuck this place. We've got dead people all around and no idea who killed them, at least not for certain."

Carrington released Hannah, took a step backward and scanned her from head to toe. "I'm just glad you're alive and all in one piece."

"Me too," she said.

Reb had quietly joined them. "Me three," he quipped with a broad smile, so sincere it made him seem younger than his thirty-five years.

Hannah was glad to see him. "Why thank you, Mr. Reb."

Reb locked on Hannah with a fixed gaze. He was so relieved she was alive, he could've hugged her. "I was just getting to know you when you went and got yourself kidnapped. Don't do that again."

Hannah laughed. "I'll try my best."

"By the way, who gave you that shiner and the swollen lip?"

Hannah blushed. She hadn't looked in a mirror for what seemed like days. "Do I look like a raccoon?"

"Absolutely. But I've always had a soft spot for raccoons."

Carrington realized he hadn't paid attention to her facial bruises. He'd been more concerned about how Hannah's experience in the helicopter might affect their relationship. He shot Reb a look that in no uncertain terms said, *Screw off, Cowboy, she's my girl.*

Reb ignored the unspoken message. He cocked his head toward the parked sedan. "We've got a doc on the way for Decker."

Hannah's eyes swirled open. "Decker's in the car? Oh, god. Is he all right? What happened to him?" She began running toward the sedan. Reb caught up and grabbed her elbow.

"Easy. He's got a concussion. One of Tanaka's perimeter explosives went off and he caught the brunt of it. He was coming to find you when it happened."

Hannah flung open the rear door. Decker appeared unconscious but was merely asleep.

"He needs medical attention, now."

Reb flashed a smile of satisfaction because his Navy SEAL connections had brought rapid response from the offshore support ship. An MH-60 Seahawk helicopter was already airborne. "Navy bird on the way with two corpsmen aboard. There's a hospital ship stationed not far offshore," he said.

Hannah crawled inside the small car and latched her arms around Decker. "You crazy fool," she said, resting her head on his chest.

Special Agent Palmer, totally exasperated by the turn of events, focused his attention on Carrington. "Who the hell are you people? Will somebody please tell me what the fuck is going on here?"

Lt. Brick began shouting and pointing at Tanaka's Gulfstream III. The aircraft's twin Rolls-Royce Spey turbofan engines were running slightly above idle speed, suggesting the pilot was preparing for takeoff.

Lt. Brick's face was a mask of pure determination. "That plane is not going anywhere. I'll shoot the goddamn tires out myself if I have to."

Special Agent Palmer sensed he wouldn't get much information from Hannah, Carrington or Reb. Instead of pressing the matter, he decided to join the fray. He jogged toward the aircraft, yanking his handgun from its holster and waving it at the pilot in the cockpit. When the plane began moving forward he aimed at the front tires and fired three times. All three bullets bounced off and the plane continued on its path toward the runway.

The Saipan Airport was not equipped with an air traffic control tower. As a result, direct communication with the aircraft relied on radios equipped with a band that the police vehicles lacked. One fast-thinking CNMI officer drove a police truck onto the runway and attempted to park it in front of the jet but the pilot increased his speed and swerved around it.

While the commotion ensued, Hannah retrieved the zippered suitcase from Whirly Man's helicopter and began lugging it toward the sedan where Decker was sleeping.

Whirly Man was no longer face down on the tarmac. He had rolled and struggled to his knees, shouting at Hannah. "Where do you think you're going with that?"

"You didn't do what you were paid to do. You didn't deliver Tanaka safely to his jet."

"You bitch! Bring that suitcase over here."

The nearest CNMI police officer struck the pilot in the head with his rifle butt, sending him sprawling to the ground, bleeding. Hannah shrugged and continued walking, dragging the suitcase toward Carrington's rental car.

Special Agent O'Reilly had overheard the exchange. He flashed his FBI credentials. "Excuse me there, miss. Please set down the suitcase. I'd like to have a look inside."

Carrington rushed to Hannah's side. "That won't be necessary. Besides, you don't have a search warrant."

"I don't need one. Now get out of my way before I have you arrested."

The Gulfstream III engines grew louder. Reb looked at Carrington for instructions. "Are we stopping that plane from taking off?"

"Those were our orders from Langley."

"The other FBI guy already tried to shoot out the tires. It didn't work."

O'Reilly sneered at Reb. "Who the fuck are you?"

Carrington stood directly in front of the federal agent, eye to eye. "He's with me."

"Well, ain't that great. And I suppose he's another member of your Argentine tourism staff."

Carrington didn't reply. Reb chuckled to himself as he jogged back to the sedan and grabbed his sniper rifle from the trunk. With a round in the chamber he dropped down on one knee, aimed and fired at the Gulfstream's front tires. He followed with two more rounds into the same target area before turning his aim to the starboard tires. The bullets tore into the thick rubber but the plane kept moving. Reb was about to send more rounds into the landing gear on the port side of the aircraft when the damage he'd inflicted became apparent. Though the plane was still moving, its path was erratic and wobbly, the pilot having difficulty steering.

Hannah cast an admiring glance at Reb. "Man of action."

Reb replied with a courtly bow. "Just a southern boy with a rifle."

Carrington was unable to hide his jealousy. "Reb, why don't you accompany this federal agent and go interview the plane pilot? Maybe he can offer some insight into where they're headed and what's going on."

O'Reilly seemed hesitant. "I still want to see what's in the suitcase. And I want to know where that guy with the rifle came from and what he's doing here on Saipan."

"By the time that happens, your pilot will have gotten away. You might even find some valuable evidence aboard. You two can talk on the walk."

With a scowl on his face, O'Reilly stomped off toward the jet.

"Go with him," said Carrington, his tone more an order meant to show he was the senior officer and in command.

Hannah watched as Reb caught up with the FBI agent.

Whirly Man, his head still dripping blood onto his Guns N' Roses t-shirt, shouted at Hannah. "Fuck you, bitch. That's my cash. You have no right to it."

Carrington gripped Whirly Man by his t-shirt. The pilot immediately took a wild swing at Carrington who ducked and landed a hard punch to the man's solar plexus. Whirly Man doubled over in pain.

Carrington gripped the back of the pilot's neck and squeezed hard. "We need to set a few things straight," he said, walking him toward the rented sedan where Decker's boots protruded from the rear door.

48

GETTING THE STORY STRAIGHT

SAIPAN
NORTHERN MARIANA ISLANDS
APRIL 1990

THE NAVY MH-60 Seahawk helicopter powerfully set down on the runway, scattering litter and any other unsecured objects in all directions. Two corpsmen hustled toward Carrington who pointed urgently at the compact sedan where Decker lay asleep.

Hannah remained at Decker's side as the corpsmen carried him toward the helicopter's open door. She kissed him lightly on the lips as they raised him into the vibrating aircraft.

The crew chief waited impassively at the door. "Any more passengers?"

Hannah shouted back. "No. Decker is the only one. Please take good care of him."

"Will do. Tell Reb the team sends its regards. He's the best."

"I certainly will."

The crew chief gave the thumbs-up. "Now keep your head down. And get even with whoever did that to you," he shouted, touching a finger to his face and pointing back at her.

Hannah shielded her eyes as the heavy blades churned the air, blowing bits of loose coral as the aircraft lifted off. She realized her facial bruises were turning purplish blue, which made her want to shout out to the crew chief, '*Already took care of that*,' but she also knew the less said in these circumstances, the better.

Donley and Lt. Brick approached Hannah as soon as she turned away from the helicopter and began walking fast, hunched over, toward the others. Lt. Brick's voice was calm but stern. "Miss Becker, or whatever your name is, we need to talk to you about what went on during your flight from Mr. Tanaka's residence."

Carrington, sensing the possibility of complications among all agencies and military services involved, rushed to Hannah's side. "Hold everything. I need to speak with her first."

Donley frowned. "And why is that?"

"Because she works for me. We work for the same company."

"And by that I presume you mean the CIA."

"That's the company."

Lt. Brick clapped his hands once and the effect was noted. He wasn't pleased. "You have five minutes."

"That's all I'll need."

Carrington draped an arm around Hannah's shoulders and guided her to where they were out of the lieutenant's hearing range. "Tanaka's dead. No doubt about that. But if a story ever surfaced, suggesting a CIA officer tossed him out of a mile-high helicopter, it wouldn't play well in Japan where he was a well-known citizen. And it definitely wouldn't be a hit among the yakuza where he ranked as an esteemed boss."

"Got it, William. So what's the official story?"

Carrington brushed back his hair with both hands and sighed. "Listen carefully. I'm going to tell you exactly what happened aboard that helicopter, and we'll get that little fucker Sadashi to swear to it, along with our pilot friend, Mr. Whirly Man."

"I'm listening, William. We don't have much time."

Carrington began to weave his tale. "Tanaka was distraught. He was convinced his heroin empire was falling apart. For that and perhaps other reasons, he was suffering from severe depression. So when the helicopter passed over Suicide Cliff, it was emotionally too much for him. In a moment of pure despair, he jumped to his death in the same spot his parents had in 1944. *Banzai! Sayonara!* He joined his ancestors."

Hannah smiled. "Not bad, William. But what about Whirly Man? Do you really think he's going to keep his mouth shut?"

"If he wants to stay out of jail and ever see any of that $50,000 in the suitcase, he'll do exactly as we say. By the way, where's the suitcase?"

"In the trunk of your car."

Hannah repeated Carrington's version of the story to Donley and Lt. Brick, who listened skeptically. Carrington was busy making deals with Whirly Man and Sadashi. Upon weighing the alternatives, both men quickly agreed to verify Carrington's version of events. Sadashi sincerely requested that the official story make note of his valiant attempt to keep Tanaka from committing suicide, which would leave him in good standing with his yakuza associates. Carrington belly laughed at the notion, feeling like a screenwriter who has been asked to modify a character in mid-production. "Consider it done, Sadashi. You are now a hero."

Carrington contacted Ashwood on an encrypted telephone line and delivered the official report, including the details of Tanaka's death by suicide. He knew Ashwood didn't believe a word of it, but as deputy director of operations at Langley, a position that placed him under constant pressure, he'd be eager to announce in-house that one of the Pacific Rim's heroin smuggling kingpins had been eliminated, courtesy of the CIA.

While Carrington responded to Ashwood's concerns, Donley and Lt. Brick pressed their interrogation of Hannah. A hard-boiled police detective, Lt. Brick had a list of questions that he asked in varying ways, hoping to catch Hannah in a lie or conflicting statement as she reiterated what had happened to Tanaka aboard the helicopter. The poor man had committed suicide, plain and simple.

Hannah offered to provide Donley and Lt. Brick with off-the-record information about the deaths of Krill, Akumu, and Sgt. Torres, but nothing beyond that. She claimed to know zilch about the deaths of Yuki and Kira, the yakuza *kobun* whose bodies lay sprawled in the underbrush near Tanaka's rented home.

Lt. Brick fired off another round of questions at Hannah. Did she know both Yuki and Kira had been shot dead with a high-powered rifle, undoubtedly the type used by the military, not some rusting antique rifle like those often found among Mariana Islands farmers or in the caves near Marpi Point? Did she realize these were acts of murder?

"I don't know anything about them. But I can tell you for certain that Akumu killed Krill with an ice pick at Tanaka's house without blinking an eye. She obviously hated the woman."

Lt. Brick wanted more. "Why would she do that?"

"I believe she was jealous of the attention Tanaka paid to Krill."

"And what about Akumu? What happened to her?"

"Tanaka shot her as she was attempting to get into the helicopter on the roof of his home."

"And why did he do that?"

"In my opinion, because she didn't obey his every

command. Akumu had a mind of her own and it led to her demise. Tanaka is a control freak. I think Akumu pushed him past his limit."

"So what happened to our dear sergeant?"

"He apparently borrowed some money that didn't belong to him, but to Tanaka. Like a bloodhound, Akumu tracked him down and when he wasn't paying attention, stabbed him with her ice pick."

Lt. Brick pursed his lips. "That fits with the cause of death. He was stabbed multiple times. Did Akumu do all of Tanaka's wet work?"

"I don't know. She may have simply taken it upon herself to kill the sergeant, thinking Tanaka would be grateful. Are we finished?"

"Almost. I'm looking into the disappearance of Yoshi Yamamoto, a master tattoo artist respected throughout the region. He's part owner of The Lucky Carp and a known heroin smuggler."

Hannah's eyes widened. "I didn't know he was missing."

Donley stood beside the police truck and used the radio to call Joe Napuna, the CNMI police chief. The prosecutor asked him to request a government helicopter to search for Tanaka's body for the purposes of an autopsy.

The chief explained the department had no such resources, nor did he have the authority to requisition support aircraft on short notice. He suggested Donley contact Whirly Man at Pacific Blue Aviation. Donley groaned as he tossed the radio microphone into the truck cab and slammed the door. The prosecutor had been prepared to arrest Tanaka for the murder of Mikito Asaki and Yoshi Yamamoto. The written press release was folded in his back pocket.

49

UNDERGROUND ART

Saipan

Northern Mariana Islands

April 1990

Mashima stood at the mouth of the cave and attempted to raise Carrington on his two-way handheld radio every hour, knowing the maximum range was less than three miles and further strained by the mountainous terrain.

Each time, he waited patiently for Carrington's response, and when it failed to arrive he returned to the cave where Hiraku slept soundly, her head resting on the satchel.

Mashima gazed at her continuously, studying the sculpted lines of her face, the small hands angelically tucked beneath her head, and the exquisite peacock feather tattooed on her left foot. He noticed her toenails were painted bright pink.

The classically black hair he found so beautiful was disguised by streaks of paint – orange, blue, red, and an occasional white line. Mashima was amused by her sense of fashion and style, undoubtedly a reflection of the Hiraku deep inside, whatever it was she had experienced in her life. He yearned to know more about her.

Hiraku was still wearing the red off-the-shoulder blouse Krill had scavenged and the men's cargo shorts tethered to her waist and held up by a length of manila rope. It was cool in the cave so Mashima covered her with his shirt, allowing his hands to linger on her small breasts and bare shoulders as she slept deeply. He contemplated touching her between the legs but knew it would be difficult to explain should she unexpectedly awaken.

As soon as Hiraku opened her eyes she began talking, her words flowing like a fountain. It was as though she hadn't spoken in months and was eager to make up for lost time. The candle provided only a flicker of dim light as she unwound so Mashima moved closer to better see her face.

When the conversation turned to her uncle Yoshi, Hiraku's eyes welled with tears.

Mashima understood her pain. "Everyone between here and Japan knows him as a top master – the finest tattoo artist in the entire Pacific Rim."

Hiraku beamed at the description of her beloved uncle. "Maybe in the whole world. Let me show you something. You may use your spotlight, but only when I tell you."

Bathed in the half-light of the cave, Hiraku removed Mashima's shirt and tossed it to him. "That was very thoughtful of you, detective. Now you no longer need to be bare-chested. I'm warm enough."

Mashima caught the toss and broke into a smile, but he didn't slip the shirt on. He was overheated despite the chill cave temperature.

Without hesitation, Hiraku turned so that her back was facing Mashima. She allowed the red blouse to fall to the floor of the cave and spread her arms like angel wings.

"Now you can turn on your spotlight."

Mashima fumbled with the light but when it finally shone he was speechless. He marveled at the masterful tattoo that covered Hiraku's back, swept over her shoulders and down her arms, some of the design disappearing around the front where it covered her ribs and, though Mashima could not see, spread upward toward her small breasts. It was the most beautiful and intricate peacock he had ever seen.

"Magnificent," he said, feeling aroused as he pressed a hand over the growing bulge in his pants.

Hiraku grinned. "Very few have seen the whole tattoo, only bits and pieces on my arms and shoulders. I wanted you to see more because I can tell you appreciate such things and you have helped me so much."

"Your uncle's artistry lives through you every day."

"I believe it does. I feel his presence always. It took him countless days to create this tattoo. Every time he had a free moment he would ask me for permission to continue. I remember being bored and frustrated from sitting still for so long, but he politely insisted."

Mashima trained the spotlight on Hiraku's back and stepped closer to study the tattoo. "Absolutely perfect." He reached out to touch a koi carp with green scales and moustache of black barbels. Next to the fish was a fierce-looking dragon, its body coiled and ready to strike. Hiraku giggled at Mashima's touch and moved away slightly, but he continued to explore the designs with his spotlight and his fingers.

"So many numbers. It's as though they're floating in air. What do they mean?"

"Some are important dates. Also my birthday. My uncle's birthday. The age of my parents when they died. Good years, bad years."

"I see. And what of these longer numbers that run the length of the curving snake?"

"My uncle had a fascination with numbers. He was also an excellent mathematician. His fingers would fly over his abacus faster than an accountant can use an electronic calculator."

"The numbers must have some meaning. Didn't he ever explain them?"

"Many days I was so tired from having to stay completely still that I just didn't ask. He was an artist and I was his canvas. I thought it impolite to question him. It would be seen as disrespectful."

Hiraku pulled the red shirt back over her head. But the lightheartedness and pride she had briefly felt soon turned to tears.

"I fear Tanaka will take revenge on Krill once he finds out she allowed me to escape."

"That was not your decision. It was hers."

"True. But inside, I hurt at the thought of it."

"Why do you think she helped you?"

"Because she and my uncle Yoshi were close friends. Yoshi trusted her. My uncle often paid for her rent because she made such little money at the casino. He didn't want her doing anything she might later regret, just to earn some extra."

"Such as?"

"Lots of men, especially the Japanese, will pay handsomely to sleep with a haole girl. They are fascinated by straw-colored hair and blue eyes."

"You really think so?"

"You're Japanese. Haven't you ever felt that way?"

Mashima blushed. "No. Never. The Americans have a saying that blondes have more fun. But I prefer black hair and dark eyes, just like yours."

Hiraku brushed aside the personal comment. "Really? No blondes in your past or future? Maybe you don't like to have fun."

Mashima didn't seem to recognize the playfulness in the

young woman's voice and instead was put off. When he regained his composure he smiled ruefully. "Perhaps because I'm only half Japanese I don't have such feelings for haole girls."

"So it's only Japanese girls for you?"

"No. I also find the Chamorro girls attractive. Perhaps because I'm half Saipanese."

Hiraku laughed. "I'm only half Japanese. Who should I find attractive?"

Mashima grinned sheepishly. "Me, of course."

"You're too old for me. I'm twenty-one. How old are you, detective? Fifty?"

Mashima was put on the defensive. "Not yet forty."

"Ah. Then the perfect girl for you would be at least thirty."

"Maybe so. I haven't had much time to think about such matters. Too much police work."

"You mean like marriage and having a family."

"Yes."

"I wish I had a family. My uncle was my only family and I knew he thought it was an important part of a person's life. He treated Krill like family. He knew she was raising Starfish and often went hungry unless she was able to take home leftovers from the hotel kitchen."

"Starfish?"

"Krill's daughter, who now may have no one to look after her. She may be an orphan, like me."

"Krill must be a very private person. I was not aware she had a child. What happened to the girl's father?"

"Nothing. He was never in the picture — at least not for long. He was a wealthy tourist who claimed he was a British ex-pat. He told everyone he was fed up with his country, its government, and its cold and rainy weather. That's what he used to say. He spent a year here on the island, drinking mostly, surfing now and then, riding his motorcycle and spending his days at the beach. Krill fell in love with him. And she thought he loved her back. But when he learned she was pregnant, he left Saipan and never looked back. I hope he returned to his land of cold rain and died of pneumonia."

"That is a tragic story. I wish we were in a position to help Starfish, but unfortunately we are not. We need to leave this island as quickly as possible," he said, suddenly wrapping her in his arms.

"I know. And it makes me angry."

"Don't be angry. Be happy that we can start a new life together."

"We?"

"I thought we might go to America together and, well, be together."

Hiraku fell silent. After an awkward minute had passed, she attempted to wriggle from his embrace but he held firm.

"What are you doing? Mashima, please let me go."

Mashima's embrace tightened until it felt to Hiraku like she was being crushed. Though Hiraku twice shouted his name, thinking it might be the last sounds uttered before she died of suffocation, it was as though he hadn't heard her.

Sensing she was about to pass out, she screamed.

"HIDEYO. LET ME GO!" SHE FLAILED HER LEGS AND TRIED TO KICK him. Mashima released her and collapsed onto one of the stone seats, his chin resting against his chest, the faraway look in his eyes hidden by the low light of the cave.

Hiraku kneeled and gently brushed his hair with the back of her trembling hand. "Hideyo, I consider you a brave man, and a dependable one, but I'm not ready to enter a relationship. My life has been horrible these past months and I'm no good to anybody, including myself."

Mashima looked up, his eyes glassy. "I would devote myself to you. It would be an honor."

"Oh, Hideyo. I'm certain you would. But I'm not worthy of such devotion. I'm a wreck and incapable of returning such deep feelings."

Mashima felt the desperate chill of rejection. His throat was dry, his eyes blinking uncontrollably. Both of his hands felt cramped. He felt the fury rise up inside him like a beast fighting to break free.

"I see."

"Do you really? My parents are dead. My beloved uncle has been mercilessly murdered. I'm homeless. I'm being stalked by the yakuza, and my only hope of survival rests with people I barely know. It's not a time to think about romance or love."

Mashima cleared his throat. "How silly of me," he said, his mind enveloped in dark thoughts as he recalled the last woman who had rejected him.

As the top of the hour arrived, Mashima again attempted to contact Carrington. He was both elated and saddened when Carrington finally responded to his radio transmission. He knew then his time alone with Hiraku was coming to an end.

Carrington's voice was brimming with concern. "Are you safe?"

"For now, yes. Hiraku is resting."

"Give me your location so that we can bring you in."

"No need. We can come to you. I have a police vehicle. We can join you within the hour, maybe a bit longer."

"Not a good idea. People are already asking questions and looking for you and Hiraku."

"We're at Kalabera Cave. Lt. Brick knows its location."

"I don't want Brick involved. His organization plays by different rules than the one I work for, and right now, you need the one with the least number of rules."

Mashima felt like a pawn shared between the local police

and the CIA, but he understood only the latter organization could provide him with the level of freedom he sought.

When answering Carrington on the radio, his exasperation went unhidden. "If you want to know the way to Kalabera Cave, just ask at any market along the road to Marpi Point. The locals will give you directions."

"I'll do that. Stay put until we get there."

Mashima let out an odd burst of laughter. "I've nowhere else to go."

Nearly an hour passed, though it seemed only a few minutes to Mashima when his radio crackled again. The static voice was Carrington's and it was filled with urgency.

"We're outside the cave. We need to be at the departure point just after dark."

50

LET'S MAKE A DEAL

SAIPAN
NORTHERN MARIANA ISLANDS
APRIL 1990

REB TRAINED his sniper rifle on the mouth of the cave as Carrington stepped out from behind a tangan-tangan tree. Carrington clutched the Beretta 92FS handgun he'd taken from Decker's thigh holster before the Navy helicopter airlifted him from the Saipan airport.

Carrington again hailed Mashima on the radio and immediately received a response.

"We're coming out."

"Anybody else with you?"

"No. Only Hiraku."

"Do you know if anyone saw you enter the cave?"

"No. Nobody. You are the first people we have seen. I hid the truck under the trees to evade aerial surveillance."

Carrington moved forward. "Good thinking. Now come out and let's get the fuck out of here."

Mashima and Hiraku squeezed into the rear seat of the small rental car. Carrington sensed the tension between them as he settled himself behind the wheel while Reb rode shotgun.

"Everything all right with you two?"

"Oh, yes," Mashima answered quickly. "I think we are all a bit tired."

Reb flicked on his mini-flashlight and studied the map. Obyan Beach was south of the airport and fronted the waters of Saipan Channel.

THE CAPTAIN OF A U.S. NAVY STURGEON-CLASS SUBMARINE awaited orders to put the insertion team ashore. The submarine was modified to carry the SEAL Dry Deck Shelter behind its sail, fitted with a detachable hatch that allowed special ops teams to move between the sub and the mobile shelter.

When the orders finally came, the submersible shelter was launched with two six-member SEAL Special Warfare teams aboard, two rigid inflatable boats, and the shelter's operations crew. The thirty-foot-long pod sped in the dark toward the island to a point where it was possible to see the beach through night-vision binoculars.

The SEALs readied the two black, rubber boats. Just outside the reef they boarded the inflatables and made their final readiness checks, patiently waiting for the flash of a coded signal from the long strand of beach. The signal, which Carrington had assigned Hannah to arrange, was merely a backup plan in case of radio malfunction.

Carrington parked the car near a grove of flame trees. "This is it. I'll be escorting Hiraku to the departure point. She and I will then leave with the extraction team."

Mashima was surprised. "Only Hiraku? What about me?"

"My orders are to extract her."

"Didn't you tell your bosses that I was of great assistance? That my life is now in danger if I stay here on Saipan?"

Hiraku was visibly upset. "You must take him with you. The yakuza will kill him."

Carrington was in command mode, assessing, weighing options, thinking logistics. Bringing Mashima along might complicate the plan. It came down to weighing more risk versus potentially little reward. Besides, he wasn't certain how much room the SEAL teams would have in their boats. A lot of details were still in play and he wasn't about to overload them with an unnecessary passenger.

"Mashima, there's still work to be done here. Reb and Mariel will need your help. After that, we'll see what can be done to get you to the U.S."

Mashima's hopes were dashed. He felt betrayed but wasn't about to give up. "Why should I believe you? Once you're gone, once the others leave, I'll be fed to the wolves. Or, more likely, the sharks."

"Because I'm your best hope."

"And what if I'm your best hope?"

"What are you saying?"

"I'm saying it would be to your advantage take me with you. I have all the information your bosses seek about the drug trafficking."

Hiraku grabbed the satchel that hung from Mashima's shoulder. "It's true. It's all on the disk."

"What disk?"

"The floppy disk. The one Krill gave to me."

"You have it?"

"Yes. It's right here in this bag."

"And you've seen what's on it?"

"No."

"Then how do you know it's not blank?"

"Because it was Krill who put it in my pocket. She knew she was in great danger, but she hated Tanaka and this was her way of getting back at him. She was angry that he murdered my uncle Yoshi."

"Let me see the disk."

"No. You can see it when we are safe," she said.

Carrington roughly pulled on Hiraku's arm and attempted to wrestle the satchel from her grip. Mashima rushed toward Carrington but stopped abruptly when Reb put a pistol to his head.

Hiraku pressed the satchel to her chest. "Stop this! All of you!"

Carrington released his hold on the satchel and turned to Reb. "Go meet Mariel down on the beach and take Mashima with you, but let's be clear on one thing, me and the girl are the only people getting on the boat."

When Mashima again objected Carrington lost his temper. "Right now, my orders are to leave this island with her," he said, glancing at Hiraku. "Mashima, I'm sure if you cooperate with the government's investigation, that will be taken into consideration. You'll likely be called to testify."

Mashima blanched. His eyes welled with tears. "You are handing me a death sentence."

Carrington didn't answer. He stomped down the trail that wound around a Japanese concrete pillbox from World War II and led toward the darkened beach. Hannah was concealed in the brush when the others traipsed past.

"Over here."

Carrington held up a hand to halt those behind him. He crouched near Hannah. "Did you try the radio?"

"Yes. No go. I tried twice to raise the sub."

"What about the light?"

"No. I was waiting for you. Didn't want to give away my position until it was absolutely necessary."

"Let's give it a try."

Hannah flashed the light, using Morse code to signal the inbound SEAL team.

Minutes later they heard the whine and purr of an outboard engine and saw the silhouette of two rubber boats with SEALs aboard streaming through the surf. A light flashed from the closest inflatable. Hannah answered.

When the first boat nudged the sand three of the six SEALs bounded onto the beach and took up defensive positions. A fourth remained in control of the boat while the remaining two unloaded watertight equipment boxes and stacked them on the sand.

The second boat came alongside and it, too, pushed its way onto the sand. Once again, three SEALs leaped onto the beach, weapons ready to unleash a barrage of firepower. The fourth stayed at the helm while the last two passed additional watertight boxes of equipment to those ashore.

Hannah kept watch on their surroundings. Carrington was next to her, their shoulders touching. He wanted to wrap his arms around her and maybe even kiss her goodbye, but decided against it. Things had become awkward between them. Feeling unsettled, he gazed sadly at Hannah and simply said, "Be safe. I'll see you back at Langley."

Hannah avoided Carrington's eyes. She slipped the Glock pistol from its clip on her waist and pulled back the slide to make certain a round was already in the chamber.

Reb smiled. "I'll watch out for her."

Carrington felt those words like a gut punch but he didn't show it. He nodded to Reb. "Once you leave the beach, stay focused on the ship. You went through BUDS, so I know you're familiar with the equipment that's being unloaded. Might be an updated timer or modified fuse, but everything else is standard issue."

"How long do we have to make this happen?"

"No change in our orders since we last heard from Stu. As far as Langley is concerned, the quicker, the better."

Ignoring Mashima, Carrington reached for Hiraku's tiny wrist. "Let's go. We need to get you off this fucked-up island."

Hiraku didn't look back. She followed the SEALs who led them to the boats, instructed her and Carrington on where to sit for balance, and pushed the first of the bobbing crafts back into the surf. The second SEAL team helped carry the boxes of equipment to Carrington's rental car before following the return route in the darkness. The Dry Deck Shelter was waiting for them, positioned just offshore. Once the rubber boats were again safely inside the mobile shelter, the craft headed for the submarine where it reattached itself to the deck.

51

SPECIAL DELIVERY

WITH ALL THE equipment stashed in the trunk and back seat, the compact rental car was striking the hard coral whenever it took a road bump. The trunk and most of the rear passenger compartment were packed full. Mashima was barely visible since three of the boxes filled with C-4 were stacked on his lap.

Hannah drove from Obyan Beach to Chalan Kanoa and parked beside their hotel. It was still night so they unloaded the equipment, exhausted by the time the last box was brought inside. Hannah took the first watch while Reb inspected the gear.

The two sets of Draeger diving rebreathers, which gave off no telltale bubbles, were packed in cases alongside twin sets of fins, masks, wetsuits, knives, and waterproof spotlights. The other crates held timers, Limpet mines and C-4 explosive packaged to resemble heroin bricks. The bulky portable computer terminal, which would allow them to communicate via the ARPANET, was securely padded in a large suitcase.

Reb had become familiar with most of the equipment while undergoing his Basic Underwater Demolition (BUDS) training at the Navy's special warfare base in San Diego, California. The SEAL school was officially named Naval Amphibious Base Coronado where candidates conducted maneuvers in the surf along the infamous Silver Strand beach.

The SEALs on his team had blown plenty of concrete and metal structures to smithereens as part of their ocean and surf skills.

"Sure glad somebody at Langley was thinking ahead far enough to send us the Draegers," said Hannah. "We trained with these at The Farm, but I could use a refresher. Regulating the oxygen with the tri-mix gas was always a bit daunting."

Reb looked at her with warm and appreciative eyes. "I'll go over everything with you before we hit the water, especially the air supply monitor."

Mashima seemed overwhelmed by all the special equipment. "Won't the guards on the ship see your bubbles and start shooting?"

Reb explained. "We'll approach ship during daylight. Nobody will see our bubbles because there won't be any. But it's still going to be pitch dark once we're in the shadow of the hull."

Hannah picked up the two spotlights and tested them. The beams illuminated the hotel room walls. "Thank you, Langley."

"Amen," said Reb. "We need to set up a surveillance site from where we can watch the comings and goings aboard the freighter."

Mashima smiled for the first time in hours. "I'll talk to

Father Garcia. He's a friend who has no love for the yakuza and his church is across from Sugar Dock. I'll go see him first thing in the morning."

Reb nodded approval. "That's welcome news, Mashima."

"Perhaps your superiors will see the value and in appreciation ensure my passage to the United States."

"You know that sort of decision is above my pay grade, but I'll certainly put in a good word for you."

Mashima offered a slight bow. "Thank you."

"If your friend is agreeable and willing to take the risk, we'll offload this equipment at the church tomorrow evening once it's dark."

Hannah disappeared into the bathroom and quickly returned wearing a thin black wetsuit. She hoisted one of the Draeger rebreathers, slung it across her chest and cinched the straps. She also tried on the mask and fins.

Reb chuckled. "Looks like you're ready to go."

Over the next hour, Reb sorted the explosives and explained where and how the Limpets must be attached to the freighter's hull. He also showed Hannah how to set the fuse timers, emphasizing they would need to swim away from the area as quickly as possible.

"I'm excited that we're doing this together," she said. "Sorry, but with all that's been happening, I forgot to tell you the flight chief aboard the helo that airlifted Decker told me to give you his best. In fact, he said you're the best."

Reb guffawed. "I don't know about that. He was just talking like a brother SEAL."

"I guess that's why Stu didn't order an entire SEAL team."

"Believe me, it was discussed as a possibility, but Stu's bosses in DC didn't want to risk any political embarrassment in the event something went wrong. It might be looked upon as a hostile military action. The people here are already touchy about the presence of our fleet and the growing number of support ships in these waters."

"So it's just you and me."

"Just you and me." Reb held up an open palm and Hannah swatted it.

52

VICE GRIP

SAIPAN
NORTHERN MARIANA ISLANDS
APRIL 1990

MASHIMA KNOCKED on the door to the Blue Pacific Aviation office where he found a dazed Whirly Man half way through a bottle of tequila. The pilot was sorting through dozens of faded color photographs spread across a long wood table. The images were mostly of young American soldiers standing around olive-green Huey helicopters, smoking or brandishing their weapons, acting macho, with the jungle in the background.

Mashima's eyes locked on a small cluster of photos. One showed a crashed Huey helicopter badly twisted and burned, another a downed Huey medevac with a large red-and-white cross emblem painted on its hull.

The stub of a marijuana cigarette lay in the ashtray on the table. A bony stray cat was hunched over, gnawing on a half-eaten tuna sandwich. The animal didn't flinch as Mashima approached.

Whirly Man raised his head in a fog. "Well, well, if it isn't my favorite little Jap detective. Did you come to arrest me for flying your Jappo brothers yesterday? Aiding and abetting fugitives from justice? I guess you don't need to worry about Tanaka anymore."

"I would certainly like to hear from you what happened aboard your helicopter, at least the moments leading up to and those following Tanaka's death."

"What's to tell? You already heard it all from the girl, Mariel, or is her name Hannah?"

Whirly Man shakily poured himself three fingers of tequila in a smudged glass. He held up the bottle, offering it to Mashima.

"Thank you for your offer, but I'm on duty."

"Suit yourself. More for me."

"It appears you have already had quite a few."

"Any law against that?"

"Certainly not."

"Why do you give a fuck what happened to Tanaka? His death means one less scumbag on Saipan."

"If he was murdered, then yes, it's my responsibility to find out who did it."

Whirly Man laughed. "Ah, I forgot. You are Detective Mashima, seeker of truth."

"Can you share with me your version of events?"

Whirly Man sliced a wedge from a fresh lime, sipped his tequila and bit into the fruit, which puckered his lips. "It went down just like the spy girl said it did. Tanaka freaked out when we started flying over the cliffs near where his parents took the plunge back in '44. One minute he was there, and the next he had the door open."

"So you are telling me for the record that he jumped to his death?"

"That's what happened."

Mashima stepped toward the door and rested a hand on the knob, purposely pausing for effect. He slowly turned and glanced back at Whirly Man. "I don't believe you. I think he was pushed."

"Think what you want. I'm telling you the truth."

"Would you be willing to take a lie-detector test?"

"Go fuck yourself, Mashima."

Mashima returned to the police station in Garapan to make amends with Chief Napuna for failing to keep him in the loop about the American special ops team on his island.

The chief was sitting at his office desk in front of an oscillating fan, the breeze from which was disturbing the incident reports clutched between his fingers.

"What is it, detective? I'm very busy at the moment."

"May I come in?"

"Only if you can offer some explanation about what's going on. Asaki is dead. Tanaka is dead. His loyal servant and alleged assassin Akumu is dead. Krill, the Lucky Carp night manager, is dead. Sgt. Torres is dead. At least four of Tanaka's bodyguards are dead, maybe more. All these bodies are piled up on our little island, not to mention the Lover's Lane couple, a case that troubles me deeply yet remains unsolved. And let us not forget that Yoshi Yamamoto is still missing and presumed dead. Oh, and in case you hadn't heard, a well-known Japanese fashion model was raped in her room at the Hotel Nikko."

Mashima stood uneasily, shifting his weight from one foot to the other. He remained silent.

"What do you make of all this, detective? I get the distinct feeling you know a lot more than you are telling me."

"I've spoken to the Blue Pacific Aviation helicopter pilot. He tells the same story as the travel agent."

"I assume you are referring to Mariel Becker, or Hannah, or whoever she is? We called the Argentine company she supposedly represents and they confirmed she is in their employ, as is her male companion, who goes by the name Jake Marson. Suddenly neither she nor Mr. Marson can be found."

"I'm sorry to say I don't know where she is, nor do I know where Mr. Marson is at this very moment. Their hotel room is unoccupied and their rental car isn't parked nearby."

"Did you question the other man who was in the helicopter?"

"Yes. Mr. Sadashi. He believes, as does the pilot, that Mr. Tanaka took his own life due to personal stress."

"And where is Mr. Sadashi?

"He returned to Tanaka's house where he had been staying but did not want to remain overnight because the police teams were still gathering evidence and the scene was very bloody. Mr. Sadashi indicated he would get a hotel room. He was ordered not to leave the island, but he has not been charged with any crime. When we last talked, he was distressed that he was unable to act as a second after Tanaka decided to take his own life. If Tanaka had waited until they were back on the ground, Sadashi claims he would have ensured his boss a more merciful and honorable death.

The chief clasped his hands together and rested them atop the stack of reports. "So where were you when all this tragedy was unfolding?"

Mashima felt a chill wash over his body and again shifted his stance. "I was helping Hiraku, Yoshi Yamamoto's niece, who feared she would be killed by the yakuza."

"And why would she believe that?"

"She was being held captive by Tanaka and tortured. Tanaka learned she and her uncle had secretly met with the CIA. He wanted to know what she and her uncle had told them."

"And where is Hiraku now? Missing like the others?"

Mashima cleared his throat before speaking. "I believe she may be under Mr. Marson's protection."

Chief Napuna hissed with exasperation. "Are you saying you turned her over to the CIA?"

"Yes, chief."

"Please give me one good reason why."

"Because she has information about the drug smuggling that the yakuza do not want shared with law enforcement. Her life is in danger and I have no way to protect her."

"The two FBI agents were here this morning. They claim Mariel Becker told them some wild story about how Tanaka's associate, Akumu, killed Krill with an ice pick, only to be shot to death by Tanaka at his home."

"I believe that is the truth."

"They were also told Akumu murdered Sgt. Torres, but that she did it freelance and not under orders by Tanaka. Do you believe that, too, is the truth?"

"Yes, chief. The wounds were consistent with the story. But it was Tanaka and his bodyguards who murdered Asaki and threw his body into the surf before kidnapping and murdering Yoshi Yamamoto. Tanaka had a videotape of Yamamoto's horrible death. He was proud of it."

"And where might that videotape be now?"

"I believe Hiraku has it."

Chief Napuna buried his face in his hands. "You should have kept me informed as these events occurred. Instead, you left me in the dark and looking foolish, especially to the two FBI men."

Mashima bowed solemnly. "Please accept my apology. It was never my intention to shame you in any way."

"Get out! I can't bear to look at you. Maybe you can go do some real police work for a change. Knock on some doors. Find out who killed the couple on Lover's Lane. It's the sort of crime that leaves people feeling unsafe, and we don't want that here on Saipan."

Mashima stepped backward until he bumped against the office doorframe. Startled, he turned into the hallway and walked briskly to his truck.

53

CRUNCH TIME

Washington, D.C.
April 1990

Stu Ashwood was waiting at the safehouse a half-hour drive from Dulles International Airport when Carrington arrived with Hiraku. Both the CIA officer and his guest were jetlagged and moving lethargically.

Over the next two hours, Ashwood gently asked the young woman many questions, the session tempered by his constant reminder that time was of the essence.

"There are people in the field right now whose lives could be jeopardized if they don't receive some very important information within the next few hours."

"I understand the predicament," she said.

Carrington handed over the floppy disk and the videotape. The disk buzzed and whirred when inserted into the desktop computer. Eventually the monitor illuminated and displayed a lengthy series of notes.

Two casually-dressed men had listened quietly from where they leaned against a far wall in the soundproof room. Neither had been introduced. They were in their late twenties, maybe early thirties. As Ashwood slowly scrolled through the text, Carrington and the other two men gathered behind him.

Carrington had considered trying to open and read the disk while aboard the submarine, but Ashwood advised against it. Security was always a concern and since the sensitive situation was far from over, the deputy director didn't want to risk adding more variables.

Two separate files on the floppy disk were crudely-drawn maps.

Hiraku glanced at the computer screen and her eyes welled with tears. "I helped my uncle draw them."

The first map purportedly showed seaborne smuggling routes from Thailand to the United States. The second outlined aerial paths from the Philippines to Tinian Island. Other files listed identities or nicknames of those involved along the supply chain, boat names, the addresses of warehouses in Thailand, the Philippines and Hawaii, and specific docks used at key shipping ports.

Ashwood abruptly stood and offered his seat to one of the men copiously scribbling notes on a yellow legal pad. "I'll leave you two to analyze this intel. Put together a report and try to have it ready for me within the hour. I know that's lot to ask, but I'll need enough to justify our operation in case anyone over at National Security decides to start asking questions. The Defense Department is already in the loop because of the sub and the SEALs."

Ashwood slipped the videocassette into the VCR player perched on a table several feet away and, with arms folded and jaw locked, watched as Yoshi Yamamoto was eaten alive.

Hiraku had covered her eyes and was sobbing. "Please, I can't watch this."

Carrington set a hand on her shoulder but she continued to wail.

When the video ended, Ashwood pulled up a wheeled office chair next to Hiraku. "I didn't want to put you through this again, but I need direct confirmation that the victim is the man you refer to as your Uncle Yoshi."

Hiraku nodded, barely able to swallow.

Ashwood glanced at the two men studying the floppy disk. "For the record, gentlemen, note this woman has confirmed the identity of Yoshi Yamamoto in the videotape."

"Will do, sir."

Ashwood poured a glass of water from a pitcher on the table and offered it to Hiraku who drank it in a fast series of gulps. "You've provided a great service by working with our officers in Tokyo and now by handing over this information. Before you leave here, we'll begin the process of giving you a new identity and a new start here in America. But until then, we need to know more about your meetings with CIA Officers Stevens and Cahill. It's my job to find out who killed them."

Hiraku answered more questions about the secretive meetings. There had been five all together over approximately two years, or at least that was to the best of her recollection. The first had taken place in London when a man and woman had introduced themselves to her Uncle Yoshi in the dining room of the posh hotel where they were all staying. Hiraku recalled both were good looking in an American way.

Yoshi Yamamoto, the famed tattoo artist, routinely serviced a short list of wealthy clients in London who enjoyed a touch-up or enhancement to their tattoos. Hiraku initially assumed the two Americans were among them, though neither wore clothing that revealed any ink work. She remembered concentrating on her dessert of tiramisu at the hotel, and how she slowly devoured it with a small fork, feeling bored and distracted while the others talked about adult subjects.

"My uncle seemed nervous later that night, but I didn't ask him why. He drank a whole bottle of sake and read the newspapers long after I went to bed," she said. "And he didn't meditate, which is something he always did."

Approximately two months later, the same Americans showed up in Zurich, where Hiraku was celebrating her nineteenth birthday.

Carrington leaned forward in his chair. "Tell us more."

"I love that city. It was my first time in Zurich. My uncle took me shopping for clothes and to fancy restaurants. We had so much fun, except for the business meetings at the bank, which were very long and I had to sign my name too many times," she said. "We went back to Switzerland the following year when I turned twenty and again we saw the Americans. They were skiing at the same resort."

Hiraku smiled inwardly as she recalled their skiing lessons at St. Moritz in the Swiss Alps, she and Uncle Yoshi laughing uproariously as they tumbled down the slopes. She had felt like a celebrity. She wished he were still alive.

The final two meetings had taken place in Tokyo – one in a parking lot and the other along a darkened roadside near Narita Airport.

Ashwood was most interested in how the information about the meetings with Stevens and Cahill might have been leaked. *Did Hiraku and her uncle share with anyone their plan to permanently leave Tokyo and the world of the yakuza? Did they tell a close friend, believing their words would travel no farther? Did she mention it in passing to one of her girlfriends? Could someone at a supermarket, the beach, an automotive repair shop, or along the street have overheard her and her uncle talking about moving to America? A bartender, perhaps? A casino customer? An exotic dancer? A prostitute? Did Hiraku notice anything unusual during any of these meetings with the Americans, such as the same stranger turning up more than once?*

Ashwood wondered why the two seasoned CIA officers had not been more careful. Perhaps they had been, which meant whoever gave them up was an insider, someone they trusted.

Carrington recalled discussing the deaths of the two CIA officers with Mashima, who claimed that as a professional courtesy the homicide detectives in Tokyo had informed him that Stevens and Cahill were last seen driving a Chevrolet Blazer stolen from Narita Airport.

If Mashima's story was accurate, the Tokyo police learned about the stolen vehicle from a paid informant who saw what looked like a man and woman hot-wiring the ignition of the SUV and speeding away from the parking garage.

Ashwood had sent a forensic team to examine the vehicle days after it had been discovered dumped along a side street in the Ginza. No matching blood or fingerprints. But that was expected since the vehicle had been towed to a police pound. As a crime scene, the Chevrolet Blazer was as useless as they come. Yes, the ignition had been hot-wired, but that wasn't unusual in a case of car theft.

Ashwood constantly asked himself: *Could Stevens and Cahill still be alive? It wasn't unheard of for intelligence and security agencies like the CIA or the KGB to trade captive spies. If so, where were they being held? And how to find out?*

54

CHURCH SERVICE

Saipan
Northern Mariana Islands
April 1990

Father Garcia was administering confessions when Mashima entered the church, which, because of its diminutive size, in Europe or South America might be described as a chapel. Mashima got in line behind three parishioners — two old women clutching rosary beads and a middle-aged man with a wooden leg. When Mashima's time came to enter the veiled booth with its heavy curtains, the priest was surprised to see him.

"I'm sorry to say I'm not here to make a confession today, Father Garcia, though I'm sure there are plenty of sins that need cleansing. I'm here to ask for your help."

"Please go on, Hideyo."

"The freighter that is tied up at Sugar Dock, it's filled with heroin. Yakuza heroin. My friends from America are going to help me sink it. We just need a place to temporarily store our equipment until that happens. We can't leave it at their hotel."

"And you want to store these materials in the church?"

"Yes, father. I believe in this mission. If it's successful, it will send a message to the yakuza that Saipan is not a place where they can safely do business."

The priest was silent but Mashima could see his lips moving in prayer. Finally, he said, "How can I help?"

Mashima gave him the details and immediately returned to the Chalan Kanoa Beach Hotel where Hannah and Reb were relieved to learn they now had an available stash house, an observation post, and use of the church's white van.

Hannah grabbed her pistol off the dresser and tucked it into her belt. "We should move this gear to the church now." She slung one of the cumbersome Draeger rebreathers over her shoulder and marched out the door carrying her wetsuit, mask, fins and weight belt. Reb and Mashima followed with the second dive set, underwater lights and other equipment. They quickly returned for the heavy Limpet mines, which would be more buoyant once in the water, and finally the C-4 bricks and detonators. An hour later, everything was stacked and covered with a tarp in the church basement. Boxes of food from the upcoming weekly food pantry were piled atop the tarp along with a stack of folding chairs.

Mashima bowed to the others. "Time for me to sleep. I'll see you all in a few hours."

"I'm tired as well," said Father Garcia. "Time to save our strength. The next few days may be very exhausting." He turned to Hannah and Reb. "If you'd like, sleep in the small bedroom on the first floor. Not up to hotel standards, but surely better than sleeping on the floor. I'll leave fresh sheets for the bed."

After a flurry of thanks, Hannah grabbed two cold beers from the church refrigerator. She popped open both bottles with her SOG knife and handed one to Reb. "Let's go up to the tower."

Reb followed her up the stairs. They both leaned against the tower's waist-high cement wall and gazed out over the water.

"I never got to thank you for saving Decker."

"I didn't do it as a favor to you. I did it because he was in harm's way and I was in a position to do something about it."

Hannah took a long pull from the beer. "If that's the way you want to put it, that's fine with me. But whatever the reason, it was a brave move. Decker would have done the same if the situation had been reversed."

"What makes you say that?"

"He saved my life once in Boston. That's how we met."

"I get it. One of my SEAL brothers saved my ass in the desert. He nearly died doing it, but if it wasn't for him, I'd be decomposing in a sand dune right now."

Hannah swigged her beer. "I returned the favor to Decker in Cuba. So I guess he and I are even."

"Fair enough. I know it's none of my business, but it seems like some uneasy history exists between you and Decker and you and Carrington."

Hannah didn't answer immediately. She studied the countless stars. "It's complicated. Men can be such a pain in the ass."

"Frankly, I'm glad they're both out of the picture here. I don't want any of that to interfere with what we need to do. We've got to be clear headed."

"It wouldn't interfere."

"So what's the story with you and Decker?"

"Long over. Decker is married to the desert and the jungle and any other place where war is the theme of the day. Oddly, it's what keeps him alive."

"And what about Carrington?"

"William has been a great mentor. Taught me a lot from my very first day on the job. He's a brilliant analyst and strategist."

"Are you in love with him?"

"No. I respect him. I even admire him. He's a close friend."

"Decker told me you like to ride horses, drink wine, and spend hours in art museums looking at paintings that he finds confusing. Oh, and that you have a thing for turtles. I guess that's the sort of stuff you both did in Boston."

"For a while, yes, we did. We shared an apartment on the harbor and everything seemed right. But after the mission in Cuba nothing was ever the same. Decker was gone again. I cancelled the apartment lease and put everything in storage, not that there was anything either of us really want or need."

"You mean it got complicated, with Carrington?"

"Yes, that and other things. But I don't even know why I'm telling you all this. It doesn't really matter. We could die tomorrow. This mission sounds risky."

"Think of it as just a leisurely swim."

"Easy for you to say. You've probably spent more time in the water than most dolphins."

Reb laughed easily. "That could be true. But you don't need to worry. I'll be with you the whole time."

"You probably say that to all the girls."

"And what girls are those?"

"I'll bet you have ten girlfriends spread from Memphis to Madagascar."

"You have some seriously mistaken ideas about me. I like women. I won't deny that. But some day, I'd like a wife and kids. I think you know what I'm saying. A family. Sounds corny, but that's what I think about when I'm out there and people are trying to kill me. I think about getting back home to something that, ironically, doesn't even exist."

"It's not corny. I know exactly how you feel. I just haven't met the right guy. I'm 31, but I'm not tossing in the towel. Most of the girls I grew up with are already married with kids. So if I don't die trying to sink this ship, I'm going to move to Southern California and learn to surf."

"Well, I'm 35 and not ready to die. There are plenty of things I'd like to do before that happens."

Hannah extended an arm without looking over at Reb and clinked her beer bottle to his. "Nor am I. So tell me, Alabama boy, what is it you want? What's on your bucket list?"

"I'd like to spend some time in Africa, on a safari, only I'd be carrying a camera instead of a rifle. I'd like to visit Paris and drink lots of wine while sitting at a café table along the Seine. Italy, too. And Greece. What about you?"

"Argentina. Ever since I became Mariel Becker, the Argentine travel agent, I've been intrigued by Buenos Aires. It was part of my research before coming here. I love horses. I'd like to ride them in the Pampas and camp out with the cowboys. I was on my high school equestrian team, but my parents could never afford a horse."

"Well, if there's time before we leave, I can help you with the surfing part. I checked out the waves here. Not quite the challenge of Hawaii, but fun nonetheless. I can imagine a tent on the beach, three or four boards of different sizes planted upright in the sand, cold beers, juicy burgers on the grill, and a bonfire after sunset. Maybe even roasted marshmallows, though I've never liked them."

"Sounds perfect. I'll take you up on that. I'll even make the burgers and let you in on my dad's secret seasoning. Oh, and one more thing – I'd like to get a tattoo, maybe a small turtle."

A wise man in the Deep South once said to Reb, *how you treat a woman will determine the woman you see.* Hannah was a fighter and from what he'd seen and heard, a definite bad ass — serious-minded, someone who relishes being in control — but Reb sensed there was a softer side to her that could easily be light-hearted. He imagined she would be an amazing lover. The thought of it caught him off guard.

"What are you thinking about?"

Reb seemed suddenly embarrassed. He nervously rubbed his chin through his black beard. "You."

"Me? And what do you see?"

"Somebody who I like very much. A friend."

Reb was glad they had gotten to talk before heading out on the mission. They had been hyperaware of each other's presence, but unable to share a private moment.

Reb raised his beer bottle. "I'll have your back when we enter the water. We'll get in and out."

Hannah smiled. "And then you can teach me to surf."

Hannah awoke in the middle of the night, surprised to find her arms wrapped around Reb who was sleeping soundly. She studied his handsome face – wild black hair and beard, ruddy complexion, high cheekbones. She tried to push thoughts and fears about the mission out of her head, so she let her mind wander.

Why was it she always seemed to find herself entangled with complicated men like Decker and Carrington, rather than a seemingly straight-shooter like Reb? Would she ever be satisfied living a simple life with kids and a husband, instead of secret missions and special ops?

Looking at Reb, she laughed quietly to herself as she envisioned what their children could look like.

55

THAT SINKING FEELING

Saipan

Northern Mariana Islands

April 1990

Ashwood's analysts at Langley quickly recognized simple codes embedded in the text on the floppy disk. One note indicated a second yakuza-funded freighter was laden with unprocessed heroin and scheduled to sail from Thailand to the Philippines in late April, where its cargo would be transformed into white powder, loaded aboard a C-47 airplane and flown to Tinian. Carrington relayed the information to Hannah via the ARPANET along with the names of two Saipanese fishermen who were routinely helping the yakuza move the heroin from Tinian to Saipan for the next seaborne leg to Hawaii.

When Hannah shared the intel, Mashima's face flushed red with anger. "The Camacho brothers. They live near the village of San Roque but keep their boat moored near Sugar Dock."

"According to what's on the disk, these two guys are ferrying white powder from Tinian to the ship docked in Saipan," she said.

"That doesn't surprise me. They've been trouble since they were born. Let me see what I can find out."

Tano and Adai Camacho, both in their late twenties, had stopped by a roadside beer shack after a day of fishing and drank a couple of cold Budweisers. They'd caught three fat grouper, which lay in the bed of their pickup wrapped in palm fronds, and planned to cook them on the barbecue when they arrived home. The brothers were shocked to find Tano's wife naked, gagged, bound with heavy fishing line and seated atop the four-burner stove in their kitchen. Both immediately went for their knives, but Mashima stepped from the shadows holding a silencer-equipped pistol that was pointed directly at them.

"Put down your knives or you'll be dead in two seconds. I'm not in a good mood."

The brothers exchanged glances, trying to determine their next step. Tano's wife began wriggling wildly, threatening to topple off the stove. Before Tano could take a step, Mashima fired a bullet into the wall behind the stove, inches from the terrified woman's head.

"Next round goes between her big brown eyes. Now drop your knives and put your hands where I can see them. We've got some things to talk about."

Mashima stood beside the stove, pistol in one hand, cigarette lighter in the other. As a tease he turned on one of the stove's gas burners and, when it failed to ignite, flicked open the cap on the lighter. The woman went completely still, her eyes wide with terror. The brothers dropped their knives.

Mashima turned off the gas. He told the brothers they were suspected of international drug trafficking and the United States government had evidence to prove it. "If I arrest you right now, you'll spend the next twenty years in prison. The government will seize your boat and possibly your home. Your family will go hungry. I can only imagine what will happen to her," he said, cocking his head toward the stove. "Or, you can do what I say and avoid that unpleasant fate."

Tano spoke first, his voice hoarse from fear. "We're not the only ones helping."

"I never said you were."

"What do you want us to do?"

"I need you to carry some packages aboard the freighter when you return with the final load of heroin tomorrow."

"What's in them?"

"That's my business, not yours. You'll bring them aboard and pack them in the hold with the bricks of heroin."

"But the guards will know something is wrong. They carefully watch everything we do."

"No they won't. The packages will look no different than the heroin bricks. We'll get them to your boat an hour before you set out for Tinian. Besides, Tanaka and his closest associates are dead, including Akumu. Nobody is running the show — at least not yet. If you stumble into any difficulty, there's a man on board the ship named Sadashi who will help you."

The brothers appeared stunned by the news of Tanaka's death. "Why are you doing this?"

"Because the drugs you help the yakuza sell do a lot of damage."

"But we need the money," said the younger Camacho. "There are no jobs in Saipan. How will we live?"

"As far as I'm concerned, your days of drug smuggling are over. But to sweeten our agreement, you can keep whatever illegal profits you've already earned. Otherwise I'll bring in a team to dig up every inch of your property until we find out where your stash is buried."

The Camacho brothers agreed and Mashima moved toward the front door, never letting go the pistol. He gave them a satisfied smile. "Now you may use your knives. I believe this woman would appreciate being cut loose."

Hannah couldn't ignore the worry she felt after Mashima told them what he'd done, but she had to admit it was a better plan than relying solely on the Limpet mines, which would be magnetically-attached to the steel hull exterior below the water line. The Limpets would blast small holes into the hull but were not powerful enough to sink the ship.

Once the bundled bricks of C-4 were co-mingled with the heroin, the fishermen would tape triangle-shaped C-4 charges onto the ship's primary seawater intake pipes. The 12-inch-diameter pipes were deep in the ship's hold, located in the sea chest, an indentation in the hull where valves control the intake of seawater for firefighting or other purposes.

Before leaving the ship, the fishermen would uncoil the thin strand of antenna wire already attached to detonators in the shaped C-4 charges and leave it on deck or hanging over the side, wherever it would be least noticed.

Early the next morning, Hannah watched as the Camacho brothers chugged out of the harbor, their fishing boat running a bit heavy in the water. She ached from squatting and kneeling in the church tower from where she could watch the 260-foot cargo ship.

It was humid in the tower, forcing her to wear a kerchief headband to keep the sweat beads from running down her face. Reb smiled when he saw her.

"Hey, Rambo. Love the look."

"Wait until you've been here for a couple of hours before you start poking fun."

Reb was carrying a small tray on which two clear glasses filled to the brim were balanced. "Sorry. I'm just used to 110 in the shade," he said. "These are from Father Garcia. It's called Tuba. Some sort of traditional Filipino coconut wine made from the sap of a palm tree."

It had taken two hours for Reb, Mashima and the Cama-
chos to load the C-4 bricks into the fishing boat. Reb explained
how to attach the shaped charges on both sides of the seawater
intake pipes.

It was nearly nightfall when the brothers returned from
Tinian and began offloading their cargo onto the freighter. The
yakuza guards paid scant attention, choosing to smoke on the
foredeck while discussing the death of Tanaka and how it
might affect their future in the organization.

Even through night-vision binoculars, Hannah couldn't tell
whether the Comachos were following the plan. She merely
hoped the explosives had made it aboard. When the Cama-
chos' boat pulled away from the cargo ship, its waterline rode
high, indicating it carried no unusual extra weight.

56

THE BEST MADE PLANS

SAIPAN

NORTHERN MARIANA ISLANDS

APRIL 1990

WITH THE MISSION only hours away, Reb suggested they give their equipment a final check and get some much-needed sleep. Father Garcia promised to wake them an hour before dawn. The priest proved good to his word. He had two cups of steaming hot coffee waiting in the white church van. He dropped off Hannah and Reb with their dive gear and explosives along a palm-shaded stretch of beach approximately a half mile from Sugar Dock. He wished them luck, made the Sign of the Cross, and returned to the church to finish digging a hole at the rear of the property where the ground was softer.

At daybreak, a slight breeze rippled the surface of the water. Hannah and Reb made their way toward the freighter. The water was barely thirty feet deep. Reb was the stronger and more experienced swimmer, comfortable in the ocean day or night. He strapped on two Limpet mines with a special harness. Hannah forced herself to keep up, burdened by a single Limpet that created drag as she swam. But she was determined. Concentrating solely on swimming toward the ship, she momentarily lost sight of Reb and panicked. Reb swam to where she could easily see him. He gave the diver-OK sign, patting the top of his head, and Hannah returned it.

The tide was incoming and schools of fish raced in all directions. Hannah briefly marveled at the underwater wonders. The parrotfish looked like miniature moving rainbows. A giant green moray eel swirled along the sand bottom and hid behind an outcropping of boulder coral. Hannah was trying her hardest to relax and stamp out the nervousness pulsing through her body. She was about to point out a huge hawksbill turtle when the tiger shark appeared and began to circle.

Reb gulped. He hadn't brought along the bang stick. It didn't seem necessary and he was already carrying plenty of equipment. Now he wished he had.

Hannah stopped swimming. Her heart was pounding as she floated, arms and legs straight out like a big X, as though moving less might make her invisible. The shark came closer, brushing her wetsuit. Hannah felt the hard tail as it muscled against her ribs.

Reb had heard about tiger sharks but never encountered one. They were a dangerous species known to attack humans. This one was about ten feet long.

The shark made another pass at Hannah. Reb kicked his fins and put himself between Hannah and the shark. He held out his dive knife, but it felt like fighting an Abrams tank with a BB gun. The shark opened its mouth. The rows of teeth were frightening. They spelled death.

Reb grabbed hold of Hannah's left arm and together they began swimming. The shark seemed puzzled by the prey's change in shape. It circled behind them and darted ahead, as if playing a game. Reb braced for the worst just as a plump grouper swam into view. The shark struck it with ferocity, blood clouding the turquoise water. Hannah thought her heart would explode.

Reb swam faster, forcing Hannah to do the same. He needed to put some distance between them and the bleeding grouper. The ship lay dead ahead. Once beneath the hull, although it was daybreak, the sea was dark and they switched on their spotlights.

Just as they'd practiced at the hotel, they magnetically attached the Limpet mines to the hull below the waterline where the devices could not be seen from the ship deck. Reb double-checked his two mines on the starboard side. Both were secure. He set the mechanical fuse timers for ninety minutes, giving them plenty of time to escape to the beach. He swam beneath the hull to the port side where Hannah was struggling to affix the Limpet.

Reb could tell she was exhausted. He helped her press the mine against the metal hull until the magnets engaged. He set the timer and touched a finger to his wristwatch, giving a thumbs-up while extending his arm to show the route to the beach.

Hannah nodded. *Time to go.* Her legs ached with every kick of her fins, but she was filled with joy at not having been eaten by a tiger shark. And more so, that they had completed the most difficult part of the mission and were headed back to shore. She thought she might kiss the sand when they reached the beach.

On the deck of the cargo ship, one of the lookouts spotted a school of mahi mahi off the bow. He called to another guard, excitedly pointing out the dozens of fish swimming together.

"Dinner," he said in Japanese. "I'll be right back."

The man returned in less than two minutes, an unbridled smile on his face and a casting net in his hands. He reached into his pants pocket and pulled out a concussion grenade, an anti-swimmer weapon used by lookouts should they spot bubbles released by a diver or other suspicious activity.

Without hesitation he yanked the pin and hurled the grenade into the school of mahi mahi. The explosion rocked the surface, sending up a spray of saltwater and dead fish. He clapped wildly and tossed the net.

Below the surface, the grenade produced a large blast but little fragmentation. The sound — traveling about four times faster in water than in air — quickly reached Hannah and Reb. It hammered their sinuses and lungs, leaving them disoriented and gasping.

Reb recovered first, but sensed his ears and nose were bleeding. He feared Hannah was unconscious. She was no longer swimming. The inside of her mask was awash in blood. He detached the integrated weights on her rebreather and guided her to the surface, less than twenty feet above.

The tide was still incoming, the peak current pulsing through a break in the reef so that Reb and Hannah were carried toward the beach. Hannah was gasping for breath, her eyes wide with fear. She coughed mouthfuls of seawater as Reb towed her.

Father Garcia was pacing nervously when they reached the shore. He waded into the knee-deep water to assist because the divers were having trouble standing. "I heard the explosion. I thought maybe one of the mines went off accidentally. I feared the worst," he said, bending to pull off Hannah's fins.

Both Reb and Hannah were dazed. The sight of blood oozing from their ears and noses shocked the priest, who quickly helped remove their dive gear and lugged it to the van.

At the church he handed them blankets and dry clothing. Hannah collapsed on the bed. Father Garcia dabbed her nose and ears with gauze until the bleeding stopped.

Reb sat in a hardback chair and closed his eyes. He had an

intense headache. His eardrums felt like they'd been punctured, but he did his best to ignore the pain. The mission wasn't over. He watched as Father Garcia flung the dive equipment into the deep hole behind the church and began covering it with loose soil and palm fronds

Reb stood shakily. "Father, we need to go back to the beach."

"You need to rest."

Hannah appeared in the bedroom doorway, her hands braced against the frame. "I'm going with you."

Reb rushed to her side and put his arms around her. "You're in no shape to do anything right now."

"I'm fine. We don't have much time."

It was still early morning when the three Limpet mines detonated, sending birds squawking and flying in all directions. Hannah was standing behind a flame tree on the beach from where she could look across the water at the ship. She pressed the button on the radio transmitter, a toy-like device often used by hobbyists to fly model airplanes, setting off a daisy chain of powerful explosions. The rusting freighter heaved and buckled, its innards shredded by the blasts. With the seawater intake pipes severed, the hull slowly began to sink into the warm turquoise water, bubbles gushing from the sea chest and holes made by the Limpet mines.

Police and emergency vehicle sirens sounded along the waterfront. Hannah and Reb watched the chaos unfold as the local fire department arrived, but the ship, though still afloat, was already fully engulfed in flames.

"If my calculations were correct, it'll take about an hour, maybe a bit longer, before she goes to the bottom," Reb said. "With the fires burning on board, I doubt anybody will be rushing in to stop the leaks. If anything, the fire department will add more water."

Upon returning to the Chalan Kanoa Beach Hotel, Hannah

sent Carrington a terse mission update via the ARPANET. Carrington responded that a Navy helicopter would extract Reb from Tinian within the next twenty-four hours and fly him to a support ship. He instructed Hannah to reserve a seat on the next commercial flight leaving Saipan because it was risky to stay longer.

Reb hid in the church basement for the rest of the day while Hannah began packing her bags. The red light on the room phone was blinking. It was a message from Continental Airlines that her requested flight change had been approved and her seat upgraded to first class. Hannah sensed Carrington had made a few calls to the airline.

Hannah jotted down the flight information and continued packing. She found it odd that a pair of her lacy underwear was missing along with a designer bra and her new Manolo Blahnik pumps. She had been about to leave the chambermaid a twenty-dollar tip, but after discovering the theft decided against it.

Mashima showed up at the hotel an hour before Hannah's flight was scheduled to depart. "I'll accompany you to the airport. If anyone has questions, I'll be there to answer them, Miss Becker."

57

ANOTHER DAY IN PARADISE

SAIPAN
NORTHERN MARIANA ISLANDS
APRIL 1990

MASHIMA ESCORTED Hannah through Customs so nobody asked any questions when she showed her Argentine passport. He was worried it might not go smoothly since many of the CNMI police officers viewed him as a traitor in some respects for cooperating with the U.S. Anti-Drug Task Force.

Once at the gate, Mashima awkwardly hugged Hannah. "Maybe I'll see you in America, but under a different identity."

"That would be nice," she said politely, not certain whether the seemingly innocuous comment contained any hidden meaning. "I'll make sure my boss knows how much help you've provided. We couldn't have done it without you."

Mashima headed for the Blue Pacific Aviation office. Whirly Man was sober for a change, standing at a workbench with tools in both greasy hands, working on what looked like parts from a helicopter engine.

"What do you want now, Mashima?"

"Is your bird ready to fly?"

"Who's asking?"

"The same people who can return your suitcase with the $50,000 inside."

"What do they want this time?"

"A quick flight to Tinian tomorrow."

"And how do I get the money?"

"Cash. All $50,000 in the suitcase, delivered in advance. I can bring it here if you wish shortly before the flight."

"Who am I flying?"

"One of the men you brought here."

"Just one passenger?"

"Just one. Early morning. Six o'clock."

"I'll be waiting."

Mashima drove to the church to make one last pitch to Reb, knowing full well it was Carrington whose opinion would make the real difference in his immediate future.

"I'm sure you're eager to leave our little island," he said.

Reb grinned. "I wouldn't say that. It has kind of grown on me."

"I have some information regarding the two CIA agents who were last seen in Tokyo shortly after Christmas. My sources tell me new physical evidence has been uncovered."

"What sort of evidence?"

"I will gladly share everything, but first I need assurance that I will be placed in the witness-protection program."

"You know that's not something I can promise. The higher-ups at Langley make those decisions. I'm not even sure Carrington has the authority."

Mashima looked as though he was about to cry.

"I'm sorry, Mashima. Technically, since you were born in

Saipan, you're a U.S. citizen. You can move to any of the fifty states permanently if you wish. But putting you into witness protection is a different matter. It takes a lot of resources and requires a ton of paperwork."

"If I choose to live in Milwaukee or Los Angeles or New York, but I'm still Hideyo Mashima, the yakuza will find me. I need protection."

"It might help if you told me about this new evidence."

"That would require trust, and I've lost mine for the CIA. And by the way, I didn't just stop by to beg for my life. Your flight with Blue Pacific has been arranged for tomorrow. Whirly Man can fly you to Tinian, no questions asked, where I assume other forms of transportation will await you. He only asks that the suitcase containing his payment from Tanaka be delivered beforehand."

"I'll make sure to bring it. And thanks, Mashima. I wish things had worked out differently for you."

"Me too."

58

THE LANGLEY WAY

South China Sea
April 1990

Stu Ashwood was elated to learn the freighter at Sugar Dock was now underwater, its cargo of heroin all but dissolved by the salty sea. He immediately requested the Navy locate the second cargo ship, which was somewhere along the 1,300-mile smuggling route between Bangkok and Manila.

The analysts studying the floppy disk were convinced the rogue freighter was carrying one of the largest yakuza-controlled shipments of heroin in the criminal organization's history.

"Find that ship. It's somewhere between Thailand and the Philippines in the South China Sea," Ashwood barked at his staff. "Coordinate satellite coverage. Find out what vessels the Navy has in the region."

Upon receiving authorization through back channels at the

Pentagon, Ashwood sent a high-priority message to the captain of the Sturgeon-class fast-attack submarine prowling the Philippine Sea more than 1,200 miles west of Saipan Island. The submarine surfaced at pre-ordained intervals in order to use its antennae. *Change course for South China Sea. Await orders regarding second freighter target.*

Based on the submarine's current location, the order translated to a sea journey of approximately thirty-five hours, presuming the submarine could maintain its top speed of roughly 28 miles per hour. It required the submarine to pass south of Taiwan before entering the South China Sea to begin the hunt.

The submarine carried wire-guided Mk-48 torpedoes capable of sinking a fast-moving warship with little or no warning. It was merely a matter of locating the freighter and shooting it like a fish in a barrel.

Hannah meanwhile fanned through glossy magazines in the first-class cabin as she estimated the airliner's speed. She was eager to return to Langley and find out precisely what was happening with everyone involved. She was also looking forward to seeing Reb, disappointed that they both had to leave Saipan so abruptly.

A U.S. Navy P-3 Orion maritime surveillance aircraft — a four-engine, turboprop plane in service since the 1960s — located the rogue freighter two days later and transmitted its location. The submarine was already in the vicinity. The captain adjusted his course so that it intersected with the freighter. When the target was in range, the captain surfaced and prepared to fire a single Mk-48 torpedo. He soon received a second coded message from Langley: *Spruance-class guided-missile destroyer en route to assist with interdiction and boarding of freighter. Stand by.*

The captain was secretly relieved. He didn't embrace the

possibility of killing innocents among the freighter's merchant crew or sinking a ship without knowing more about its cargo.

Another message from Ashwood: *Surface and attempt to contact freighter. Fire single torpedo as a warning. Do not strike target. Repeat. Do not strike target.*

The freighter captain saw the torpedo spinning toward his ship, but he didn't slow down. He altered his course, knowing it was impossible to outrun the submarine, and uttered a brief prayer as the torpedo veered away.

If new orders arrived, the submarine commander would not redirect the next wire-guided torpedo. He'd send the freighter to the bottom.

The Navy destroyer captain didn't waste any time as his ship arrived at the intersection. He opened fire with both five-inch guns, sending warning shots across the freighter's bow. The freighter slowed to a crawl.

The heavily-armed boarding party encountered no resistance from the six yakuza and ten merchant crew. Within minutes, the first reports reached the captains of both the destroyer and the submarine. The cargo hold was overflowing with unprocessed heroin. The freighter captain, under arrest, confirmed his ship was bound for the Philippines. Beyond that, he refused comment.

Ashwood relayed the news to the CIA director who immediately apprised President Bush's top national security advisors. The interdiction by the U.S. Navy was heralded as a big win for America's war on drugs and a powerful gut punch to Japan's organized crime syndicates. It was up to President Bush's strategists to explain to the American people how such a victory had occurred in a Pacific Rim war with the Japanese that was never declared or publicized.

The freighter was escorted to the U.S. naval base at Subic Bay in the Philippines where a press conference was scheduled upon its arrival. Credit for the operation would be awarded to the Navy and to undisclosed intelligence sources that provided the smuggling-route information. No mention would be made of the CIA.

Hannah arrived in DC just as Ashwood's team was celebrating the success of the operation. She looked around the cozy Georgetown pub for Reb but he was nowhere in sight. Carrington spotted her walk in and graciously handed her a glass of champagne.

"As always, coming to my rescue," she said.

"Just glad you're back."

Carrington leaned in for a hug but Hannah's body went statue stiff. Although Carrington was her immediate superior, Hannah had turned the corner on their more intimate relationship.

"What about Decker and Reb?

Carrington coldly rattled off an update. "Decker left the naval hospital in Guam even though the doctors advised against it. No surprise there. From what I've heard, the Iraqis are about to invade Kuwait. I guess he wants to be there when the fireworks begin. He volunteered for one of the advance sniper teams."

"Sounds like Decker. And Reb?"

"Reb got picked up on Tinian by a Navy chopper. He spent a day aboard a support ship before he was ordered back to the Special Warfare Center in San Diego where he was being debriefed. We haven't heard from him since he left Saipan."

"Will he be rejoining his SEAL team?"

"I have no idea. The Navy brass only shares information when they're good and ready. Until then, we're in the dark."

The following day, Hannah repeatedly checked her phone for messages between debriefings at Langley, hoping Reb would reach out. But she received no word.

Her spirits were momentarily buoyed when Ashwood

tossed a designer box on her desk. Inside was a green kimono. "As promised," he said.

Hannah held up the elegant kimono and let the high-quality silk slip through her fingers. "It's absolutely beautiful. You obviously have very fine taste and I'll treasure it. It'll be a reminder of this mission, though there were a few moments I'd like to forget."

Hannah asked whether Hiraku was already enrolled in the protection program.

"Not yet. She has some business to take care of in Switzerland first, and we're assisting her with that. I think she'll be just fine."

"I was just thinking about Krill, the casino night manager at The Lucky Carp. I'd probably be dead if it wasn't for her. She took out two bodyguards with her pufferfish recipe, but Tanaka's crazy-ass servant killed her for it. Krill has a young daughter named Starfish. She must be heartbroken. I'd like to adopt her."

Ashwood arched his eyebrows. "That might be rather tough, considering your job responsibilities."

"I could resign."

"I don't think that would be such a great idea."

"But what will happen to Starfish?"

"When Hiraku's business in Zurich has been concluded, there will be plenty of money for the little girl's care and education. Starfish will have an endowment fund. She'll be set for life."

Hannah smiled appreciatively. "Thanks for making that happen."

"I didn't do anything. Her uncle made it happen. He was prepared. The Swiss bank account already had been opened by his niece, though I doubt she understood why at the time or just how flush it was."

"And how flush was it?"

"Just over four million."

"Now that's what I call an endowment fund."

"Once the funds have been transferred into a custodial account, a portion of it will be made available to Hiraku under her new identify, courtesy of Uncle Sam."

"She should be happy about that."

"There's more. A second Swiss account opened by Yoshi Yamamoto contains well over $50 million. It's set up as a trust for orphans abandoned by their parents and living in institutions throughout Japan. It appears he had a righteous soul."

"What happens to that account?"

"It'll likely be fought over by certain people in our national security agencies with plenty of input from INTERPOL and, of course, the bank."

"Do you think Hiraku will be allowed to keep the four million?"

"My guess is, she'll walk away with half of it. Krill's daughter will also benefit from the same account."

"And what's in my future?"

"That depends on you."

"I want to get back to work."

Ashwood grinned approvingly. "When you're fully rested, you'll head back to Tokyo and try to find out what happened to Stevens and Cahill. We received a tip from a police officer on Saipan that could be worth following up. His last name is Mashima. Perhaps you know him."

"Tokyo, here I come," Hannah said cheerfully, gently fist-pumping the air but choosing not to mention her familiarity with Mashima.

Returning to the CIA-owned apartment where she was temporarily staying in DC, Hannah discovered a small package wrapped in dull brown paper mixed in with her mail that had been forwarded. It was the size of a cigarette pack and bore no return address. She carefully tore away the paper and opened the lid. It was a silver necklace adorned with a single tiger shark tooth. She felt a rush of excitement pass through her body, knowing Reb hadn't forgotten about her, but deep inside she was already looking forward to the next mission. She'd find out who killed Stevens and Cahill, and maybe even get some payback.

59

PICKING UP THE PIECES

Saipan

Northern Mariana Islands

April 1990

Lt. Lou Brick spoke at length with CNMI Police Chief Joe Napuna and the local fire chief about what they believed caused the explosion aboard the ship that left five dead – two merchant crew and three yakuza. Two more crew were still unaccounted for but presumed lost.

Both chiefs blamed the blast and subsequent fire on shoddy maintenance and unsafe cargo materials. As Chief Napuna told the news reporters who arrived with cameras and notepads, spontaneous combustion aboard freighters past their prime was not a far-fetched theory. "We have an arson investigator arriving from Guam to assist. If it has not been destroyed, we hope to examine the ship's manifest to learn what dangerous materials were aboard."

Brick didn't buy the theory, but he really didn't care. What mattered most was the destruction of the white powder, which was no longer marketable. That was a victory.

A trio of high-ranking yakuza arrived on Saipan a week after the sinking and headed directly to The Lucky Carp.

Tony was stacking cases of beer behind the bar when they brashly burst through the front door. Sadashi was seated behind a desk in what had been Yoshi Yamamoto's small office, busily reviewing invoices for food and alcohol supplies. He spotted them through the open door and scurried to the front entrance, bowing deeply and launching into a flurry of explanations and apologies. The new visitors, silent partners in the casino resort, had already heard the story of how Sadashi attempted to prevent Tanaka from leaping out of the helicopter. They praised him for his efforts and his loyalty.

Following a ceremonial toast with sake, the yakuza bosses informed Sadashi he would be in charge of The Lucky Carp and its related enterprises, at least temporarily, until a vote was taken in Tokyo and a permanent manager appointed.

Sadashi told them he was short on casino staff because the longtime night manager was dead. He sadly relayed how Akumu had killed Krill in a fit of rage, only to be slain herself by Tanaka for murdering a local police sergeant without his authority. Sadashi said he had witnessed Akumu's death on the rooftop of Tanaka's home, as had several bodyguards who could confirm the story.

The three *oyabun* arranged a meeting the same day with Chief Napuna to learn who had killed five of Tanaka's employees – Kira and Yuki shot to death along a rocky path, two bodyguards poisoned by pufferfish, and a third *kobun* murdered just outside the cliff-side house.

Chief Napuna informed them Detective Hideyo Mashima was in charge of the investigation but no suspects had been identified. Since the five yakuza deaths did not appear related to drug trafficking, the police chief doubted the controversial

Anti-Drug Task Force would become involved. He had no answers regarding the sunken ship but extended his condolences for the three yakuza killed during the explosion. The chief was eager to be rid of these men. He had an appointment with his attorney to discuss an ongoing FBI investigation into his allegedly spending $40,000 in taxpayer dollars on an off-island junket and for a "lover's vacation." He was also hoping the deaths of The Lucky Carp's three primary owners might cause the record of his gambling debts to be misplaced. He planned to talk to Sadashi.

Ray Donley sensed his career as a prosecutor was falling apart before his eyes. The Asaki murder trial was fizzling and would soon be closed by the court for lack of evidence. It was only a matter of time before the judge dismissed the related charges against the two pot farmers who had confessed to the crime.

Donley was further perplexed now that Tanaka was dead, leaving him without a high-profile racketeering case. He agonized over the death of Akumu, whom he had hoped to charge with the murder of Sgt. Torres and bring to trial, earning him support and respect among the island police.

His only moment of triumph had occurred during a search of Tanaka's jet at the airport. Two beautiful young South Korean girls were found hiding in the main cabin. Still in their teens, they had fled a prison-like jungle garment factory for a promise of work in the bathhouses of Tokyo, not understanding the offer from Tanaka meant a life of prostitution.

Donley held a press conference to address the issues of child abduction and sex slavery, but the cargo ship explosion and spate of yakuza-related homicides on the island overshadowed it.

60

CASE CLOSED

Saipan

Northern Mariana Islands

April 1990

Mashima opened his briefcase and gently rubbed the lacy underwear between his thumb and forefinger, bringing the thin cloth to his nostrils and inhaling deeply. He ran his fingers along the bra's embroidery, tracing the delicate stitching before cupping one of the high heels in his hands like a holy chalice and filling it with sake until it overflowed.

The detective gulped until he coughed. The rice wine drizzled from his nostrils and spilled down the front of his shirt. He laughed and gently set the shoe on the kitchen table, admiring its perfection. He poured more sake into a low-ball glass, lit an incense stick, tuned his radio to a classical music station, and sat back in his favorite worn leather chair. He studied the photograph of Ray Donley and wife, Cheryl, smiling on their wedding day, then tore it into four equal pieces and tossed it into a metal wastebasket.

The voice-message light was blinking on his home phone. It was Chief Napuna, concerned that the Lover's Lane homicide file folder was missing. He had called to ask whether Mashima might have taken it home to work on the case notes. Mashima assured the chief he had not, adding his personal belief that confidential investigation files should be kept only at the police station unless required in the courtroom.

When the chief hung up, Mashima dumped the contents of the folder into the wastebasket along with the wedding photograph and carried it to the back porch where he set the papers afire with his cigarette lighter.

Back inside, he smoked a Dunhill cigarette, drank more sake, splashed cold water on his face and stood staring into the mirror over the bathroom sink. He turned slightly to better see the left side where the thick scars pulled his face into a grimace. *Hideyo? No, more like Hideous, he thought, thanks to the yakuza.* He slipped the black mask into his pants pocket and the $5,000 in cash he'd skimmed from Whirly Man's suitcase. It was a balmy Sunday night, the sky filled with shooting stars and promise, perfect for the cockfights in San Antonio.

THE END

AUTHOR'S NOTE: IF YOU ENJOYED PACIFIC POISON, I HOPE you'll read my previous novel, the serial-killer thriller DEADLY FARE as well as my mafia thriller BLOOD SONS.

KEEP READING TO FIND EXCERPTS AT THE BACK OF THIS BOOK.

A NOTE FROM THE AUTHOR

As 1990 approached, I didn't know much about the yakuza, but two intrepid government prosecutors and a hard-boiled police lieutenant — people I met routinely as a news reporter covering the crime beat in Massachusetts — were about to embark on a mission to fight heroin trafficking by powerful Japanese criminals on Saipan Island.

The mission sounded intriguing, exotic, the stuff novels are made of, and when I looked at a world map the possibility became more enticing. Apparently my enthusiasm showed through because they suggested I join them as a photojournalist in their remote Pacific island adventure.

When I pitched the idea to John Moran, the cigar-puffing executive editor at the daily newspaper in Massachusetts where I worked as a reporter and photographer, he approved a paid leave and the following week handed me a check to cover the round-trip airfare to Saipan along with some spending money. I've never met another boss like that.

Moran, who remained a hardcore newsman until the day he died, believed in the story because it had lots of connections to Massachusetts and its North Shore. He also trusted my reportorial skills. News Editors Allan Kort, Ted Grant and Bill Plante, along with the late Associate Editor Fred Goddard, supported Moran's decision, so it was green lights all around.

Once on Saipan in the Northern Mariana Islands, I bunked in a defunct CIA compound with Police Detective Lt. John LeBrasseur, one of the toughest men I've ever met. I spent my free time exploring abandoned World War II Japanese bunkers, and caves where corroded bayonets and unexploded artillery shells lay scattered about.

Howitzers and anti-aircraft guns had been transformed over the years into rusted sculptures and on the island's coral reefs, U.S. military Sherman tanks from the Battle of Saipan remained encrusted where the shells from the Japanese shore batteries had found their mark in 1944.

In shallow water off one popular beach, a Japanese Zero fighter plane rested on the coral. On another, the wing of an American bomber lay in the sand where it crashed or had washed up in a storm decades ago.

To gain a better understanding of the terrain, I joined LeBrasseur on a trek to Mount Tapotchau, Saipan's highest peak. Mount Topotchau had been the scene of brutal and prolonged fighting between Japanese forces and U.S. Marines.

Locals tended to give the place wide berth, believing the bloodshed had left it haunted.

The Battle of Saipan lasted three weeks in the summer of 1944, during which 3,144 U.S. servicemen, both Army and Marine Corps, were killed or later died of their wounds. Another 10,952 were wounded but survived. Military historians have estimated Japanese forces suffered over 25,000 dead and countless wounded.

My days on Saipan included accompanying a task force of special-ops troops to remote villages for break-of-dawn drug raids. I also kept close tabs on local murders involving the yakuza whose assassins had become a heavy presence on the island. The yakuza were suspected of funneling heroin along a supply chain that led from Thailand to the Philippines to Saipan, and onward to Hawaii and San Francisco for distribution in the United States. By 1990, that smuggling route was showing its success, the number of heroin addicts growing exponentially on America's streets.

As the investigation broadened and the terrain became more familiar, I joined LeBrasseur and a contingent of detectives from the Commonwealth of the Northern Mariana Islands (CNMI) police force on a helicopter flight to the nearby island of Tinian, where in 1945 a lengthy runway was built to accommodate the American B-29 bomber *Enola Gay,* which would drop its deadly atomic payload on the Japanese city of Hiroshima.

Our helicopter pilot was nervous because the aircraft had taken ground fire a week earlier, presumably from pot farmers attempting to evade surveillance.

Wild goats grazed along the flat coral airstrip and a small bronze plaque offered a few historic facts about the Enola Gay's bombing mission, but mostly Tinian was desolate. The airstrip had become an ideal place for smugglers to land small planes.

LeBrasseur, a seasoned detective with the Lynn, Massachusetts Police Department, had made inroads in cracking down on drug traffickers in New England. His success, as head of a county anti-drug task force, was documented in a Harvard University criminology study, which led to his being invited to replicate the tactics on Saipan.

LeBrasseur was instrumental in my ability to obtain access to the task force operations. Assistant Attorney Generals Raymond Buso and Edward Hayden, both prosecutors from the Essex County District Attorney's Office in Massachusetts, also provided friendship, support and information during my days on Saipan. The result was a series of newspaper stories on

Saipan — a package of ten articles and photos the editors submitted for a Pulitzer Prize.

To all of these men, I offer an unbridled thank you, because without them, it's unlikely I'd have had such an international adventure or written this novel.

I'd also like to extend thanks to my good friend Dan McMackin for sharing his knowledge of all things military. He is always ready to help answer my questions about weapons, tactics and protocol.

As always, I'd be remiss by not recognizing the sacrifices made by my wife, Christine, son Zack and daughter Julie, which allow me opportunity to write books while other men are engaged in far more important undertakings. Together they are my beta-reader team.

I'm also proud to note my daughter designed the book cover of PACIFIC POISON, just as she did for my serial-killer thriller DEADLY FARE and mafia novel BLOOD SONS.

If you enjoyed PACIFIC POISON, I hope you'll consider reading my previous books. Although Hannah Summers is featured predominately in all three, the books can be read as standalones.

Authors depend on reviews to keep their books in the public eye and attract new readers. If you have the time and the inclination, leaving a review on Amazon or Goodreads would be much appreciated.

ABOUT THE AUTHOR

David Liscio is an international, award-winning journalist whose lengthy experience covering crime stories led to the writing of his debut novel, the serial killer thriller DEADLY FARE.

An investigative reporter, David's work has appeared in dozens of magazines and newspapers. The recipient of more than 20 journalism honors, his feature stories have earned first-place awards from the Associated Press, United Press International, and many regional news media groups. He has reported extensively on organized crime both in the United States and abroad, in addition to writing about military and environmental subjects.

David is an avid sailor, outdoorsman, and adjunct college professor. A father of two, he lives with his wife, dog and cat on the Massachusetts coast, where for 25 years he served as a fire-fighter and founding member of the town's Ocean Rescue team.

You can contact him on his website: www.davidliscio.com or via email at bostoncrimewriter@gmail.com.

For more information:
www.davidliscio.com
david@davidliscio.com

ALSO BY DAVID LISCIO

DEADLY FARE

A SERIAL KILLER THRILLER

Fans of Vince Flynn and Nelson DeMille won't want to miss this page-turning thriller set in Boston...

**FIVE WOMEN MURDERED. A CITY PARALYZED BY FEAR.
ONLY A MATTER OF TIME BEFORE HE STRIKES AGAIN.**

When beautiful young women begin to vanish from Boston Logan International Airport, State Police Lt. Hannah Summers is the only one who sees a pattern amidst the cold case files. She knows a killer is on the loose, and she's determined to make her chauvinistic bosses believe her hunch about a gypsy cab driver — before it's too late.

As the body count rises, so does the public's panic. Under pressure from the district attorney to make the killings stop, Summers soon finds herself rubbing elbows with ex-Special Forces soldier Emmett Decker, a private investigator hired by the wealthy family of a missing local girl. The more their paths cross, the harder it is to deny they may be chasing the same monster — and that the tension between them is more than purely professional.

One thing is certain: the Boston Butcher must be stopped before any more women climb inside his cab... and wind up paying the ultimate price...

————

BLOOD SONS

A MAFIA THRILLER

Fans of Vince Flynn and Nelson DeMille won't want to miss this page-turning underworld thriller...

————

TO A MAFIA BOSS, BLOOD MATTERS MORE THAN

ANYTHING... EVEN THE SON HE SPENT FIFTEEN YEARS
RAISING AS HIS OWN.

When a DNA test reveals an accidental hospital baby-switch fifteen years prior, two teenage boys find their lives upside down and their futures uncertain. Against his will, Nicholas Cooper is abruptly transplanted from his idyllic vineyard home to the crime-ridden streets of Providence. His biological father — none other than notorious crime boss Vinnie "Cocktails" Merlino — has big plans to retake control of Cuba's once-flourishing casino scene... and those plans include his rightful heir standing by his side.

As Nick grows ever more deeply enmeshed in Vinnie's violent underworld, he unwittingly becomes the focus of a Central Intelligence Agency investigation, led by new recruit Hannah Summers. From the colorful streets of Havana to the snow-capped trails of upstate New York... through blood rites, flying bullets, Belizean jungles, and family betrayals... BLOOD SONS poses the ultimate question of nature versus nurture.

Does the blood in your veins determine the man you'll become?

You can't choose your family... sometimes, they choose you.

———

Now available for purchase in ebook and paperback.

Made in the USA
Middletown, DE
04 September 2020

16730559R00199